"Lock the door, turn off the phone, and grab a pitcher of iced tea because once you start reading *Poor Mrs. Rigsby* you won't want to stop! Kathy Herman takes us on a journey jam-packed with truth and light, redemption and renewal. This story is a mini-retreat between covers."

Lois Richer, author of *Dangerous Sanctuary*

"*Poor Mrs. Rigsby*. The choice she thought would free her from her problems turned out to be a lifelong weight on her soul. A haunting look at what happens when we try to convince ourselves we are wiser than God…the God who loves enough to redeem us from the disasters of our own making."

Carol Cox, coauthor of *A Stitch in Time*

"Oh, what a tangled web Kathy Herman weaves! And every delicious thread of *Poor Mrs. Rigsby* draws you deeper in the mystery."

DeAnna Julie Dodson, author of *In Honor Bound*, *By Love Redeemed*, and *To Grace Surrendered*

"What a treasure! Kathy Herman intertwines fast-paced prose with complicated characters and nail-biting intrigue to create what is simply complex. *Poor Mrs. Rigsby* is certainly a paradox of entertainment as the reader is transported through the poverty of worldly wealth and the riches of heavenly humility."

Deidre Pool, author of *Loving Jesus Anyway*

"*Poor Mrs. Rigsby* is a story about real people with real problems, people who could be our neighbors, or ourselves. How many of us might be tempted to grab the same solution to our problems that Sally Cox did, if the opportunity arose? Kathy Herman writes a powerful message about the only real solution to life's problems."

Lorena McCourtney, author of *Whirlpool*, *Riptide*, and *Undertow* (The Julesburg Mysteries)

"Kathy Herman does her usual, skillful job of telling us about characters so real we feel as if they live next door. *Poor Mrs. Rigsby* is both thought-provoking and pleasurable to read."

JANELLE SCHNEIDER, AUTHOR OF *FROM CARRIAGE TO MARRIAGE* IN THE COLLECTION *BRIDE FOR A BIT*

"Kathy Herman has done it again. *Poor Mrs. Rigsby* is a well-written novel, with a unique and compelling storyline that keeps you guessing. With honesty and realism, the story powerfully illustrates the words of Jesus, 'You cannot serve both God and money.'"

RANDY ALCORN, AUTHOR OF *DEADLINE* AND *DOMINION*

Poor Mrs. Rigsby

[A NOVEL]

KATHY HERMAN

Multnomah® Books

POOR MRS. RIGSBY
PUBLISHED BY MULTNOMAH BOOKS
12265 Oracle Boulevard, Suite 200
Colorado Springs, Colorado 80921

International Standard Book Number: 978-1-59052-314-8

Cover image of woman by Corbis/Shepard Sherbell
Background cover image by Photonica/Joshua Sheldon

Scripture quotations are from:
The Holy Bible, New International Version
© 1973, 1984 by International Bible Society,
used by permission of Zondervan Publishing House
The Holy Bible, King James Version

MULTNOMAH and its mountain colophon are
registered trademarks of Random House Inc.

Printed in the United States of America

Library of Congress Cataloging-in-Publication Data
Herman, Kathy.
Poor Mrs. Rigsby : a novel / Kathy Herman.
p. cm.
ISBN 1-59052-314-8 (pbk.)
1. Nursing homes—Employees—Fiction. 2. Nursing home patients—
Fiction. 3. Dementia—Patients—Fiction. 4. Female friendship—Fiction.
5. Divorced women—Fiction. 6. Treasure-trove—Fiction. 7. Aged
women—Fiction. 8. Poor women—Fiction. I. Title.
PS3608.E762P66 2004
813'.6—dc22

2004007349

To Him who is both the Giver and the gift

ACKNOWLEDGMENTS

The more I write, the more grateful I am for those who support me in prayer, those who take time to encourage me—and those who patiently instruct me so that the scenarios I create are realistic.

I would like to extend a special thank you to Paul David Houston, assistant district attorney, Rusk County, Texas, for his valuable input on law enforcement and legal procedures; and for taking hours of his time to read pertinent chapters and make suggestions that have added to the realism of the scenes. Paul, I hope someday we get to meet face-to-face. You aren't *that* far down the highway!

Also, a word of thanks to Ann Tyson, RN, BSN, director of nurses, Chandler Nursing Center, Chandler, Texas, for defining and explaining the roles of the nursing home staff and their procedural responses to patient accidents and deaths.

I would like to express my appreciation to my sister Caroline Berry for answering my questions about landmarks, restaurants, hospitals, and shopping areas in the Kansas City metropolitan area. What a fun stroll down memory lane!

To my friends Shirley Lindsay, Dottie Hilsman, Sue McKay, and Rosy Halley, who drove me to physical therapy countless times during the months I juggled rehab with deadlines. Thanks for offering before I even thought to ask!

To Laverne McCuistion for your support and encouragement, and that warm smile that radiates every time I see you. You make me appreciate all the more the privilege of writing for Him.

To my author friend Deidre Pool, for the precious heart-stirring cards that arrived daily when I was on the homestretch, racing toward my deadline. Thanks for cheering me on—and asking Him for grace.

To my sister Pat Phillips, and to Susie Killough, Judi Wieghat, and the ladies in my Bible study groups at Bethel Bible Church, and my friends at LifeWay Christian Store in Tyler, Texas, for your heartfelt prayer support.

To my readers who encourage me with e-mails and cards and personal testimonies, thanks for sharing how God has used my words to touch you. It means more than you know.

To my author friends in ChiLibris, thanks for inspiring and challenging me—and for your many prayers on my behalf.

To my editor, Rod Morris, who has been my compass throughout the writing of six novels, thanks for keeping me on course. How I've grown to respect your insights and suggestions!

To the staff at Multnomah, whose commitment to "pushing back the darkness" has become my own, thanks for being light bearers with every book you publish.

And to my husband, Paul, whose thoughts are forever intertwined with mine, thanks for unselfishly allowing me to bring a host of book characters to our dinner table the past four years. Your masculine insights have added to the depth and authenticity of each story.

And most of all to my Heavenly Father, in whose Book of Life I have but a tiny part, thank You for trusting me to create stories based on the principles in Your Word—and then blessing them beyond my wildest dream. You never cease to amaze me!

"For the love of money is a root of all kinds of evil.
Some people, eager for money, have wandered from the faith
and pierced themselves with many griefs."

1 TIMOTHY 6:10

Elsie Rigsby sat in the dimly lit back room of Rigsby Transport Company, reconciling the books. The company's income had more than doubled in the past six months, and most of the new accounts were paying in cash. Though they were finally getting ahead, her husband Arnie insisted they put every nickel back in the business.

So, why did Arnie always have a roll of bills in *his* pocket? When it came to her needs, and those of their son, Harry, Arnie insisted they maintain a "moratorium on unnecessary spending." He gave her just enough money to pay household expenses and buy groceries, and not a penny more.

"It's just a set of building blocks, Arnie," she had argued. "Harry needs to play. That's how children learn."

"He's got the whole outdoors. I'm not bustin' my tail so you can buy him toys! Take 'em back."

"Then let it be his birthday present."

"The kid's gonna be two. He doesn't even know what a birthday is."

Elsie sat quietly for a moment, her finger winding the curls covering her ear. "I bought a dress for Arleta and Ned's wedding. It was on sale," she quickly added.

Arnie glared at her, his eyebrows forming a bushy line. "A storebought dress? You've got a sewing machine."

"But I'm running out of time. I've been working hard. I thought maybe just this once—"

"Well, you thought wrong! If you want something new, make it. The dress goes back…"

Elsie put down her pencil and rubbed the tightness in her neck. She had known better than to argue with him. But why should she have to do without while Arnie wasted money on his smelly cigars, his stash of moonshine, and his backroom slot machines?

Elsie looked down at the bookkeeping ledger and the stacks of money she had just counted. She slipped a hundred-dollar bill into her pocket.

Suddenly, she heard angry voices on the other side of the door. Elsie took the bill out of her pocket, her heart racing, and put it back on the stack. She sat quietly and listened to Arnie hollering at one of the drivers. She strained to hear what he was saying, and then wished she hadn't. *What are you thinking, Arnie? You're going to end up in prison!*

Elsie sat dumbfounded, her mind processing the implications of her husband's business dealings. Finally, she put the ledger in her desk drawer and locked it, then put the money and a deposit slip in a zippered bag. She hurried out the back door, furious that Arnie would be so reckless with her future and Harry's.

She crossed the street and started walking briskly toward the bank when she spotted an empty bench in Mulberry Park. She cut through the spongy grass, her eyes brimming with tears, and sat on the wrought iron bench under a towering shade tree. She blinked to clear her eyes and noticed a young couple strolling hand in hand, a small boy walking next to them waving a toy airplane and giggling with delight.

A stab of jealousy pierced her heart. Her son's father was not only stingy and mean, but also dishonest! What else hadn't Arnie told her? Or did she even want to know?

Elsie let out a sigh of helplessness and sat for a long time, her eyes on the little boy with the toy plane. She knew Arnie would deny everything if she confronted him. But did she dare confide in anyone else—even Pastor Roe? If the cops found out what Arnie was really hauling in those trucks, he'd go to jail, leaving her to raise Harry by herself. The thought of scraping even harder the rest of her life was more than she could bear.

Elsie clutched the zippered pouch containing the day's bank deposit. She rose to her feet, suddenly feeling bold and in control.

Two can play this game, Arnie. Ruin your life if you want to, but Harry and I are not going to pay for it!

1

tupid door! Sally Cox pushed the front door with her shoulder, then pushed harder and nearly fell in when it gave way. She stepped inside, hit with the fishy odor of last night's Tuna Helper, and dreading the thought of another weekend alone.

It was hard to accept that Sam had divorced her and moved in with some chick fifteen years younger than he, leaving Sally with this run-down house and all the headaches that went with it. Sam had salved his guilt by giving her *everything*. Was she supposed to be grateful? Even a paid-for house required upkeep. And she could barely afford the utilities and taxes, and had neither money nor energy to get it ready to sell.

She flopped on the couch and kicked off her shoes, careful not to let the ripped upholstery snag her panty hose. She was staring at the cracks around the light fixture in the ceiling when her orange tabby cat jumped up and lay on her chest, its eyes peering directly into hers, its paw padding her cheek.

"Well, Kiwi. It's just us girls." Sally stroked the cat's fur and wondered if Sam had any conscience left. He certainly had no shame.

With the help of Botox and expensive makeup, his saucy little cash cow looked young enough to be his daughter. She had come with a nice divorce settlement—also two teenagers and enough emotional baggage to sink the *Titanic*. Sam would eventually be miserable. At least, she hoped so.

The phone rang. Sally put Kiwi on the floor, then got up and walked to the kitchen.

"Hello."

"Mom, it's me," Leslie Saunders said. "You sound tired."

"I just got home. I'll be fine after I'm off my feet for a while."

"You still working double shifts?"

"No, I'm back to forty hours since they hired enough staff."

"Good," Leslie said. "Alan and I don't want you putting too much pressure on yourself. Why don't you take the weekend to rest?"

"Actually, I'd rather stay busy. I'm going to start back to church this Sunday. I'll be fine."

"Are you sure?"

"Absolutely," Sally said, trying to believe it.

"Promise you'll call if you get lonesome?"

"Promise. Now stop worrying, and go pay attention to that sweet husband of yours."

Leslie sniffled. "I'm really sorry Daddy left. I hate being so far away."

Sally defiantly blinked the stinging from her eyes and stuffed her emotions in the few moments of awkward silence.

"I love you, Mom."

"Love you, too. Talk to you soon."

Sally went to the kitchen table and put her head down. How could Sam have walked away from their thirty years of marriage as if she meant nothing?

It had taken Sally months to pull herself together and go looking for a job, but she soon realized how few job opportunities existed for a fifty-four-year-old woman with no current job skills. Though working at a nursing home was not the job she'd hoped for, the training had only taken eight weeks.

Sally went into the living room and spotted the pair of baby shoes that Sam had set on a bookshelf after Leslie outgrew them. They'd been there so long that Sally rarely noticed anymore. She picked up the tiny shoes and set them in her palm, noting the white polish caked in the cracked leather. Sam had kept them polished—almost every night. He'd been a good father. Not a bad husband, either, except for the fling he'd had with some secretary at work. That was twenty-five years ago, and Sally thought he had gotten it out of his system.

She went to the coffee table and picked up the TV remote.

Kiwi paced on the back of the couch and meowed repeatedly.

"Hey, you. We agreed to stick together on this. Rule number one: No whining."

2

Monday morning at 7:03, Sally turned her faded blue Subaru into the employee parking lot of Walnut Hills Nursing Center and pulled next to Karen Morgan's sassy Kia Sportage. She got out of the car, the January wind whipping her hair, and hurried toward the employee entrance, clutching her purse, her lunch, and a sack of jelly beans.

The charge nurse looked up when Sally walked in the door. "Cutting it a little close, are we?" Wanda Bradford said.

Sally smoothed her hair with her fingers, then put her lunch in the refrigerator. "I'm only three minutes late. I had to stop at Quick Mart."

"Well, I suggest you wipe the Monday morning expression off your face and start making your rounds."

Have a nice day, Wanda. Feel free to irritate somebody else.

Sally put her purse in her locker and a handful of jelly beans in her pocket, then headed down the hall toward the east wing, struggling to conjure up the incentive to get her through the next eight hours. She hoped whoever had finished out the last shift had already gotten some of the patients dressed.

She walked into room 201, pleased to find Rufus Tatum already dressed and sitting in his wheelchair.

Sally looked down at his bare feet. "You kicked your slippers off again. Let me put them on you."

Rufus shook his head.

"You can't go barefoot. You'll catch a cold."

He looked at her with the defiance of a two-year-old, then scrunched his toes.

Sally squatted and looked him in the eye. "Honestly, Rufus. Am I going to have to bribe you again?"

An impish smile stretched his mahogany cheeks.

"All right." Sally reached in her pocket and pulled out a half-dozen jelly beans. "How about it?"

As if by magic, Rufus relaxed his toes.

Sally put the candy in his sweater pocket and quickly got the fur-lined slippers on his feet. She winked at his roommate. "I'll be back in a minute, Charles."

She wheeled Rufus down to the lounge and set him in front of the TV, then went back and got Charles and parked him next to Rufus. "You two check out the news. I'll be back to take you to breakfast."

Sally hurried down the hall and turned into room 202.

Elsie Rigsby was sitting in her wheelchair, her frail hand pulling a handled comb through her fine, white hair.

"Good morning, sweetie. You look lovely."

Elsie handed the comb to Sally. "Give this to Fay."

Sally glanced at the empty bed on the other side of the room and wondered if Elsie remembered Fay was in the hospital.

"Harry's coming today," Elsie said.

Sally opened the closet and took a flowered housedress off the hanger. "Harry comes on Sundays, sweetie. This is Monday."

"Johnny's coming today," Elsie said insistently.

Sure he is. You've been saying that since I started working here. Sally helped Elsie slip out of her nightgown and into the dress, then put on her anklets and sequined slippers. "Okay, you're good to go."

Sally rolled Elsie out to the hallway and spotted Wilda Cunningham inching her wheelchair down the corridor. She positioned Elsie's wheelchair behind Wilda's.

"Sweetie, follow Wilda to the dining room." Sally chuckled to herself, knowing she would finish her rounds before they made it to the end of the corridor.

Sally scurried in and out of rooms until all her patients were ready to start the day, then positioned them at the assigned tables in the dining room. She was marking her duty roster when she noticed a nice-looking man pull up a chair and sit next to Elsie. She recognized his face from the picture on Elsie's nightstand, but his hair was long and wavy now and pulled back in a ponytail.

Karen Morgan came over and stood next to Sally. "I wonder what moved Johnny boy to grace her with his presence after all these months?"

"I doubt she realizes how long it's been. Will you look at him, pouring on the charm? He looks thrilled to see his grandmother."

Karen snickered. "Probably wants something."

"Why so cynical? Don't you like him?"

"I don't trust him."

Sally peered out across the dining room. "He seems nice. And it's the first time I've seen everyone at the table laughing."

"Yeah, Jonathan's a charmer, all right." Karen rested her hand on Sally's shoulder. "But Elsie'll get depressed when he promises to come back and then doesn't. She's not my patient anymore, but I still feel protective of her."

"The way she's been lately, she may not even remember he was here."

Karen lifted her eyebrows. "Better yet. Listen, I need to change a few beds. Take a good look at number one grandson. I doubt you'll see him again for a long time."

Sally leaned against the wall, her arms folded, and watched the man who had the attention of everyone at Elsie's table. Jonathan Rigsby looked to be about forty, give or take. She didn't see a wedding ring.

"Don't you have things to do while your patients are having break-fast?"

Sally looked into Wanda's scolding eyes. "I was enjoying the sound of laughter. Elsie's grandson's a real hit."

Wanda turned toward the table and wrinkled her nose. "Wonder why he let his hair get long? Makes him look like a hippie."

"Doesn't seem to bother her. She's eating up the attention. They all are."

"And you're eating up the clock when you should be changing beds."

Sally didn't move for several seconds, despite the scowl on Wanda's face. Finally, Sally unfolded her arms and started down the hall toward her patients' rooms.

After the sermon yesterday, Sally was finally able to admit that her resentment toward Sam was affecting her attitude—even on the job. What was she supposed to do about it: forgive him for tossing her aside and moving in with some young thing, then saddling her with a financial burden she was ill-equipped to handle? Forgiving him wouldn't change the fact that Sally had to work with a rude old sourpuss just to survive, while Sam lived comfortably on his girlfriend's divorce settlement.

She let out a loud sigh. And Wanda's indifference to her circumstances just heaped on more resentment.

Jonathan Rigsby pushed his grandmother's wheelchair into her room, then closed the door and sat on the side of the bed facing her.

"I can't get over how great you look, Grandma."

"You're sweet to say that, Johnny."

"Didn't you see the way the men looked at you? Ninety years old, and you're still getting double takes." He patted her cheek playfully, and she smiled. "So, tell me about your visit with Dad yesterday."

Elsie's face went blank, her eyes clouded with confusion.

"Your son Harry, Grandma. He brought you the daisies in that vase."

She looked over at the nightstand. "Aren't they lovely? Harry stayed and had chicken pot pie."

"Ah, you *do* remember." Jonathan studied his grandmother. "Uh, Dad said he talked to you about getting your affairs in order."

Elsie turned her head and caught his gaze. "I did no such thing."

Jonathan wiped the perspiration from his forehead. "It's really hot in here. Do you mind if I turn the heat down?"

"Go ahead, dear. Hand me the afghan so I won't get chilled."

Jonathan draped the afghan over her legs, then turned the thermostat from eighty to seventy-five.

"Arnie lied to you," Elsie said. "I never talked to him about getting my affairs in order."

"Grandma, you talked to your son Harry. Your husband Arnie's been dead for two years."

"Arnie never gave me a cent more than I needed. Harry knows that."

Jonathan stood next to the window, his thumbs hung on his jeans pockets. Was she more aware than she was letting on?

She had money, all right. The trick was getting her to tell him where it was while she could still remember, and before his father got it out of her—or Medicaid found out and made her pay for the nursing home.

Jonathan sat again on the side of the bed, his hands clasped between his knees. He hated what he was about to do. He hoped his grandmother wouldn't remember, but even if she did, who would take her seriously?

3

Harry Rigsby held out the TV remote and surfed between the Weather Channel and ESPN, then hit the off button. He was hungry but couldn't muster the incentive to get up off the couch for another stale peanut butter sandwich. Daytime TV was boring. In fact, *daytime* was boring. Where had he gotten the idea that retirement would be great? The doorbell rang. He heard the front door open, then felt a draft on his stocking feet.

"Dad, it's me."

"Yeah, hurry up and close the door."

Jonathan Rigsby came into the living room and flopped in the chair facing the couch.

"Why aren't you workin'?" Harry said. "I thought you got accepted for that warehouse job."

"I didn't like the supervisor's attitude. I turned it down."

"Must be nice."

"Like you've got room to talk?" Jonathan said. "You dumped plenty of jobs in your day."

"Yeah. Yeah. Always gotta throw it in my face, don't you?"

"Hey, Mom and Bill are paying me to watch the house while they're out of town. It's not like I'm doing nothing."

Harry rolled his eyes. "Yeah, that's a rugged assignment."

"By the way, I saw Grandma this morning."

"Got in your semiannual duty, did you?"

Jonathan sighed. "What's eating you? Didn't your Social Security check get deposited?"

"Yeah, sure. By the time I pay the bills, I'll be lucky to have enough left for groceries."

Jonathan's eyes dropped to Harry's belly. "Doesn't look like you're starving."

"Wait'll I get the gas bill."

"You can always go sit with Grandma. She keeps the thermostat at eighty—compliments of Medicaid."

"Yeah, her worries are over."

Jonathan smirked. "I'll remind you of that when I put *you* in a home."

"Thanks for nothin'." Harry picked up the couch pillow and threw it at Jonathan. "So where'd your mother go?"

"She and Bill are in Key West. They'll be gone till the end of the month."

"Must be rough. Gracie's darned lucky that husband of hers gets a nice fat pension check every month."

"You get no sympathy from me, Dad. It's your own fault."

"Yeah? Well, take a lesson. Unless you change your ways, you're gonna end up in the same boat."

"I doubt that," Jonathan said.

"Then you better get yourself a good job and start savin'. Tryin' to make it on Social Security's no picnic."

"I've got time to figure it out," Jonathan said. "A lot can happen between now and then. Besides, everyone I know lost money on their 401k's when the stock market took a dive. That's no guarantee."

"What did you and your grandma talk about?" Harry asked.

"I did most of the talking. She and her cronies did a lot of laughing. Made me feel good to see them having fun, you know?"

"What made you suddenly decide to go see her? You haven't been out there since the Fourth of July." Harry studied his son's face.

"Hey, I went because you laid a guilt trip on me. But I'm glad I did. She still recognized me."

"The whole time?"

"Nah, she got me mixed up with you, and you with Grandpa. But some of the time she seemed with it. I'm going to try to see her more often. Why are you looking at me that way?"

"Just wonderin' why this sudden burst of concern."

"I don't know. I guess seeing how fast she's slipping made me realize how much she means to me."

"Or how much money she has?"

Jonathan rolled his eyes. "You're the one who thinks she's holding out, not me."

"Come on. Even my old man accused her of rat-holing. Ma always had money when we needed it, and he didn't give her squat. She had to be skimmin' money from the company. Where else would she get it?"

"Even if you're right, it all belongs to Medicaid now."

Harry wanted to slap the grin off Jonathan's face.

Sally Cox walked into Elsie Rigsby's room, surprised to find her still asleep. She couldn't remember Elsie ever sleeping through lunch. Then again, she was ninety years old—did it really matter?

Sally started to leave, then noticed Elsie's eyes had opened. "You *are* awake."

Elsie stared up at her, but gave no indication she understood.

Sally took her hand and gently squeezed it. "You're still pretty groggy. I guess the excitement of having your grandson visit wore you out."

Elsie blinked but didn't respond. A tear trickled down the side of her face and rolled onto the pillow.

"Hey, what's the matter?" Sally sat on her bedside and dabbed the tear with a tissue. "Are you in pain? I'll get the nurse."

Elsie held tightly to Sally's hand. "Just a bad dream, dear," she whispered. "I'm a little frightened."

"Don't be. I'm here."

Elsie's eyes were bloodshot and seemed clouded with confusion. "Who are you?"

"Sally Cox. I work here."

"Where?"

"Walnut Hills Nursing Center, where you live."

"In St. Louis?"

"In Kansas City."

Elsie's fingers pressed into Sally's arm. "Harry won't know where to find me!"

"It's all right. Harry knows exactly where to find you. In fact, he was here just yesterday."

Elsie seemed trapped in a blank stare, and then her eyes widened. "Yes…he brought me daisies."

"That's right. And your grandson Jonathan came this morning. You had a wonderful time."

Elsie turned loose of Sally's arm and grabbed at the covers. She seemed agitated. "I want to go to sleep."

"You slept through lunch. How about if I get your tray? Roast chicken and sweet potatoes. I know you like that."

Elsie clamped her eyes shut and pulled the covers up to her nose. Sally patted her hand. "Okay, sweetie. Enjoy your beauty sleep. I'll check on you later."

Sally went out in the hallway and saw Wanda Bradford walking in her direction. It was too late to turn around.

Wanda pointed to her chart. "I see Mrs. Rigsby wasn't in the dining room for lunch."

"She's pooped from her grandson's visit and has slept most of the day."

"Since when is it our policy for patients to miss meals?"

"There's nothing wrong with Elsie's appetite," Sally said. "She's just worn out from the excitement. I'm sure she'll eat her dinner."

"All I need is her son accusing us of neglect."

"Maybe he should've been here to see how excited she was to see her grandson. I've never seen Elsie that enthused about anything before."

"You're not paid to amuse or enthuse, Ms. Cox. Your job is to make sure your patients stay on schedule with their daily activities. Is that clear?"

"I don't see how her sleeping through one lunch could hurt any—"

"I *said*, is that clear?"

There was that churning in her gut again. "Whatever." Sally felt satisfied with her irreverent response and almost wished Wanda would report her to the director of nurses. But she figured it would take more than one disrespectful response for her to get fired from this dreadful place. They were already short staffed. And it wasn't as though people were standing in line to work there.

Wanda shot her a crusty look. She started to say something, and then turned around and started down the hall, mumbling something as she went. Sally pictured her wearing a black hat and riding a broom.

"What are you staring at?" Karen Morgan asked.

"I'm not sure. It calls itself Wanda."

Karen laughed. "You'll get used to her. She's got a Day-Timer for a heart. We think she's really a robot. Is she on your case?"

"Yeah. Elsie Rigsby slept through lunch, and Wanda's nose is out of joint."

"Let me guess: She's worried the family will accuse us of neglect?"

Sally nodded. "How'd you know?"

"She always thinks that. As long as you're doing your job, blow it off. The woman gets paranoid about a hangnail."

Sally sighed. "How long have you worked here?"

"Four years."

"And how long did it take you to look forward to coming to work?"

Karen put a hand on her shoulder. "Look, we've all had to learn how to deal with Wanda."

"So how about letting me in on it."

"Avoid her whenever possible. And never let on that she intimidates you."

Sally watched as Wanda turned the corner and disappeared from view. "Have you tangled with her much?"

"No. Someone told me early on to keep her at an arm's length and do what I was hired to do."

"I thought that's what *I* was doing."

Karen licked her thumb and rubbed a spot off Sally's name tag. "But if *I* can tell Wanda intimidates you, she sure can. You've got to send a different signal."

"How do I do that?"

"You'll figure it out. Just don't let her run you off. I've seen how good you are with your patients. You're an asset to this place."

Sally caught her eye. "You really think so?"

"Absolutely. I have a feeling Wanda sees it, too."

"Then why does she hassle me?"

Karen lifted her eyebrows. "Because she *can*."

Jonathan Rigsby turned the corner in the hallway and nearly bumped into Sally Cox. "Oops, sorry. I wasn't paying attention."

"I'm afraid your grandmother's been sleeping the day away. I guess all the attention this morning wore her out."

He smiled. "No kidding?"

"She was awake earlier, but seemed disoriented and wanted to go back to sleep. Said something about having a bad dream. She was really out of it."

Jonathan took off his gloves and stuffed them in his coat pockets. "I planned to stay through dinner. Is it okay if I sit with her?"

"Sure. My shift is ending. But if she sleeps much longer, the charge nurse will insist someone wake her up."

"Yeah, okay. Thanks."

Jonathan went to Elsie's door and knocked softly. "Grandma, it's me." He slowly entered the room and saw her curled up under the covers. She looked so small.

He closed the door and sat on the side of the bed. He put his hand on his grandmother's back and felt her take in a breath and then let it out. He felt at the same time guilt—and relief. He hoped the small dose of Rohypnol he had given her that morning would wear off without causing serious side effects. She shouldn't remember a thing....

"Here, Grandma, I brought you an extra orange juice," he had said. "With all this cold weather, you need your vitamin C. We don't want you getting sick."

Elsie drank it down, then handed him the empty carton, a proud look on her face.

"Good girl. Your cheeks look rosier already."

Jonathan got up and rinsed out the carton and threw it in the trash. He pulled the door shut, then sat on the side of the bed and made small talk until his grandmother sat motionless in the wheelchair, her eyes glassy. He leaned over, his face close to hers, and spoke softly.

"Grandma, I need to talk to you about something *very* important: the money you took."

She sat staring at her fingers.

"The IRS knows you have it."

She looked over at him, her speech slow and deliberate. "No one knows."

"The IRS does."

"How could they?"

Jonathan shrugged. "They do. And they've threatened to take it all."

She stared blankly for several seconds, then her eyes turned to slits. "Lou never would've told them."

"Well, they know about it. And they're going after it. So unless you tell me where it is, they're going to get it all."

Elsie's eyebrows gathered, her fingers grasping Jonathan's wrist. "It's buried," she whispered. "Stacks and stacks of hundreds."

Jonathan's heart raced. He squatted in front of the wheelchair and put his face in front of his grandmother's. "Where is it? Tell me so I can keep it safe."

"Lou and I agreed we wouldn't tell."

"Your brother Lou?"

She nodded.

"Grandma, he's dead. He'd *want* you to tell me. How else can I help you?"

Elsie's eyes grew wide and fearful. "You mustn't tell anyone I fixed the books."

"I won't. I promise. Tell me where you buried the money, and I'll go get it for you."

"You can't bring it to me! I'm hiding it from Arnie!"

"Shhh!" Jonathan took hold of her arm and squeezed. "Keep your voice down. I won't tell Arnie anything. Just tell me where it is."

She looked beyond him, panic in her eyes, and tried to pull her arm free. "Let go of me, Arnie! It's mine! You owe me!"

Jonathan covered her mouth tightly with his hand, his heart racing. "Shhh. Take it easy, Grandma. It's me, *Johnny*. I'm trying to protect your money. You need my help."

Seconds later, her muffled cries turned to whimpering, and she quit fighting him. Jonathan slowly took his hand off her mouth and then gently stroked her hair, his eyes gazing into hers.

"Grandma, the truth is, Arnie knows where the money is, and he's going to steal it. You have to tell me, or he's going to blow every nickel."

Suddenly, her eyes looked wild and darted all over the room. She held out her hands and acted as if she were picking something. "Look at all the lovely flowers...red ones...white ones...yellow ones...purple...orange—"

"Grandma, where are you?"

"Shhh...be still...it's peaceful here...so quiet..."

Jonathan put his lips to her ear. "Where's the money?"

"Buried right here. Behind the angel. Arnie doesn't know."

"Where exactly? Tell me where."

She smiled, her eyes set on something beyond him. "So peaceful...the money's safe here...she can't tell...never can tell..."

His grandmother babbled on and on for several minutes, but nothing she said revealed where the money was. Jonathan got her settled down for a nap. He tucked the covers around her shoulders, then got up and paced. So close! And yet so far! He went over to her closet and brought out a shoe box stuffed with old black-and-white photos. He remembered seeing one of her and his grandfather standing under a trellis in a flower garden. Maybe that's what she was talking about.

If he could find the picture he was looking for, maybe his grandmother could tell him where it was taken. And if his hunch proved to be correct, he might be able to find the money without ever creating suspicion.

4

On Tuesday morning, Sally Cox went in the employee entrance of Walnut Hills Nursing Center three minutes early, and with a manufactured confidence she hoped Wanda Bradford wouldn't see through. The smell of coffee permeated her senses.

"Good morning, Wanda. What's brewing?"

"Hazelnut," Wanda said.

More like witch-hazelnut! Sally smiled without meaning to.

"Do you find that amusing?"

"Uh, no. I'm just eager to get started."

"Good. Make sure Mrs. Rigsby gets back on schedule."

"I will."

"And no more standing around when your patients are at breakfast."

"No, that's the best time to clean their brooms—rooms! I meant rooms."

Wanda looked over the top of her glasses. "Sounds like one of us has already had enough caffeine this morning."

Sally timed in, fumbled to get her name tag on, and then headed down the hall, stifling her laughter.

"You look like a different person today," Karen Morgan said.

"Thanks. I feel better. Guess I just needed an attitude adjustment."

"Well, if you need another one, I'm available. See you later."

Sally walked to the east wing and decided to check on Elsie first. She pushed open the door to Elsie's room, surprised to see Jonathan Rigsby sitting on the side of the bed, unshaven, and wearing the same clothes he had on yesterday.

"I didn't expect to see you this early," Sally said.

"Actually, I slept in the chair all night." Jonathan reached back and tightened the rubber band on his ponytail. "Grandma seemed so groggy. I just wanted to be sure she was all right."

Sally turned to Elsie in the wheelchair. "How are you feeling?"

"Dreadful, I must say. This headache won't go away."

"Did you tell the nurse?" Sally asked.

Jonathan nodded. "Yeah, someone gave her Extra Strength Excedrin a few minutes ago."

"It's not working!" Elsie snapped.

"You just need some nourishment, Grandma. You've hardly eaten in twenty-four hours."

"I'm not hungry."

Jonathan winked at Sally. "That's what you say now. Just wait'll you see what they're serving."

"I don't want any."

"Raisin French toast, covered with banana slices and oozing with warm maple syrup. I know you can't resist *that*." Jonathan's voice was playful and prodding. "I'll have some with you."

Elsie's face was suddenly animated. "Will you? I'm so tired of eating alone. No one comes to see me anymore."

Sally smiled at Jonathan and shrugged. "Would you step out so I can get her dressed?"

"Sure. I'll go say hi to Rufus."

Sally went to the closet and took a purple housedress off the hanger. She noted the name marked on the inside: Maude Freeman. How hard could it be to get the laundry delivered to the right room? Not that Elsie would know the difference.

"Here you go, sweetie. Let's get you out of that gown. It's nice to see you wide awake. You could hardly keep your eyes open yesterday."

Sally noticed some bruises on the inside of Elsie's left wrist. She was sure they weren't there yesterday. "How did you get these?" All Sally needed was for Wanda to cite her for not reporting it, and then accuse her of abuse.

"I had a bad dream."

"Yes, you did." Sally gently ran her thumb over the black-and-blue area. "That must've been *some* dream."

Elsie scrunched her eyebrows. "What dream was that, dear?"

Sally sighed. "Nothing. Are you ready to go have raisin French toast?"

"Well, of course, I am. I've been asking for it. What took so long?"

"Your grandson Jonathan is here. He's going to have breakfast with you."

"Oh, my. Then he must have passed his driver's test!"

Sally stood outside the open door of Wanda's office and knocked.

"Come in." Wanda peered over her glasses, then glanced at her watch. "I thought you'd be cleaning rooms."

"I noticed some bruises on Elsie Rigsby's wrist when I got her dressed. They weren't there when I left last night."

"You're sure about that?"

"Positive."

Wanda removed her glasses and sat back in her chair. "And how do you account for them?"

"I can't. Elsie was groggy all day yesterday. She seemed confused. Said she'd had a bad dream. Maybe she'd been thrashing in her sleep. She does that sometimes."

Wanda's eyes narrowed. "I wonder why no one else reported it?"

"I don't know, but if she banged her wrist, the bruises wouldn't have shown up right away."

"I'll have to file a report. Her son will have to be notified. She isn't bruised anywhere else?"

Sally shook her head. "Not that I could see."

"All right, Sally. I'll come take a look."

"Elsie doesn't seem to be in any discomfort. You might tell her son that."

Wanda raised an eyebrow. "I've been doing this a long time. I don't need to be told how to report accidents to the families."

"Of course not. Uh, I'll get back to work now."

"Thank you."

Sally turned and left the office. That went better than anticipated. She wondered if Harry would take it in stride or make a big fuss about it. At least Jonathan hadn't overreacted.

Harry Rigsby threw off the afghan and got up from the couch. He was on his way to the kitchen when he saw Jonathan coming up the front steps. Harry opened the door and hurried him inside. "I wondered if you'd come by."

"I brought you lunch," Jonathan said and handed Harry two sacks. "Why are you scowling?"

"Some woman called from the nursing home. Your grandmother's got bruises on her wrist."

"I know. I was there."

"And I'm tryin' to figure out why."

"Why Grandma has bruises? Or why I was there?"

"Both."

"I stayed with her last night because she seemed groggy and out of it when I went back over there for dinner. I was worried about her."

"Since when?"

"Will you get off my case! I'm trying to be nice to Grandma. I'd think you'd be glad."

"So, what do you think the bruises were from?"

"I don't know. I never even noticed them. You know the nursing home has to report every little thing."

"Yeah, I know. But I hear lots of stories. I don't want 'em mistreatin' her."

"Grandma seemed fine at breakfast this morning. Ate everything they put in front of her and then snatched a piece of French toast off Rufus's plate. It was really funny."

"Good. That makes me feel better. So, what's in the sacks?"

"Double cheeseburgers and onion rings in one. Cokes in the other. Thought you might like something different for a change. Or would you rather *stick* with peanut butter?" Jonathan laughed.

Harry gave him an elbow in the ribs. "Come on, I'm starved."

Harry went in the kitchen and sat at the table across from Jonathan. He pulled everything out of the sack, then grabbed a double cheeseburger, pulled down the wrapper halfway, and took a bite. "Thanks for leavin' off the onions. Really hits the spot."

"You're welcome. Oh, by the way," Jonathan took a photograph out of his shirt pocket, "Grandma and I were going through her box of pictures. Any idea where this one was taken?"

Harry took the photograph and held it at arm's length, then brought it closer. "Looks like Aunt Clara and Uncle Roy's place."

"Wasn't Roy your dad's brother?"

"Yeah. His son Wilbur and I used to get in trouble together when we were kids."

"Did they live in St. Louis, too?"

Harry stuffed an onion ring in his mouth. "No, they lived in Dexter Springs." He handed the photo back to Jonathan. "I loved that place. Spent a lot of time out there as a kid."

"Nice picture of Grandma and Grandpa. Cool-looking trellis."

"Aunt Clara had a flower garden in back of the house—second to none. Uncle Roy always used to brag on her, said she had the greenest thumb on Milton Street."

Maybe greener than she thought. Jonathan put the picture in his pocket. "So, where was this town in relationship to St. Louis?"

"About halfway between St. Louis and Kansas City. You remember...that's where my old man's buried." Harry shot him a look. "Oh, that's right. I forgot you were off on some wilderness adventure."

"Come on, cut me some slack. I still feel bad about it."

"Yeah, I know."

"Do Aunt Clara and Uncle Roy still live there?"

"Nah, they've been dead a long time. I heard one of their grandkids owns the place now."

"Good memories, eh?"

Harry nodded. "Yeah, I'm glad you stumbled onto the picture. Kinda fun thinkin' back."

"Grandma may not remember looking at the pictures with me, but I'm glad to have the time with her."

"I don't know what's got into you, Jon. But I appreciate it."

"It's the least I can do." Jonathan lifted his eyes. "Grandma's not going to be around forever."

Sally checked in on Elsie Rigsby just before her shift ended and found her sitting in her wheelchair next to the window in her room.

"What've you got there?" Sally said.

"Family photographs." Elsie took a photo from a tattered shoe box and held it up, her frail hand shaking. "That's my Harry the day he started school."

Sally pulled up a chair next to Elsie, glad to share one of her lucid moments. "Yes, I see the resemblance."

Elsie stared at the photo for several seconds, then put it back in the box and picked up another. "This is me."

Sally took the picture and studied it. "Will you look at that figure? You were a real beauty, Elsie. Don't tell anyone I said so, but you're still the prettiest lady in this place."

"Here's one of Harry on his second birthday."

"I remember when my Leslie was two. They're so animated and excited about everything. Did you have a big party?"

Elsie's expression turned suddenly dark. "We were pinching pennies in those days!"

"Boy, can I relate to that," Sally said quickly. "Well, I'm sure *whatever* you did to celebrate was special."

The wrinkles on Elsie's forehead deepened. "Arnie made me take them back."

"Take what back?"

Elsie seemed agitated. She snatched the picture from Sally and put it back in the box.

"Come on," Sally said. "Let's go down to the sunroom. It's a lot cheerier."

Elsie looked up as if she had just noticed Sally. "Harry never comes to see me anymore."

"Well, you have *two* visitors today: Rufus and Wilda. They're down in the sunroom, waiting for you."

"They are?"

"Yes, indeedy. And you wouldn't want to keep them waiting now, would you?" Sally combed Elsie's hair and eyebrows with her fingers, then straightened the collar on her housedress. She put a tiny dab of moisturizing cream on her cheeks and rubbed it in. "You look lovely." She reached for Elsie's beaded purse and put it in her lap. "Let's go greet your guests."

Sally pushed the wheelchair out the door and almost ran into Jonathan. "Oh, sorry. I was just taking your grandmother down to the sunroom. She has guests." Sally winked. "Rufus and Wilda have come to see her."

"Why are *you* here?" Elsie said to Jonathan.

"To see my favorite grandmother."

Elsie folded her arms tightly. "Don't think I'm going to forgive you just like that!"

Jonathan squatted next to the wheelchair. "Grandma, it's *me*, Johnny. I promised I'd be back this afternoon."

"Does your father know what you're up to?"

Jonathan shot Sally a bewildered look, then stood up and whispered, "Has she been this out of it all day?"

"Off and on. We had a nice conversation just a few minutes ago. She showed me some old snapshots of her and your dad. Funny how one minute she seems alert and responsive, and the next she's off somewhere."

Jonathan rolled his eyes. "Might as well blow off most of what she says anymore."

"For what it's worth, I think your coming to visit is making a difference."

"Thanks, I'd like to think so." Jonathan unlocked the wheelchair. "Come on, Grandma. Let's don't keep your guests waiting."

Elsie clutched her beaded purse and began to mumble. "Arnie made me take them back. I didn't want to. He *made* me."

Sally watched for a moment as Jonathan pushed his grandmother's wheelchair down the hall, then went back in and began to straighten Elsie's room. She set the shoe box of photographs on the nightstand, glad the sweet old woman could still recall some of her past. Sally thought it sad that after all the years Elsie had been married to Arnie, she never spoke fondly of him.

"Are you hiding in here?" Wanda Bradford said.

Sally let go of the box and turned toward the door. "No, I'm straightening Elsie's room. She took out these photos and showed them to me. She needed someone to talk to. I think it did her good."

"You're a certified nursing assistant, Sally. You're not paid to play psychologist."

Sally stood, her temples throbbing. "I wasn't aware that being kind wasn't part of my job description. I guess I'm done for the day."

Wanda looked over the top of her glasses. "I've watched you with patients. You're good, Sally. And more caring than most—except for that annoying chip on your shoulder."

Sally bit her lip and fiddled with her uniform pocket. *Look who's talking!* "Sorry. I thought you were unhappy with my work. Guess I don't have much self-confidence yet. I haven't had a job in a long time."

"Well, I'm not one to compliment you just for doing your job, so don't expect it. And since I'm the one who has the most say in your future here, it would behoove you to be more cooperative with me."

Sally nodded. "I have been a little defensive."

Wanda seemed distracted for a moment, and then her face softened. "Sally, listen to me. I started out as a CNA. I loved working with patients, trying to make a difference in the quality of their lives. I allowed myself to get emotionally attached. Then one by one, they started to fail. And eventually die." Wanda sighed. "The sadness spoiled it for me, and I almost opted out of nursing school. I learned the hard way the importance of keeping an emotional distance between the patients and me. You're not going to be here long if you get depressed." Wanda looked over the top her glasses. "And frankly, we need good people like you."

5

On Wednesday morning, Jonathan lay in bed, thinking about the significance of the photograph in light of the information he'd been able to get out of his grandmother. Everything seemed to fit. He'd hardly been able to sleep, now that he had something substantial to go on.

He sat up on the side of the bed and rubbed his eyes. It was 7:15. He picked up the phone and dialed.

"Yeah?"

"Dad, it's me."

"I'm surprised *you're* up this early. So, how was your grandmother yesterday afternoon?"

"We had a good time entertaining guests in the sunroom."

"What're you talkin' about?"

"Oh, that gal who works the day shift told her Rufus and Wilda had come to visit. Grandma bought it. It was pretty cute."

"I told you she's slippin' fast."

Jonathan switched the phone to the other ear. "Dad, I'm going to be gone a few days. I got a tip on a big factory in Pittsburgh that's hiring. Pays really good. I want to check it out."

"I thought you didn't want to live back East again? And what about Gracie and Bill's place? I thought they were payin' you to housesit."

"I'll put a hold on the mail and the paper. They won't even know I'm gone. Besides, Mom's been on my case to find a job."

"Since when can you afford to drive all that way, just to check out a job you'll probably find somethin' wrong with anyway?"

Jonathan smirked. "This one sounds like it's going to pay off. I'm hitching a ride with a buddy of mine who's been unemployed for a while. We're splitting expenses and can switch off driving."

"What about your grandmother?"

"I won't be gone long. Wouldn't hurt you to check in on her a little more often."

"Oh, so now you're gonna lecture me on how to treat my own mother?"

"Do whatever you want. I'll call you, okay?"

"Yeah, sure you will, Jon. See you when you get back." *Click.*

Jonathan hung up the phone. So he lied to his dad. If his hunch was correct, he might not have to look for a job—ever!

The patients in the east wing of Walnut Hills Nursing Center were lethargic and undemanding, and Sally decided to take a short break. She walked into the employees' lounge and saw Karen Morgan sitting alone at a table.

"Now *that's* a pair to draw to," Sally said, eyeing Karen's Hershey bar and diet Coke.

Karen chuckled. "Thought I'd skip the calories in the soft drink. Makes me feel like less of a glutton. You're free to join me, but I warn you—I'm stingy with my chocolate. I never share."

"That's okay, I brought my own snack." Sally sat in the chair facing Karen and opened the wrapper on a blueberry muffin she'd picked up at Quick Mart.

"How're you and Wanda getting along?" Karen asked.

"We had a breakthrough yesterday. She cautioned me about playing psychologist. She's not as insensitive as I thought."

"You've got to be kidding. The woman has ice water for blood."

Sally smiled. "Not really."

"Well, I'm glad things are better. I don't want to lose you. There's way too much turnover in this place."

Sally took a bite of muffin and savored it for a moment. "Elsie sure is somber today. I wonder why Jonathan isn't here yet? He always knows how to cheer her up."

"I warned you he'd leave."

"He wouldn't do that to Elsie again."

"Oh, but he would."

"Don't be so cynical. He's probably got other things to do this morning."

Karen rolled her eyes. "Wanna bet he won't be back before Easter?"

"My guess is he'll be here to have lunch with her."

"Wake up and smell the coffee, Sal. Johnny boy never stays any-where for long. Doesn't even have a permanent job. If you ask me, he's too old to be so footloose."

"I didn't see a wedding ring," Sally said. "Has he ever been mar-ried?"

Karen snickered. "Twice. No kids, though. Just as well."

"You're awfully negative about him. Sure you're not projecting your anger at your old boyfriend onto him?"

Karen shook her head. "Look, I'm not into men bashing, if that's what you think. Jonathan's always been nice to me. But something about him seems phony. Besides, I was the one who saw how depressed Elsie got each time he promised to come back and then didn't show for months at a time."

"I doubt she'd even realize the time lapse now," Sally said. "But I think you're wrong about him leaving."

"We'll see. I've seen this same scenario played out a few times. I guess he could have a sudden personality change, but what are the odds?" Karen stood and gathered her trash, then looked at Sally. "I'm really glad things have eased up between you and Wanda."

"Thanks. Me, too."

Sally slid out of the chair and dumped her wrapper in the trash, then headed back to the east wing.

Harry Rigsby pulled a sweatshirt over his flannel shirt, and then slipped on a hunting vest that was too tight to zip. The only thing that could make January feel any colder was ice or snow. And the only thing that could motivate him to go see his mother in the middle of the week was the heat in her room. Not that he minded spending a little time with her. But the whole nursing home scene was depressing. Besides, he never knew from one moment to the next whether or not his mother was on the same page.

He went out to the kitchen and poured himself some coffee, then sat at the table and let the mug warm his hands. The thick frost on the kitchen window made it impossible to see out.

What a sorry life for a healthy sixty-five-year-old man! His mother had always been after him to make something of himself and be a good support to Gracie and Jonathan. But Harry piddled the money away on what he wanted, giving little thought to how it was depriving his family—until that day he came home early....

Harry had left work in the middle of the afternoon, running a fever and feeling as if a brick wall had fallen on him. He pulled in the driveway and noticed Gracie out on the porch with Jonathan. When he walked up the steps, he saw two large suitcases on the porch and two sheepish faces looking up at him from the porch swing.

Harry looked at the suitcases and then at Gracie. "What *is* this?"

"You weren't supposed to be home for hours," Gracie said. "I—I didn't want you to see us leave. But I can't live this way anymore, Harry."

"What're you talkin' about?"

"I'm through talking. It doesn't do any good. You don't care about anyone but yourself."

"What's your beef, woman? You've got a roof over your head, food in your belly, clothes on your back. I worked my tail off so you can have a home. And now you're just walkin' out?"

"A home is more than a house, Harry." Gracie dabbed her eyes. "And a family is supposed to share and grow together. We're dying."

"That's bunk!" Harry started to grab Gracie's arm. Jonathan stood up.

"It's her choice, Dad."

Harry looked up at his fifteen-year-old and wondered when he had grown into a man. "You leavin', too?"

Jonathan nodded.

Harry threw his hands in the air. "Okay then, go! Both of you! See if I care!"

Harry turned on his heel, yanked open the front door, and went inside. He stormed out to the kitchen and grabbed the aspirin bottle. A car pulled up out front. He pulled back the curtains and saw a cab driver open the trunk and help Jonathan put both suitcases inside. Then Gracie and Jonathan got in the cab and drove out of his life....

Harry had been sure they'd come back. They didn't. But a bigger surprise was how little he missed them once he got over the shock. His life went on as before, only with fewer interruptions. He was free to hang out with his buddies, play cards, watch TV, go bowling, fishing, hunting—whatever he felt like doing. And he could always find some-one to sleep with. But as the years ticked away, he realized something was missing. That's when he tightened the ties with his folks. Harry was so much like his dad that they never got along well. But Harry had a soft place for his mother. She had been the nurturer when his father was self-absorbed in whatever struck his fancy at the moment.

Harry wasn't sure he had ever loved anyone besides his mother. He'd been fond of Gracie as long as she served his needs. And every now and then he felt something for Jon he couldn't explain. Was it love? Pride? He wasn't sure. He wasn't one to feel deeply about things. It was Jonathan who'd come looking for him after the kid's second marriage failed ten years ago. And though there was always tension between the two of them, Harry couldn't deny a growing attachment to his son.

He took a sip of coffee and let the liquid warm him. He had himself to blame that he was alone and forced to live on a fixed income. But if his mother had money put away somewhere, she'd want him to have it. She certainly wouldn't want Medicaid to take it all.

Harry felt a twinge of guilt for wanting to get his hands on his mother's money. Even after Gracie left, she had never asked him for a cent. Harry had managed to spend everything he earned on himself. And it was never enough.

Sally watched Elsie pick at her lunch for over forty-five minutes, then decided enough was enough. She took Elsie back to her room, got her tucked in for a nap, pulled the blinds, and then sat on the side of her bed.

"There you go," Sally said. "A nice nap will chase away the blahs." Of all the days for Elsie to be lucid, it would be the day Jonathan didn't show up.

Sally got up and looked out in the hallway to see if Wanda was around, then shut the door and again sat on the bed. "I know you're disappointed Johnny didn't come today. He probably had to work."

"Nonsense. Johnny doesn't have a job."

"Well, maybe he's looking for one."

Elsie sighed. "What he's looking for is my money."

"What money is that?"

"The money I kept from Arnie."

"Does Jonathan know where it is?"

Elsie's eyes grew wide, her fingers digging into Sally's arm. "Johnny's after my money, just like Harry and Arnie. They're all greedy. They're not getting a cent!"

"Okay, sweetie. Take it easy. No one's going to take your money."

Elsie motioned with her finger for Sally to lean forward. "If anything happens to me," she whispered, "promise me you'll get the money and give it to the poor."

Sally nodded and patted Elsie's hand. "Of course I will. Don't you worry." Sally looked deep into Elsie's eyes. Poor thing was so confused. "Are you ready to take a nap now?"

Elsie held tighter to Sally's hand. "Dig behind the stone. Lou and I buried the money there."

"Okay, sweetie. I'll find it. I'll make sure it goes to the poor."

Elsie loosened her grip and let her arm fall to her side. "It's been safe with Sophie all these years. Arnie never knew."

The door swung open and Wanda Bradford walked over to the bed, a clipboard in her hand. "And how is Mrs. Rigsby doing?"

"She's all set to take a nap," Sally said, her heart pounding. "And I'm about to go check on Mr. Tatum."

Wanda shot her a scolding look, then looked at the clipboard. "Her blood pressure's a little high. How's her appetite?"

"Not as good as usual, but she's disappointed her grandson didn't come today."

Wanda looked at Elsie. "Are you in any discomfort, Mrs. Rigsby?"

"Well, of course I am. No one comes to see me. How am I supposed to feel?"

Wanda turned to Sally, an eyebrow raised. "Mrs. Rigsby seems quite alert and responsive today, wouldn't you say?"

Sally stood, her back to Elsie, and lowered her voice. "Not really. She's been different since Monday. She seems confused."

"I'll have the doctor take a look at her," Wanda said. "Isn't Mr. Tatum waiting for you to take him to the shower?"

"Uh, yes. I was just leaving."

"You have eleven other patients, Sally. Surely Mrs. Rigsby can take a nap without your help." Wanda held her gaze a moment and then walked out of the room.

Sally waited until Wanda's footsteps grew faint, then sat on the side of the bed and brushed hair off Elsie's forehead. "I'll check in on you later."

Elsie's eyes seemed to plead. "The money's in Dexter Springs. With Sophie. Don't tell Johnny and Harry."

"Okay, sweetie. I won't. Now get some rest."

Sally got up and walked to the door, then stared at the tiny person under the covers. When she turned to leave, she found herself nose-to-nose with Harry Rigsby.

"Oh, excuse me." She took a step backwards and let him in the room.

"How's my mother?" Harry asked.

"She's about to take a nap. Seems a little down today. She was expecting Jonathan to come by."

"Yeah, weren't we all?"

"Pardon me?"

"Oh, nothin'. Jon took off and won't be back for a few days. Guess she's stuck with me."

"I'm sure she'll be thrilled for the company."

"If she even knows me. She seem out of it to you?"

"A little confused, maybe. Fretting about money. Nothing that made sense."

"Yeah, she's liable to say anything," Harry said. "Last time I was here she thought she was some rich lady with a fat bank account. So, where're those bruises I got called about?"

Sally followed Harry over to the bed and was surprised when Elsie held up her wrist.

"Uh, there," Sally said. "Your mother thrashes in her sleep sometimes. She must've hit it on the bed rail."

"Doesn't look too bad. Good thing for you."

Sally paused and counted to ten. "Excuse me. I need to check on another patient."

"Yeah, go ahead. Think I'll stick around. Feels nice and warm in here. Sure beats watchin' TV in that meat locker I live in."

Sally left the room and started to walk away, then heard Harry's voice and decided to stand outside the door and listen.

"Wanna tell me why *you're* frettin' about money? I'm the one who needs it."

"Is that you, Arnie?"

"Oh, stop fakin'. I know you understand me. How much longer are you gonna play this game? Dad's been gone a long time. When you're gone, the money's gonna rot somewhere. Is that what you want?"

"They served corn chowder for lunch," Elsie said. "I've never liked corn chowder."

"Ma, please. One of these days you're gonna forget where it is. Just tell me. I promise I'll split it with Jon."

Elsie started to sing, "Are you sleeping, are you sleeping, brother John. Brother John. Morning bells are ringing. Morning bells are ringing. Ding ding dong—"

"Okay, Ma. Have it your way. What I don't get is why you rat-holed money and won't even share it with your own son. You're stingier than Dad was."

Sally heard the TV go on. She waited a few seconds, then walked across the hall to Rufus and Charles's room, wondering how much of what Elsie told her was true.

Jonathan arrived in Dexter Springs just after 10:00 PM, bought a six-pack of beer, and drove around until midnight, getting a feel for what he wanted to do.

He turned into a shopping center and parked in the back of the Wal-Mart parking lot, away from the security lights. He crushed the last empty beer can, pitched it on the floor, and got out. He took the shovel out of the trunk and put a flashlight in his coat pocket, then started walking up Milton Street.

He approached the house he had driven by earlier, that once belonged to his great uncle and now belonged to his cousin Layton— at least, according to the listing in the phone book. The lights were out in the house. He snuck around to one side and was surprised to find the gate on the chain-link fence unlocked. He went into the backyard and decided not to use the flashlight. In the moonlight, he could see the outline of what appeared to be a shed in the very back of the lot, and trees around the perimeter—and something that looked like a trellis.

The moonlight made it easy to see, but it also made him easy to spot. He stopped and looked back at the house. The lights were still out.

He walked under the trellis and into what had to be a flower garden, relieved to see it was smaller than he had imagined. No flowers were blooming in the January chill, but he saw bushes and walkways and statues.

"Grandma, where's the money?"

"Buried right here. Behind the angel..."

Jonathan examined the garden statues and saw that the tallest one was an angel. Surely after all these years, the statues had been replaced several times. But he was feeling lucky. What did he have to lose?

Jonathan began digging behind the angel until he'd worked up a good sweat—and created a conspicuous mound of dirt. Why would anyone bury the money any deeper than this? He heaved a sigh and leaned on the shovel, disgusted that it was turning out to be more complicated than he had thought. He shoved the angel with his foot, and laughed derisively when it fell over and broke in two.

Suddenly, he heard a deep, throaty growl behind him. Jonathan stood completely still, his heart racing, and tightened his grip on the shovel, then quickly spun around, swinging the shovel and hitting something with a loud thud. A German shepherd yelped, and then lay motionless.

Jonathan heard footsteps pounding the ground and saw a man running toward him.

"Hey, what'd you do to my dog!"

The man ran into him, and they both went sprawling to the ground.

Jonathan was sure it was Layton. He scrambled to his feet and grabbed the shovel and swung it wildly. He struck Layton in the chest, knocking him on his back, then straddled him and jammed the shovel handle against Layton's throat. He looked into his cousin's eyes, wide and full of panic, and loosened his grip on the shovel.

In the next instant, Layton pushed Jonathan off his chest and wrestled the shovel from him. He got to his feet and backed up. "Don't come any closer! I don't want to hurt you, but I will."

Jonathan charged his cousin, thinking he would knock him down and make his escape. A second later, he felt as if a stick of dynamite had gone off in his head. He stumbled and fell, vaguely aware of the cold ground under his cheek—and then nothing.

Just after 2:00 AM in Dexter Springs, lights from law enforcement vehicles flashed in the inky darkness as city police and sheriff's deputies strung yellow crime scene tape behind a modest, two-story Cape Cod.

Inside, Layton Rigsby sat on the couch, one arm around his wife, and the other around his son.

"I—I didn't mean to kill him," Layton said, his body trembling. "I was just defending myself."

Sheriff Todd Baughman lifted his eyebrows. "ID says his name's Rigsby, same as yours."

"I think he's my cousin."

"You think? Come on, Layton. Either he is or he isn't."

Layton pulled his wife and son closer. "I haven't seen him since we were teenagers. I already told the police that."

"Then why do you suppose he was on your property?"

"I don't know. He was digging for something."

"Any idea what that might be?"

Layton shook his head.

"How'd you know he was out there? Was your dog barking?"

"No, Duke was asleep in Murray's room. I got up to use the bathroom. The moon was bright, and I saw someone digging in the flower garden. I told Sylvia to stay inside, and I went and got Duke and a flashlight, then went out back. I thought maybe one of Murray's friends was playing a joke. Duke ran ahead and cornered the guy. Next thing I know, the guy swings his shovel and hits Duke in the head and knocks him out. I rushed the guy, knocked him to the ground, and asked why he hurt my dog and what he was doing out there.

"He didn't answer me. He just pushed me off, got up, and started swinging the shovel like some maniac. Hit me in the chest and knocked me flat on my back. Next thing I knew he was pushing the shovel handle against my throat, and I couldn't breathe. I thought he was gonna kill me. Finally, I got him off me and grabbed the shovel away from him. I told him to stay back, that I didn't want to hurt him. But he came at me, and I hit him with it. God help me, I didn't mean to kill him. It was self-defense!"

Sheriff Baughman looked at the woman. "Did you see what happened, Sylvia?"

Sylvia Rigsby nodded, wiping a tear from her cheek. "I was watching from the window. The man swung around and hit Duke with a shovel. I saw Layton and the guy fighting, and I ran to get the rifle. But when I got out there, Layton was kneeling next to the man and told me to call 911—that he was dead." She put her hand over her mouth and muffled the emotion.

Sheriff Baughman's eyes moved to the frightened teenager on the couch. "Murray, did you see anything?"

"No, sir. I woke up when I heard my mom crying—when she called 911."

The sheriff wrote something on his report, and then looked at Layton. "Do you know the name of his nearest relative?"

Layton raked his shaking hands through his hair. "Uh, yeah. His father is Harry Rigsby. Last I heard he lived in Kansas City."

6

On Thursday morning, Harry Rigsby walked two Kansas City police officers to the front door, then went to the kitchen and stood, his back leaning against the countertop, his mind racing like a runaway train.

Identify the body? He had never considered that his son might die before he did. How was he going to afford to bury him? Jon had no life insurance. He wasn't even a veteran. Gracie and Bill would have to pay for it. He wondered how Gracie was handling the shock, or if the authorities in Key West had found her yet.

Harry spotted his coffee mug on the kitchen table and went over and sat, his eyes fixed on two empty Coke cups piled on top of the trash. So, that's why Jon had brought him lunch, and then seemed so interested in the photograph! Had his grandmother told him the money was buried in Aunt Clara's flower garden, or was he just acting on a hunch? Either way, it was hard to fault him. Harry would've done the same thing if he'd known where to look.

But why didn't Jon just make up a story about why he was digging, instead of getting into a fight with Layton? His mind flashed back thirty years to Jon and Layton laughing and wrestling together. He blinked the stinging from his eyes, then took a sip of coffee. He quickly spit the cold liquid back in the mug, then got up and dumped the rest of it in the sink.

He had to pull himself together. Right now, he needed to focus on driving to Dexter Springs to identify Jon's body.

Harry walked into his mother's room just as Sally Cox had finished blow-drying Elsie's hair.

Sally looked up. "Oh, you're back again today."

"I need to talk with my mother," Harry said, wondering why Sally always stared at him as if she could read his mind. "Think you could give us a minute—*alone?*"

"Uh, of course. Sorry." Sally put the blow-dryer in the nightstand and left the room.

Harry pulled up a chair next to his mother's wheelchair and took her hand. "Ma? I got bad news. I don't know if you're gonna get this or not, but there's no easy way to say it. Jon's been killed."

Elsie looked up, her eyes wide and alert. "How?"

"He was out at Uncle Roy's old place, diggin' in the flower garden in the middle of the night." Harry waited for her to react and was surprised when she didn't. "Roy's grandson Layton owns the place now. Saw someone diggin' out back and went out to run him off. They fought. Jon charged him, and Layton hit him in the head with a shovel. Never even knew it was Jon till the police found an ID on the body."

A tear ran down the side of Elsie's face.

"We both know why Jon was out there. He was lookin' for the money, wasn't he?"

Elsie sat still, her eyes clamped shut, her chin quivering.

"For cryin' out loud, will you just tell me where it is? Jon lost his life tryin' to find it! Now I gotta go identify the kid's body, and I don't even have enough to bury him!"

Elsie's eyes flew open. "God knows I loved that boy. But he was foolish. So foolish." Tears splashed onto Elsie's housedress.

Harry took a handkerchief out of his pocket and wiped her face. "Look, I don't know when they'll release Jon's body. But sometime soon I gotta bury my only son. I'm beggin' you, Ma, at least give me enough for that. Don't make me go to Gracie for the money."

Elsie shook her head and mumbled on and on about something that didn't make sense.

Harry dropped her hand. "Thanks a heap for your generosity, Ma. Really warms my heart." He rose to his feet. "It'll take the rest of the day to get over there and back. Don't wait up."

He left her room and shut the door harder than he had intended to. He brushed past Sally Cox and walked toward the front entrance.

7

On Friday morning, Sally Cox sat in the employees' lounge at Walnut Hills Nursing Center, her mind racing and her eyes tracing the letters on a can of Orange Crush.

Karen Morgan got something out of the vending machine, then walked over and sat across the table from Sally. "Did you hear what happened to Jonathan Rigsby?"

Sally nodded. "It was on the morning news. Really sad."

"More like freaky. What do you suppose he was doing in his cousin's yard—looking for a body?" Karen chuckled. "Sorry, bad joke."

Sally sighed. "The whole thing's a bad joke."

"Does Elsie know what happened?"

"Harry told her. Poor thing just shut down."

Karen lifted her eyebrows. "There was something about Johnny boy I never trusted."

"That's what you said."

"You still aren't convinced he's a weirdo?"

"I'm convinced he was good with Elsie, all right?"

"Sorry," Karen said. "Joking helps me cope. It's really not funny. But why was he digging in his cousin's yard in the middle of the night? You have to admit it sounds ghoulish."

"I suppose the police will figure it out. In the meantime, I have to deal with Elsie. She didn't need this."

"Honey, nobody needs this. How's Harry?"

Sally shrugged. "*He's* the one I don't trust."

"Really?"

"You didn't hear me say that."

Karen smiled and leaned forward. "Okay. But at least throw me a bone."

"I hate the way he manipulates Elsie. He's self-serving and sneaky."

"Like father, like son, eh?" Karen glanced up at the clock. "I took my break earlier. I need to get back. But if you want to talk about it, or if you need help with Elsie, I'm available."

"Thanks."

Sally waited until Karen left the lounge, then took two Excedrin out of her pocket and washed them down with the last of the Orange Crush. If Harry didn't know where the money was before, he did now. The creep! Was she willing to let Harry rip off Elsie and then rip off the system? Shouldn't she at least let him know that she was onto his greedy little scheme?

Then again, all she needed was for Harry to deny everything and make a scene with the administrator. If Medicaid got involved, it would be Sally's word against his. And Sally could be out the door—and out of a paycheck.

Sally crushed the soda can, then got up and put it in the trash. He should be ashamed. What kind of son tries to extort money from his failing mother? How much money could one old woman have socked away? Sally sighed and shook her head. "Poor Mrs. Rigsby."

Sally knocked gently, and then went in Elsie Rigsby's room. The old woman looked frail sitting in her wheelchair, staring at the snowflakes floating down outside the window.

Sally pulled a chair next to her and sat. "Beautiful, isn't it? I used to love the snow when I was kid. I grew up in the East, where we had snow all winter long. I think I learned to ice-skate before I learned to walk."

Sally sat in the quiet and wondered if Elsie even knew she was there.

"Arnie would never let me buy ice skates for Harry."

Okay, sweetie. Let's keep you talking! "How come?"

"Arnie was stingy. Tight as they come."

"Times were hard. I suppose money was hard to come by."

"Not for Arnie." Elsie sat quietly for a moment, then turned to Sally, a defiant look on her face. "I fixed the books. I couldn't let him ruin us!"

Sally touched her hand. "Of course you couldn't, sweetie. It's all right."

Elsie's eyes brimmed with tears. "Johnny would've taken it all."

Sally got up and pulled the door shut, then sat again and took

Elsie's hand. "Did Johnny go to Dexter Springs to dig up the money?"

Elsie clutched Sally's arm and whispered, "It's safe with Sophie. You can't tell Harry."

"Don't worry, I won't." Sally looked into the old woman's eyes and for a split second seemed to be in her soul. "Elsie, who's Sophie?"

There was a knock at the door. Sally jumped, her hand over her heart.

"Ma, you awake?"

Harry Rigsby came in and stood peering down at them. "Why's the door closed? What's wrong?"

"Nothing's wrong. Your mother and I have been watching the snow. She's a little depressed."

"Yeah? Well, she's not the only one."

Harry's eyes seemed to probe. Had he heard anything?

"I'm sorry about Jonathan," Sally said. "I know this has been horrible for all of you."

"Well, you can go now."

"They'll be serving lunch in fifteen minutes. Will you be bringing your mother down to the dining room?"

"Yeah, sure. Whatever."

Sally left Elsie's room, her heart pounding and her thoughts spinning out of control.

Sally checked in on Elsie several times during the afternoon, disgusted that Harry had planted himself in Elsie's room, watching TV and taking naps. She could hear him snoring clear out in the hallway.

Sally had finished her rounds for the day when Wanda Bradford tapped her on the shoulder.

"Sally, the police are here, wanting to talk to employees who had contact with Jonathan Rigsby. I told them to start with you, since you spent more time with him and with Elsie than anyone else."

Thanks for nothing, Wanda. "All right," Sally said. "Where are they?"

"They're set up in the staff meeting room. They're waiting for you there."

"I doubt if I'll be much help."

Wanda's expression was uncharacteristically kind. "Relax. Just tell them what you know. By the way, is Mrs. Rigsby doing any better?"

"It's hard to say. Harry's been with her most of the day, being the dutiful son."

"You look tired, Sally. Talk to the police, then take the weekend and get some rest. I know this has taken its toll on you."

You don't know the half of it! Sally walked down the hall and turned into the staff meeting room. Two police officers looked up and rose to their feet.

"I'm Officer Dan Shaw, and this is Officer Mark Albright of the Kansas City Police Department. We're working with law enforcement from the Dexter Springs area to question people who knew Jonathan Rigsby."

Sally shook hands with each. "I'm Sally Cox, a CNA on the day shift. Elsie Rigsby is one of my patients."

"Then you knew her grandson?" Officer Shaw asked.

"I can't say I knew him. But I had a couple of days to observe him with his grandmother."

"Please, sit down and make yourself comfortable." Officer Albright nodded toward a vinyl chair. "This will only take a few minutes. Just routine."

Sally sat and tried to relax.

"We'd like to record this conversation," Officer Shaw said. "It would save a lot of time."

"That's fine."

He pushed the button on the recorder. "We're talking with Sally Cox, a certified nursing assistant at Walnut Hills Nursing Center in Kansas City. All right, Ms. Cox, when was the first time you met Jonathan Rigsby?"

"Monday morning of this week. He came to visit his grandmother, Elsie Rigsby, who's one of my patients. I saw him with her at the breakfast table."

"What was your impression?"

"He and his grandmother seemed glad to see each other. And the people at Elsie's table instantly warmed up to him. I had never seen them that interactive or laughing that much."

"Did you have occasion to speak with him?"

"Off and on. He hung around most of the morning until Elsie wore out. Then he left, and she slept the afternoon away."

"Did you observe anything odd about his behavior? Did he say anything that struck you as unusual?"

Sally shrugged and shook her head. "No, he was extremely attentive to his grandmother. In fact, Jonathan came back to have dinner with her and ended up spending the night. Said he was worried something might be wrong with Elsie because she could hardly wake up and seemed lethargic. I think he just wore her out."

"You mentioned he was at the breakfast table. Was that out of the ordinary?"

"I don't know what his routine was when he came to visit," Sally said. "Like I told you, I never met him until this past Monday. But one of the other CNAs told me he had a habit of showing up, promising to come back, and then disappearing for months. You might want to ask Karen Morgan. Elsie used to be her patient and she has some strong opinions about Jonathan."

"Do you?"

"It's hard to have an opinion when I hardly knew him. The only thing I can tell you about Jonathan is that he was attentive to his grandmother, and she seemed to enjoy his company." *And that he was after the poor woman's money and thought nothing of ripping her off. The creep!* Sally's heart pounded so hard her name tag was moving.

"Okay, Ms. Cox, that's all for now," Officer Albright said. "Here are our business cards. If you think of anything else, please contact us."

Sally nodded. "Then you're through with me?"

"Yes, ma'am," Officer Shaw said. "You're free to go. We appreciate your cooperation."

8

After dinner, Sally Cox put on her heavy sweats and tennis shoes to walk off the canned chili that felt like a brick in her stomach despite the Maalox. She grabbed a flashlight and went outside on the front porch. She looked up at a scant spattering of stars in the city sky and wondered if Sam was out walking with his "sweet young thing."

She pulled the hood up over her head, then skipped down the steps and out to the sidewalk, grateful that the snow hadn't stuck. For once, she was actually glad to have the weekend to think.

Her mind raced with Elsie's words: *Arnie was stingy. Tight as they come. I fixed the books. I couldn't let him ruin us! Johnny's after my money, just like Harry and Arnie. Dig behind the stone. Lou and I buried the money there. It's been safe with Sophie all these years. Arnie never knew. You can't tell Harry.* What did it all mean? Who was Lou? And Sophie? Had they told Jonathan where to find the money?

Sally had a sinking feeling there was a lot more involved than just a little savings one sweet old grandmother had tucked away. It didn't matter now. Thanks to Jonathan's foiled attempt to retrieve it, Harry knew where it was.

If anything happens to me, promise me you'll get the money and give it to the poor.

Sally saw car lights coming toward her. A red Camaro slowed and pulled next to the sidewalk. *Oh, no. What's he doing here?*

Sam Cox rolled down the window. "You shouldn't be walking alone when it's dark."

"I wasn't alone until you left. Did you drive all the way over here just to rub my nose in it?"

"Don't get mad, Sal. I was in the neighborhood. Saw you walking and thought I'd say hi."

"Okay, hi—now good-bye." Sally resumed her walking.

Sam made a U-turn and followed alongside in the other lane. "At least tell me how you're doing. Leslie said you got a job over at that nursing home in Walnut Hills."

"It's more than a job. I'm a certified nursing assistant." *With lousy pay, a lousy supervisor, and a lousy mess on my hands.*

"That's great. I'm glad you're doing well."

"Better than well, Sam. Give your conscience a rest. Shouldn't you be home with Ms. Botox and the kids?"

"Look, it's been eight months," he said. "Do you think we could at least talk civil?"

"For what purpose?"

"There's no reason we can't be friends. Maybe we could have coffee sometime."

Sally stopped, her arms folded, and glared at him. "I don't think so."

"It'd make Leslie happy."

"That's Alan's job."

A wall of silence stood between them. Sally wanted to run, but felt as though her feet were cemented to the sidewalk.

"I never meant to hurt you," Sam finally said. "I wish you could understand that."

"You didn't just happen to be in the neighborhood, Sam. Why are you really here?"

"I told you. I miss talking to you."

"Talk to Ms. Botox."

He let out an exaggerated sigh. "Her *name* is Allison. And we do talk. But sometimes I miss talking to you, okay?"

"No, it's not okay. I've got my own life now. And I don't have anything to talk to you about."

"We used to be friends."

"We used to married."

Sam shook his head. "All right. You have a right to be mad. But if you ever get to the place where you can forgive me, I'd like us to be friends."

"Good-bye, Sam. Have a nice life."

"Just think about what I said, all right?"

Sam rolled up his window and drove off. Sally started walking, tears clouding her eyes and a north wind nipping her face. How dare he show up with no warning and get her emotions all stirred up! He had a lot of nerve thinking she would forgive him or ever consider him a friend.

Sally crossed the street and walked past New Hope Bible Church and glanced at the words on the lighted sign out front:

If Jesus is Lord of your life,
trust Him to provide what you need.

Sally walked faster, then started to jog. *Provide* was a relative term. She was already working as many hours as they'd give her and still couldn't pay all her bills. She'd probably spend the next eleven years scrimping, and then retire on a fixed income—assuming Social Security hadn't gone bankrupt yet. Hardly cause for rejoicing.

Harry Rigsby walked in the front door, tossed the newspaper on the couch, and turned up the thermostat. At least the snow flurries hadn't amounted to anything. He peeled off his coat and gloves and lay on the couch, his hands behind his head.

He hadn't expected to feel this sad about Jon's death. He and the kid had never been close. So why had Harry just spent the evening wandering around the Country Club Plaza, peering in store windows, and freezing half to death?

He picked up the remote and turned on the TV, wondering if Gracie and Bill were home yet. He knew Gracie would be devastated and full of questions. What was he supposed to say to her? The image of their son at the morgue was one he would just as soon put behind him.

Harry closed his eyes, the sound of Jon's laughter ringing in his ears. It didn't seem that long ago that Jon was just a boy. Harry realized he was smiling. A memory of Jon's winning basket at the family reunion was still vivid in his memory. But he had so little recollection of what his son had been like as a kid.

He glanced at his watch. Gracie and Bill's plane should have landed over an hour ago.

Gracie Garver stepped in the house and turned off the security alarm, then held open the door while her husband brought in the luggage from the garage.

"Honey, go sit down," Bill said. "I can get this."

Gracie walked through the kitchen and down the hall to the guest bedroom. She stood in the doorway and observed the room as Jonathan had left it: bed unmade and clothes piled in the chair. Tears stung her eyes. Maybe the police were wrong. Maybe it was all a mistake. She felt her husband's arms slip around her.

"You don't have to deal with this right now," he said.

"It's not like I can turn it off." Gracie sniffled. "My son tried to kill his cousin. I have to live with that."

"Honey, we don't know what was going through Jon's mind."

"He had problems. Don't tell me he didn't."

"The kid was shiftless. He wasn't violent."

"Then why isn't he here, in this bed—instead of some stainless steel drawer in the county morgue?" Gracie wiped the tears from her cheeks.

The phone rang.

"I'll get it." Bill kissed the top of her head, then walked out to the kitchen, Gracie on his heels.

"Hello...? Yeah, they did...We just walked in.... Not very well, how about you...? I'm sure it was.... Hold on, let me see if she can come to the phone."

Bill turned to her, his hand over the receiver. "It's Harry. You want to talk to him?"

Gracie wrinkled her nose. "I suppose I should." She cleared her throat and took the phone. "Hello, Harry."

"Guess the cops found you. Heck of a way to find out your kid's dead."

Gracie held her hand over her mouth and fought back the emotion. "The sheriff said you identified Jon's body."

"Uh, yeah. I drove over there yesterday afternoon."

"H-how did he look?"

"Like Jon."

"That's not what I meant."

"What do you want me to say? He had a pretty nasty head wound. Looked like Layton wasn't takin' any chances."

Gracie dabbed her eyes. "What was Jon doing there? As far as I know, he hasn't even talked to Layton since you and I divorced."

"I dunno. Jon told me he was goin' to Pittsburgh for a job interview."

"Why would he lie? What was he hiding? Doesn't the sheriff know *anything?*"

"Just what Layton told him: that he confronted a man digging in his yard, who clobbered his dog and then tried to choke him with a shovel. Swears he had no clue it was Jon till sheriff's deputies found his ID."

"What makes them think Layton's telling the truth?"

"The sheriff goes to church with Layton's family. Has known them for years. Layton's wife backed up everything he said, and his wounds are consistent with his story. Plus, Layton was so shook that the paramedics had to give him somethin' to calm him down. Sounds legit."

Gracie blew her nose. "I keep expecting Jon to walk through that door. I can't believe I'm never going to see him again."

There was an awkward lapse in the conversation.

"Harry, are you still there?"

"Yeah, I'm here. We gotta talk about funeral arrangements."

"I shouldn't have to bury my son—" Gracie's voice cracked. "It wasn't supposed to be this way."

"Yeah, I know. Jon didn't have life insurance, and I sure don't have that kind of—"

"Save your breath. Bill and I know better than to expect anything from you!"

"I'd pay for everything, if I had it."

"I need to go. I'll call you when I can think."

She hung up the phone and went back to the guest bedroom. She sat on the side of the bed and picked up one of Jon's T-shirts and held it to her cheek. Was there ever a time she hadn't worried about him? Bad grades. Skipping school. Drugs. Countless jobs. Two divorces. Overdrawn bank accounts. Bill collectors. All her efforts to teach him responsibility had failed.

It didn't help that Harry had made no effort to be a father to Jon. But Bill had treated him like a son. And still, Jon's bad choices had seemed to rumble in the distance like a building storm. Nothing they had done ever caused him to settle down. But nothing had prepared her for this.

Gracie let her tears fall on the T-shirt, as if that would somehow wash away the sense of failure and finality that consumed her.

9

Harry Rigsby sat at the kitchen table, his fingers wrapped around a mug of lukewarm coffee, his eyes stuck on Tuesday morning's obituaries in the *Kansas City Star.*

Jonathan Rigsby

Graveside services for Jonathan Harold Rigsby, 40, are scheduled for 10 AM Tuesday at Round Hill Cemetery with Rev. Richard Akins officiating under the direction of Jackson Heights Funeral Home, Kansas City. Mr. Rigsby died January 17 in Dexter Springs.

He was born December 29, 1963, in St. Louis, Missouri.

Survivors include his father Harold Ray Rigsby; his mother Grace Elizabeth Garver; stepfather William Earl Garver; and his grandmother Elsa Mae Rigsby, all of Kansas City. He was preceded in death by his paternal grandfather, Arnold Harold Rigsby of Kansas City; and his maternal grandparents, Jonathan and Eva McClendon of Dexter Springs, Missouri.

Harry folded the newspaper and set it aside. Precious little could be said about Jon's accomplishments or his background. Pity. Harry doubted anything would have changed had Jon lived a full life. The kid was just like his old man. He felt a twinge of sadness that he hadn't been a good role model, but wondered why Jon hadn't taken after Gracie. She'd been a good mother. And his stepfather, the big shot shoe store owner, would certainly have given Jon an "in" had he been the slightest bit motivated to work hard.

Harry glanced at the clock. In less than three hours, he would be standing in the cold at some gravesite Gracie and Bill had chosen, saying good-bye to his only son. Other than the ordeal of watching Gracie sob over Jon's casket at the funeral home, none of this seemed real. At least Bill and Gracie were paying for the whole thing. That was one headache he didn't have to contend with.

Harry had considered requesting permission from Elsie's doctor to allow her to attend the graveside service, and then decided against it. *If* she were lucid enough to know what was happening, the grief—not to mention the harsh weather—would take its toll on her. But even more than that, he was never sure what she might say. And he didn't want to raise any eyebrows. So far, the authorities seemed stumped as to why Jon was digging on Layton's property, and Harry wasn't about to crack open that door.

Sometime soon, he'd have to figure out a ploy to get Layton to let him do some digging where Aunt Clara's flower garden had been. Maybe he'd tell Layton that, years back, Harry's folks had buried family heirlooms there. If Layton didn't seem receptive, maybe he'd just tell him the truth and offer to split the money. It's not as though Layton was rolling in the bucks. But it was way too risky to do anything for a while.

Harry vacillated between resentment and tenderness for his mother. Her sadness over Jon's death was genuine, but her miserly withholding of her money infuriated him. What earthly good would it do her now? Why would she even consider letting it go to waste? He wasn't about to give up on her until he found out where she'd put it.

Sally Cox sat in the employees' lounge, a can of Coke in her hand and the morning paper open to the obituaries.

Karen Morgan poured a cup of coffee and sat at the table facing Sally. "Jonathan Rigsby's graveside service should be getting underway."

Sally glanced at her watch. "Still can't believe he's dead."

"It's weird, all right. How's Elsie this morning?"

Sally leaned forward and lowered her voice. "Depressed. But heaven forbid I should mention it, lest Wanda think I'm psychoanalyzing her."

"Doesn't take a rocket scientist to figure it out."

"Ah, but I'm being *paid* to make sure Elsie completes the activities of daily living—not to play psychologist. Like I'm supposed to ignore it?"

"You can't. Just don't tell Wanda everything you know."

Sally lifted her eyebrows. "She's a mind reader."

"Nah, she's not *that* good." Karen blew on her coffee, her gaze set on Sally. "You've gotten pretty close to Elsie."

"She's a sweetheart."

"I've always thought so. Does she still go on and on about things that don't make sense?"

"Sometimes. But other times she seems as present to me as you do right now. Just the other day we looked through some old photographs of her and Harry. It was fun getting to interact with the real Elsie, you know?"

"So, what did she have to say?"

Sally shrugged. "It's not so much what she said. Just that she was able to remember some things."

Karen took a sip of coffee, her eyes peering over the top of the cup. "Sounded to me like she didn't have a very happy life. Sure never had anything nice to say about that husband of hers."

"You noticed that, too?"

"Arnie Rigsby must've been a real tightwad. Elsie said he never gave her an extra cent for anything—and that Harry and Jonathan were as greedy as he was."

"Elsie told you that?" Sally said, her heart racing.

Karen nodded, her finger wiping the lipstick off the rim of her cup. "She told me all sorts of things. Hard to know what was real and what wasn't." There was a long pause, then Karen looked up, her eyes probing. "Elsie actually told me once she's rich. Wonder where *that* came from?"

Sally folded the newspaper and pushed it aside. "Probably wishful thinking. If her husband was as tight as you say, she must've done without. She doesn't talk to me about things like that."

Karen downed the last of the coffee. "Well, onward and upward. I've got to get back to work."

"Me, too. I've still got three patients to get showered before lunch."

Sally got up and tossed the Coke can in the trash, then walked toward the east wing, wondering just how much Elsie had told Karen Morgan about the money—and if Karen had figured out that Jonathan had died trying to find it.

Sally completed her list of morning duties and decided to check in on Elsie before lunch. She knocked gently, then entered Elsie's room and found her sitting in the wheelchair next to the bed, a Bible closed in her lap, tears streaming down her cheeks.

Sally sat on the side of the bed and handed Elsie a Kleenex, then patted her hand. "I'm so sorry about Jonathan. I know your heart is heavy today."

Elsie blinked, but said nothing.

"Sweetie, I'd give anything if I could take some of your sorrow. I really would. I want you to know that."

Elsie looked down, a tear splashing onto the worn leather cover of her Bible. "If only I could've trusted Him."

Sally put her hand on Elsie's shoulder. "I think you were wise not to. Jonathan didn't sound very responsible."

Elsie sighed. "I'm talking about *God*." She put her face in her hands. "I didn't trust Him to take care of us. So, I took money from Arnie's business—to make *sure*."

Sally's mind raced to fit the pieces to the puzzle. Is that what Elsie had meant by "fixing the books?"

A few moments passed in silence, and then Elsie looked over at her. "I saved almost all of it for Harry. But Lou warned me not to trust him with that much money."

"Sweetie, remind me who Lou is."

Elsie dabbed her eyes and looked indignantly at Sally. "My older brother. Can't you remember anything?"

"Is he still living?"

"Well, of course, he's not living. I'm ninety and I've outlived almost all my family—even my grandson." Elsie blew her nose.

"What about Sophie…is *she* still living?"

Elsie drew in a breath, her eyes wide. "Who told you about Sophie?" she whispered.

Sally heard footsteps, and then Harry's irritating voice resonating behind her. "Well, here you are *again*."

Sally got up and turned around. "You mother's sad about Jonathan, and I was trying to comfort her. I'm sorry for your loss. I know it's been difficult."

"You got that right. How about you go do whatever it is you do and give us some privacy."

Sally squeezed Elsie on the shoulder. "I'll check in on you later. Lunch is in twenty minutes."

Sally brushed by Harry, glad to be out of his presence and disgusted to think that he was all Elsie had left. She stepped into the hallway, surprised to see Karen Morgan standing outside the door.

"That man really grates on me," Karen said.

Sally lifted an eyebrow. "Yeah? You're not the only one."

"Wish I could blame it on his son's death, but Harry's always been abrasive. So, how's Elsie doing?"

"Sad. And confused."

"Why? What'd she say?"

"Nothing that meant anything—rambling, mostly. But I sensed that having someone hold her hand was comforting."

"Especially when the only close relative she's got is scary Harry." Karen looked at her watch. "I'd better scoot. It's almost lunchtime."

Sally nodded. "I need to make sure Rufus has his slippers on. You know he kicks them off, just so I'll bribe him with jelly beans?"

Karen chuckled. "He's a rascal, all right. See you in the dining room."

Harry sat on the side of Elsie's bed, his elbows on his knees, his chin resting on his palms. "What's the point in cryin' now, Ma? Jon's dead and buried. I'm the one who's humiliated that Gracie and Bill had to pay his funeral expenses."

Elsie looked up at him. "Gracie's a generous woman."

Harry rolled his eyes. "Yeah, so you've told me a million times. Too bad Jon didn't turn out like his mother."

Harry got up and closed the door, then paced in front of the window. "You've gotta stop holdin' out. There's no reason for you to hang on to the money. You're gonna be in this place till you die, and not one cent of it's gonna do you any good."

Elsie sat with her head bowed, as if she didn't hear a word he said.

Harry went over to her wheelchair and squatted, his hand tilting her chin upward until he could see her eyes. She avoided his gaze.

"It's just the two of us now, Ma. And you might not be here much longer. I got nobody else. I can barely make ends meet as it is. And with Jon gone, who's gonna take care of me when I can't? That money would go a long way in securin' my future."

Elsie's lips became a taut line, and she turned her head.

Harry let go of her chin. "You treat me like some reject. I'm your son, for cryin' out loud!"

She looked up at him, her eyes brimming with tears. "Then act like it."

Harry got up and sat on the bed, pretending not to notice his mother's sniffling. He glanced at the picture of Jon on her nightstand and was struck with a horrible thought: What if Jon *had* found the money, and Layton made up the story about Jon attacking him? What if cousin Layton had killed Jon for the money and outsmarted the cops?

Harry peeled off his sweater and wiped the perspiration from his forehead. Maybe it was time he made another trip to Dexter Springs.

There was a knock at the door.

"Excuse me," Sally said. "It's time for lunch. Will you be taking your mother to the dining room, or would you like me to?"

Harry rose to his feet and picked up his coat and sweater. "Uh, you take her." He looked over at Elsie, his voice laced with sarcasm. "Thanks for all the understanding, Ma. Let's do this again real soon."

He turned on his heel, brushed past Sally Cox, and headed for the main entrance. He reached in his pocket and pulled out a ten-dollar bill and four ones. Could he really afford the drive to Dexter Springs? Then again, how much would it cost him if cousin Layton had pulled a fast one?

10

Sally Cox laid her coat and today's mail on the back of the couch, then reached down and lifted Kiwi into her arms. "Come up here and let me love on you. I haven't had a hug all day."

She sat on the couch and held the purring ball of fur in her lap. "It's only Tuesday, and I'm already beat. There's a lot to be said for being a cat."

The phone rang, and Sally decided to let the machine get it.

This is Sally, leave a message and I'll call you back. Beep...

"Sal, it's Sam. I've been thinking about our conversation the other night. I just wanted to say I'm sorry I made you uncomfortable. But I was serious about missing talking to you. My offer to have coffee sometime is still open. Take care." *Click.*

"Ha! Hear that, Kiwi? Sam thinks he can waltz back into my life like nothing ever happened. Fat chance."

The phone rang again.

"I'm not getting up. Go away, whoever you are."

Beep. "Ms. Cox, this is Tri-State Gas Company, reminding you that your account is past due. Please contact us immediately so we can work out a payment agreement. The number is—"

"I don't want the number," Sally hollered. "I can't pay you till my next paycheck."

She put Kiwi on the floor, then got up and hung her coat in the closet. She put on a wool jacket and zipped it, then turned the thermostat down to sixty.

How tempting it was to go out back and bring in some logs and get a roaring fire going. But how could she afford to let the heat go up the flue and turn the rest of the house into an icebox? A hot bath would be a whole lot cheaper.

Sally grabbed the mail and walked out to the kitchen. She threw the catalogs in the trash, then stuffed an overdue notice for property taxes into a drawer. "Thanks a lot, Sam. Sure glad you *gave* me this place."

She started reading through a newsletter from church and noticed a new Sunday school class was being offered on the Beatitudes. She felt that annoying churning in her stomach. "The poor in spirit get blessed. And the poor in cash get harassed. No justice."

Sally pushed the newsletter aside and took a frozen dinner out of the freezer and popped it in the microwave. She filled one of Kiwi's bowls with fresh water and the other with Friskies, then sat at the table.

Her thoughts turned again to her conversations with Karen Morgan and with Elsie. It was possible Elsie had told Karen many of the same things she had told Sally. It was also possible that Karen was fishing for information, trying to fill in the blanks.

Sally wished it were in her power to get the money and give it to the poor, just as Elsie had asked her to do. But finding out where it was was next to impossible, and Harry was steps ahead of her. Besides, legally it belonged to Medicaid—and after what Elsie told her, probably the IRS. If Harry got his hands on it, Sally could blow the whistle. But unless that happened, it was smarter to play dumb—and not breathe a word of what she knew to anyone, especially Karen Morgan.

She wondered how much money Elsie and Lou had actually buried. It was enough to make Jonathan fight to his death. And for Harry to keep putting pressure on his ninety-year-old mother. And for Elsie to have confessed her guilt after all these years. Then shouldn't it be enough to keep Sally's curiosity in check—and her nose out of it?

She grabbed the pot holders and took her dinner out of the microwave and plopped it on the counter. She had the strangest feeling that if she didn't walk away now, she wouldn't be able to.

Harry Rigsby parked his Ford Falcon in front of a two-story Cape Cod house and turned off the motor. The place seemed smaller than he remembered it. For a split second he could almost hear Uncle Roy calling everyone over to the picnic tables for Aunt Clara's fried chicken, corn on the cob, and lemon meringue pie.

Harry got out of his car and noticed the engine smelled hot. Great. All he needed was to get stuck in Dexter Springs overnight and have to shell out more money for car repairs. He walked up the front walk and rang the doorbell, his heart pounding.

The porch light came on, and a teenage boy opened the door.

"Yes?"

"May I speak with Layton, please?"

"We're in the middle of dinner."

"Sorry for the bad timing, but would you tell him Harry Rigsby is here to see him?"

The boy looked as though he'd seen a ghost, then turned and yelled over his shoulder. "Dad, you'd better come in here!"

A man with a receding hairline appeared behind the boy, his eyes wide, his jaw hanging—and his face and neck cluttered with cuts and bruises. "Harry? I—I'm surprised to see you!"

"Sorry to drop in like this," Harry said, noting that Layton still bore the Rigsby family resemblance. "I drove over to the sheriff's department to get Jon's things and decided at the last minute to stop by before I headed back."

"Uh, come in. Please." Layton held open the door and buttoned his top button as if to hide the bruises. "Sorry we didn't drive over for Jon's funeral. Didn't seem appropriate, under the circumstances."

"Hey, where'd you guys go?" a woman's voice called from the other room. "Dinner's getting cold."

"Sylvia, would you come in here a minute?" Layton said.

A few seconds later, an attractive woman about forty paused in the kitchen doorway, then walked toward them, her eyes set on Harry.

"Sylvia, this is Jon's father, Harry Rigsby."

"Yes. I—I've seen pictures of you," she said, holding tightly to Layton's hand, her pale cheeks suddenly turning a scalding pink.

"And this is our son, Murray," Layton said. "Man, this is really awkward. Why don't we sit down and let the shock wear off."

Harry sat in a recliner, closest to the fire. The others sat together on the couch, Layton in the middle.

"I probably should've called first," Harry said. "But then I thought, as long as I'm in town, we should make things right—since we're family and all."

Layton's chin quivered. "You can't know how sorry I am about what happened. I had no idea it was Jon. I never would've—" Layton's voice trailed off, and he hung his head.

Sylvia wiped a tear from her cheek. "It's been a nightmare for us, too."

Layton looked up at Harry, his eyes pooled with regret. "Why didn't Jon just come and tell me he wanted to dig something up? How was I supposed to recognize him out there in the dark? I can understand him getting scared and hitting my dog. But I can't imagine why he tried to choke me with a shovel. I thought he was going to kill me." Layton dabbed the corner of his eyes with his thumb and forefinger. "Man, we used to play together. What was he thinking? I'd do anything to change it."

"Yeah, I'm sure." Harry let out an exaggerated sigh. "Jon had been under lots of stress for a long time. Couldn't seem to hold a job or keep a wife. He must've finally cracked."

"It's a cryin' shame," Layton said. "The sheriff's department brought out some equipment and dug around out there. Didn't find anything. Went all over the yard with metal detectors. All they found were rusty nails, some change, a brass button—junk like that. Can't imagine what Jon thought he was going to find."

"Me neither." Harry shifted in his chair. "Look, it's been a hard day. I need to get back. I just didn't feel right about leavin' without lettin' you know I don't blame you."

Layton leaned his head against the back of the couch and closed his eyes, one hand clutching tightly to Sylvia's hand, the other to Murray's. "Thank you. That means a lot."

Harry stood, and Layton got up and walked him to the front door.

"If there's anything I can do, Harry—anything. Don't hesitate to ask."

Harry patted him on the shoulder. "I'll check back soon and see how you're doin'. Should've done it years ago."

"Please, tell Gracie how sorry I am."

"Yeah, I will. Take care."

Harry walked down the front walk, sensing three pairs of eyes watching from behind. He got in the car, relieved when the motor turned over the first time. He looked up and waved at the three Rigsbys standing at the front door. If they were covering up something, they deserved an Oscar.

Harry drove down Milton Street and turned onto the main highway toward I-70, convinced that Layton hadn't found the money—and neither had the sheriff. So what was it about that old photograph that had enticed Jon to this location?

Harry decided that it was time for him to sort through his mother's shoe box of old pictures. Perhaps a stroll down memory lane would produce just the clue he needed to end this scavenger hunt once and for all.

Gracie Garver lay curled up on the couch, nestled in her husband's arms, her eyes watching the embers in the fireplace, her heart aching with grief.

"You awake?" Bill Garver whispered.

"How can I sleep when my son's out there in the cold, buried under six feet of dirt?"

Bill pulled her closer. "Shhh. That kind of thinking will drive you crazy."

"Harry didn't shed a tear. Not one."

"Harry keeps his feelings to himself."

"His *son* died, Bill. The only one he's ever had—or ever will have. What is he, a robot?"

"He's Harry. What can I say?"

There was a long stretch of silence. Gracie's mind raced with the same unanswered questions that had plagued her from the beginning.

"Jon had never been to Arnie's brother's place. How did he know how to find it?"

"Gracie, the man was forty years old. How hard could it be to find out where his great-uncle used to live?"

"But why would he want to after all these years? Roy's been dead for a long time. Jon didn't even know him."

"Honey, we've already been over this. He must've known his cousin owned the place now. You said they were close as kids. Maybe Jon wanted to reconnect."

"This wasn't a reunion, Bill. Jon was looking for something! And why did he tell Harry he was going to Pittsburgh for a job interview?" Gracie exhaled loudly. "Harry thinks he flipped, but he doesn't know the first thing about Jonathan. Never did."

"Maybe you should talk to his grandmother."

Gracie shook her head. "I haven't seen Elsie in years. She might not even recognize me—or care to talk to me. I did divorce her son, after all."

"But you two loved Jon more than anyone. She knows that."

"Harry says she's not in touch with reality anymore. I never know how much of what he tells me is true."

"Then check it out for yourself."

"Maybe I will, when I feel better. She must be sad, too. How depressing that Harry's all she's got left."

"At least he still goes to see her. I'll give him that."

Gracie ran her finger along the satin hem of her robe. "Harry's completely self-serving. But if he's ever cared about anyone besides himself, I suppose it's his mother." Gracie sat up and started rubbing her temples. "This is going to drive me crazy. Why would Jon make up a story about a job interview, take a shovel from the garage, then drive all the way to Dexter Springs to dig in a place he'd never been before?"

"I don't know. But Jon seemed as sane as they come."

"I'll struggle with this the rest of my life." Gracie put her face in her hands. "If only we'd been home. Maybe this wouldn't have happened."

Bill pulled her closer. "You're going to make yourself sick, thinking that way."

11

Sally Cox arrived at work early on Wednesday morning and headed for Elsie's room, hoping to spend a few minutes with her before clocking in. She knocked gently on Elsie's door, and then walked in to find Karen Morgan sitting on the side of the bed, holding Elsie's hand.

"I didn't expect to find *you* in here," Sally said, trying to mask her annoyance.

Karen smiled and looked at Elsie. "Guess we're both concerned about our girl here."

Sally couldn't tell whether Elsie was glad to see either of them.

Jeffrey Horton breezed through the doorway and over to where Sally was standing. "Excuse me, ladies. I wasn't aware the shift had changed."

"I'm not on the clock," Karen said. "I'm just visiting with Elsie."

"Then wait till visiting hours like everyone else."

Karen rolled her eyes. "Get a grip, Jeffrey."

"Look, I may be the lowly male CNA, but surely I'm capable of handling my patients without *your* help?"

"Sarcasm isn't a virtue," Karen said. "Nor is compassion a vice."

Jeffrey's eyes narrowed. "Ever so clever. Why don't you let me tend to Mrs. Rigsby, and try *compassioning* on your own side of the building?"

Karen let go of Elsie's hand and brushed the hair off her forehead. "You'll have to excuse Jeffrey, honey. He was absent the day they taught manners."

"I'll come back later," Sally said. "I just wanted to see how Elsie was doing before I started my day."

Jeffrey held his gaze on Karen. "And I'd like to end mine without so many *chiefs* in the room."

Karen smirked. "Good-bye, Jeffrey. You can have the whole tepee to yourself. Come on, Sally, before he starts beating his war drum."

Sally followed Karen out of the room. "What was *that* about?"

"Don't worry about it," Karen said. "Why are you mad because I came to see Elsie?"

"I'm not mad. Just disappointed. I came in early so I could spend a few minutes with her off the clock. Wanda's back on today, which means I'll have to watch my p's and q's."

"Well, there's no need to turn it into a turf war."

"Don't overreact, Karen. It's no big deal."

"Tell that to Jeffrey. Well, at least Elsie doesn't seem depressed today."

"How could you tell?"

"Because she's madder than blazes at Arnie. She told me he talked ugly to her yesterday."

"She's got him confused with Harry," Sally said.

"I know. But as long as she's venting, she won't get depressed. She might be a bit cantankerous, though. Be warned. She's liable to say anything. I wouldn't take her too seriously."

"I know how to handle Elsie."

"Of course you do. See you later."

Sally watched Karen walk down the corridor and round the corner. What a pain in the neck she was turning out to be! Sally glanced at her watch, then began ambling toward the office. She was lost in thought when she became aware of footsteps rapidly approaching from behind.

"Sally, wait!" Jeffrey said. "What happened back there wasn't directed at you. I just get tired of Karen horning in."

"What do you mean?"

"For the past couple weeks, she's been in Mrs. Rigsby's room almost every morning. Makes me feel like a total incompetent."

"I guess after being Elsie's CNA all that time, she can't just stop caring."

"Well, I wish she'd care on someone else's shift. I don't like her breathing down my neck.

"Why don't you tell her?" Sally said.

"I've tried. Confrontation isn't my strong point, especially with someone almost twice my age."

"You could talk to the director of nurses."

Jeffrey shook his head. "No one respects a whiner. Besides, I really don't want to make waves when I'm this close to graduating. The night shift works out great with my school schedule."

"Yeah, I hear you."

"Karen acts like she owns the woman. Kinda weird, if you ask me."

"Ever hear what they talk about?"

Jeffrey rolled his eyes. "Are you kidding? Karen stops talking when I walk in—like she's in junior high or something. It's really irritating. Sorry to dump all this on you."

"That's okay," Sally said. "Maybe I can think of a way to discourage Karen from invading your space."

"Yeah, I wish."

Sally's morning started off fast, and then went into high gear.

Rufus Tatum had awakened with a cold and was clingy—and as uncooperative as a child when it came to taking his medicine. The med tec had to enlist Sally's help to get anything down him.

Wilda Cunningham wouldn't eat her breakfast. Or let Sally bathe her. Or stop bossing her roommate.

Neither patient in 207 went willingly to therapy. One patient in 205 had the stomach flu and kept missing the plastic bucket. Another in 204 fell and cut his elbow. The pair in 206 bickered constantly over the room temperature.

Sally was way behind schedule making beds and bathing patients. She was feeling frazzled and a little sorry for herself, when someone tapped her on the shoulder. *What now?*

"You're going to self-destruct before lunch," Wanda said.

Sally threw up her hands. "I can't keep up with them. Suddenly, they're all high maintenance."

"Do what you can. You can't be everywhere at once."

"I feel like a mother with a house full of demanding children."

Wanda smiled. "In a way, you are. Is there anything I can do to take the edge off at the moment?"

Sally let the words sink in. "Uh, if you're serious, Wilda Cunningham's been waiting for quite a while to go to the sunroom. I need to clean up a bathroom mishap in 203 and change the bedding."

"All right, I'll take her. I was going that direction anyway."

"Thanks," Sally said, her feet moving again. "I really appreciate it."

Sally finished the cleanup in 203, then stuck her head in Elsie's room and found her asleep in bed. Poor thing must be depressed, no matter what Karen Morgan said.

Sally spent the remainder of the morning tackling one challenge after another, surprised when she realized it was almost lunchtime.

She went in 201 and put the back of her hand on Rufus Tatum's forehead. He still felt hot. She got him in the wheelchair and pushed his side table in front of him and adjusted it. "They're bringing your lunch tray in here. I'll come back and cut up your food, okay?"

He wrinkled his stuffy nose and shook his head.

Sally squatted, reached in her pocket, and held some jelly beans in her palm.

He eagerly reached for them, and Sally closed her hand. "*First* you eat, then we talk jelly beans."

He nodded, a twinkle in his eye.

Sally patted his knee. "I'll be back when they bring your lunch tray." She rose to her feet victorious and turned to his roommate. "Come on, Charles. Let's get you to the dining room."

Sally got ten of her patients settled in the dining room, and then went back to get Elsie, hoping Harry wasn't with her. She walked in, surprised to find her still asleep.

Sally gently shook her. "Wake up, sweetie, it's time for lunch."

Elsie lay on her side, still as a stone.

Sally sat on the side of the bed and gently massaged her back. "I know you're sad about Jonathan. But you have to keep up your strength."

Elsie didn't budge.

"You'll feel better if you eat something. They're serving chicken and dumplings. Let's get you into the wheelchair." Sally tugged at Elsie's arm. "Come on, sweetie, work with me. You can't skip lunch."

Sally took hold of Elsie's shoulder and rolled her on her back, struck by how pale and fragile she looked. "You have to get up. Come on." Sally picked up her hand. It was limp—and cold. Sally put two fingers on Elsie's wrist and tried to get a radial pulse, then felt her carotid artery. Nothing!

"Elsie!" Sally slapped her on the cheeks. "Wake up, Elsie. Come on. Open your eyes. Look at me."

Sally's heart sank. She ran out into the hallway and spotted Wanda coming out of room 201. "Something's wrong with Elsie!"

Sally hurried back to Elsie's bedside, Wanda close behind.

"I came to take her to lunch!" Sally said. "She won't wake up! I can't find a pulse!"

Wanda sat on the bed, put the bell of her stethoscope against Elsie's chest, and listened intently.

"Come on, sweetie, breathe," Sally whispered.

Wanda held open one of Elsie's eyelids, and then the other. She paused, as if she were saying a prayer, and then rose to her feet. "She's nearly gone. There's nothing we can do. She and her son signed a DNR."

"So we just stand here and let her die?"

Wanda put her hand on Sally's shoulder. "It was Elsie's wish that she not be resuscitated. Considering how her mind's been slipping, this is a blessing. It'll be much easier on you if you can look at it that way." Wanda glanced at her watch. "Stay with her. I'll go page the doctor."

Stunned onlookers moved away from the doorway and let Wanda pass.

Sally inched closer to the bed, unable to take her eyes off the tiny woman she had cared so much about. Elsie's lips looked bluish. There was no rise and fall of her chest. No color in her face. No hint of life.

12

Sally Cox opened her eyes, aware of Kiwi's purring, a howling wind, and tree branches scraping the gutter. She remembered coming home from work and crashing on the couch without even taking off her coat.

The streetlight shone through the picture window, causing eerie tree shadows to sway back and forth across the living room walls. The forecast called for only snow flurries, but she would have welcomed a blizzard if it meant she could stay home tomorrow.

How sad that Elsie had died of a heart attack—and on the one day Sally had been too busy to spend time with her. She wondered how Karen was taking it.

She also wondered about Harry. Losing his son and his mother less than a week apart couldn't be easy, not even for him. But she doubted it would take him long to get over it, once he got his hands on Elsie's money. Sally sighed. What difference did it make now?

The phone rang. She put Kiwi on the floor, then groped her way to the kitchen and flipped on the light.

"Hello."

"Sally, it's Karen. I called you three times and left messages. Why didn't you call me back?"

"Uh, I didn't hear the phone." Sally let her eyes adjust to the light, then glanced up at the clock. "I was so wiped out when I got home, I fell asleep until a few minutes ago. I can't believe it's after eight."

"I heard you were the one who found Elsie."

"Yeah, I went to take her to lunch and couldn't wake her up. Really sad."

"You didn't notice any symptoms prior to that?"

"No, I would've reported it."

"Did she say anything strange? How did she act?"

"She was quiet at breakfast. I disagree with your assessment. I think she *was* depressed."

"Did you spend time with her, trying to draw her out?"

Sally sighed. "I have eleven other patients who ran my wheels off, okay? Each time I checked on Elsie, she was napping. I thought it was her way of escaping. What should I have done—got her up to ask how she was feeling?"

"Sorry. I'm just trying to understand what happened."

"Well, that's two of us. The only thing that was different was her mood. She was grieving over Jonathan."

"Well, not any more. Poor thing's finally at peace. I wonder what kind of service Harry's going to have for her?"

"I don't know, but I'd like to go."

"He might decide not to do anything," Karen said. "All Elsie's family is dead—and I don't think he's close to anyone on his father's side."

"This can't be easy after he just buried Jonathan. But I have to believe he'll have *some* kind of service for her. I'm sure Elsie had everything prearranged."

"Did she tell you that?"

Sally waited several seconds before answering. "She was ninety, Karen. She buried her husband a couple of years ago. She had to have thought about it. There's no way she would have left those details up to Harry."

"Maybe not her burial, but what about the service?"

Sally exhaled loudly. "Why don't we just wait and see what arrangements he makes? She was his mother, not ours."

"Maybe so, but I treated her better than he did."

"So did I. That's beside the point. Listen, talking about this is depressing. I'm going to take a hot bath and go to bed. I'll see you in the morning."

Harry Rigsby sat on the couch in his living room, wrapped up in an afghan, staring at the television screen. He glanced at his watch and realized he'd been watching TV for over an hour and didn't even know what was on. He picked up the remote and turned it off.

It had taken him less than thirty minutes to gather his mother's belongings at the nursing home. Everything she owned was in two cardboard boxes on the floor of his hall closet—everything except the money.

Harry sighed. What miserable excuse for a son would think about money at a time like this? His mother was dead. Dead!

Harry swallowed the emotion. Though he'd lived most of his life doing what he pleased, his mother had always stood by him, even after Gracie left. She had encouraged him to get his priorities straight and his finances in order, to remarry and make a new life for himself. She said she'd help him financially if he'd shape up.

How many times had he blown his paycheck and asked her to float him a loan till the next pay period—and then didn't pay her back?

When he turned fifty, his mother told him she wasn't going to loan him any more money.

"I'm getting old, Harry," she had said. *"I won't always be here to clean up after you. From now on, you'll have to fund your own irresponsibility."*

How was he supposed to know she was serious and would never give him another cent?

He maxed out his credit cards and teetered on the edge of bankruptcy before he finally got serious about living within his means. At least he was able to keep his house, even if he never saved a dime. But now that he was retired, his meager Social Security checks weren't enough. Unless he could find his mother's money, he was destined to live out his days barely scraping by—or being forced back into the workforce.

Thankfully, his mother had prepaid her funeral expenses, right down to the cost of transporting her body to Dexter Springs. All she had asked of Harry was to see to it that she was buried next to his father and the date of her death was engraved on their headstone.

He wondered who he should notify of his mother's passing. Was it worth the long-distance charges to call a handful of great-nieces and -nephews—ones who hadn't seen her for years and probably never gave her a second thought? He didn't think so.

But he should call Gracie. She'd been close to his mother before the divorce. Surely, she'd want to know, even if she was still grieving Jon's death.

Harry got up, his hands in his pockets, and wandered around the house, feeling an inexplicable urge to talk to someone familiar.

Gracie Garver was folding the last of her husband's T-shirts and putting it on the washer when she heard the phone ring.

"Bill, can you get that…? Bill?"

The phone rang a third time, and she hurried to the kitchen.

"Hello."

"Gracie, it's Harry. Hope I'm not interruptin' anything."

"I'm just folding laundry." She glanced at the clock. "Why are you calling? Is something wrong?"

"Yeah. Ma passed away today."

Gracie walked over to the kitchen table and sat. "How did it happen?"

"The doctor said it was probably a heart attack. One of the gals who works there found her."

"I'm really sorry, Harry. This must be overwhelming."

"Yeah."

"What are you going to do about a funeral service?"

"Most of her family's dead. Think I'll just have a graveside service."

"You burying her next to Arnie?"

"Yeah."

"When?"

"Day after tomorrow."

Gracie grabbed a notepad and pencil. "What time? Bill and I will come."

"Two o'clock?"

"All right."

"That's real decent of you, Gracie. Especially after what you've just been through."

She wondered if Harry had any idea how she felt. "I liked Elsie. I want to be there."

"You remember how to find McClendon Cemetery?"

"Remind me. It's been two years."

"Get off I-70 and go south on 127 till you see the yellow farmhouse, then turn right on the gravel road and go about two miles. You'll see it."

"I remember now. Will anyone else be there?"

"I don't think so. I don't even know who else to call."

There was a long pause. She could hear Harry breathing and thought she heard him sniffling.

"Harry, are you all right?"

"Yeah, sure. I knew it was comin'. Guess you're never really ready."

Gracie doodled on the notepad. "Do you want Bill to help you with the details? You're probably not thinking clearly."

"Nah, I'm okay. Just kinda hard realizin' everybody's gone, you know? I feel like an orphan or somethin'."

"I'm sorry. I know it's hard."

There were several seconds of dead air. It seemed as though he didn't want to hang up.

"Harry, you sure you're all right?"

"Yeah. Just a little stunned is all."

"Well, if you need help, call. Otherwise, we'll see you at the cemetery Friday at two."

"Yeah, thanks. I appreciate it."

Gracie hung up the phone and realized Bill was standing in the doorway.

"What's the deal?" he said.

"Elsie died today. I don't think I've ever heard Harry sound so...well, *lost*."

"Tough break for Harry. A double whammy."

Gracie paused, surprised at the compassion she felt. "Bill, I took the liberty of telling him we'd go to the graveside service. It's at two on Friday. We might be the only other ones there."

"No problem."

"It's in Dexter Springs. I hope you don't mind driving over there."

Bill pulled up a chair and put his arm around her. "I don't mind. But are you ready for that?"

"I'll be okay. The old cemetery isn't anywhere near Layton's place. In fact, it's not even in town. It's at the edge of an old farm Elsie's father owned at one time."

13

Sally Cox arrived at work on Thursday morning, still nursing last night's headache and lacking the incentive to start her rounds. She was putting her coat and purse in her locker when she became aware of someone standing behind her.

"What a shock about Mrs. Rigsby," Jeffrey Horton said.

Sally closed her locker and turned around. "Yes, it was."

"I didn't know till I came in last night, and the charge nurse filled me in. I felt bad for you. Must've been tough finding her like that."

Sally blinked the stinging from her eyes. "I can still see her face. I hope she didn't lie there and suffer."

Jeffrey put his hand on her shoulder. "Sounds like she just quietly slipped away. Not a bad way to go."

"I keep telling myself that. I feel guilty, though. Like I should've known."

"Hey, don't go there. You'll drive yourself nuts. We should all be so lucky to live to ninety and then die without pain."

Sally sighed. "I know that in my head. My heart hasn't caught up, though. It's going to feel strange without her."

"Not for long. They're bringing Fay Emerson back from the hospital this morning and admitting a new patient to fill the vacancy in that room."

"Didn't waste any time, did they?"

Jeffrey shrugged. "Life goes on, Sally. They need us, too."

"You're right. This is the first time I've lost a patient. I suppose I'll get used to it."

"I doubt that. But you'll learn to keep it in perspective." Jeffrey looked at his watch. "I need to head to class. Hope you have an okay day, all things considered."

"Thanks. I'm going to try."

Sally went to the computer and clocked in, then headed for the east wing. She turned the corner and saw Karen Morgan in the hall-way, too late to avoid her.

"There you are," Karen said. "I've been waiting for you."

"I need to get busy. It's after seven."

"There's a graveside service for Elsie on Friday in Dexter Springs."

"Yeah, I saw it in this morning's paper. I'm scheduled to work on Friday."

"I'm sure you could get the day off if you wanted to go."

"I can't afford to take off a whole day."

Karen rolled her eyes. "So trade shifts with someone or pull a double. That's what I'm doing."

"You're going?"

"Of course I am. We could go together. My Sportage could use a good run on the highway."

"Actually, that would solve a problem for me," Sally said. "I'm not good at finding places. I don't even know where Dexter Springs is, much less the cemetery."

"Oh, I called Harry and got directions. It's a little country ceme-tery outside the city limits. It won't be hard to find. Harry actually sounded pleased we were coming."

"You told him *I'd* be there?"

"You said you wanted to go."

"Well...all right. I'll see if I can get my schedule changed."

Sally went through the morning, avoiding room 202 until Fay Emerson was brought back from the hospital. Sally got her settled and her things put away, all the while careful not to look across at the empty bed. She was just leaving when Wanda walked in.

"Just the person I want to see," Wanda said. "We're getting a new patient, Dottie Fredericks, and I need you to make up bed A and get everything ready. She's being transported by ambulance and should be here within the hour."

"All right," Sally said.

"It won't be as hard as you think. The sooner you do it, the easier it'll be. When you're finished, would you stop by my office?"

"Uh, sure," Sally said. "I'll just be a few minutes."

Sally gathered the linens and made the bed, concentrating her thoughts on the items she needed to pick up from the grocery store instead of the image of Elsie's lifeless body.

She checked the closet next to the bed and double-checked the A basket in the bathroom to be sure it was empty, then left room 202 and walked to Wanda's office.

Sally stood outside the door and knocked gently.

Wanda looked up, the lines on her forehead relaxed. "Come in and sit for a minute."

Sally was glad for a chance to get off her feet and didn't have the emotional energy to feel intimidated.

Wanda took off her glasses and folded her hands. "How are you doing today?"

"Okay."

"I was looking for a more descriptive answer."

Sally saw the sincerity in her eyes. "I'm feeling sad. And a little guilty. But I'm able to do my job."

Wanda got up and shut the door, then leaned on the bookshelf, her legs crossed at the ankles, her hands in her pockets. "I still remember the first patient who died on my watch: a man named Willis Harcourt. He had a stroke while I was busy with other patients. I came in to check on him and found him dead—much the same scenario you experienced yesterday. I remember reeling with all kinds of feelings: anger, guilt, self-doubt, grief, regret, defeat, despair—you name it, I felt it." She looked out the window, and then at Sally. "The truth is, there was nothing I could've done to prevent what happened. It was his time to go.

"Of course, I didn't see it that way at first. I felt an inordinate sense of responsibility for Mr. Harcourt's death. Plus, I was appalled at how undignified his passing seemed. Death isn't pretty. And it took a long time for me to let go of that image.

"But years of working in this business have made me realize something that continues to sustain me. It's not their destiny we're entrusted with, only their care. We're caregivers, Sally. Not saviors. Their days are numbered by the One who made them."

Sally took her index finger and thumb and dabbed the corners of her eyes.

"I doubt if you'll ever forget losing your first patient either. But you can't let it defeat you. What you do is immeasurable. And merciful. It's a noble profession. Not many people are willing or able to get this close to the dying. Thank God for people like you."

Sally put her face in her hands and stifled her sobs.

Wanda sat in the chair beside her and waited until she had finished crying.

"Sally, we got off on the wrong foot, but I think we're starting to find our rhythm. I told you the other day that I have to put a buffer between my patients and myself. And I suggested you do the same. The simple truth is, I'm a coward. I can't handle getting too close to patients. Actually, I admire people like you who can. Just don't let it burn you out. Find your comfort zone and learn to stay within it. And, for what it's worth, I think you're a fine CNA. I wish I had more like you."

Sally plucked a Kleenex from the box on Wanda's desk and blew her nose. "I appreciate you saying that."

"Are you all right to go back to work?"

Sally nodded. "I'm fine. I think I just needed to let it out. Thanks."

Harry Rigsby hung up the phone, satisfied that the plans for his mother's graveside service were in place. The preacher at Dexter Springs Community Church had agreed to say a few words at the cemetery. And the two women from the nursing home were going to be there. Plus Gracie and Bill. At least he wouldn't have to bury his mother alone.

Harry considered telling Layton, but decided to wait until it was over. If Layton and his family showed up, he didn't know how Gracie might react. Besides, he didn't want her to know that he'd paid Layton a visit the day of Jon's burial.

Harry wondered how strange it would feel, riding solo all the way to Dexter Springs in a limousine designed to transport family members. He couldn't very well ask Gracie and Bill to ride with him, though he would have welcomed the company.

He hated that his hands were shaking, and he knew it wasn't because it was sixty-five degrees in the house. He'd been a loner all his life. Never needed anybody else. Why did he suddenly feel so empty— and out of control?

He went to the hall closet and dragged out the two cardboard boxes he had packed up at the nursing home. He opened the larger box and reached inside for the shoe box of photographs. He took it over to the couch and began to look through the pictures.

He found the one Jonathan had shown him—the one of his parents standing under the trellis in Aunt Clara's flower garden. His mother looked pleasant, his father distracted. His old man had always seemed to be somewhere else, even when he was in the same room. But what struck Harry was the vacant look in his mother's eyes. He picked up another photo of her. Then another. And another. The look was always the same. How had he missed it all these years? Had he been so busy taking advantage of her that he never bothered to see her pain?

Harry wondered what kinds of problems his mother must've had to contend with, being married to *Arnie*. Though his parents never talked openly about it, Harry sensed that his father's booming trucking business had been involved in something shady. He'd heard his parents arguing about it a few times but never dared ask questions.

He dug deeper in the box and found a sepia photo of his parents on their wedding day. He didn't remember ever seeing it before. His mother was a knockout! Hourglass figure. White dress. Long curls. Smiling eyes! His dad looked strong. Dark suit. Striped tie. Slicked-down hair. Boastful eyes.

Harry tried to imagine what they were like back then—so young and full of life. Surely they had loved each other, at least in the beginning. He got glimpses of it from time to time, but usually they seemed indifferent toward one another, like their minds and hearts were completely separate. Maybe losing their firstborn had wrecked whatever happiness they'd had. Hard to say. They never talked about her.

The best memories Harry had of his parents were those at Uncle Roy and Aunt Clara's place. It was there his father seemed relaxed and playful, and his mother girlish and affectionate. He could still hear the sound of their laughter, distinct from the others, and yet somehow part of a symphony of souls related by blood, but held together by choice.

Harry sighed. How ironic that the one place that had held such fond memories was now stained with Jonathan's blood.

He put the box on the floor, then lay on the couch, two pillows behind his head and his feet up over the back. It wasn't even time for lunch, and already he'd run out of things to do.

Sally left work precisely at 3:00. But instead of going home, she drove to Starbucks, ordered coffee and an oatmeal raisin cookie, then sat at the corner table, watching people come and go.

Near the front window, two obnoxiously loud young women, sporting fashionable leather jackets and salon nails, sat facing each other at a table for four, Saks Fifth Avenue shopping bags displayed on the empty seats.

Across from them sat a college-age couple, their heads buried in textbooks, seeming oblivious to the laughter across the aisle.

Near the center of the room, two tables were pushed together, and five men sat discussing some kind of business venture, their voices resonating and fading like the bass of a stereo.

At the table closest to Sally, a woman sat leafing through *Better Homes and Gardens*, her profile remarkably like that of Nan Bingham, who had moved to Jefferson City during the time Sally was in the throes of grief over her failed marriage. How she wished Nan still lived nearby. Her absence had left a big void.

Sally finished her coffee and popped the last bite of cookie into her mouth, then gathered her mess, lamenting that she could have gone home, brewed a fresh pot of coffee, and had store-brand cookies for a fraction of what she had just spent. She started to leave when she saw Sam coming in the front door.

I don't believe it! She grabbed the back of a chair and stood facing the wall, her heart pounding. Had he seen her? She nonchalantly lowered herself to the chair, dying to look over her shoulder. A few seconds later, she heard his voice.

"Sal, what a surprise!"

She winced. "You got that right."

"As long as you're here, let me buy you a cup of coffee."

"Thanks anyway, Sam, but I was just leaving."

He pulled out the chair beside her and sat. "What's your hurry? You're done working for the day."

"How would you know?"

He smiled. "Okay. Wishful thinking."

Sally pretended to be annoyed. He still had that charming grin. She could resist almost anything but that.

"Come on, one cup of coffee, and then I have to get back to work. Besides, there's nowhere else for me to sit. The place is packed out."

"All right," she said, instantly wishing she hadn't.

"Would you like your usual?"

Sally glanced over at him. "Yeah, right. Like you remember."

"Hey, it's me, Sam Cox, memory extraordinaire. You'll have either a regular coffee with extra cream—or a chocolate latte with a generous sprinkling of nutmeg on top. Which will it be?"

Sally forced her mouth not to smile. "Chocolate latte."

"I'll be right back."

Sally went around and sat on the opposite side of the table. A minute later Sam was back with her chocolate latte, exactly the way she liked it.

"So, how's the job working out?" he said.

"Really well. Couldn't be better." *I can't pay the property taxes or the gas bill, but I'll die before I admit it to you!*

"Have you talked to Leslie lately?"

Sally shook her head. "No. It's been really busy at work. And yesterday, one of my patients died."

"I guess that's what old people do in nursing homes."

"Honestly, Sam. Do you think you could be any colder?"

"Sorry, I didn't mean anything by it. But don't you have to expect that kind of thing?"

Sally took a sip of latte, then wiped the froth off her lip. "It doesn't matter if you expect it, it's still a loss. There's something sacred about the passing of a life. You can't understand unless you've experienced it."

"Yeah, you're right."

There was a long, uncomfortable pause. Sally wished she were home, soaking in a hot bath.

"I might as well tell you," he said. "You're going to hear it from Leslie anyway. Things are strained between me and Allison. I doubt we'll be together much longer."

"Oh," Sally said flatly.

"Is that a caring 'Oh' or a sarcastic 'Oh'?"

"Let it be whatever turns your crank, Sam. I don't care what you do."

"Well, I wanted you to hear it from me."

Sally noticed his hands shaking. She was *not* going to feel sorry for him. "So, this is why you wanted to have coffee with me?"

"No, I've wanted to do this for a long time. I didn't have the guts to ask till I ran into you the other night."

"Sam, cut the game playing. You're lonely, and I'm the only person you've got to talk to."

He took a sip of coffee. "You're the only person I *want* to talk to."

"That's nice. But I don't share your need to be friends. Friends don't cheat. Friends don't humiliate. Friends don't leave the other financially strapped. Friends don't—"

"Okay, I get the point."

"No, I don't think you do."

"Sal, I don't expect you to forgive me. But you know me—good and bad—better than anyone. I just need you to listen—" His voice failed, and he tightened his grip on the paper cup.

"Okay, I'm here. Talk."

Sam paused, then looked up and held her gaze. "Allison's son Kenny got picked up for questioning after some gang initiation. One of his low-life buddies beat the tar out of an eighty-one-year-old man. Kenny wasn't charged with anything, but he's a time bomb waiting to go off. The kid's hanging out with a dangerous crowd."

"How old is he?"

"Fourteen, going on two. Won't listen to anything I have to say. I've had better dialogue with a bowling ball."

"Does he listen to his mother?"

Sam shook his head. "Kenny doesn't listen to anybody but his peers."

"Where's his father?"

"Ah, the good Dr. Landon? He pays Allison a big chunk of money every month but has zero interest in the kids. She's at her wit's end. All she talks about is getting Kenny out of Kansas City."

"Can you blame her?"

Sam sighed, his eyebrows gathered. "She wants us to move to Louisiana, closer to her mother."

"So go. You love her, don't you?"

"Love her? I don't even know if I *like* her."

Sally raised her eyebrows. "Gee, you mean sex doesn't conquer all?"

Sam looked out the window, his cheeks flushed. "Okay, I deserved that. But I have to be realistic. I'm fifty-five years old, and I'm not going to quit my job and mess with my pension fund. And frankly, I can't imagine life with Allison and two problem teenagers in some little burg in Louisiana—close to *Mom*."

"So, she told you to get lost?"

He shook his head. "I haven't told her yet."

"Same old Sam. You do love to drop those bombs."

"I doubt this'll be a bomb. Things are so strained she already knows. I just need to confront it head-on."

"Then be a man and do it. You didn't have any trouble dumping me."

Sam's eyes watered, and he quickly blinked several times. "I'm sorry, Sal. I didn't realize at the time how cruel it was. I was so obsessed with having a younger woman running after me that I lost sight of what was important."

"Let's stick to the subject. So, when are you going to tell Allison the truth?"

"As soon as I find a place to live."

Sally folded her arms and sat back in her chair. "Oh, no you don't. There's no way you're moving back in."

"Take it easy. It never even occurred to me."

"Good. Because it's *not* an option."

"Actually, I'm on a waiting list for a studio apartment close to the Plaza. I should know something by the weekend. All I want is for us to be friends. I think it took being away from you to realize how important real dialogue is. Allison and I never did much of that."

Sally started to make a snide remark, and then didn't. "I'm sorry, Sam. I'm still trying to get over you walking out on me. I don't know if I can ever view you as a friend."

"Ever?"

"I don't know. I'll have to get back to you on that one." Sally pushed back her chair and stood, then hung her purse strap on her shoulder. "Thanks for the latte."

14

Harry Rigsby waited for the driver to open the door and then slid out of the limousine, shading his eyes from Friday's brilliant sun hanging in the southern sky. Except for an occasional nippy breeze, it was surprisingly comfortable for January.

He walked slowly across the crunchy grass, through the wide-open gate, past the faded headstones of relatives he had never known, and stopped under the green canopy where his mother's casket had been placed.

He felt ashamed at how meager the red carnations looked, mingled with the greenery draped over the casket. He'd sprung for fifty bucks, and that was a push. He could imagine what Gracie would think. He glanced at his watch. It was only 1:40.

The name "Rigsby" on the polished gray headstone caught his eye, and he vividly remembered the day two years ago when they buried his dad. Harry had felt no emotion, other than relief that it was all over. Today all kinds of emotions competed for his attention. Regret. Helplessness. Anger. Self-pity. And sadness—deep, unrelenting sadness. A kind he had never experienced before, and feared would never go away.

He walked down to the grave of the infant sister he had never met. He'd always resented his mother's obsession with a kid who lived only three months. Now he wished she were standing with him through this.

Harry was aware of gravel crunching and a car slowing to a stop. He quickly wiped his eyes and swallowed the emotion he hoped hadn't stolen his ability to speak. He turned around and saw a familiar white Eldorado.

Gracie and Bill got out and walked toward him arm in arm. He both dreaded and relished their arrival.

Harry nodded at Gracie and held out his hand to Bill. "Thanks for comin'," he said, shaking Bill's hand harder than he had intended to.

"We're very sorry," Gracie said. "Elsie was a lovely lady."

"Yeah, she was." Harry escorted them to the casket. "I kept things simple, the way Ma wanted it."

"Give us a minute, okay?" Gracie said.

"Yeah, sure."

Harry walked out from under the canopy. Gracie took Bill's hand and bowed her head.

A black Suburban pulled up. Harry saw a tall young man in a black topcoat get out of the car and walk toward him, a Bible in his hand.

"Harry?" the man said. "I'm Pastor Jim from Dexter Springs Community Church."

Harry shook his hand. "Thanks for comin'."

"It's my pleasure. How are you holding up?"

"So-so. It's no picnic."

"I know it's hard. I'm glad I can be here to make this part easier for you." Pastor Jim stood for a moment, his eyes moving slowly across the headstones. "What a wonderful old cemetery. You said your mother's family is buried here?"

"Yeah, her dad owned this land. She was a McClendon, so I guess I'm related to everybody here. Never met most of 'em."

"I'll bet there's a lot of history here."

Harry shrugged. "Guess so. If you're into that sort of thing."

"I am. My wife and I are working on our family tree." Pastor Jim looked over at the casket for several seconds, and then at Harry. "You said your mother was a Christian. You didn't say whether or not you are."

"Nah, it was her thing. I never went in for all that religious stuff. Neither did my ol' man."

Pastor Jim rubbed his chin with his fingers. "I put a lot of thought into what I'm going to say today. Some of it's geared around the Christian hope. I made the assumption that it would be all right."

"Sure. Ma would like that."

The pastor glanced at his watch. "It's not quite two, but if you're ready, we can get started."

"Uh, two ladies from the nursing home said they were comin'. Maybe we should wait a few minutes."

"Of course." Pastor Jim looked up at the bluebird sky. "The

weather certainly has cooperated. Couldn't ask for a lovelier January day."

"Yeah, after the cold snap and all the flurries, this is a real surprise."

There was an awkward lull in the conversation, and Harry stared at the ground, his hands in his pockets. He felt the pastor's hand on his shoulder.

"Excuse me, I should go introduce myself to the others."

"Yeah, good idea." Harry stayed where he was, rocking from heel to toe. He looked across the gravel road to an open field and watched a flock of blackbirds spring into the air, a swirling mass of black dots that descended behind a row of trees.

He tasted dust and noticed a green Kia Sportage had pulled up behind the pastor's car, and the two women from the nursing home were walking over to him. He couldn't remember their names.

"Thanks for comin'," he said. "Did you have any trouble finding it?"

The younger woman shook her head. "Not at all. I'm Karen Morgan. We spoke on the phone. I think you know Sally Cox."

Harry shook hands with both of them. "Yeah, I appreciate you comin' all this way. Ma would be real proud to know you're here."

Sally discreetly put her hand in her coat pocket and wiped it on the lining. That's as close as she ever wanted to get to Harry Rigsby.

She followed Harry over to the casket, where he introduced her and Karen to Pastor Jim and to Gracie and Bill Garver.

Sally felt bad she hadn't thought to bring flowers. Harry certainly hadn't knocked himself out.

"If you'll all take a seat," Pastor Jim said, "we can get started."

The young pastor remained standing, his eyes moving slowly from person to person.

"Each of you is here today because you cared about Elsie Rigsby. When Harry asked me to say a few words, I accepted, but had no idea what I could say that might encourage you and pay tribute to her.

"I didn't know Elsie, but I wish I had. I look around this quaint old cemetery and hear history calling from each of these headstones—a family's heritage sealed in the wind, impossible to erase.

"Elsie was born a McClendon, but she married Arnie Rigsby and took his name for almost seventy years before she laid him to rest right here, knowing one day she would be buried beside him.

"Elsie lived ninety years, longer than most of us will. And she saw the world change in amazing ways, good and bad, while her own life was filled with joys and sorrows as her Creator saw fit to allow.

"She gave birth to a daughter who died at three months old. But God provided a son, Harry, for her to love and to nurture and to raise. And it's for Harry that we offer our support at this time and in this place—that he may remember and honor the woman who gave him life…"

Sally thought she was going to be sick. *Remember and honor the woman who gave him life?* All he wanted was her money.

"We take comfort today," Pastor Jim said, "in knowing that most of Elsie's earthly life was spent in good health, surrounded by people who loved her. And we take comfort, knowing that Elsie's eternal life will be spent in glory, surrounded by people who love God, those who were sealed by His promise in the gospel of John, the third chapter, the six-teenth verse: 'For God so loved the world that he gave his one and only Son, that whoever believes in him shall not perish but have eternal life.'"

Sally felt the words wrap around her like a down comforter.

Pastor Jim opened his Bible and, with confidence in his voice and compassion in his eyes, read Psalm 23: "The LORD is my shepherd, I shall not be in want…"

Sally thought about all the years Elsie had been in want and had resorted to taking money from Arnie's business. How bad had things been for such a sweet lady to take such drastic measures? It was obvi-ous from Elsie's confession that it had still bothered her.

Pastor Jim finished reading the psalm, then bowed his head. "O Lord, we commit to You the spirit of Your servant, Elsie, who was born again by Your Spirit and who now dwells forever in Your presence. We who know and love You have the assurance that we will see her again in that place where there will be no more tears—and no more death."

Sally wiped her eyes. *Good-bye, sweetie. Be at peace.* She opened her eyes and snuck a glance at Harry, her heart suddenly colder than the breeze that bit her face. He seemed somber enough, but she knew it was an act.

"Would you sing with me 'Amazing Grace'?" Pastor Jim said.

Everyone stood, and the young pastor, whose voice reminded her of Steve Green, led the small group through all the verses. Much of the time, he was the only one singing.

Sally couldn't take her eyes off Harry. The more she thought about how he had badgered Elsie for the money, the madder she got. Why should he be allowed to take what his mother didn't want him to have?

Sally realized the singing had ended.

"That was nice," Karen said. "I'm glad we came."

"Yeah, me too."

Everyone stood around and made small talk for a couple of minutes, and then the pastor shook Harry's hand and left. Then the Garvers left, and the limousine driver walked over to Harry and said something. Harry nodded and wiped off his glasses and came and stood next to Karen.

"Thanks again for comin'."

"We were glad to be a part of it."

Sally nodded, but couldn't bring herself to say anything to Harry. His red-rimmed eyes irritated her all the more.

"Can you find your way back okay?" he said, motioning to the limousine driver that he'd just be a minute.

"Oh, sure," Karen said. "But before we go, would you mind if we take a look around the cemetery? This is such a neat place."

"Sure, whatever."

Harry walked back to the limousine. The driver let him in and then drove off, leaving a trail of white dust hanging above the gravel road.

Karen fastened the top button of her coat and put on her gloves. "Well, are you coming?"

Sally shrugged. "It's getting windy. And colder."

"Come on, it's not every day you get to see something like this."

"Okay, but I really don't want to be here when they lower Elsie's casket."

Sally strolled with Karen through the small cemetery, reading names and dates on the headstones and wondering about Elsie's ancestors. Had they come from Scotland? Ireland? Some of the stones dated back to before the Civil War.

In the middle of the cemetery stood the largest monument, topped with an elegant statue of the risen Christ, the name "McClendon" etched in bold letters across the stone.

"I'll bet they were Elsie's parents," Sally said, moving closer to read the dates. "Why am I not surprised the only Rigsbys buried here are Arnie and Elsie? Arnie was probably too cheap to buy plots, so he gladly took the freebies from his wife's family."

Karen snickered. "You're probably right."

Sally walked slowly, her hands tucked warmly in her pockets, her head tilted toward the sun rays filtering through a basket weave of bare branches. A chilly gust of wind spun a whirlwind of leaves and dust across her path, and her eyes fell on a Celtic cross, engraved with the names, "Louis and Martha McClendon." She did the math. If the man were living, he'd be ninety-four. Was this Elsie's brother?

"Can you imagine how beautiful this place must be the other three seasons of the year?" Karen said, moving on.

Sally spotted a small monument at the end of the row. "Look at the angel. That's different." She walked ahead of Karen and stopped in front of the headstone, admiring the beautiful guardian angel carved out of white marble. Her eyes dropped down to the name. She froze, her heart doing flip-flops.

"Well, what do you know. There is another Rigsby buried here," Karen said. "This must be the baby daughter Elsie lost. The dates make sense."

Sally's mouth felt like cotton, and no words would come. All she could do was stare at the name engraved on the headstone:

SOPHIE ANNE RIGSBY

15

Sally Cox sat in the passenger seat of Karen Morgan's Sportage, her eyes closed and her head leaned against the back of the seat. What did Karen know about Sophie? She'd certainly played dumb when she saw the name on the headstone.

And what did Harry know? Maybe he'd already dug up the money and had been waiting until Elsie died to spend it. Then again, if he'd found it, why would he have badgered his mother to tell him where it was?

"You going to sleep all day?" Karen said.

Sally's eyes flew open, her hand over her heart. "Girl, you scared me to death!"

"Sorry. We're already to Independence. Want to get something to eat before I take you home?"

"Maybe something light," Sally said. "If I remember right, there's a soup and salad place at the first turn off."

"Sounds great." Karen glanced over at her. "You're sure wiped out."

Sally looked out the side window. "I'm not wild about funerals. Plus, Harry wears on me."

"I thought he behaved rather well today."

"He played the part," Sally said.

"Pastor Jim did a nice job. Can't be easy doing a burial for someone you don't know—and with only five other people present."

Sally nodded. "It really was nice. I think Elsie would've approved."

"Do *you* believe she's in heaven?"

"I'm not the Judge. But if she chose to trust Jesus as her Savior, I do. That's what the Bible says."

"Don't tell me you're a Christian—and one of the 'born-again' variety, no less?"

Sally wanted to deny it, and then didn't. "Actually, I am. Though my faith's been pretty shallow lately. I've got some anger issues about Sam leaving. I've only been to church once in months."

Karen snickered. "So, who needs church? I can worship God anywhere—even driving down the highway."

But do you?

"Is that the place you're talking about—across from the truck stop?"

"That's it."

Gracie Garver picked up the empty cartons of Chinese takeout and threw them in the kitchen trash can. The trip to Dexter Springs had brought back all the emotions she'd felt at Jonathan's burial—and all the unanswered questions. She was haunted by her son's unexplained behavior. And the thought that she would have to bear this burden the rest of her life was overwhelming.

Harry had seemed so pathetic at the cemetery. She wondered what he would do now that he had no one. She felt sorry for him—but not sorry enough to get involved in his life. He'd made his own bed.

She turned to her husband. "Bill?"

"Hmm?" Bill Garver sat at the kitchen table, his head buried in the newspaper.

"I wonder if I should go talk to Layton."

He lowered the paper and looked over his half-glasses. "What brought that on?"

"I'm never going to rest till I know why Jon did what he did."

"May never happen, honey. The sheriff's convinced it's a dead end."

"That's because the sheriff doesn't love him—" Gracie choked back the emotion. "I had to bury my only child, and no one knows why!"

Bill patted the chair next to him. "Come here."

Gracie sat, and he put his arm around her.

"Elsie's funeral brought it all back. You've got to give it time."

"Please don't tell me time heals all wounds! I can't handle another platitude."

"What would you ask Layton if you saw him?"

She shrugged. "Probably nothing he hasn't answered before. But I could see his eyes, his expression."

"Honey, do you really think if his story didn't add up, the sheriff wouldn't have seen it? They questioned the guy for hours on end."

"I don't know. But *if* he knows more than he's saying, it would be hard to keep it from me."

"Gracie, you haven't seen the man since he was a kid. You don't know anything about him."

"He's just a grown version of the little boy who stayed at our house, who ate at our table, and who played with my son. If he was holding something back, I'd see it in his eyes, Bill. I just would!"

"All right, take it easy. I'm on your side. But, what if, after you talk to him, you feel like he's *not* holding back? Will you be willing to accept that?"

Gracie threw up her hands. "You don't want me to talk to him!"

"I didn't say that."

"You think the sheriff's assessment is right?"

"I'm reasonably sure he's done a thorough job."

"Well, I have reasonable doubt!" Gracie dabbed her eyes. "A mother's vote should count for something."

Bill pulled her closer and stroked her hair. "All right, honey. I can see how important this is to you. When do you want to talk to him?"

"He's probably home for the weekend," Gracie said.

"You going to drop in unannounced, or are you going to tell him you're coming?"

"I think I should tell him. He can prepare a canned speech if he wants, but I'll see through it."

Bill took off his glasses and folded the newspaper in half. "I'll drive you over there. I can wait in the car or go do something else. I don't think you should try this by yourself."

Sally took a sip of tomato basil soup and wrapped her hands around the warm mug. "Mmm...does this ever hit the spot."

"It's delicious," Karen said. "Glad you suggested this place."

"We've had quite a day. Thanks for driving. I get so nervous when I have to go looking for something."

"No big deal. I like driving. I'm glad we went."

Sally nodded. "Me, too. It was nicer than I thought it would be."

"Didn't you just love that old cemetery?"

"I wonder who owns it?" Sally said.

"I suppose the heirs. I'm under the impression that the cemetery wasn't part of the deal when the farm was sold. I think it still belongs to the family."

"Wasn't it sad about Sophie?" Sally said, her eyes studying Karen's. "Did Elsie ever mention to you that she'd lost a child?"

"Why would she talk about something that happened sixty-eight years ago?"

"I don't know. She talked to you about Arnie."

"She talked to everyone about Arnie. He must've been something else. I have a feeling Harry's a cookie-cutter version of his dad."

Sally raised her eyebrows. "In some ways. But Harry seems lazy. I got the impression Arnie was a workaholic, even if he was a tightwad."

"Elsie got in plenty of digs about Arnie the cheapskate, all right."

"Can you imagine how lonely it must've been outliving everyone in her family? Do you suppose she had brothers or sisters?"

Karen took a pat of butter and spread it on a warm piece of bread. "One time Elsie told me she had a brother who was an undertaker. I'm assuming he's gone now. Probably buried in that cemetery somewhere."

Sally continued all through dinner to phrase things in a way that would cause Karen to trip over herself. But she never did. Still, Sally had the feeling Karen knew more than she was letting on.

Harry took out another piece of bread and covered it with ketchup, then folded it in half and took a bite. Why couldn't he stop stuffing himself? The fifty bucks he'd spent on flowers should've gone to groceries. If he didn't slow down, he wasn't going to make it until the next Social Security check got deposited.

He felt satisfied about his mother's burial. He didn't believe in heaven or hell or God or any of that stuff. But since she did, he wanted to do right by her. He didn't know why the song got to him. Something about the way the preacher sang it made the words seem almost true. Harry couldn't imagine being anywhere for *ten thousand years*. It was all he could do to think about facing tomorrow.

He figured he'd better call Layton and let him know about his mother's death. Layton would understand why he hadn't been invited. But Harry wanted to stay in his good graces. Whether the sheriff found it or not, it was likely the money was buried where that old flower garden used to be. He'd just have to strike a deal with Layton to let him dig for it. Or find a time when Layton and his family were out of town.

Sally eased into the warm bath water and immersed herself up to her neck. She doubted she was going to sleep well tonight. Was it possible that she was the only one who knew where the money was, and that she could get it, give it to the poor, and silently gloat that Harry could never touch a penny of it?

On the other hand, how courageous was she—or how foolish? Was it realistic to think she could dig up the money by herself? And if she got caught, what could she say that anyone would believe? Harry would play dumb. And she might end up in jail, trying to prove that all she wanted was to give Elsie's money to the poor.

16

Gracie Garver sat at the kitchen table, watching Saturday's sky slowly turn the color of molten lava. She felt warm lips pressed against her cheek.

"Good morning, honey," Bill said. "Coffee smells great."

"It's almost ready. I've got some bagels warming in the toaster oven."

"Looks like the weather's not going to be a problem," he said. "You still determined to go?"

Gracie nodded. "I'll call Layton around nine and see if he's going to be home this afternoon."

"You seemed restless last night."

"Believe me, I'm not looking forward to this. Plus, I guess Elsie's burial brought back a lot. I'm still glad we went. When she was my mother-in-law, we got to be good friends."

"Yeah, I gathered that."

"You know, Bill, I can't believe I never thought to ask Harry if we could bury Jon in McClendon Cemetery. At least he'd be with family..." Gracie put her hand to her mouth. "He's just out there by himself, as if he doesn't belong to anyone."

Bill gently took her arm. "Hey, you can't start second-guessing things. I thought we found a wonderful spot."

"We did." Gracie wiped her eyes. "I'm just sad we couldn't get him a burial plot next to ours. Seeing Elsie's family all buried together...well, it was nice, that's all. Not many families even know who came before them."

Bill patted her arm. "Coffee's done. I'll get it. You want cream cheese or butter on your bagel?"

"Cream cheese."

A minute later, he came back and set a cup of coffee in front of her and a plate of bagels on the table.

Gracie smiled. "Thanks."

"I might go talk to the sheriff while you're at Layton's house," Bill said. "Just to see what the status is on the case."

"Oh, I'll just bet he's ready to close it. That doesn't mean I am. I'm under no illusion that Jon didn't have problems. But his encounter with Layton makes no sense to me at all."

"I know. Me, either. And who knows? Maybe Layton does know something he might tell you that he wouldn't tell the police. But don't get your hopes too high."

Sally Cox woke up to a ringing sound and realized it was the phone.

This is Sally, leave a message and I'll call you back. Beep...

"Ms. Cox, this is Dr. Brennan's office. Your account is ninety days past due. We need you to contact us and make arrangements to pay—"

Dr. Brennan wasn't going to get paid any faster than anybody else. What did they expect a woman to do when she didn't have health insurance—skip the mammogram and Pap test? Sally sighed. She was eligible for health benefits through the nursing home, but they only paid half the premium. She would have to pay off some old debts before she could afford to enroll in the program.

"Thanks a lot, Sam! Sure glad you *gave* me everything!"

Kiwi jumped on the bed and then on Sally, one paw resting on Sally's cheek.

"Where've you been? It's almost nine thirty." Sally stroked the cat's fur and let the purring calm her nerves. "I'm not going to think about bill collectors today. I only get one day off this weekend, and I'm not letting anybody ruin it."

The doorbell rang.

"Why don't *you* get that?"

Sally chuckled. She put Kiwi on the floor and put on her bathrobe on the way to the front door. She looked through the peephole. *What now?*

Sally combed her hands through her hair and smoothed her robe, then pulled on the door several times until it opened. "Why are you here?"

"I got the studio apartment." Sam handed her a piece of paper. "That's my address and phone number, in case of an emergency."

"You could've phoned."

He put a Starbucks sack in her hand. "I brought you coffee. And a big cinnamon roll."

"Forget it, Sam. I'm not going to be your *friend*."

"You don't want it?"

"I'm sorry about Allison, but you're going to have to find someone else to talk to. I can't do this." She handed the sack back to him.

"Sure you can. You won't."

"Okay, *I won't*. That's my prerogative."

"You're awfully grumpy for a woman who just got offered a freshly brewed large coffee with extra cream and a warm jumbo cinnamon roll."

Why did he have to have such a charming smile?

"Look, Sal. If you really want me to leave, I will. I just thought you might like to celebrate with me. I'm a free man."

"Well, that's certainly something I can get excited about. But we're *not* friends. I'm making that perfectly clear right up front."

"Okay, we're not friends. Would you mind if I came inside? It's freezing out here."

"I've only got one day off this week. I've got things to do."

"So do I. I'm moving out, but not till eleven o'clock. Allison will be gone for a few hours. It'll be less stressful. Come on, don't make me waste this stuff."

"Oh, all right." Sally stepped aside and let Sam in, thinking she needed her head examined.

"The place hasn't changed a bit," he said.

"I'm sure it's a big comedown after living with Allison."

Kiwi came over and rubbed against Sam's leg. He reached down and picked her up. "Did you miss me?"

Sally rolled her eyes. She took the sack from him, walked out to the kitchen, and placed the two coffees and two cinnamon rolls on the table. "Are you coming or not."

"Yeah, I'm coming. I'm just lovin' on ol' Kiwi here. I've missed having a cat. Allison hates cats."

Sally gripped the edge of the table and bowed her head. "Sam, this is too weird. I can't do it. I appreciate the thought, but I don't want you here. I really don't." She spun around and looked past the charming grin she knew was a ploy. "You need to leave."

"You kicking me out?"

"I'd rather you go voluntarily." She could almost hear the hissing of Sam's ego deflating.

He slipped his hands in his pockets and stared at the floor. "Okay, I'll get out of your hair. Keep the coffee and rolls."

"You sure?"

"Yeah." Sam seemed to hesitate, then looked up, his eyes wide and almost mournful. "I blew it, Sal. I know that. I'm sorrier than you'll ever know. And I doubt anything will ever make it okay. But I don't want to lose your friendship. I'm going to keep trying. You can slam the door in my face, hang up on me, and avoid me like the plague. But I'm still going to try."

Sally blinked several times. "I'm sorry, too, Sam. But I don't know how to be *just* friends."

"We could learn."

She shook her head. "It'd never work. There's too much chemistry."

They stood staring at each other until the scream of a siren broke the spell.

Sam walked to the front door and hesitated as if he had something else to say, then yanked the door open and ran down the steps. He got in his red Camaro with a U-Haul trailer in tow and drove off without looking back.

Sally went out to the kitchen, Kiwi on her heels. "Too bad you're a finicky eater. I'm going to devour this cinnamon roll and freeze the other one. Why are you looking at me like that? He's the one who left. Don't get soft on me now, just because he said he missed having a cat. You can't believe a word the man says."

Gracie Garver sat outside Layton Rigsby's home, nestled in the soft leather of the Eldorado, her heart racing faster than her mind.

"It's not too late to scrap the whole thing," Bill said.

Gracie looked out the passenger-side window at the Cape Cod house she hadn't seen in forty years. It hadn't changed much.

"You want me to go with you?" Bill said.

"No. I can do this."

Bill took her hand and kissed it. "I'll wait till you're inside, then I'll head over to the sheriff's office. Call my cell phone when you're ready for me to come get you."

Gracie slowly took in a breath and let it out. "Okay," she said, her hand on the door handle, "I'm ready." She got out of the car and looked back at Bill's reassuring eyes, then bunched up the fur collar around her neck and walked toward the house.

She tripped on a crack in the sidewalk and almost lost her balance. Why hadn't she worn flats? She felt the color rush to her cheeks when she realized a man was standing in the doorway.

He walked down the steps and met her halfway. "Hello, Gracie."

The words sounded trite, but what did she expect him to say? Layton had aged. Put on thirty or forty pounds. But the mouth, the eyes, the stance were the same. He stood staring at her, his eyes filled with dread, his weight shifting from one leg to the other.

Gracie put her arms around him for several seconds, then stepped back, surprised and glad he hadn't resisted.

"You're grown up," she said.

"Yeah. You haven't changed much, though."

"We both know that's a lie."

"Uh, why don't we go inside where it's warm?"

Layton went up the steps and held open the door. Gracie stepped inside and inhaled the sweet aroma of something freshly baked.

"Why don't you sit here by the fire?" Layton said. "My wife and son went over to Wal-Mart. They should be back soon. I'd like you to meet them."

Layton sat on the couch, his hands clasped between his knees, his eyes downcast. A full minute crept by without either of them saying anything.

Gracie wondered what had made her think she could handle this alone. "I guess you're wondering why I wanted to see you."

"Before you go on, I...I need to say something. I can't tell you how sorry I am about what happened. I never would've hurt Jon—" Layton's voice cracked. "I didn't know it was him, Gracie. I swear it."

"Tell me what happened."

Layton sighed and continued to stare at the floor. "I got up to go to the bathroom in the middle of the night and saw a guy out back diggin' a hole. I thought maybe it was one of my son's friends, playing a joke. I let my German shepherd out, and by the time I got out there, Jon had already hit my dog with the shovel and knocked him out. I knocked him to the ground and asked what he'd done to my dog, and what was he doing in my yard. He didn't say anything, just tried to choke me with the shovel handle. He kept pushing it harder and harder against my throat. I couldn't breathe. I finally threw him off and grabbed the shovel away from him. I told him I didn't want to hurt him, but he came charging at me..." Layton shook his head from side to side, then wiped a runaway tear. "I was afraid he'd kill me."

Gracie felt as if her heart were a crystal vase shattering into a million pieces.

"What was I supposed to do? I have a wife and son. If only Jon would've told me it was him." Layton put his face in his hands. "I don't know what else to say. I have to live with it the rest of my life."

Gracie reached in her purse and snatched a Kleenex. "Layton, do you have *any* idea what Jon was looking for?"

"No. But whatever he thought was out there must've seemed mighty important."

Gracie dabbed her eyes. "It doesn't make sense. Something's missing. Jon didn't just come over here with a shovel and risk his life and yours on a whim."

"Harry thinks he flipped out."

"What makes you say that?"

"He came and talked to me—the evening after Jon's funeral."

Gracie raised her eyebrows. "Harry drove over here?"

"Yeah. Said he had to pick up Jon's belongings at the sheriff's office. And wanted me to know he didn't blame me for what happened. I've got to hand it to him, it took guts to come here."

Gracie paused and let that one go by. "What else did Harry say?"

"Not a lot. Mostly that Jon had trouble with marriages and jobs, and had been under lots of stress."

"So, that was his explanation for Jon's strange behavior?"

Layton shrugged. "I guess so."

"I don't agree with Harry. There must be another explanation." Gracie felt her eyes move like searchlights deep into Layton's heart. "Tell me what you think, even if it's just a hunch. Please...I have to live with this, too."

Layton cracked his knuckles, then got up and stood by the mantel, his hands in his pockets.

"Why speculate?"

"Why not? It might lead to something. My son is dead and nobody can give me one good reason why."

Layton hung his head. "The sheriff said he'd been drinking. But that doesn't explain why he came all the way—"

The phone rang.

"Excuse me." Layton went out to the kitchen. "Hello? Oh, hi Harry…. I'm so sorry to hear that…. No, I completely understand…. But you don't have to worry about that anymore, Gracie's here…. Same questions the rest of us have….You want to talk to her…? Okay, I'll be here…. I'm so sorry about your mother. Talk to you later. Good-bye."

Layton came back and sat on the couch. "That was Harry. He told me about his mother dying. I'm sorry I didn't know."

"I'm surprised he's just now telling you," Gracie said.

"He was afraid you might be upset if I came to the burial—since you and I hadn't talked yet."

"Very thoughtful of him." Gracie tried to relax the wrinkles on her forehead. Since when did Harry have a relationship with Layton?

Gracie nestled in the car seat, hoping the warmth of the heater would stop her shaking.

"At least, now you know," Bill said.

"Know what? That Layton didn't lie about Jon attacking him? That's comforting."

"That's what you went to find out."

"Well, I've got a bulletin for you—Harry went to see Layton the night of Jon's funeral."

"Harry drove all the way over here?"

"Uh-huh. Told Layton he went to the sheriff's office to pick up Jon's belongings. We already had all Jon's things."

"Maybe Harry needed to confront Layton."

Gracie rolled her eyes. "Harry told Layton he didn't blame him for what happened. Harry doesn't do anything that's not self-serving. I wonder what he really wanted?"

"Give the guy a break, honey. Maybe seeing Layton was a way to handle his grief."

"What grief? Did you see a tear?"

"People grieve in different ways."

"I know that. But Harry's too cheap to fill his tank just to go tell Layton he didn't blame him. He could've called him for next to nothing."

"Well, that's not the kind of thing you like to tell someone over the phone."

"Really?" Gracie said. "Harry didn't have any trouble calling Layton to tell him Elsie had died."

"How do you know that?"

"Harry called right before I left. He even told Layton he hadn't been invited to the burial because it might upset *me*. Since when does Harry care about that?"

"What other motive could he have?"

Gracie's eyes narrowed. "That's what I want to find out."

Sally Cox went to the freezer and took out the second cinnamon roll Sam had left her and popped it into the microwave.

"I might as well get it over with," she said to Kiwi. "I'll never sleep with this thing in the house. Yes, this is pigging out. That's what humans do when they're stressed. I don't expect a finicky eater like you to understand."

Sally poured herself a glass of milk, then opened the microwave and carried her snack to the kitchen table.

She glanced up at the clock: 11:00 PM straight up. She was glad she was scheduled to work tomorrow. Who needed another day to worry about Elsie's money, Harry's greed, or Sam's wanting to be her best friend?

Sally tried to imagine herself married to Sam again, but the mental images of his sizzling liaisons with Allison Landon threw cold water on any embers of passion Sally might still have.

Kiwi jumped up on the kitchen table and stretched on her belly until her nose was just inches from the cinnamon roll, her yellow eyes intent on the glass of milk sitting next to it.

Sally chuckled. "Okay, I get the hint." She got up and poured a little milk in a saucer and placed it on the floor, then sat at the table. She took a big bite of the cinnamon roll, thinking she might as well rub it on her thighs because that's where it was going anyway.

A sense of hopelessness tore at her heart. She was relatively fit for fifty-four. But she would never look as good as Allison no matter how hard she tried. Of course, she wasn't spending a fortune at the plastic surgeon's office either.

"Anybody can look good if they have enough money," Sally said to Kiwi. "How am I supposed to compete with that? Liposuction.

Tummy tucks. Botox. A little less here. A little more there. Whatever happened to aging gracefully?"

Sally had surmised all along that Sam's attraction to Allison wouldn't last. His middle-aged ego had seemed to be on the prowl for any young tigress that would affirm his manhood. Sally shook her head. What had Allison's teenagers thought about their mother and Sam living together? It had devastated Leslie.

Sally licked the icing off her fingers and put her saucer and glass in the dishwasher. So much for comfort food.

17

Gracie Garver sat wrapped in a Polartec bathrobe, the dawn outside her kitchen window a soft pink blanket folded on the horizon. She opened her eyes wide and blinked several times, then brought her hand to her mouth and captured the last of a yawn. What a miserable night!

"You awake over there?" Bill whispered, as he sat across the table from her.

"I'm watching the sun come up."

"Are you still stewing about Harry going to see Layton?"

"I wouldn't say I'm stewing. But I *am* curious. And bothered."

"Honey, why don't you just ask him about it?"

Gracie sighed. "Harry never gives me straight answers."

"You haven't tried having meaningful dialogue with the guy in twenty-five years."

She picked up an emery board and slid it back and forth over her thumbnail. "Why on earth would I want to? I still don't like the man. And I certainly have no respect for him."

"Harry may not be the demon you think he is. People change. Or at least mellow with age."

"Whose side are you on, anyway?"

Bill leaned forward and pressed his lips to her cheek. "Maybe instead of choosing sides, we should all try to work together. The goal is to find out what caused Jon to go to Layton's. Once you know that, I think you can deal with the truth—good or bad."

Harry downed the last of his coffee and looked up at the clock: eight o'clock. He picked up the phone and dialed the number he had tacked on the bulletin board in the kitchen.

"Hello?"

"Gracie, it's Harry. I hope I'm not callin' too early."

"No. What is it?"

"I was just wonderin' how your visit with Layton went yesterday. I'm glad you finally decided to break the ice. Probably helped a lot."

There was a long, disconcerting silence.

Gracie exhaled loudly. "Why didn't you tell me you went to see Layton the day of Jon's burial?"

"I don't know. Guess I figured you'd be sore. What difference does it make?"

"I guess that depends which side of the fence you're standing on. Didn't you think I would want to know what he had to say?"

"Not really. He didn't tell me anything the sheriff hadn't already told us."

Gracie's voice went up an octave. "What right did you have to tell him you didn't blame him for Jon's death? The case is still open. We don't even know what Jon was doing there."

"Good grief, woman. The kid had no idea it was Jon who attacked him. He needed to know I believed it was an accident."

Silence.

"Gracie, what's eatin' you?"

"I don't trust you, Harry. You hadn't had contact with Layton in twenty-five years, and you used up a tank of gas to run over to Dexter Springs to tell him you don't blame him for Jon's death? Why didn't you just call him? And why did you lie to him that you went by the sheriff's office to pick up Jon's things?"

"Will you calm down?" Harry held the phone away from his ear.

"I don't want to calm down! My son's dead, and I want answers!"

"Yeah, well, we don't have answers. That's just the way it is. I already told you what I think."

"I don't care what you say, Harry! I don't believe Jon flipped out! I think he knew exactly what he was doing, beer or no beer. But until *I* know what that was, I'm never going to let it go!"

Harry counted to ten, then spoke with a calculated calmness. "Our son was sick and went off the deep end. I know it's hard to hear, but that's the story."

Silence.

"Gracie, what do you want from me?"

"I want to know what you're not telling me!"

"You know everything I know. Difference is, I'm willin' to accept the obvious. Now, suppose you tell me why *you* went to see Layton?"

"To confront him. I knew if I could see his face, I'd know whether or not he was telling the truth."

"And?"

"I think he's told us what he knows. But I'm not so sure *you* have."

"What's that supposed to mean?"

"When Bill and I left for Key West, Jon was as happy as I've seen him in a long time. He was excited about reconnecting with his grand-mother. So, what happened between then and the time he ended up dead in Layton's backyard?"

"I don't have a clue."

"I think you do."

Harry brought his fist down on the table. "You're nuts!"

"That's your answer for everything. Well, I'm *not* nuts, and neither was Jon!"

"I'm hangin' up the phone, Gracie. I can't talk to you when you're like this. Go take a pill or somethin'—"

Click!

Harry heard the dial tone and was surprised that Gracie had hung up first. He didn't like it one bit that she was suspicious. He didn't want her sniffing around if he was going to strike up a deal with Layton.

He couldn't let her get to him. He'd have to be patient and wait it out.

Gracie loaded the lunch dishes in the dishwasher, then wiped the smudges off the kitchen cabinets and ran a damp mop over the floor. She went in the living room and dusted the tables, then sat on the couch and thumbed through a new issue of *National Geographic*. She closed the cover and looked up, her eyes colliding with Bill's.

"You're as jumpy as a turkey in November," he said.

"It's Harry's neck I'd like to wring. That man infuriates me like nobody else can."

"Don't let him ruin your day. He's not worth it."

"Why do I let him get to me?"

"I don't know, honey. But you're going to have to stand your ground if you two are going to communicate." Bill held up the enter-tainment section of the newspaper. "You want to get out for a while, maybe catch a movie?"

"Truthfully, I'd like to get the guest room cleaned out."

"Think you're up to it?"

She raised her eyebrows. "I'm mad enough to try it."

"Okay. Holler if you need help."

Gracie walked to the guest room and stood in the doorway for a moment. Was she ready to pack Jon's things away?

She went over to the armchair and picked up a pair of Levi's on top of the clothes pile. She could do this. She *had* to do this.

Gracie checked the pockets, then tossed the soiled jeans on the bed. She picked up an Old Navy sweatshirt and dropped it on top of the jeans, then grabbed a white T-shirt and started a separate pile. She put the plaid flannel shirt she had bought him for Christmas on the jeans pile. Piece by piece, she sorted through the mound of clothes Jon had dumped in the chair, then took the clothes into the laundry room and started the first load.

Gracie went back to the guest room and stripped the sheets off the bed, then remade it with only the comforter and pillow shams.

She sat on the side of the bed and rested for a moment, surprised to feel more relieved than grieved. She opened the top drawer of the nightstand, ready to throw out the junk Jon had accumulated: candy wrappers. Pizza coupons. Pennies. Pens. Paper clips. A car lube flyer. A buy-one-get-one-free combo meal coupon. A book of matches. The cardboard backing from a notepad.

She started to toss the cardboard but noticed some deep impressions on it. She held it up and could make out "541 Milton St." in the center, surrounded by doodles of flowers, arrows, and dollar signs.

Gracie walked to the living room where Bill sat in his favorite chair.

"Look at this."

Bill gave her a blank look. "What is it?"

"Look at the impression. Jon wrote down Layton's address."

"Where'd you get this?"

"In the nightstand in the guest room."

Bill tilted his head slightly up and then down, looking through his bifocals. "Well, we already know Jon went there."

"But look at the doodles. John never drew flowers and dollar signs."

"How could you know that?"

"I'm the one who cleaned out all his pack rat piles. Jon always drew stars and arrows and cubes. Ever since he was a little boy."

Bill took off his glasses and looked at her. "Does it matter?"

"Yes, it matters! A mother should know her own son—" Gracie blinked the moisture from her eyes, then looked at Bill. "I'm scared I'm going to wake up one morning and find out I didn't know him at all."

"Honey, are you sure you're up to this?"

She nodded. "It's exhausting. But I really want to finish."

"Okay. How about if I make us a batch of Billy Garver's Texas Chili for dinner?"

"What did I do to deserve you?" she said, the corners of her mouth turning up.

Bill winked, then folded his glasses. "Talk nice to me, and I'll throw in corn bread and a fresh green salad."

By three o'clock Sunday afternoon, Sally Cox was glad to end her shift. Things seemed so strange without Elsie. Dottie Fredericks was a nice lady, but Fay Emerson was crabby as a stew pot in Baltimore since she'd come back from the hospital. Even Rufus wasn't cooperative in spite of the jelly beans. Sally was starting to remember why she hadn't liked her job in the first place.

At least her relationship with Wanda had improved. Maybe with time, Sally would start to enjoy coming to work again. It's not as though she had a choice.

"Hey, girlfriend, time to go home."

Sally turned around, surprised to see Karen Morgan. "What are you doing here? I thought you'd be home vegging after your double shift yesterday."

"I've been running errands. Thought I'd buzz by for a minute before I go to the Laundromat."

Sally smiled. "Well, that explains it. I'd avoid that place as long as possible."

"I checked the schedule and we're both off Tuesday. I'm thinking of taking some silk flowers to put on Elsie's grave. And Sophie's. Want to tag along?"

Sally's heart raced. "Uh, well...maybe. I mean, I haven't thought that far ahead. Can I get back to you?

"Sure." Karen met her gaze and seemed to be analyzing her. "You okay?"

"Yeah, I just need to get off my feet." *As if that's going to solve anything.*

"Okay. See you in the morning."

Sally clocked out, then put on her coat and gloves and headed for the car, dreading the thought of another macaroni-and-cheese dinner.

She pulled out of the parking lot, shivering from the cold, and turned the heater fan as high as it would go. She turned off the radio, wishing Sam were that easy to silence. Finally, a surge of warm air wrapped around her ankles.

Sally let the hum of the road and the toasty warmth soothe her and felt her eyelids grow heavy. She nodded off for an instant and opened her eyes just as she came over the crest of a hill where a line of cars was stacked up at the stoplight. She slammed on her brakes, aware of her tires screeching and her purse falling on the floor, and came to a stop just inches short of a white Mazda.

"Sorry!" she said to the man whose eyes glared at her in the Mazda's rearview mirror.

The light turned green, and Sally pulled through the intersection and into the Pizza Hut parking lot, her heart hammering and her hands shaking, all too aware she hadn't paid her car insurance.

Sally's eyes clouded over and tears spilled down her cheeks. She put her forehead against the steering wheel and began to sob and then sob harder, wondering if it was going to be like this the rest of her life.

18

Harry Rigsby put down Monday's newspaper. He surfed every TV channel at least five times, then hit the off button on the remote. How was he supposed to concentrate with Gracie so ticked off? For twenty-five years she couldn't have cared less what he did. And now, the one time he needed a little space, Gracie decided to stick her nose in and complicate everything.

Harry got up and went to the kitchen. He picked up the phone and dialed the number tacked on his message board.

"Hello?"

"Bill, it's Harry. Can I please speak with Gracie?"

"I don't think that's a good idea. She's pretty upset after your call yesterday."

"Yeah, I figured. That's why I called back. I'd like to mend that fence before this creates problems."

"You need to tread lightly, Harry. She's fragile."

"Yeah, guess we both are. Think she'll talk to me?"

"I'll go ask, hang on…"

Harry wrapped the phone cord around his wrist several times and then unwound it, remembering how much he despised "making up."

"Hello, Harry," Gracie said.

"Thanks for talkin' to me. I wanted to apologize for gettin' upset with you before. We're both still a little testy. Jon's death did a number on us."

"That's an understatement."

"Yeah, sorry. I'm not good with words. I feel bad it upset you that I went to see Layton. I wasn't tryin' to keep anything from you. It was one of the hardest things I've ever done. It was hard to talk about it, you know?"

"You didn't shed a tear when Jon died."

"Cryin' won't bring him back. Besides, I'm private about my feelin's. You know that."

Gracie sighed. "I probably overreacted. I'm not myself these days."

"Yeah, I hear ya. It's been tough for me, too. Think I'll go out to the cemetery this afternoon. It might help."

There was a long pause. Harry wondered if she was buying it.

"I finally cleaned out Jon's room yesterday. I found a used-up notepad in the nightstand. The impression left on the cardboard had Layton's address and some doodling that didn't seem in character."

"Doodlin'?"

"Yes. Arrows, flowers, and dollar signs. For as long as I can remember, Jon drew arrows and stars and cubes."

"The kid was forty, Gracie. He was away more than he was there. How could you know what he doodled?" Harry was aware he was talking too fast.

"It might mean something. I'm turning it over to the sheriff."

"Seems like a stretch."

"Maybe. At least, it's *something*. That's more than we had before."

"Yeah, okay. Listen, I gotta go. Just wanted to clear up what happened yesterday."

"All right, Harry. Thanks for the apology. I'm sorry, too."

Harry hung up the phone and started pacing. "Flowers, arrows, and dollar signs? For cryin' out loud, Jon! Why didn't you just put it in neon lights?"

Sally sat in the employees' lounge, nibbling on a granola bar, aware of Karen Morgan out in the hallway talking on her cell phone. Sally glanced up just as Karen turned off the phone and put it in her pocket.

Karen came in the lounge and slid into a chair across from Sally. "Men. What is it about 'it's over' they can't understand?"

"So, what's the deal? I thought you broke it off with that guy a long time ago."

"Yeah, well…Danny's a little dense," Karen said. "So, have you thought any more about tomorrow?"

Sally felt the color rush to her face. "I have a confession to make: I'm tapped out. I can't afford to kick in on the flowers. Or help with gas. Or eat out."

"That's okay, I'll loan you the money."

Sally sighed. "I can't afford to pay you back, Karen. My bills are piling up. I'm going to have to get a second job."

"Well, listen. I was going to gas the car and buy the flowers, whether or not you decided to go. And I'll treat you to lunch."

"I can't let you do that."

"Why not? You'd do it for me, if the tables were turned."

Sally studied Karen's eyes and saw only sincerity. "All right. I'll swallow my pride this time. I can still see those pathetic-looking carnations on Elsie's casket. I like the idea of silk flowers."

"I'd like to put some on Sophie's grave, too. I wonder if anyone's even been to that baby's grave since Elsie stopped going?"

"I'm sure Harry didn't bother." Sally carefully watched Karen's facial expressions. How she wished she could confide in Karen and enlist her help to get Elsie's money and give it to the poor! But what if Karen insisted the money be turned over to Medicaid? Or the IRS? Or worse yet, what if she reported Sally and got her fired? Or in trouble with the law? All Sally wanted at this point was closure.

Sally blinked to clear her eyes.

"Hey, you okay?" Karen said, putting a hand on Sally's arm.

"Yeah. I just have a lot on my mind."

"Finances that bad, eh?"

Sally sighed. "Yeah."

"Have you thought about credit counseling?"

"Not really. My problem isn't how I'm spending money. I just don't have enough. I don't need an expert to tell me that. I can't pay my car insurance. And my property taxes are overdue. I knew it would catch up with me, but I was hoping it would take longer. I'm going to have to look for a second job right away."

"I'm sorry. I know your ex left you in bad shape."

Sally raised an eyebrow. "Do you think?"

Karen rose to her feet. "I need to get back to work. Why don't I pick you up at your house in the morning around nine o'clock? We'll have a relaxing day. It'll get your mind off all this."

"That'd be great, Karen. Thanks."

Sally put the wrapper back on the granola bar and put it in her pocket. How much longer could she build up all this pressure before she exploded? She wanted to pray but couldn't seem to find the words. God hadn't helped her up to this point. If she was going to get out of this mess, it was up to her to figure out how.

Gracie Garver walked through a bulletproof security door in the Craddock County Sheriff's Office after being cleared by a man in uniform.

"Was all that security clearance necessary?" Gracie whispered, one hand holding her husband's, the other holding tightly a Ziploc bag that contained the notepad. "How am I supposed to relax when they make me feel like a criminal?"

Bill Garver squeezed her hand. "Come on, honey. It's for everyone's protection. You never know what kind of weirdos are lurking around these days."

"Maybe we shouldn't have come. I'm probably way off base," Gracie said.

"Can't hurt to turn it over. You'll feel better. And the sheriff will see we're serious about cooperating and reluctant to have him close this case until they've explored every avenue. Come on, honey. Stand by your guns."

The receptionist smiled. "May I help you?"

"Yes, I'm Gracie Garver. I called earlier and made an appointment to see Sheriff Baughman."

"Yes. If you folks will have a seat, the sheriff will be right with you."

Gracie sat next to Bill in the waiting room, feeling as though she were a schoolgirl in the principal's office. "I hate this," she whispered. "I feel like everyone's staring at us."

"No, they're not."

"I'll bet they think Jon was some kind of monster."

"Honey, stop it. We're here to turn over the notepad. No one's going to judge us."

Gracie knew better. How could they not? They had to be wondering what kind of parents raise up a son who's capable of attacking his cousin with a shovel and trying to choke him. Let them think whatever they want. How could they know how hard she'd tried to be a good mother?

"Mr. and Mrs. Garver, the sheriff will see you now."

Gracie stood and followed the receptionist down a long, paneled hallway that faintly smelled of old wood and reminded her of St. Andrew's Church, where she and Harry were married.

The receptionist stopped in front of the last office, then turned around and waited for Gracie and Bill to catch up.

Opaque glass covered the top half of the dark wood door, the word "Sheriff" stenciled in gold letters across the middle of the glass.

"Go right in," the receptionist said. "Sheriff Baughman's expecting you."

Gracie walked in and looked up at a tall, rugged man with a badge on his uniform. He was young enough to be her son, but his face looked weathered beyond his years.

"Mr. and Mrs. Garver, I'm Sheriff Baughman. It's nice to finally put faces to the names." He reached out and shook hands with each of them, then motioned to a taller man who had risen to his feet. "This is Investigator Ralph Knolls. He's handling your son's case."

"Nice to meet you," Knolls said.

"Sorry I missed you on Saturday," the sheriff said. "May I get you some coffee? Hot chocolate? This old building never heats up real good."

Gracie shook her head. "Nothing for me."

"No, I'm fine, thanks," Bill said.

"Please sit down. May I see the notepad you told me about on the phone?"

Gracie handed the Ziploc bag to the sheriff. "It might not mean anything. But Jon...well, he just never doodled flowers and dollar signs. I know that sounds ridiculous, but there are things a mother knows that no one else pays attention to."

The sheriff put on latex gloves and took the cardboard out of the bag and examined it carefully. "You say your son didn't usually draw flowers and dollar signs?"

"That's right."

"Is the address written in his handwriting?"

Gracie nodded.

"Hmm..." The sheriff looked intently at the impressions on the notepad, and then at Gracie. "What do you think the significance is of the flowers and dollar signs? You obviously have some thoughts about it."

"Well, I can't be sure if it's even related," Gracie said. "But the spot where my son was digging used to be his great aunt's flower garden many years ago."

The sheriff raised his eyebrows. "You think he was digging for money?"

Gracie shrugged. "I don't know. Maybe. I'm convinced he knew exactly what he was doing. I just don't know what that was."

"Are you now saying your son was involved in something illegal?" Knolls said.

"No!" Gracie said, more adamantly than she meant to. "I haven't changed my feeling about that. Jon was fiscally irresponsible, but he never seemed bothered by his debts. I don't think he'd break the law to get money, if that's what you're implying."

The sheriff put his hands behind his head and leaned back in his chair. "We turned over the soil at the crime scene and went over it with metal detectors. We didn't find anything buried there."

"Yes, I know."

"I'll have the notepad dusted for prints. Are you the only other person who touched it?"

"We both handled it," Bill said.

The sheriff sat up straight, his arms folded on the desk. "Okay, we'll see what prints show up. We'll also talk to Layton Rigsby again. I'm pretty convinced he's telling the truth about what happened. But if there was money involved, we need to make darn sure *he* doesn't have it. Your thoughts?"

Gracie hesitated, and then decided to say it. "This probably means nothing, but I wish you'd talk to Jon's father again. I realize he's my ex-husband, and I don't trust him on a good day. But I get the feeling he knows more than he's saying."

"You think he was involved in this?" the sheriff said.

Gracie shook her head. "No, I'm not saying that. Call it intuition, but I think Harry knows more about why Jon went to Layton's place than he's admitting."

"Maybe I'll talk to him myself."

Bill took Gracie's hand. "We'd appreciate anything you can do and want to cooperate fully."

The sheriff rose to his feet. "Okay, then. Let me get moving on this. I'll let you know if I come up with something. If you think of anything else, just call me or Investigator Knolls."

19

Sally stood in front of the picture window in the living room, watching through the dingy sheers for Karen Morgan's Sportage to pull up. Sam had driven by earlier but didn't stop. Thank God for small favors!

She glanced at the unopened mail still piled on the back of her couch. Mostly bills. Yesterday, when she got home from work, three messages from collection companies were on her answering machine. How dare they call on Sunday! Was nothing sacred?

Not that Sally had made Sunday sacred in a long time. She kept trying not to be mad at God for her circumstances. But she was. And it was pointless to pretend otherwise. Where was this *provision* He'd promised? She was teetering on the edge of financial ruin. How could she give God the first 10 percent when keeping 100 percent wasn't covering her expenses? A lot of sense that made.

Sally heaved a sigh of exasperation. She could understand why Elsie had taken money out of Arnie's business. It might've been wrong, but it had probably saved her a lifetime of worry.

Karen's Sportage pulled up, and Sally grabbed her purse, then bent down and rubbed Kiwi's neck. "Don't you dare let Sam in while I'm gone."

Sally locked the door, then skipped down the steps and got in Karen's car.

"Good morning. Ready for a diversion?" Karen said.

"More than ready."

"Take a look at the flowers on the backseat."

Sally peered over the back at two lovely silk bouquets made of white mums and a variety of greenery. "Looks so real. I like the variegated holly with it."

"I found a great sale—half of half," Karen said. "I bought some spring flowers for later."

"It's really nice of you to do all this."

A smile spread across Karen's face. "It's fun. And I'm anxious to see the old cemetery again. I'm enthralled with cemeteries. Couldn't have asked for a prettier day, either."

Karen drove several blocks through Sally's old neighborhood, then took the on-ramp onto I-70 and merged with a rushing tide of traffic moving far more swiftly than the bumper-to-bumper traffic in the westbound lanes.

As they drove eastward toward Dexter Springs, Sally nestled in the bucket seat, her eyes closed, and let the morning sun bathe her face. At least for today, she could ignore the ominous foreboding that her life was headed for disaster.

Gracie Garver pushed open the kitchen door, her purse hung on her shoulder and a bag of groceries under each arm.

"Honey, let me get those," Bill said. "What're you in such a hurry about?"

"Something occurred to me while I was grocery shopping, and it won't leave me alone."

"About what?"

"The notepad."

Bill opened one of the sacks and started stacking the canned goods in the pantry. "Go on, I'm listening."

"I was walking to the checkout, and something came back to me out of the blue: Arnie used to make wisecracks about Elsie rat-holing money. She would roll her eyes and laugh it off, but it created some real tension between them. Harry and I used to talk about it."

"What does that have to do with the notepad?"

Gracie sat at the table. "Well, what if Arnie was right? What if Elsie did have money hidden away? And what if Jon, for whatever reason, thought it was buried in Aunt Clara's flower garden? That could explain him doodling flowers and dollar signs around Layton's address."

Bill turned and looked over his shoulder, his eyebrows raised. "Honey, that's a mighty big jump. More like a Grand Canyon leap."

Gracie sighed. "I know. But what if?"

Bill was quiet for a few moments. He put the perishables in the refrigerator and then sat at the table next to Gracie. "I've got to be honest: This seems way out there. On the other hand, it could explain Jon's renewed interest in his grandmother. Honey, what's wrong? Why have you got that blank look on your—"

"That's it!"

"What?"

"That's what Harry knows but isn't telling—that Jon went to Layton's to dig up Elsie's money!"

"Honey, Jon didn't find any money."

"But I think Harry knew what Jon was trying to do."

"Then why didn't he just tell the sheriff that?"

"*Because…*" Gracie's eyes narrowed. "Harry's still hoping to find it."

Bill sat for a moment, seeming to process the implications. "Do you have any idea how crazy this sounds?"

"Yes, I do. But it makes sense. Think about it."

"A ninety-year-old woman with buried treasure…why didn't she just give it to Harry years ago instead of watching him struggle?"

Gracie smirked, her hands folded on the table. "Because he would've blown it—just like Arnie."

"You think she told Jon where it was?"

"I wondered about that. But I don't think so. Jon was no more responsible with money than Harry or Arnie."

"So, how do you suppose Jon knew where to go digging?"

Gracie raised an eyebrow. "Want to bet Harry knows? He's not going to volunteer anything, especially if there's a chance he can get to the money first."

Bill put his palms to his temples. "I think we'd better slow down. This is a serious accusation. If Harry knew his mother had money…"

"He could be up on Medicaid fraud charges. Shouldn't we tell the sheriff about this?"

Bill sat back in his chair, his arms crossed. "Might want to talk to Harry first. If we're going to stir up a hornet's nest, we darned sure better be right."

Sally looked out her passenger-side window at the cloud of white dust kicked up by Karen Morgan's Sportage, trying to commit to memory the turns they had made since exiting I-70. It wouldn't be hard to find her way here again.

Karen pulled the car to the side of the road and turned off the motor. "Okay, girlfriend. We have arrived."

Sally got out of the car and took in a whiff of country air and gravel dust. She looked out across McClendon Cemetery and decided it was even prettier than she remembered.

"Here you go." Karen tossed her one of the mum bouquets.

"These are so pretty. I'll bet Elsie would rather have silk flowers than those pathetic carnations Harry put on her casket."

"Scary Harry?" Karen said, a grin on her face. "Come on, let's go dress up Elsie and Sophie's graves."

Sally opened the wrought iron gate and walked toward Elsie's headstone, spotting the freshly packed dirt where the green canopy had been. She stopped and stood in front of the simple, polished gray stone, noting that the date of Elsie's death had not yet been engraved. "Hello, sweetie," she whispered.

"Go ahead and put the flowers in the holder," Karen said.

Sally bent down and put the mums in the holder, then stood back and admired them, flooded with unexpected emotion. She stood quietly for a moment.

"Much better," Karen said. "That looks nice."

Sally nodded, too choked up to say anything, but aware of Karen standing beside her. Neither woman said anything for a minute.

It was hard to think about Elsie's body being down there, under the cold, dark earth. At least her spirit was at peace. Sally wondered if Elsie knew she hadn't kept her promise.

"Come on, let's put these on Sophie's grave."

Sally meandered toward the older side of the cemetery, the breeze tousling her hair and guilt tormenting her conscience. Elsie's pleading voice couldn't be silenced in this place. And Sally felt the pressure mounting again.

"There it is." Karen picked up her pace.

Sally followed her to the end of the row, where the marble guardian angel stood watch over Sophie's grave. Karen squatted and reverently placed the mums in the flower holder. She was silent for a moment, then rose to her feet. "I wonder if Elsie's life would've been different if Sophie had lived?"

"What do you mean?" Sally said.

"Daughters tend to be friends with their mothers. Sophie would've watched out for her. Poor thing might as well've had nobody in the end."

"It's not fair, is it?"

Karen glanced over at Sally. "I think Elsie thought of us as daughters, don't you?"

"I don't know how she thought of us. We were certainly fond of her."

Karen put her hands in her coat pockets and looked up at the sky. "We treated her more like a mother than Harry did. Good thing she didn't leave him anything. The creep doesn't deserve it."

Sally's heart pounded so hard that she felt a little woozy. "How do you know she didn't leave him anything?"

"Because she was on Medicaid, silly."

Sally gave a slight nod. "Oh, yeah."

Karen closed her eyes and tilted her head back, letting the sun bake her face. "What a gorgeous day."

Sally stole a glance behind Sophie's headstone and saw that the ground had not been broken. Surely, if Harry had known where the money was, he would've gotten his hands on it by now.

"Come on," Karen said. "Let's walk around a little more before we head back."

Sally sat in the corner booth at the Dexter Springs Burger King, finishing the last of a double cheeseburger. "This is good, Karen. Thanks."

"You're welcome."

Sally took a sip of diet Coke. "Is something bothering you? You're awfully quiet."

"I was just thinking about your situation. Must be awful having bill collectors calling you day and night."

Sally sighed. "Now, that ought to give me indigestion."

"Yeah, sorry to bring it up. But you asked."

"That's all right. It's just below the surface anyway."

"Have you thought about where to apply for a second job?"

Sally poked the ice in her cup with the straw. "I don't know. Some place that needs a sales clerk or a waitress or a part-time CNA. Makes me exhausted just thinking about it."

"Sam really hung you out to dry, didn't he?"

"Yeah, he did. Could we talk about something else? This is depressing."

"Sorry." Karen glanced at her watch, and then at the empty tables around them. "Are you in a big hurry to get home?"

"Not especially. Why?"

"I've got a proposition I'd like to run by you."

"What kind of proposition?"

Karen folded her hands on the table. "What if I could help you get enough money to pay your debts—and maybe stay out of debt permanently?"

Sally laughed. "Yeah, right. Legally?"

Karen looked up, her eyes serious and searching. "That's up to you."

"Oh, brother. Now I *am* curious."

Karen glanced over at the employees behind the counter. "Come on, let's take a drive. I'll fill you in."

"You're not trying to get me into one of those multilevel marketing deals, are you?"

Karen smiled. "No, this is much simpler and much faster."

20

Sally Cox sat looking out the window, her eyes feasting on the rural countryside, while Karen Morgan drove the car up and down the hills around Dexter Springs. Off to the west, the sky was turning a golden pink.

"Okay, Karen, it's getting late. Tell me where we're going."

"In circles," Karen said.

"What?"

"I'm killing time."

"Why?"

"Because I want you to be intrigued and open-minded."

"What's the big mystery?"

Karen made a right turn on an unmarked road, then pulled the car onto the grassy shoulder and turned off the motor. She leaned back on the seat, her arms folded. "I've got some serious business to discuss with you. I've thought about this long and hard, and it's time to see if you're interested."

"In what?"

Karen looked out the front window, her eyes seemingly fixed on a row of blackbirds perched on a weathered fence post. "Did you know Elsie had money?"

Sally felt her neck muscles tighten, her heart racing faster than the jackrabbit that shot across the road.

"Yes or no?"

"How would I know?"

"Look, Sal, it's time to stop the game playing. Elsie talked to both of us. She told me stuff. She told you stuff."

Sally shrugged. "Okay, I knew."

"I thought so. Did she tell you if anything happened to her, to give the money to the poor?"

Sally looked over at Karen. "Yes."

"Well, that's what I plan to do. And I think I know where the money is."

"Behind Sophie's headstone," Sally said.

Karen smiled, her eyebrows arched. "I thought so. Which brings me to my proposition."

"Which is?"

"Well, you're poor, aren't you? I think Elsie would be pleased for you to have the money."

"Karen, what are you saying?"

"Look, we can run by Wal-Mart and buy gloves, flashlights, shovels. I say we wait until dark and go digging. It's either there or it isn't. If it is, then it was destined to be ours. Who knows? Maybe it's the answer you've been praying for."

Sally felt her face get hot and hoped she wasn't blushing. She hadn't even bothered to pray. But would God approve of this? "Did Elsie tell you she got the money by fixing the books in Arnie's company?"

Karen laughed. "No. Isn't *that* a kick?"

"It's a kick all right. It also means the money belongs to the IRS— and to Medicaid. What you're suggesting is criminal."

"Hey, when you asked if it was legal, I said it depends on you. I don't have a problem with it. What they never had, they won't miss. It's a drop in the bucket to them. But you? It could change your life. Don't tell me you've never thought about it."

Sally could hardly believe she was even considering this. "What do you stand to gain from this?"

"Half. I'll keep what I need and give the rest to the poor."

"This is a huge risk. And there might not be much money."

Karen smiled. "Elsie told me she buried stacks and stacks of hundreds. Sounds like it's worth exploring. Look, if you want to give away your half, feel free. But I think Elsie would be happy to know her money got you out of financial trouble—and that Harry never got his hands on it."

Sally sank into the seat. "Karen, no. What if we get caught?"

"We won't. Nobody ever comes out here. But we can't sit on this. You need to decide right here, right now: Are you in or out?"

Harry Rigsby sat at the kitchen table, rummaging through the shoe box containing his mother's old photographs. He held up the picture

Jon had shown him of Elsie and Arnie standing in Aunt Clara's flower garden, and began to question whether Jon had been on the right track.

The sheriff never found anything buried there, and it's not as though he hadn't looked. Layton seemed too honest and too remorseful to have taken the money before the sheriff arrived. So where was it?

Harry slammed his fist on the table. He got up and started pacing, panicked at the thought that he might never know where his mother's money was hidden.

The phone rang and he grabbed it. "What?"

"Did I call at a bad time?" Gracie Garver said.

"I'm just havin' a bad day. Whaddya want?"

"I'm afraid what I have to say may add to it. Bill's on the other line. We need you to level with us about something."

Harry winced. "What now?"

"We need to know why Jon went to Layton's."

"What is this? How should I know?"

"Don't mess with us," Gracie said. "We already have the answers. We just want to hear your explanation."

"I don't know what you're talkin' about."

There was a long pause. Harry could hear her breathing.

"Jon was looking for your mother's money, wasn't he?"

"What money? Ma was broker than a bag lady."

"This is not the time to play hardball," Bill said.

"What're *you*, the umpire? This is none of your business."

"Look, Harry." Bill's voice was tight and controlled. "This is the first time I've stuck my nose in your business in the twenty-five years I've been married to Gracie. But if Jon was at Layton's looking for Elsie's money, your not telling the sheriff is withholding evidence."

"What is it about 'I don't know' you two don't get?"

"Harry, don't get huffy," Gracie said. "I remember Arnie making wisecracks about Elsie rat-holing money. If she did, and you knew about it, you could be up on Medicaid fraud charges. This is serious."

"What? Now you're threatenin' me?"

"I don't care what happens to you! I'm trying to understand why my son's dead. Do you get *that*?"

"And you think I don't?"

There was a long, agonizing silence.

"Look, Harry," Bill said softly. "I think we all want to understand what was going on in Jon's head."

"Yeah, well, there's no way to know that, is there? What am I, a mind reader?"

Gracie let out a loud sigh. "Jon drew flowers and dollar signs around Layton's address. That's just too big a coincidence not to mean something."

"Maybe so," Harry said. "But I don't know anything about Ma havin' money. My ol' man talked like that my whole life. And they still ended up with nothin'. Which is the same as I've got, in case you didn't notice."

"Which is all the more reason why you'd like to find the money."

"Think what you want, Gracie. You're way off base."

"We'll let the sheriff decide."

"Good. Bring him on. I got nothin' to hide."

Karen parked the car next to the road and turned off the lights. Sally opened the door and stepped into the frigid January night.

"It's pitch black out here," Sally said, her breath turning to vapor.

"The sky's clear. We'll get our night vision pretty quickly. Come on, help me with this stuff."

Sally reached in the backseat and put her gloved hands around the handle of a shovel wedged between the seats, and turned it until she got it out of the car.

"Here." Karen handed her the flashlight and lawn bags. "I'll get the other shovel and the tool box." Karen took the things out of the car and placed them on the ground. "Okay, stay here while I hide the car behind those trees."

Karen pulled the car off the road and turned off the headlights and the ignition. In the stillness, Sally heard the swishing of leaves on the gravel road, footsteps crackling over twigs—and her conscience reminding her of the gravity of what she was about to do. She was relieved when Karen reappeared and began walking toward her.

"Lead the way," Karen said, bending down to get her shovel and tool box.

Sally held the flashlight in front of her and leaned the shovel against the wrought iron fence. She opened the gate and walked slowly across the cemetery, her heart pounding in protest.

"You okay?" Karen said.

"Yeah, I'm fine." Sally felt a churning in her stomach. God's promises to provide hadn't worked for her. What was she supposed to do: go bankrupt waiting for His help?

"Hey, slow down," Karen said. "I can't see where I'm going."

"Sorry."

Sally waited for Karen to catch up, then turned down the last row and trudged slowly toward Sophie's grave, wondering about the time so many years ago when Elsie and Lou had come here to bury the money. What had been going through their minds? Who could've imagined that one day, two CNAs from Walnut Hills Nursing Center would come calling in the night like two grave robbers, ready to make good on a promise—and to make off with whatever was buried there?

Harry slammed down the phone. He let out a string of curse words he would like to have shouted at Gracie and Bill.

He marched to the hall closet, put on his coat and gloves, pulled a stocking cap down over his ears, and left the house for a brisk walk.

There was no way was he going to let Gracie ruin this for him! Getting his mother's money was his last hope for any quality of life—and telling the sheriff what he knew wouldn't bring Jon back. Why couldn't she just back off and leave things alone? All he needed was her and Bill ganging up on him!

Harry thought carefully about the questions the Kansas City police had asked him when they questioned him after Jon's death. Harry had been genuinely stunned to find out Jon hadn't gone to Pittsburgh on a job interview, but to his cousin Layton's—and with a shovel, no less. And his shock over Jon's death had been real. Harry hadn't had to manufacture anything. The cops bought it that he didn't know anything.

Gracie could squawk all she wanted. Some stupid doodles on a notepad weren't enough to prove anything. Besides, how could the authorities charge Harry with Medicaid fraud when he had never laid eyes on this money his mother had supposedly stashed away? For all he knew, it was a myth. At least, that's what he planned to tell them.

Sally looked up at a sea of stars that twinkled like diamonds on black velvet. She thought of her wedding ring tucked in the corner of her lingerie drawer—and the reason she took it off.

"Keep your eyes on the ground," Karen said. "You keep moving the flashlight, and I can't see where I'm going."

Sally held the beam of light in front of her. "I see Sophie's angel just up ahead." For a moment she wanted to run all the way back to Kansas City.

"Are you cool with this?" Karen said. "Because once we get going, there's no turning back. I can't afford to have you panic."

"I'm fine."

"Remember to keep your gloves on. We don't want prints on anything."

Sally nodded. "I got it."

Karen walked around to the back of Sophie's headstone. "Shine the light over here. Let me see how hard the ground is." She put the sharp end of the shovel in the ground, put her foot on the metal, and gave it a good push. "Hey, it's not too bad," she said, dumping the first scoop of dirt. "Why don't you dig there on my right, and we'll meet in the middle. If the money's where Elsie said it was, we should hit something. I can't imagine she buried it very deep."

Sally left the flashlight on and set it at the angel's feet. She began digging. One scoop. Two. Three. A pile. "This isn't as hard as I thought it would be."

"We aren't through yet, girlfriend. Keep digging."

"What was that?" Sally listened intently, her weight resting on the shovel.

"It's just the wind. Keep digging."

Sally continued to dig, every now and then looking over her shoulder, ridden with an eerie feeling that the McClendons were eyeing her with disapproval. Or maybe God was.

"Hey, I hit something!" Karen said. "Get the flashlight!"

Sally grabbed the flashlight and shone it on the ground.

Karen squatted and knocked on something hard.

"Can you tell what it is?"

Karen shook her head. "Not yet. Let's keep digging."

The two women feverishly dug around the object until it began to take shape, then Karen put down her shovel and dropped to her knees, her face just inches from whatever lay in the shallow hole.

"Oh, no!" Karen whispered. "What've we done?"

"What's wrong?" Sally's heart felt as though it might stop beating at any moment. "What is it? What's down there?"

Karen brushed away the dirt, then looked up, her eyes wide. "It's a coffin!"

21

Sally Cox got down on her knees beside Karen, her body shivering more from the gruesome discovery than from the cold. "We have to stop. Someone must've set the headstone the wrong way."

"It doesn't make sense," Karen said. "Elsie would've seen to it that things were done right."

"Well, maybe Arnie wouldn't pay for a headstone right away. Maybe the grass grew over it and she forgot which end was which. I doubt the McClendons kept a map of where the bodies are."

Karen brushed the remaining dirt off the top of the coffin. "On the other hand, why is it buried this close to the surface? It's only down about two feet. And it's not in a vault. Come on, let's keep digging."

"But what if we're wrong? What if Sophie's remains are in there!"

"Then we'll close it up and put everything back the way we found it. But I don't think we're going to find a baby skeleton in here. Elsie said she had a brother who was an undertaker. Can you think of a safer place to hide your money than a coffin?"

"Her brother's name was Lou, and he helped her bury the money. Elsie told me."

Karen let out a loud whoop. "Okay, let's get this thing out of here. I think we've hit pay dirt!"

"Shhh! Someone might hear you."

Karen laughed. "Yeah, I could wake the dead. Come on, dig."

The two women dug around the coffin until it was completely exposed and there was room for them to step into the hole. Karen got on one end and Sally the other, their hands braced under the coffin.

"Okay," Karen said, "one, two, *three…*"

Sally's back was taut, her heart fluttering, as she and Karen ever so slowly strained to lift the child-sized coffin up out of the hole, then dropped it on the ground.

"We did it!" Karen said, sounding short of breath. She climbed out of the hole and laughed. "You okay?"

Sally arched her back. "I can't believe how heavy it is!"

"Let's get this thing open!"

Gracie had been trying to make some headway on a crossword puzzle for over an hour but had hardly made a dent. Was she being too judgmental about Harry? As indifferent as he'd been to Jon growing up, the relationship between father and son had improved considerably in recent years. She couldn't imagine that Harry would have supported Jon doing anything unlawful. And maybe she was wrong about Elsie's money. Maybe she had been hasty in accusing Harry. The whole idea *was* a bit far-fetched.

"A penny for your thoughts," Bill said.

"Oh, as usual I'm starting to doubt my instincts."

"They're usually pretty good."

Gracie closed the crossword puzzle book. "But what if I'm wrong? This could ruin Harry."

"I don't see how," Bill said. "If he really doesn't know anything about his mother having money—assuming, of course, there *is* money—he doesn't have anything to fear from the law."

"I suppose not."

"You don't sound convinced."

Gracie sighed. "Truth be known, I couldn't care less whether or not he gets his mother's money. I'm mad at him for pretending he didn't know that Jon went to Layton's to find it. But I could be wrong. What if he didn't know?"

"And what if he did?"

"Bill, you know Harry disgusts me. But I don't want to make his life any harder. Maybe we shouldn't go to the sheriff until we have more to go on."

Bill put down the newspaper. "Stand your ground, Grace. You've let Harry walk on you ever since I've known you. If he's innocent, he's got nothing to worry about. But if he got Jon involved in some quest to find Elsie's money, he has some responsibility for getting him killed."

"It's so hard to think that—" Gracie put her hand to her mouth and swallowed the emotion.

Bill got up and knelt by her chair, his arm around her. "This is not about Harry. It's about Jon—and our finding out exactly what happened. There's nothing to be gained by withholding this from the sheriff."

Gracie wiped the tears from her cheeks. "You're right. It's just so awful to think that his own father might have put him up to it."

Sally sat on her heels, the flashlight in her hands, aiming the beam of light on the dirt-encrusted coffin.

"I wonder how this thing opens," Karen said. "I don't see a lock." She ran her fingers along the middle where the lid met the bottom. "There's a latch. It feels stuck." Karen picked up a screwdriver and tried to pry the latch open. "Darn! This thing is stubborn. I can't get it to budge...wait...there...I think I've got it...yeah, it's moving!" Karen glanced up at Sally. "Okay, here goes." She slipped her fingertips under the lid and began to slowly raise it.

Sally clamped her eyes shut, horrified to think Sophie's remains might be inside. Why had she agreed to do this?

A second later, Karen let out a wicked laugh. "Will you take a look at this? Say good-bye to Walnut Hills."

Sally's eyes flew open, and she saw stacks and stacks of hundred-dollar bills, each bound and neatly packed into the coffin.

Karen stripped off her gloves, grabbed a stack of money, and counted it. Fifty hundreds? That's five thousand dollars! All these stacks look the same." She dug down to the bottom and pulled up more stacks. "We're rich, Sal. There must be a couple hundred thousand in here. Maybe more. Quick, get a lawn bag."

Sally zipped open the box of lawn bags and knelt next to Karen. She tore one bag off the roll and fought with it until it opened, then held it while Karen stuffed it with money.

"Get another bag," Karen said. "We can split the money later."

Karen worked quickly, and within a couple of minutes, the coffin was empty.

Sally tied the top of each lawn bag in a double knot, wondering if she had ever been more afraid than she was at this moment. Her eyes searched the darkness, half expecting the entire Dexter Springs Police Department to converge on them at any moment.

"Okay," Karen said, putting her gloves back on. "Let's get this back in the ground."

The two women got down in the hole, then lifted the coffin and set it where they had found it. They climbed out and quickly filled the hole around it with dirt, then packed it down as best they could and raked their footprints with the blade of the shovels.

Sally could hardly catch her breath, more from fear than exertion. "What should we do with the shovels?"

Karen took Sally's shovel and nodded toward a row of trees about fifty yards behind them. "Light the way."

Sally led with cautious haste, her eyes on the ground in front of her, her heart in her throat. When she reached the tree line, she stopped, aware of Karen swishing past her on the left.

"Keep the light on the trees so I can see," Karen said.

Sally held the flashlight steady and watched as Karen tossed the shovels, one at a time, into some heavy underbrush, then hurried back to her, a look of elation on her face.

Karen threw her arms around Sally and squeezed, swaying her back and forth. "We did it! We're free! Thank you, Elsie! Thank you! Come on, we'd better get the money before Arnie's ghost tries to take it back!" Karen's giggling filled the night.

The women made their way back to Sophie's grave and checked the ground to be sure they weren't leaving anything behind.

"Just a minute," Karen said. She took the bouquet of mums out of the holder and placed them on another grave. "We don't want to draw attention. We can bring flowers another time. Okay, girlfriend, let's go. We should stop at Elsie's grave and move those flowers too."

Sally picked up one of the trash bags and slung it over her shoulder, then shone the beam of light on the ground in front of her and traced her steps back to Elsie's grave. She stood silent, trying to assimilate what she had just done.

Sally was aware of Karen taking the flowers off Elsie's grave, and seconds later, coming and standing next to her.

"You think she knows?" Sally said.

"Are you kidding? Elsie's grinning from ear to ear. Wait," Karen whispered. "Did you hear that?"

"What?"

"I think Arnie just turned over in his grave." Karen laughed so hard she lost her balance, dropped the bag of money on the ground, and landed on her behind.

Sally giggled in spite of herself. But as she trudged back to the car, taking her first steps of financial freedom, her burden seemed even heavier than before.

Karen lifted the rear hatch of the Sportage and put the bags of money and the toolbox inside. "I am *so* jazzed! Just think how much peace of mind this will buy." She pulled Sally close, her arm around her, and looked up at the sky. "Thanks to Elsie, our troubles are over. When we drive away from here, nothing will ever be the same."

22

Sally Cox pushed the front door with her shoulder, and then pushed again until it gave way and she stumbled into the living room with one of the bags of money.

"Come on," she whispered to Karen.

She waited until Karen stepped inside, then bolt-locked the door, flipped the light switch, and pulled the drapes.

Sally exhaled a sigh of relief. "*Now,* I feel safe."

"Why are you so paranoid?" Karen said. "No one followed us. You act like Arnie's ghost is chasing you or something."

Kiwi meowed as if to scold Sally for being late, then paced in front of the couch, her back a fluffy arch.

Sally reached down and picked up Kiwi and smiled when she started to purr. "Sorry I'm late. But you'll thank me when you're eating Fancy Feast from now on."

"Okay," Karen said. "Where do you want to count the money?"

"Let's use the kitchen table."

Sally led the way to the kitchen and set the bag on one of the chairs.

Karen brought the other bag and dumped the contents in the middle of the table, delivering a distinctive, musty smell. "Will you look at this? We've died and gone to heaven!"

"You don't believe in heaven."

"Well, if I did, this is it!" Karen picked up a bundle of bills and planted a kiss on it. "Who says money can't buy happiness? Or at least *rent* it?" Karen looked across the table at Sally. "Just think, no more bill collectors."

Sally glanced over at her answering machine and noticed there were seven messages.

"Okay," Karen said, rubbing her hands together. "Let's see how much we've got." She arranged the bundles on the kitchen table, and then reached in the bag and stacked the remaining bundles on top of the first. "That'll simplify everything: There's an even number. Watch while I count them."

If Sam could see me now, Sally thought.

"One, two, three, four..."

Sally tried to decide which bill to pay off first. *Debt free!* She could hardly imagine what it would be like.

"Nineteen, twenty, twenty-one..."

Sally's heart raced as she did the math. She fantasized about paying cash for a new car. Fixing up the house. Getting a salon hair cut. Buying stylish clothes. A membership at the gym. Eating out. Getting Kiwi's shots.

"Forty-eight, forty-nine, *fifty!"* Karen looked at Sally, her eyes wide and brimming with tears. "Fifty stacks of five thousand...*a quarter of a million dollars!"*

Sally stood staring at Karen, then at the money, trying to absorb the magnitude of what it could mean. All the way home from Dexter Springs, she had felt as though someone would surely pinch her, and she would wake up just as financially strapped as before.

"A hundred and twenty-five thousand dollars each," Sally said, her eyes burning with tears.

Karen came around the table and threw her arms around Sally, crying, laughing jubilantly, and then crying some more.

Sally wept, as though a geyser of stress was erupting, releasing the pressure she had been holding inside for months.

Karen took a step back and leaned against the countertop. "I'm going to give two weeks' notice and look for something else. No more Walnut Hills. No more Depends. And no more Wanda."

"I'll probably stay," Sally said. "I'm not qualified for anything else. But now I can afford the medical insurance and won't have to get a second job. Imagine being debt free...and having all the spending money I could ever want. It's too good to be true."

"By the way, did anyone know you were going to the cemetery today?"

Sally shook her head. "No."

"Good. I didn't tell anyone either."

"You think someone will notice the fresh dirt behind Sophie's grave?"

"I doubt if anyone goes there anymore," Karen said. "But no one would suspect us. Besides, we didn't leave a fingerprint on anything, and we covered up our footprints. Any other evidence of our being there could be explained by the fact that we had walked around the cemetery after Elsie's service."

"We had on different shoes."

Karen moved next to Sally, a smile stretching her cheeks. "Then I suggest we give these shoes to Goodwill as soon as possible. We can certainly afford to buy new ones." She nudged Sally's arm with her elbow. "And we don't have to wait till they go on sale."

Sally savored that thought for a moment. She could pick out any pair of shoes she wanted—and pay cash for them.

Karen glanced at her watch. "Two thirty! We're going to be zombies. I'm so pumped I doubt I'll sleep a wink, but I need to try."

"You want to crash here?" Sally said. "I've got a spare bedroom."

"Thanks, but I think it'd be smart to have my car parked in my space when the sun comes up. We pulled this off without a hitch. Let's not get sloppy now." Karen's eyes seemed to search Sally's. "This is just between us, right? You're not going to get sanctimonious on me and turn yourself in or something?"

"No, this stays between you and me and Elsie. Though I'm not sure I believe it yet."

"Well, believe it, girlfriend. This is a gift—the answer to all your problems."

Karen put half the money in a lawn bag and tied it, then slung it over her shoulder. She hugged Sally with her free arm and walked to the front door. "I'll see you at seven."

After Karen left, Sally went back to the kitchen and stared at the one hundred and twenty-five thousand dollars stacked on the table she'd bought at Hank's Discount Warehouse right after she married Sam. She picked up one bundle of hundreds and fanned one end of the bills through her thumb and forefinger, the musty smell like perfume to her senses. *Thank you, sweetie. Rest in peace.*

She put each of the bundles in the lawn bag and took it to her bedroom closet, then set it on the floor and pushed it back behind her long hanging things.

Sally quickly undressed, and realized she was shivering. She put on her threadbare flannel pajamas, then went out in the hall and turned the thermostat up to toasty. She climbed into bed and pulled the comforter up over her, relishing the rush of warm air coming from the vent.

She turned on her side, Kiwi nestled in her arms, and closed her eyes, letting every muscle of her body melt into the mattress. She thought of the white Toyota Camry with luscious leather seats that had been parked next to her at Safeway...the houndstooth wool pantsuit she had seen at Hall's...the buttery-soft leather pumps at the Jones Store...the medium-rare steaks served at the Plaza III...and—

If anything happens to me, promise me you'll get the money and give it to the poor. Sally hugged Kiwi a little tighter. Wasn't *poor* a relative term? Surely Elsie would be pleased to know that her money had bought Sally peace of mind and more—and probably saved her from bankruptcy.

But as Sally's mind floated between wakefulness and sleep, her conscience accused her of taking the easy way out—of twisting Elsie's words to suit her own circumstances.

And what about Karen's half? Did Sally really think Karen would give what she didn't need to the poor? Hadn't Sally known all along that it was just talk—a ploy to get her to agree to dig up the money? Plus, Elsie's money was ill-gotten in the first place. It belonged to Medicaid and the IRS.

Sally tossed from side to side. Let Karen deal with her own conscience! Sally *was* poor and accountable only for how she chose to spend her half. Plus, the money was a drop in the bucket to Uncle Sam. The government was rich enough.

Why was she entering into this battle anyway? It was too late to change what had happened—not that she wanted to.

Sally was trying to shut off her mind, her body begging for sleep, when suddenly she had an ominous sense that she was being watched. Her eyes flew open, and she sat up, her heart racing. Was that a shadow moving across the window?

She got out of bed and hurried to the front door, then double-checked the bolt lock and flipped the porch light on. She went to the basement door and slid the chain lock, then to the kitchen and double-checked the keyed lock on the back door. She flipped on the porch light and peeked through the curtains. No one was in the backyard. She listened intently. The neighbor's dog wasn't barking.

Kiwi meowed and rubbed against one of Sally's legs, then the other.

"You're a lot of help. Where's a watchcat when you need one?"

Sally took the cordless phone off the cradle and carried it back to the bedroom and locked the door. She put the phone next to her pillow and got back in bed, the covers pulled up to her chin, confident that no one could get to her without breaking at least two locks. It was probably her imagination anyway.

She lay in the stillness, her eyelids heavy, her body limp with exhaustion, and felt herself drifting off to sleep...

Suddenly, the night grew thick and oozy, almost alive. Sally's heart began to pound and then pound harder until she thought it would burst. In the darkness, she saw something even blacker moving slowly across the floor, then up the far wall and across the ceiling. It didn't have a voice, but hovered over her, its steely coldness causing her to shudder.

Kiwi arched her back and hissed, then let out a slow, menacing growl.

Sally turned over on her stomach and buried her face in the pillow, consumed with terror beyond her imagination. She waited for what seemed an eternity, aware of something breathing on the back of her neck.

Something evil. And it wasn't leaving.

23

S ally was aware of an obnoxious buzzing noise and Kiwi's paw padding her cheek. She groped for the off button on the alarm clock, relieved when the racket finally ceased. She lay quietly for a moment, making sure she was awake and the awful nightmare was over.

She slid out of bed and stumbled out to the kitchen, every muscle in her body sore and aching. She poured water in the coffeemaker and put a coffee filter pack in the basket, then turned it on.

She pulled out a chair and sat, her elbows on the table, her chin resting on her palms. Her excitement over the money had been over-shadowed by that horrible nightmare. And now she felt guilty again. It's not as though the money had benefited anyone where it was. Elsie would probably have given the money to Sally herself, had she known of her financial predicament.

It's never too late to do what's right.

Sally sighed. Yes, it is! Putting half the money back in the coffin wasn't going to absolve her—not that she was physically capable of it anyway. And turning her half of the money over to the authorities would raise questions about how she got it. Karen Morgan would never support her story. So, unless Sally wanted to land in jail, she had no choice but to stick with the plan.

She might as well get her debts paid off as soon as possible; though how to deposit enough money in the bank without creating suspicion posed a big problem. But she couldn't just waltz in each creditor's office and flash hundreds of dollars around either. Maybe she could use her Visa card to pay bills, and then pay Visa at the end of the month. But she couldn't use cash to pay that bill either. Sally sighed. This was more complicated than she had realized. Maybe Karen could tell her how to handle it.

Sally got up and poured herself a cup of coffee.

The love of money is a root of all kinds of evil.

There was that churning in her gut. All she wanted was to get out of debt. How evil was that? She had trusted the Lord until she thought she would drown in a sea of debt. And He hadn't thrown her a life preserver. What was she supposed to do? Not paying her debts was just as wrong. And Elsie's money was a gift—the means to Sally's being debt free.

So, what about a new car? Nicer clothes? Eating out? A membership at the gym? How does that go to help the poor?

Sally got up and dumped her coffee in the sink, then headed for the shower. She had enough pressure without arguing with herself!

Sally walked in the employees' entrance at Walnut Hills Nursing Center and went to the computer to clock in. She felt a tap on her shoulder.

"How are you feeling?" Karen Morgan said.

"Sore. How about you?"

"*Fabulously* sore," Karen said. "I actually slept like a baby. Judging from the bags under your eyes, I'm guessing you didn't?"

"Not really. I had this creepy nightmare."

"Well, you can go to bed early tonight." Karen lowered her voice. "Can you believe we actually pulled it off? I can hardly wait to give notice."

"What reason are you going to give?" Sally said. "They'll want to know why."

"I'm telling them my mother's sick. That's true, in a way. She just had a knee replacement. But she lives in Miami."

Sally looked over Karen's shoulder and didn't see anyone. "How do I get the money in the bank so I can pay bills?"

"You can make deposits of up to ten thousand dollars without having to fill out a Currency Transaction Report for the IRS. If they look at you weird, just keep it light. Tell them you sold off some antiques you inherited."

"They're bound to get suspicious if I do this repeatedly."

Karen grinned. "You can have accounts at more than one bank."

Sally saw Wanda walking toward them and gave Karen's arm a double squeeze.

"Good morning, ladies," Wanda said. "I do hope you're eager to get started."

"It's going to be a beautiful day," Karen said. "Supposed to be sunny and almost fifty degrees."

"That's what I hear." Wanda looked at Sally. "We need to tread lightly around Fay Emerson. She couldn't sleep, and she's cranky as an old bear. Jeffrey Horton had his hands full most of the night."

He's not the only one. "Okay. Thanks for the heads-up."

Sally put her purse in her locker and some jelly beans in her pocket, then started walking with Karen down the main hallway.

"You don't seem very excited," Karen said.

"I just don't like deception."

"Who does? But it's a small price to pay for financial freedom."

"Yeah, I suppose."

Karen smiled. "I'm going to the Subaru dealer to look at Foresters after work. Want to go?"

"Think I'll pass. By three o'clock I may be too stiff to walk to my old car, let alone go looking for a new one."

"Okay, see you on break," Karen said.

Sally turned down the hallway to the east wing, realizing that it was just one week ago that she had found Elsie dead. Already, she and Karen had claimed Elsie's money, twisted her wishes to suit their own, and washed their hands of any wrongdoing. Sally felt that churning in her gut again. At least one of them actually believed it.

Harry Rigsby heard the doorbell ring. He folded the newspaper and went to the front door and looked through the peephole. Sheriff Baughman? *Oh, brother, here it comes.*

"Hey, sheriff. What brings you out this way?"

"Would you mind if I come in for a few minutes?" Sheriff Baughman said. "I had some business in Kansas City and thought I'd kill two birds with one stone."

Harry led the way into the living room. "Make yourself comfortable. I assume this is about Gracie's harebrained idea."

"What idea is that?" the sheriff said.

Harry raised his eyebrows. "How about you tellin' me what she said?"

"Okay." The sheriff took off his hat and sat on the couch. "She and her husband think you know why your son was on Layton's property."

"Yeah, I know what they think. It's bunk."

"Then what do *you* make of the doodling?"

"Nothin'. The kid drew flowers and arrows and dollar signs. You oughta see some of the stuff I doodle. Big deal. Gracie's making way too much of this."

"Then you don't believe your mother had money hidden away?"

Harry rolled his eyes. "My Ma was as broke as a bag lady. She never had anything. Gracie knows that. I don't know where she came up with this crazy idea that Jon was after some private stash my mother had. The woman's still in denial." Harry paused for a moment and studied the sheriff's face. "Look, I can't blame her for wantin' to know why Jon did what he did. Don't we all? Well, it's not gonna happen. Some things we just have to accept."

"So you still think Jon flipped out?"

"I'm sayin' I haven't got a better explanation why he'd make up a story about a job interview in Pittsburgh, and then end up dead in his cousin's backyard. The whole thing's insane."

Sheriff Baughman's eyes were piercing. "So you have no idea why Jon was digging on Layton's property? Even though your ex-wife seems convinced he was after your mother's money."

"What money? My folks had nothin'. Why would Ma keep money hidden when she could've used it?"

"Maybe she was miserly," the sheriff said. "Or she didn't want to pay Medicaid."

Harry put on the most pained look he could muster. "How can you malign my mother this way? The poor woman struggled her whole life to make ends meet. She died penniless. And now you're tryin' to pin somethin' on my son that makes no sense at all."

Sheriff Baughman fiddled with the lining of his hat. "From where I sit, Mrs. Garver's explanation makes more sense."

"Can't help that," Harry said. "There's no money. And no reason that I know of for Jon to have been diggin' on his cousin's property."

"So you don't want to amend your story?"

"No. And I resent bein' put in this position. Gracie and Bill are graspin' at straws, and I'm gettin' just a little tired of everyone caterin' to 'em."

Sally shoved the front door with her sore shoulder, then turned around and pushed it with her behind until it finally opened. She went inside and slammed the door shut, vowing to get the stupid thing fixed if it took the entire hundred and twenty-five thousand.

She dropped her purse and the mail on the back of the couch and picked up Kiwi, who was already purring.

"I'm glad you're feeling perky," Sally said. "I'm so tired I nodded off at the stoplight."

She went into the kitchen and remembered she'd forgotten to play back yesterday's messages. Now the machine was full. She hit the replay button.

"Ms. Cox, this is Tri-State Gas Company—" Sally hit the delete button.

"This is Mona at Dr. Brennan's office. We need to arrange—" Delete.

"Sal, it's Sam. It's 8:30. I'll catch you later—" Delete.

"Hey, Sal. It's Sam. It's 10:15. Would you please give me a call?" Delete.

"Sal, it's me again. It's 11:45. I'm getting worried. Call me when you get home." Delete.

"This is Sam. It's 12:25. Call me when you get in. I don't care what time it is." Delete.

"It's Sam. It's 1:30 in the morning. I honestly expected more from you." Delete.

Sally rolled her eyes. "Who does he think he is, my father?"

She went through the remaining messages, all from collection agencies, and deleted them one by one, then took the Friskies out of the cabinet and filled Kiwi's bowl.

The doorbell rang.

"Go away. I don't want any."

It rang again, and she went to the front door and looked out the peephole, then yanked on the warped door until it opened. "Ouch! What do you want, Sam?"

"What were you doing last night?"

Sally's heart raced faster than the squad car zooming past her street. "I beg your pardon?"

"You going to tell me who the guy is?"

"What guy?"

"The one who stayed over. I saw his Sportage in the driveway—at 2:00 this morning!"

"You've got a lot of nerve spying on me. What I do is none of your business."

"I was worried when you didn't return my calls."

She raised her eyebrows, but kept her voice down. "We're divorced, Sam. I don't want to talk to you. I don't want to be your friend. And I sure as heck don't plan on checking in with you."

"Babe, listen. I know I hurt you, but please don't stoop to this to get back at me. You're better than that."

Sally rolled her eyes, her hand on her hip. "Don't flatter yourself. You're way off base."

"Then who was here?"

"A gal from work. We went to dinner and a movie, and then killed a pot of coffee and a batch of brownies and talked half the night. As if it's any of your concern."

Sam looked at her sheepishly. "Oops."

"Shouldn't you be at work?"

He smiled. "You're tired. I can always tell."

"That's nice. Good-bye now." Sally started to close the door, and he held it open with his hand.

"Leslie wants you to call her. Says it's important."

There was that charming smile.

"Fine. Good-bye, Sam." Sally pushed the door closed and locked it.

She watched through the peephole as he got in his Camaro and drove off. *Of all times for him to be watching out for me!*

She looked down at Kiwi. "Yes, I know he called me 'babe,' but don't get any bright ideas. I'm not starting up anything. I don't care if he's crazy about cats."

Sally went out to the kitchen and poured a cup of cold coffee and put it in the microwave. She picked up the phone and dialed Leslie's number.

"Hello."

"Hi, honey. It's Mom."

"Hi! I missed you over the weekend. So how have you been? Are you enjoying the new church?"

"I only went the one time. It seemed flat. It's probably me. I'm not feeling very spiritual these days."

"How are things at work?"

"Okay. Except one of my patients died last week, and it's been an adjustment. She was a real sweetie."

There was a long pause. Sally heard whispering.

"Leslie, who are you talking to?"

"Uh, Alan took the day off. We have some great news and could hardly wait to tell you: I'm pregnant...Mom...?"

"Oh, Leslie." Sally's eyes filled with tears and spilled over onto her cheeks. "This is wonderful. I'm blubbering all over myself. It's so exciting. Does your father know?"

"I called his cell phone a little while ago. He was excited, but I made him promise not to tell you. I'm so relieved he's not with Allison anymore."

"Me, too. I think her problems scared him off."

"Daddy said you've had coffee with him a couple of times."

Sally paused, her fingers tapping the table. "That's a gross exaggeration. He ran into me at Starbucks. And he brought coffee to the house one morning, and I sent him on his way."

"So, you're not seeing him again?"

"Is that what he told you?"

"Well, I—uh, not really. I guess I was hoping."

"We're civil again, Leslie. But that's as far as it's going. Let's talk about you. When's your due date?

"June 23."

Sally jotted it down on her calendar. "Are you going to find out the baby's gender ahead of time?"

"I don't know yet. Alan wants to. I'm not sure. How do you feel about it?"

Sally realized she was smiling. "I think it'd be fun to know. Oh, Les, I can't believe you're going to be a mother. And I'm going to be a grandmother!"

"Maybe you could take some time off when the baby gets here. We'd love to fly you up here and have you stay with us for a couple of weeks. But I don't know if you can afford to miss that much work."

"Oh, don't worry about that. I'm sure I can work something out."

"You don't have vacation yet, and we don't want it to be a financial hardship."

Sally looked over at the empty table and pictured the bundles of money stacked on it. "It won't. I'm doing much better. In fact, I'm thinking of having the house fixed up. Maybe I'll turn your old bedroom into a nursery! Wouldn't that be fun?"

"Mom, I hear sunshine in your voice."

"It's about time, don't you think?"

Sally sat staring at the ten o'clock news, but mentally rehashing the big news of the day: Her baby was having a baby. It didn't seem possible. How fun it would be shopping for a grandchild! And now she could afford to buy designer children's clothing—the kind she used to drool over but could never afford. She felt that churning in her gut again. Her conscience was starting to be a real pain in the neck.

Kiwi jumped up on the couch and nestled in Sally's lap.

"You're spoiled rotten, you know that? You're going to be a real brat when the grandbaby comes."

Sally relaxed to the sound of Kiwi's purring, her own eyelids growing heavy. She got up from the couch and stumbled toward the bedroom. She put on her pj's, pushed the on button on the alarm clock, then turned off the lamp and nestled under the covers.

She lay quietly, giving herself completely to the mattress beneath her, aching for a good night's sleep. Her thoughts turned to nothingness as she felt herself drifting off to sleep...

What was that sound? The darkness was *breathing*, just inches from her face. Sally didn't dare move. Couldn't move. Heaviness, black and menacing, seemed to press down on her with paralyzing weight. She held her eyes shut, her fingers clawing at the comforter, her flesh covered in goose bumps. She tried to scream, but nothing came out.

Kiwi hissed and let out an eerie growl, then jumped off the bed and shot out the door.

Sally struggled to find her voice, then realized she was talking. "What are you? Go away! Leave me alone!"

It seemed as though the presence was laughing at her, amused by her feeble attempt to take charge.

Sally opened her eyes and saw only blackness. Thick blackness. That breathed. And laughed. And toyed.

She grabbed her pillow and hugged it, sensing that whatever was in the room was evil—and dangerous. *Lord, help me! Protect me!* She breathed in and held it, and then exhaled in short, rhythmic whispers the Name above all names. "Jesus...Jesus...Jesus..."

Sally lay still, soaked in perspiration, her heart racing. She opened her eyes, surprised to see Kiwi curled up next to her.

She reached over and turned on the lamp, then sat on the side of the bed, hugging herself and shivering from more than just the cold.

24

Sally Cox put her hand to her mouth and caught a yawn, then turned into the parking lot of Walnut Hills Nursing Center at 6:50 AM and pulled into the space next to Karen Morgan's Sportage.

Karen was just getting out of the car. "Hey, girlfriend. How are you feeling today—sleep any better?"

Sally sighed. "Not really. I'm having the most horrendous nightmares."

"I'm sorry. Hey, I picked out the Forester I want—silver with black leather seats. Really sharp. Once I figure out how to get enough money converted into a cashier's check, I'll be ready to roll. I'm so excited."

"I wish I were as comfortable with the money as you are."

"You're going to buy that Camry, aren't you?"

"I don't know. It's a lot of money."

"Of course it is, silly. That's why you need help paying for it. That's what the gift is for. You've got to stop second-guessing yourself. Why don't you come over tonight, and we can figure out some of the logistics, like how to make deposits without creating suspicion. Hey, better yet, why don't we go out to eat first—steaks at Plaza III?" Karen smiled. "I'll even treat."

"Oh, that sounds so good. By the way, before I forget to tell you, Leslie's pregnant."

"That's great!" Karen threw her arms around Sally. "All the more reason to dine out and celebrate, *Grandma.*"

Sally chuckled. "That sounds so funny. But I'm thrilled about it."

"Just think of all the baby gifts you can buy with your own little bundle." Karen laughed. "Sometimes I just take the money out and stack it. Stare at it. Dream about what I want to do with it."

"Have you decided whether or not you're going to give any of it away?"

"I think Elsie would be happier knowing we got the money than perfect strangers. Please don't tell me you're going to give yours away?"

"Are you kidding? I can't bring myself to cash even a hundred-dollar bill, much less divide it up for charity. It's all still in the bag."

"Why is this so hard for you, Sal? If we hadn't dug up the money, it would've just rotted and helped no one."

"I know. I'm working on it. My conscience won't give me a break, though."

"That's because you're one of those born-again Christians."

Sally felt the heat color her cheeks. *Some Christian.*

"Listen," Karen said, "you can guilt yourself to death and ruin the best thing that's ever happened to you. It's your choice. I, for one, am going to enjoy every last cent—and never look back."

Harry Rigsby sat at the kitchen table, scraping dried mustard off the vinyl tablecloth with his thumbnail.

If Jon were alive, the two of them could spend time watching the sports channel or renting movies—maybe some good "shoot 'em ups." And after the weather warmed up, they could go fishing. Or grill some hot dogs and watch baseball.

Who was he kidding? He'd never spent time with Jon in his life. But all of a sudden, he wished he had.

How much had he missed by being self-indulgent? His entire life he had focused on himself. And now that's all he had—but without the money to feed his old habits. No poker. No boozing. No bowling. No billiards. No "going to the boats." All of which equated to no *friends.* At least he could still afford to buy a few lottery tickets.

The phone rang. Harry hoped it wasn't Sheriff Baughman.

"Hello."

"Harry? It's Layton. I hope this isn't an inconvenient time."

Harry stretched the cord into the living room and sat on the couch. "No, not at all. How are you?"

"I'm fine. I feel so bad about your mother dying, especially right after Jon. I just wondered how you're doing."

"Oh, you know, it's tough," Harry said, swinging the phone cord like a jump rope. "I get lonesome. But I'm gettin' by. You do what you gotta do."

"Yeah, I'm really sorry. Listen, I had the day off, so Sylvia and I took some flowers out to the cemetery to pay our respects to Elsie. We noticed a fresh grave on the other side of Sophie's headstone. Who passed away?"

"Nobody that I know of."

"Hmm…there hasn't been anything in the obits about a burial at the McClendon Cemetery, except your mom's."

"I don't know what to tell you, Layton. I haven't heard anything. You sure it's not just bare ground that needs grass seed?"

"No, this is reddish dirt. Freshly packed. Doesn't even look like it's been wet yet."

Harry got up and walked back to the kitchen. "I dunno. It's news to me."

"Okay. I was just curious. By the way, Todd—I mean, Sheriff Baughman came by the house Monday night with some doodling that Jon did: some flowers and dollar signs drawn around my address. The sheriff wanted to know if I had any idea what it meant."

"Do you?"

"No. But if Jon was digging for money, he picked the wrong flower garden. There's nothing out there."

The wrong flower garden! Harry switched the phone to his other ear, his heart beating like a punching bag. He remembered his mother planting a neat little hedge around Sophie's grave and adding flowers all along the inside border. She kept it manicured for years. It was a real showplace till she got too old to tend it, and everything died off and got thrown away.

"Did I say something to upset you?" Layton asked.

Harry took a slow, deep breath. *Stay cool.* "Nah. It's just hard realizin' we're never gonna know the answers to this stuff."

"Probably not. I'm really sorry."

"Yeah, no one's blamin' you, Layton. Listen, thanks for the call."

Harry hung up the phone and paced like a caged lion. He remembered his mother's reply one time when he had asked about the money. She said it was a *dead* issue, then smiled wryly and walked away. It was all starting to make sense.

Harry raked his hands through his hair. Who could've known to go digging behind Sophie's grave? Was it possible that Gracie and Bill knew where Elsie buried the money and accused Harry of knowing something to cover up their own scheme? He didn't see how they could know anything when Jon didn't. Besides, Gracie didn't need it.

Harry wondered if he should drive over to the cemetery and take a look. At *what*, a pile of dirt? He hit his forehead with the palm of his hand. The whole thing was making him crazy.

Only one thing mattered now: finding out who'd been digging and what he'd found.

Sally savored the last bite of the best filet mignon she had ever eaten, then laid her fork on the plate. "Unbelievable."

"Get used to it," Karen said. "You can buy all the steak dinners your heart desires. This one's on me."

The waiter cleared the dishes and ever so neatly removed the bread crumbs from the tablecloth. "Would you ladies care for dessert?"

Sally smiled. "You mean that wasn't it?"

"I'll have strawberry cheesecake," Karen said. "My friend would like chocolate mousse."

Sally lifted an eyebrow. "How'd you know?"

"You mentioned it to me somewhere along the line. How you and Sam always ordered it when you ate here."

Sally winked at the waiter. "Looks like I'm having chocolate mousse."

"Coffee?"

Karen nodded. "With cream."

"The same for me, thank you." Sally looked over at Karen. "Actually, Sam and I ate here only once—on our twenty-fifth anniversary."

"You had thirty, as I recall."

"Hard to believe, eh?"

"Ever miss him?"

"Not if I can help it."

"Was he just a real creep?"

Sally took a sip of water. "Not usually."

"Was he a lousy husband?"

"Not at all. Till he got involved with Allison."

"Ms. Botox?"

Sally smiled. "Yeah. The thing is, I don't really think he cared that much about *her*. It had more to do with him panicking at turning fifty-five."

"Guess he decided to exceed the speed limit, eh?"

Sally's eyebrows scrunched together. "That's one way of putting it. He did cheat one other time, though, when Leslie was little. He had just turned thirty that time. Thought life was passing him by. So he made a pass—at a gal named Lotus."

Karen chuckled. "*Lotus*? For real?"

Sally nodded. "So help me. It lasted a month or so. I didn't find out till after the fact. I was pretty shook. Locked him out of the bedroom for a long time."

"How'd he get back in your good graces?"

Sally rolled her eyes. "Sam doesn't just 'get back in my good graces,' he charms his way in. I don't remember exactly what changed my mind. But I honestly don't think he cheated after that. Until Allison came along."

"Well, *Allison* is certainly a more palatable name than *Lotus*." Karen smirked. "But *Ms. Botox*? Now, that's priceless."

"Have you ever been married?" Sally asked.

Karen rolled her eyes. "Unfortunately. Right out of high school. Talk about a fiasco. Never again."

"Is that why you broke up with that guy you lived with?"

"Look, even if I were dumb enough to get married again—which I'm not—I'd never pick Danny. He's too weak. Plus, he's a real cheapskate. He'd never take me to a place like this."

"So what was the attraction in the first place?"

"We were smashed. We met at a party and seemed to hit it off—and ended up spending the weekend together. Right after that, he moved in. Things were great till he got laid off and started drinking all day, and stuck me with all the bills. I finally got fed up and told him to leave. That was months ago. Last week, he started calling again, begging me to take him back. Said he's got a great computer job at that big Sprint office in Overland Park. I haven't returned his messages. I keep hoping he'll give up and stay out of my life."

"You really mean that?"

Karen wiped the lipstick off the rim of her water glass. "Danny's a leech. I don't want him around, especially not now that I've actually got money."

The waiter appeared with the desserts and placed them on the table, then poured the coffee and stepped back. "You ladies enjoy."

Sally took a bite of chocolate mousse and let it melt in her mouth. "Mmm…is this ever delicious!"

"Okay," Karen said, "let's change the subject for a few minutes."
She lowered her voice. "You asked me how to get enough money in the
bank so you can pay your bills. Did you understand what I said about
making multiple deposits under ten thousand dollars?"

"Sure, but with my luck, someone would question it."

Karen patted her hand. "Just stay confident and friendly. If it
makes you feel better, tell them you're selling off your grandmother's
antiques. I already opened accounts in four banks, and as soon as I start
making deposits, it won't take long to get the money in there."

"When did you have time to open four accounts?"

Karen blushed. "Uh, I thought ahead. I figured if we found the
money, I'd be ready."

"Aren't you afraid someone will notice the deposits and throw up
a red flag?"

"No. Why would anybody at the bank go sticking their nose in
my business when they *want* the money in there?"

"I don't know. I'm such a chicken. I guess I feel so guilty that I'm
afraid it will show."

Karen shook her head. "What am I going to do with you? I really
wanted you to get out of debt. That was the whole point."

Sally wasn't buying that for a moment. "I'm sure I'll calm down
soon. Right now, I'm more comfortable taking it slow."

"Well, I'm going to be driving a Forester by this time next week,
mark my word. Life is just going to keep getting better and better. You
can get on board or hoard. It's up to you."

The waiter came back to the table. "So, how was everything?"

"Amazing," Sally said. "I'm not sure which I enjoyed more: the
steak soup, the steak, or the dessert."

Karen nodded. "Everything was great."

"Will there be anything else?"

"No, we're ready for the check," Karen said. "You can give it to
me." She glanced over at Sally, a smile on her face, then laid a crisp
hundred-dollar bill on top of the bill and handed it back to the waiter.
"See how easy that was?"

Sally pushed the front door with her shoulder and winced, then turned
around and pushed again with her behind, nearly losing her balance
when it opened and she stumbled backwards into the living room.

"I hate this stupid door! That's the first thing I'm going to spend money on!" She closed the door, aware of Kiwi's indignant meowing.

"Did you miss Mama? I brought you a can of Fancy Feast. I know it's a guilt offering, but you're going to love it."

Sally went out to the kitchen and opened the can, then spooned half the contents into Kiwi's bowl. "All right, here you go. If it's half as good as my dinner was, you'll be hooked for life."

Sally put the bowl on the floor, then hit the Play button on the answering machine.

"*Ms. Cox, this is Tri-State Gas Company*—" Delete.

"*Ms. Cox, this is Regis-Barrett Financial calling on behalf of Dr. Brennan's*—" Delete.

"*Sal, it's me. Can you believe we're going to be grandparents? I know you won't call me back. I just wanted to say 'Congratulations, Grandma.'*" Delete.

"*Ms. Cox, we really need you to call us about your overdue*—" Delete.

"*Uh, Sally. This is Harry Rigsby. It looks like some kids've been vandalizing the cemetery. When you were out there lookin' around, did you happen to notice whether or not there was fresh dirt behind my sister Sophie's headstone? Please give me a call at*—" Off.

Sally replayed the message and jotted down the phone number. She picked up the phone and dialed Karen's number.

"Hello."

"Karen, it's Sally, I just got home and—"

"You got one, too? A message from scary Harry?" She laughed.

"It's not funny. Who would've ever thought he'd go back out there?"

"Doesn't matter. We just play dumb. Yes, we noticed the dirt, but didn't think a thing about it."

"You want us to tell him we saw it?"

"Sure. We thought it was a fresh grave. How incriminating can that be? Plus, if we say we saw it the day of Elsie's funeral, that'll get us off the hook for Tuesday night. Not that anyone even knew we were together, right?"

Sally felt that churning in her stomach. "You think we should call him back tonight?"

"You can if you want. I'll catch him sometime tomorrow. I don't think we should seem too eager. Just make sure we tell him the same thing."

Sally sighed. "That we saw the dirt and thought it was a fresh grave?"

"That's it. Be sure to keep your voice relaxed. And ask how he's doing these days. There's no way he suspects *us* of anything."

"Okay."

"Hey, someone's got their finger stuck in my doorbell. I've gotta go. There's nothing to worry about. We covered ourselves coming and going. Call me back after you talk to Harry."

Sally disconnected, then dialed the number Harry had given her. "Hello."

Sally recoiled at the sound of Harry's voice. "It's Sally Cox, returning your call."

"Yeah, thanks. Sorry to bother you with this. I'm just tryin' to pinpoint when the vandals started dumpin' dirt out at the cemetery. Did you see anything after Ma's burial when you were lookin' around?"

"Actually, I do remember seeing dirt behind Sophie's headstone. I assumed it was a fresh grave. In fact, Karen and I commented on it at the time. We wondered who else had died."

"Nobody. Vandals probably dumped the dirt there. Little troublemakers. I'd like to catch 'em in the act. You're absolutely sure you saw the dirt there on Friday?"

"Yes," Sally said. "Positive."

"Yeah, okay. Thanks. That's all I was wantin' to know. I'll tell the sheriff."

"I hope you're doing okay since your mother died. I know it's been difficult."

"Yeah, it has. Hard without Jon, too."

"I can only imagine. I've thought of you a number of times." Sally could hardly say the words and wondered if lying would ever get easier. "Well, I hope I've been of some help."

"Oh, yeah. More than you know. Thanks for callin'."

Sally disconnected and called Karen back. The phone rang and rang. "Come on, pick up."

"This is Karen. I'm probably out gallivanting somewhere. Don't hang up without leaving a message." Beep.

"Karen, it's Sally. I talked to Harry and told him we saw the dirt and thought it was a fresh grave. I don't think he suspects we took the money, or even has a clue that's what the digging was about." Sally stopped to catch her breath. "I don't know how you can be so nonchalant about this. I'm a nervous wreck keeping a hundred and twenty-five thousand dollars in my closet! Call me back." *Click.*

Sally took the phone with her to the bathroom. She turned on the water, hoping that soaking in a hot bath would help her sore muscles relax so she could sleep.

Why couldn't she just enjoy the money the way Karen did instead of always worrying that she was going to get caught? They *had* covered their tracks. No one else knew. Sally sighed. Except her stupid conscience!

She turned off the water and eased into the tub, letting her entire being sink into the warmth.

Kiwi put her front paws up on the side of the tub, her tiny nose twitching as she sniffed the steamy air.

"You big chicken. Why don't you come closer?"

Sally chuckled, then closed her eyes and laid her head against the porcelain. What a nice evening she'd had with Karen. Guilt or no guilt, it had been fun dining at the Plaza III. And it wouldn't take much coaxing for Sally to do it again.

Maybe by the weekend she'd be comfortable enough with the money to take a couple hundred dollars and buy baby clothes to send to Leslie. She imagined holding her grandchild in her arms and felt tingly all over.

The bathroom light flickered and then went off. Her eyes flew open, her heart racing. She saw light under the door and exhaled a sigh of relief. Just a burned-out bulb.

She got out of the tub and fumbled in the dark for her towel, cringing at the thought of having another of those awful nightmares. Maybe she would take a Tylenol PM and knock herself out.

25

On Friday morning, Sally Cox arrived at work twenty minutes early and pulled her old Subaru into her usual spot. Karen Morgan wasn't there yet. Sally finished listening to a song on the radio, then got out and walked toward the employees' entrance.

She opened her eyes wide and blinked a couple of times, resisting the urge to yawn for the umpteenth time. She opened the door and spotted Wanda at the coffeepot.

"Good morning, Sally," Wanda said. "Aren't you feeling well?"

"I took a Tylenol PM last night, and I'm still a little sluggish. Plus, I forgot to put on makeup. I'll go do that now, before my shift begins. I think I'll have a cup of that coffee, too."

"Fay Emerson is starting to warm up to you."

Sally put her lunch in the refrigerator. "You're kidding? How can you tell?"

"She told Jeffrey Horton he should be kinder. That he could take a lesson from that bottle brunette on the day shift." Wanda's mouth curled up at each corner. "I think you've made a breakthrough."

Sally laughed. "Whodathunk?"

"I heard Karen Morgan gave notice."

"Yeah, she did."

"I hate to see her go. She was good."

"Yeah, she was." Sally poured herself a cup of coffee.

"I expected you to have more passion about her leaving," Wanda said. "You two are good friends, aren't you?"

"Oh, kind of. I don't see her outside of work, but I'll miss her being here. I'd better go put on my makeup before I clock in."

Sally went into the ladies' room and quickly applied foundation to her face, adding a dab of concealer under her eyes and then blush to her cheeks. She couldn't believe how haggard she looked. She put on lipstick and pressed her lips together. If only she had something to cover up her guilt. She glanced at her watch, wishing she'd had a chance to talk to Karen about last night's call to Harry.

Sally came out of the ladies' room and put her purse in her locker, then clocked in and walked to the east wing. She went into room 201. Rufus Tatum was already dressed and in his wheelchair, his feet bare, his slippers on the floor. He looked at Sally and wiggled his toes.

"Okay, Rufus, here you go." She held out six jelly beans so he could see, then put them in his sweater pocket. "Don't spoil your breakfast."

She put on his slippers, then wheeled him down to the patient's lounge and parked him in front of the TV.

She went back to get Charles ready for the day, and then moved on to the next room. And the next. She was coming out of room 210 when she bumped into Wanda.

"Oh, I'm sorry," Sally said, noticing Wanda's somber expression.

Wanda took Sally by the arm and led her down the hall and into her office. "We need to sit down. I've got something very disturbing to talk to you about."

Sally sat with her hands gripping the sides of a vinyl chair, knowing she was about to be forced into a humiliating confession. Maybe it was better this way.

Wanda pulled up a chair and sat facing Sally. "There's no easy way to say this: Karen Morgan was found murdered."

Sally sucked in a breath and couldn't let it out. *Murdered?*

"She was found strangled in her apartment. A neighbor heard Karen's alarm clock ringing for twenty minutes and became concerned. He knocked on Karen's door, and when he didn't get an answer, tried to open the door and found it unlocked. He discovered Karen's body on the kitchen floor and dialed 911."

Sally stared at nothing, her mind racing with questions. Did someone murder Karen for the money? Who could've known she had it? Had Harry gone over there? Did whoever killed Karen know that Sally had the other half of the money?

"Sally, are you all right, dear?"

"No, I don't think I am. I can't believe this. Why would anyone want to kill Karen?"

"The police don't have any suspects yet."

"Was it a burglary? Was her apartment ransacked?"

"I don't know. The police haven't established a motive for her killing. They don't think she was sexually assaulted."

Sally wrung her hands, and then buried her face in them and shook her head from side to side. "This is horrible. Just horrible."

"The police are here and will no doubt want to question you," Wanda said.

Sally looked up. "Me? Why?"

"Actually, all of us. They'll get set up in the staff meeting room, and then interview us one by one." Wanda took hold of Sally's arm. "Are you going to be all right? I could call in someone to take your shift."

"No, don't do that! I need to stay busy."

"This is a lot for you to handle. First Jonathan, then Elsie. Now Karen. Maybe you should take some time off."

"No, I'll go crazy at home. I need to keep working."

"How can you meet your patients' needs if your mind and emotions are elsewhere?"

Sally looked at Wanda, her eyes pleading. "I can do it. Please. I need to stay busy. Plus, I can't afford not to work." *And I'm terrified to go home!*

Sally kept looking at her watch as if that would slow down the time. What was she going to do when it was time to go home? Who could she turn to? *Lord, I'm so sorry I let Karen talk me into this. I don't know what to do.*

Sally felt a tap on her shoulder. "The police are ready for you now," Wanda said.

"Have you already talked to them?"

Wanda nodded. "Go on. I'll keep an eye on things."

Sally walked down to the staff meeting room and knocked lightly on the open door.

"Come in."

Sally went inside and saw the same two police officers that had questioned her about Jonathan Rigsby.

The men stood. "Ms. Cox, you may remember me from last time. I'm Officer Dan Shaw." The older of the two held out his hand and shook hers.

The younger officer did the same. "Officer Mark Albright. Sorry we have to keep meeting under these circumstances."

"Please, sit down and relax," Officer Shaw said. "I know this has been a big shock."

Sally sat, feeling numb enough that she wasn't panicked about talking to them. *Easy does it, Sally. Keep your voice controlled. Don't talk too fast.*

"What was your relationship to Karen Morgan?"

"We were business associates—both certified nursing assistants—CNAs."

"How long had you known Karen?"

"Since I started working here. About three months."

"Did you hang out together outside of work?"

"No. Well, we had dinner out once."

"And when was that?"

Sally's heart hammered. "Last night."

Office Shaw lifted his eyebrows. "What time did you have dinner?"

"I left the house around six o'clock. And got home at nine fifteen."

"Where did you eat?"

"The Plaza III."

"Just the two of you?"

"Yes."

"Do you have a receipt of some kind to verify that?"

Sally shook her head. "No, sir. Karen paid for it."

He looked down at his hands. "I see. By any chance, were you two romantically involved?"

Sally shot him an indignant look. "No, of course not."

"The Plaza III is a classy place. Pricey. Was there a reason Karen paid for the dinner?"

"Look, we worked together. Karen knew I was having trouble making ends meet. She wanted to do something nice for me. That's *all.*"

Office Shaw nodded. "Okay. Please don't take offense at any of these questions, Ms. Cox. We have to explore every angle. Since you might have been the last person to see her alive, we need to know everything you know. If you've got nothing to hide, you have absolutely nothing to fear. This is routine."

"Have you ever been to Karen's apartment?" Officer Albright asked.

"No, I haven't. I'm not even sure where it is."

Sally suddenly remembered the message she had left on Karen's recorder. Had Karen erased it? Her heart beat so fast her name tag was moving. She realized she was wringing her hands and stopped.

"Where were you last night between nine thirty and eleven thirty?"

"Home."

"Can anyone verify that?"

Sally tried to smile. "My cat? I live alone."

"Do you know if Karen was seeing anyone?"

Sally's eyebrows gathered. "She lived with a guy for a while—a Danny something. But she broke up with him before I started working here. I don't know of any others."

"Was it a volatile relationship?"

"I don't know. Karen just said he was a skinflint and wouldn't take her to nice places."

"Any idea where this guy lives?"

"No," Sally said. "But I think he works at the Sprint office in Overland Park. Does something with computers."

"Do you know if Karen had ever been married?"

Sally nodded. "She told me she married right out of high school. It didn't last long. But she never discussed the details with me."

"Did she ever mention a neighbor—Michael Rich?"

"No."

Officer Albright wrote on his report. "Okay, thanks."

"Can you think of any reason why someone would want to hurt Karen?" Officer Shaw asked.

Yes, a hundred and twenty-five thousand reasons! "No, everyone liked Karen."

"What about Jeffrey Horton?"

Sally couldn't believe the implication. "I don't know. He and Karen grated on each other. But he wouldn't kill her!"

"Again, Ms. Cox, don't be offended. We have to ask these questions."

Sally sat in the employees' lounge, her uneaten sandwich in front of her, feeling as though it would take too much energy to chew. The grilling she had gotten from Officers Shaw and Albright had lasted for over an hour. Neither had given any indication that they suspected a burglary. But they hadn't mentioned finding a big stash of money either.

Sally replayed in her mind what she remembered leaving on the answering machine. She had been so anxious she couldn't remember for sure, but knew she had given away more than she should have, including the amount of money she had hidden away.

She had been afraid to tell the police about Karen's doorbell ringing or about the first phone call, for fear it would draw attention to the message left on the machine.

She knew Karen had caller ID. If the police had found it, surely they would have questioned Sally about the money. Her heart was filled with dread. What if the killer had been with Karen when Sally called back? He would've heard everything Sally said—and seen her phone number! If the police didn't find the money, the killer must have taken it. Why would he have deleted the message unless he didn't want anyone to know what he was up to?

Sally cringed, wondering if Karen, desperate for her life, had heard Sally's voice on the machine but was helpless to tell her what was happening.

How she wished she could just hit the delete button and erase this ugly chapter from her life. *It's never too late to do what's right.* Sally's eyes burned with tears. If only that were true!

What kind of grandmother could she be behind bars? Leslie's heart would break when she found out. And the thought of facing Sam and Wanda with what she had done was overwhelming.

Sally wondered which she feared most: that someone was out to kill her? That she would finish out her life in jail? Or that she would lose the respect of everyone she cared about? How had she allowed herself to get caught in this trap? All she had wanted to do in the beginning was get Elsie's money and give it to the poor. She felt that churning in her gut. *All right*, she screamed at her conscience. *The money didn't rightfully belong to Elsie!*

She could almost feel Karen's hand on her shoulder and hear her contagious laughter. What a waste! Something deep inside Sally wanted to groan and wail and mourn that Karen had entered eternity an unbeliever, lost in darkness—forever!

Had Sally, even once, chosen to be a Christian example of faith or hope or love? Then again, how effective would it have been to sow a seed of faith in Karen's heart when her own was hardened by hurt and disappointment and bitterness? In her anger at God, Sally had abandoned her values and willfully accompanied Karen down a murky path of greed and deceit—and collaborated with the enemy. Sally shuddered. How dare she call herself a Christian?

The dark, breathing presence that had occupied her dreams now seemed to be an impenetrable black cloud separating her from everything good and decent. She felt as though she had sold her soul to the lowest bidder.

26

Sally Cox drove slowly around the block three times, her eyes peeled for any sign of an intruder—or anything that seemed out of place. Finally she pulled in the driveway and turned off the motor. She sat for a few minutes, wishing she were a kid again, swinging on the big rubber tire hanging from her grandfather's walnut tree.

Karen Morgan's murder was all over the news. It still didn't seem real. Sally felt sure that the phone would ring and it would be Karen's voice and it would all have been a horrible mistake.

Sally looked up at the winter sky and dreaded the darkness that would fall by dinnertime. She got out of the car, intensely tuned in to her surroundings, and walked to the front door, terrified of spending the weekend alone.

She took the letters out of the mailbox, then put the key in the lock and pushed the door with her hip several times until it gave way. She shut the door, turned the bolt lock, and pulled the drapes. She made sure the basement and back doors were locked and checked the locks on each of the windows, lamenting that she had talked Sam out of putting in an alarm system years ago.

If an intruder were to break in, what was she going to fight him off with, a broom handle? She was scared of guns and even more afraid of knives, fearing any attacker would turn the weapon on her. Sally pictured the killer's hands around Karen's neck, and then blinked away the image.

Sally was suddenly aware of Kiwi meowing her little heart out, and reached down and picked her up. "I didn't mean to ignore you, baby. It's been a horrible day. Be glad you're feline and don't have a clue what's going on. And that you have nine lives."

Sally went over and pushed the play button on the answering machine. All the messages were from bill collectors, and she quickly deleted them all.

She spooned the other half of the Fancy Feast into Kiwi's bowl and sat at the table, feeling like a stranger in her own skin. She reached over and turned on the radio, hoping to catch the news on the hour.

The phone rang and she sat frozen, waiting for the answering machine to pick it up.

This is Sally, leave a message and I'll call you back. Beep…

"*Sally, it's Jeffrey Horton, I just—*"

Sally grabbed the receiver. "Jeffrey, it's me. I'm here."

"Oh, good. I was hoping to catch you when you got home. Do you believe this?"

"No—" Sally choked back an unexpected wave of emotion. "It's horrible."

"The cops came out to the college and nabbed me when I came out of class. Questioned me pretty extensively. I suppose I'm a suspect since Karen wasn't my most favorite person and everybody at work knew it. But I sure didn't kill her!"

Sally took the phone to the table and sat. "Yeah, that's what I told them."

"Thanks. Unfortunately, I don't have a good alibi. I was at home with my laptop, working on a research paper until ten thirty when I left for work."

"Don't feel bad. The police wanted to know what I was doing between nine thirty and eleven thirty. I told them I was home. They wanted to know if anyone could confirm that, and I told them just my cat."

"You're a suspect?" Jeffrey said.

Sally drew imaginary circles on the table with her forefinger. "I might be the last one to have seen her alive. We went out for dinner last night. I got home at nine fifteen. I called her when I got home, and she had to get off the phone because the doorbell was ringing. I keep wondering if it could've been the murderer at the door. Gives me a sick feeling."

"Yeah, I'll bet. Hard to imagine what was going on over there. I saw on the schedule you have the weekend off. You just going to hibernate and try to deal with this?"

"No, I've got friends visiting from Topeka," Sally said, without really knowing why. "Think we'll go down to the Crown Center and out to Stephenson's for lunch. And maybe to the art gallery. And the Plaza. I'm glad because I don't want to be alone."

"You know, it was really weird, the cops wouldn't speculate about a motive. Did they with you?"

"No. But it seems as though we can rule out sexual assault or burglary."

There was a long pause. Sally wondered why.

Jeffrey sneezed. "Excuse me. I think I'm coming down with something. I'll tell you one thing—I would've loved to have been a fly on the wall when the cops questioned the neighbor who found her."

"Why?"

"*He's* the one who stands out to me. He could've rung the doorbell, had some kind of confrontation, strangled her, and walked right back to his apartment. And the next morning, played the hero."

"But why would he go over there just to kill her?"

"Maybe he didn't like her any more than I did."

Sally shuddered and let her silence register her disgust.

"Hey, sorry," Jeffrey said. "I really didn't mean that."

"I can't believe you'd even joke about it. I'm sure the police will ask him all the right questions."

"Yeah. But you do realize the cops don't release everything they know to the media? They always hold back something that will identify the real killer and weed out the attention seekers."

Sally got up and leaned against the countertop. Why was Jeffrey giving her the creeps? "I've never heard that."

"It's true. Don't you watch cop shows?"

"No."

"Well, take it from me—they're not going to reveal everything they know until this thing's over."

Sally sat on the couch, listening to Kiwi's purring, wishing she were as calm as her trusting pet.

Her conversation with Jeffrey wouldn't leave her alone. Jeffrey's access to Elsie had been equal to Sally's and Karen's. What if Elsie had told him about the money, and he'd gone digging behind Sophie's headstone and found the coffin empty? The first person he would've suspected of taking it was Karen Morgan, especially since it was obvious the digging had been recent.

Jeffrey didn't seem like a murderer—not that Sally knew what a murderer was supposed to look and sound like.

She ran her hand over Kiwi's fur. One thing she felt sure of: If the money was still in Karen's apartment when the police arrived, then the killer knew nothing about it—which meant Sally's message was probably left on Karen's answering machine. And that seemed unlikely, since the police would have confronted Sally with it by now.

She couldn't rule out Jeffrey.

And who was this Michael Rich who had discovered Karen's body? Was it possible he could've seen into Karen's apartment when she brought home the money? Sally sighed. She couldn't even alert the police to that possibility without incriminating herself. Besides, if Michael could see in, probably anyone could have. Sally couldn't imagine Karen being careless enough to leave the drapes open if the money was out of the bag.

And what was her ex-boyfriend like? Sally didn't even know Danny's last name—just that he was a skinflint and Karen had broken off her relationship with him. Did he still have a key? Had he been nosing around the apartment when Karen was gone? Then again, if he had been, why wouldn't he just take the money and run off with it? It's not as though Karen could report the theft to the police.

Sally's head was spinning with "what ifs." She wanted to go outside and run off some of the tension, but leaving the house was too risky.

The phone rang. Sally jumped, her hand over her heart. She put Kiwi on the floor, then went out to the kitchen and waited for the machine to answer it.

This is Sally. Leave a message, and I'll call you back. Beep...

"Sal, it's Sam. I just wondered if you knew the lady who got murdered—the one who worked at Walnut Hills—"

Sally picked up the receiver. "Yeah, Sam. I knew her."

"Oh, you are there," he said. "I thought maybe you were out running."

"I wish I were."

"I guess you had a tough day."

"That's putting it mildly. The police grilled everyone—me for over an hour. It's just a horrible—" Sally put her hand to her mouth. *Not now. Not with Sam.*

"Hey, you want some company? I was about to go running. I could do it just as easily in your neighborhood as mine."

Sally fought with herself, and then gave in quickly. "Sure. Come on over."

"I'll be right there."

Sally hung up. Was she desperate or what? She had enough trouble without opening *that* door.

Harry Rigsby drove past Karen Morgan's apartment building, not surprised to see curiosity seekers gathered outside, alongside a respectable media presence. That explained why Karen didn't call back.

But why had Sally lied about her and Karen seeing the dirt at the cemetery? He could think of one good explanation: The two women had pulled off the heist sometime since Friday. And Sally had just eliminated the only other person who knew.

Sally and Karen, more than anyone else, had time and opportunity to coax his mother into telling where she had hidden the money. He could just hear them sweet-talking her, buttering her up till she spilled it all. And then acting so caring at the cemetery. Man, what a couple of con artists. It was hard for him to believe these two broads actually pulled it off.

He smirked. Too bad Sally's cold little scheme would be short-lived. He would confront her and force her to split the money with him. It's not as though she could tell the police anything with him holding Karen's murder over her head.

Sally ran until her legs felt as though they would go out from under her. She stopped and bent over, her hands on her knees, and tried to catch her breath.

"Hey, weekend warrior, slow down," Sam said. "You're going to stroke out if you don't take it slower."

Sally nodded, still panting. "Yeah…I know."

Sam came and stood next to her, puffing as hard as she was. "We're too…old to…keep up this pace."

Sally turned and smiled at him. "Speak for yourself."

"Listen, I'm spent. You want to get coffee or something?"

A car drove slowly past them, the male driver seeming to be looking for a street number. Sally stood up straight, her eyes following the car until it disappeared.

"Why are you so nervous?" Sam said. "You've been jumpy since we left."

"I don't know. I guess I'm rattled about Karen's murder."

"Sure you are. But it has nothing to do with you."

Sally started running again. She crossed the street and headed down the block toward the house, Sam laughing and trying to keep up. She kept pushing until she reached the house, then bounded up the steps and leaned against the front door, completely winded.

Sam sat on the steps. "Good grief, woman. You're trying to kill me, aren't you?"

Sally shook her head, but couldn't turn her panting into words.

A minute passed before either of them said anything.

"You want to go to Starbucks?" Sam finally said.

"No! I—well, I think I'd rather stay home. I'm kind of tired."

"Okay, I can take a hint. But I enjoyed running with you. Maybe we could do it again sometime."

Another car drove by slowly. Was that Jeffrey's VW? She was sure it was! Or was it?

"Sal, come down here a minute." Sam patted the step.

Sally sat next to him. "What?"

"You want to tell me what the heck's wrong with you?"

"Nothing. I'm just exhausted."

"Babe, we've been out here for almost an hour and you haven't even mentioned Leslie being pregnant. Don't tell me nothing's wrong." He took her chin and turned her face toward him. "After all these years, don't you think I know when you're not being honest with me?"

"I can't," she said, instantly wishing she hadn't.

"Why not?"

Sally got up and went to the front door. "I just can't, that's all."

Sam came up behind her, his palms against the door, his arms on either side of her. "I don't want to violate your space. But promise you'll call if you need to talk?"

She nodded.

Sam turned around and went down the steps.

Sally fumbled to get the key in the lock, her hands shaking, her heart doing flip-flops, and then spun around just as he was about to get in the car. "Sam, wait!"

He came back to the steps. "Yeah?"

"Why don't you come in," Sally heard herself say. "I'll make us some coffee."

"Really? That'd be great."

Harry drove slowly down Wells Street, squinting to read the house numbers, when he spotted Sally's blue Subaru parked in the driveway and a red Camaro parked out front. He was able to make out "416" painted on the curb.

The house was stone. Long front porch. Chipped paint on the eaves. Cracks in the front steps.

The drapes were pulled in the living room and the blinds pulled on the other windows. He wondered who the red Camaro belonged to. He knew Sally was divorced.

Harry turned off the motor and put his hands in the pockets of his hunting jacket. At least he knew where she lived now. Eventually, whoever was in there would have to leave.

27

Sally Cox opened the freezer compartment of the refrigerator and pulled out a package of French vanilla decaf coffee she had ground at the grocery store. "It's not Starbucks," she said to Sam, "but it's really pretty good."

"Sounds great to me," he said, stroking Kiwi's fur.

Sally opened the bag and spooned six tablespoons into the Mr. Coffee and turned it on.

She walked over and sat at the table across from Sam, feeling guilty for inviting him in just because she was afraid to be alone.

"Sal, what's bugging you? You look like you're ready to jump out of your skin. You having hot flashes again?"

She shook her head. "That's the least of my worries."

"So, talk to me. An ex-husband ought to be good for something besides target practice." There was that charming smile.

"It's been a difficult day. Karen's murder really shook me up."

"Did you know her well?"

"We took coffee breaks and lunches together at the nursing home. I really hadn't known her long."

"I heard on the radio she was forty-three. Was she single?"

"Divorced. She lived with a guy for a while, then broke up with him a few months ago. I suppose he's a suspect. But then, who isn't at this point?"

"What do you mean?"

Sally shrugged. "It's a long story."

"Don't tell me you're a suspect?"

Sally got up and took two mugs out of the cabinet. "I didn't say that." She poured coffee in each, then added a splash of nondairy creamer to hers.

"You didn't have to, babe. You're hands are shaking."

Sally set the mugs on the kitchen table, then grabbed some napkins and started wiping up what she'd spilt.

Sam put his hand on hers, and she didn't push him away.

"I can't force you to tell me what's wrong, but I promise I'll listen without comment. It might make you feel better to get it out."

Sally avoided his eyes. She glanced up at the clock. When the coffeepot was empty, Sam would get in his car and leave. And she'd be alone—and as vulnerable as Karen was.

Sam sipped his coffee, his penetrating eyes peering over the top of the mug.

Sally dabbed the moisture on her upper lip, then took her index finger and wiped the lipstick off her cup. For the first time in her life, she was too cowardly to level with Sam.

"I don't think you should be alone tonight," he said, leaning back in his chair, his arms crossed. "I'll sleep in the spare bedroom. You won't even know I'm here. I know what you're thinking, but—"

"All right."

Sam raised his eyebrows. "All right?"

Sally nodded. "But this is not an invitation for anything else," she quickly added. "My bedroom is off limits. Are we in agreement on that?"

"Yeah, sure. I'll just feel better if someone's with you. I don't remember ever seeing you this rattled."

"I'm scared, Sam. I don't know how to explain it to you."

He took a sip of coffee. "Okay. I'll sack out with Kiwi."

Sam Cox lay wide-awake in the spare bedroom, Kiwi curled up on his chest, his curiosity on tilt. In the thirty years he'd been married to Sally, she'd never acted so skittish. And why hadn't she at least *mentioned* Leslie's pregnancy? How weird was that?

He couldn't imagine that Karen Morgan's murder had frightened Sally enough to make her receptive to his staying overnight. There had to be more to it than that.

Sam nudged Kiwi till she moved off his chest, then turned on his side and pulled the covers up to his chin. Had Leslie's bed always been this uncomfortable? It's a wonder the kid grew up without back problems.

He tried to picture how his daughter would look with a round belly and that beautiful glow he'd seen in the faces of other expectant mothers. It seemed only yesterday that he was in the delivery room, and Leslie had made her debut…

"She's all red and wrinkled," Sam had said, just as the doctor cut the umbilical cord. "Her feet are purple. Is that normal?"

"Yes. She's beautiful," the nurse said. "Let's get her cleaned up, and you can hold her."

Leslie stopped crying when the nurse placed her in Sam's arms. He gazed into her eyes, which looked like two ripe olives set below the little pink cap on her head, and all the apprehension he'd had about being a dad seemed to melt into a pool of awe. This tiny creature seemed to know him, and it was hard to believe that just minutes before she'd been curled up in Sally's womb, oblivious to the world outside. He fell in love with Leslie at that moment and wondered if anyone or anything could stir him the way she had…

Sam rolled onto his back, his hands behind his head. If only he had remained as devoted to Sally. It had been foolish getting involved with that young gal at work…what was her name? He couldn't even remember. He had turned thirty and she was only twenty-two and a real flirt. He'd kicked himself a hundred times since for being so weak.

But Sam had remained faithful after that and concentrated on being a good father to Leslie, hoping that his unwavering devotion to his daughter would also get him back in Sally's good graces. It did eventually. And after Sally's bitterness finally wore off, things were good—until Sam turned fifty-five and woke up in a tempestuous midlife crisis.

He sighed. Talk about messed up! He remembered how flattering it had been having a younger woman go after him. His flailing ego had been easily seduced into thinking that a new beginning with Allison would somehow prolong his youth.

But the sex wasn't enough. And when he finally came to his senses, he realized he didn't even *like* Allison. He'd thrown away a good marriage for a cheap imitation that hadn't fully satisfied any of his desires.

Sam heard a scream coming from Sally's room!

He threw off the covers and raced down the hall. He flung open Sally's door and found her shivering on the side of the bed.

"What happened?" he said, putting her robe around her shoulders.

Sally buried her face in her hands. "I keep having the same horrible nightmare. It seems so real."

"What's it about?"

"The darkness seems to be alive and breathing and moving all around me. Then it hovers over me like it's coming to get me. Makes my skin crawl, just thinking about it."

Sam turned on the lamp. "See? No one here but me and Kiwi."

Sally nodded. "I know. So why does it feel like there is?"

"You say you've had this nightmare before?"

"Several times lately. I'm almost afraid to go to sleep."

"Would you like me to make you some hot tea?"

"No, thanks...but would you mind sitting in the chair for a while? I really don't want to be alone in here. I took something and will probably fall asleep again. I might have the same dream."

"Yeah, sure. I'll be right here."

Sally crawled under the covers, her eyelids heavy.

Sam turned off the lamp, then went over and sat in the rocker and put Kiwi in his lap.

Harry Rigsby saw a light go on in Sally's house. And then go off again. Whoever was in there wasn't coming out tonight. He might as well come back in the morning. What could Sally do with the money between now and then anyway?

Out of the corner of his eye, Harry thought he saw someone creeping in the dark along the side of the house. He could barely make out someone standing next to a tree. His heart raced, his eyes focused intently on the shadow. Someone tall. Dressed in dark clothing. What was going on? Did someone else know about the money?

Maybe he didn't have this whole thing figured out after all.

Sam sat in the quiet in Sally's bedroom and thought he saw a shadow move across the window. He got up and stood against the wall and peeked between the blinds.

Was someone standing under the maple tree? He wasn't sure. Of all times for his rifles to be locked up at his apartment.

"Sam, what are you doing?" Sally whispered.

"We may have a prowler."

Sally sat up in bed. "Where?"

"On the side of the house." Sam searched the darkness and didn't see anyone. "I could swear someone was out there. I'm going to take a look."

"No, don't!"

"Don't worry. I'll surprise the creep." Sam went out to the kitchen, took a flashlight and a hammer out of the utility drawer and set them on the counter, then grabbed an empty vinegar bottle out of the trash and broke the bottom end with the hammer. He went out the front door and stood on the porch, aware of the neighbor's dog barking.

He went down the steps and around the side of the house, the broken bottle in one hand and the flashlight in the other.

"I know you're out here. Why don't you stop sneaking around and come out here where I can see you?"

He shone the flashlight on the trunk of the maple tree and across the entire side yard and didn't see anyone. He peeked over the fence into the backyard. He walked around to the other side of the house and slowly moved the beam of light across the darkness, then went up the front steps and back into the house.

Sally met him in the living room. "Did you see who it was?"

"There's nobody out there. I think we're both a little edgy."

"Are you sure?"

"Yeah, false alarm. Sorry, babe."

Harry ducked behind the steering wheel, relieved when the guy went back inside. Then he saw the tall, shadowy figure move slowly through the yard next door and disappear.

Harry had a sinking feeling. He felt sure he could intimidate Sally into splitting the money, but once he did, who else might he have to contend with? He had never planned on things turning violent. Was it worth the risk? He thought about his mounting bills. And his cold house. And how sick and tired he was of eating ketchup sandwiches. He had to at least confront Sally and find out what she knew. But first, he'd sleep on it. Clear his head.

He started the car and pulled away from the curb and saw someone peeking through the curtains. He tightened his grip on the wheel. Rats! That's all he needed.

Sally stood at the bedroom window, her heart racing. Was that Harry Rigsby's white Ford Falcon? She watched the taillights disappear and tried to read the license plate but couldn't make out the numbers. If he'd been prowling around outside, then he must know about the money. He must have strangled Karen and was coming after her!

"Babe, are you all right?" Sam said. "You're shaking again."

"I just need to lie down. The thought of a prowler..."

"There's nobody out there."

"I know. Like you said, I'm a bit edgy. I'm going back to bed."

"Okay. I'll be in the other bedroom if you need me."

Sally waited until Sam left, then crawled under the covers and turned on her side, her mind racing faster than her pulse. There must be someplace she could go where Harry wouldn't find her. Someplace to think, to figure out what to do about the money.

The only right thing to do was turn it over to the police, but how could she face a jail sentence—and the devastation it would cause Leslie, especially now?

Sally felt the emotion tighten in her chest and then a deluge of tears spilling out. She buried her face in the pillow and muffled her sobs. How could she have allowed herself to be deceived into thinking the money was the answer to her problems? *Lord, what have I done?*

28

Sally Cox opened her eyes to daylight and the smell of coffee brewing. She forced herself to defy the gravity of depression and got out of bed. She slipped into her flannel robe and went to the kitchen.

"Ah, there you are," Sam said. "I was hoping the aroma would wake you up. I ran by my apartment and got some Starbucks Breakfast Blend."

Sally noticed the egg carton and various spice bottles on the counter. "What are you making?"

"A Spanish omelet. By the way, you're low on picante sauce, so I put it on your list."

Sally yawned and rubbed her eyes. "What time is it?"

"Ten. I was afraid you'd sleep right through this masterful showing of culinary talent." There was that charming smile. "But here you are, just in time." He pulled out a chair and held the back. "Sit down, madam, and I will gladly serve you."

Sally sat in the chair, and Sam pushed her up to the table. She watched as he whipped the eggs and added her last bell pepper and onion, already chopped into small pieces.

"Now, a tablespoon of picante sauce," Sam said. "A dash of salt. A few shakes of pepper. A little chili powder." He reached into her almost empty refrigerator and took out the green container of Parmesan cheese. "A couple of hearty shakes for that cheesy flavor, and we're in business." Sam whipped it all together and poured the mixture into an already-hot Teflon skillet, then pushed down the button on the toaster. "Four slices of wheat toast coming up. And," he said, filling a mug with coffee, "Breakfast Blend, with a big splash of nondairy creamer." He set the mug in front of her and went back to the stove.

"Thanks." Sally blew on the coffee, enjoying the aroma of breakfast cooking, but uncomfortable with Sam making himself at home. "I guess you'll be leaving after breakfast."

"I suppose so. Unless you'd like me to stay another day. I don't mind."

Sally took a sip of coffee. "I think I'll be okay now. I was just so exhausted last night I couldn't think straight." She could tell by his expression he didn't believe her.

Sam whistled while the omelet cooked. The toast popped up, and he buttered all four slices and cut each in half.

"You going to church tomorrow?" Sam said.

"I don't know. Are *you?*"

Sam nodded. "Yeah, I thought I'd start going again. They may stone me before I get in the door, but I've been a prodigal long enough. You want to go together?"

"I switched churches. I've been going to that Bible church down the street."

"New Hope? Really? You like it?"

Sally sighed. "Truthfully, Sam, I've had a difficult time concentrating on anything spiritual in the past eight months."

He looked at her sheepishly. "Yeah, I'm sure. I've probably been banished from Redeemer anyway. Maybe I should try New Hope."

Wouldn't hurt me to go either. Sally sighed. What was the point? Regret wasn't enough to right her relationship with God—or mend her relationship with Sam.

"Bad idea, eh?"

"Sam, don't get me wrong. I appreciate your staying here with me last night. But I'm not ready to go to church with you."

"Yeah, okay. I understand. But I think I'll go. I need to get my slate wiped clean. I can't believe I let myself get this messed up. What time is the service at New Hope?"

Sally had to think to even remember. "Uh, eleven, after Sunday school."

"Okay, two Spanish omelets coming up." Sam brought everything to the table, and then sat across from her. "You want to say grace?"

"I'm not awake yet," she said. "Why don't we just eat?"

Harry emptied a box of corn flakes into his bowl, then got up to get milk and remembered he didn't have any. He was sick and tired of running out of groceries before his Social Security check got deposited.

He had driven by Sally's around eight and found the red Camaro still parked out front. Who was this guy? Harry felt pushed to resolve the money issue with Sally as soon as possible—before the mystery person got to her. He wondered if he should be bold enough to ring her doorbell.

His mind was spinning with all sorts of questions. Had Sally murdered Karen? Or had someone else—perhaps whoever had been sneaking around in the dark? But who else could have known about the money, except someone else at the nursing home? Hard to say who those broads had gotten to help them.

This was so unfair! Why should he have to stoop to this to get what was rightfully his?

The doorbell rang. What now?

Harry walked to front door and looked through the peephole. What did *she* want? He opened the door and forced a smile.

"Hello, Gracie. Did you come to drop another bomb?"

"We need to talk."

Harry noticed Bill waiting in the car. "About what? Every time I talk to you, my day ends up ruined."

"We were shocked and horrified to hear Karen Morgan had been murdered. She was such a nice young woman."

"Yeah, she was. Hope they catch the scum who did it. You didn't come all the way over here to talk to me about that though."

Gracie fiddled with the button on her coat. "I called Layton last night, just to see how he and Sylvia were doing. He said they'd been out to the cemetery and put flowers on Elsie's grave."

"Yeah, that was real nice of 'em. What's your point?"

"Layton mentioned seeing fresh dirt on the other side of Sophie's headstone. Did someone else in Elsie's family die?"

"Not that I know of."

"And you don't find it odd that someone's been digging there?"

Harry shrugged. "I'm not gonna lose any sleep over it. Look, I've got stuff to do. Wanna tell me what you're driving at?"

"All right. Did you finish what Jon started? Did you dig up Elsie's money?"

"Huh?"

"Jon was close—just not close enough. Elsie didn't bury the money in Aunt Clara's flower garden. She buried it behind Sophie's grave, didn't she?"

Harry threw up his hands. "Here we go again. How many times

do I have to tell you Ma didn't have any money? End of story."

"No, it's not," Gracie said. "If you knew Jon went to Layton's to dig up the money, then you have some responsibility for what happened to him."

"*What?*"

"Don't raise your voice at me, Harry. Bill and I are onto you. And we won't let you benefit from Jon's death."

Harry shook his head. "You're a real piece of work, you know that, Gracie? Did you even talk to Sheriff Baughman? He was over here the other day. I told him everything I know—*again.*"

"Yes, as a matter of fact, I did."

"Then you know he hasn't charged me with anything."

Gracie shot him a look of indignation. "I'm not dropping this, Harry. You robbed Jon of a father's love all his life. And you let him die doing your dirty work, just so you could defraud Medicaid and live it up on Elsie's money."

Harry dropped his head to his chest and shook it from side to side. "This is grief talkin'. You're way off."

"Is that so? Well, let's just see how far the money goes with all of us breathing down your neck."

Sally stood at the front door and watched Sam get in his car and drive away, then set the bolt lock and hurried to the bedroom closet.

She reached behind her long bathrobe and pulled out the bag of money and set it in the bedroom chair. She dragged two suitcases out of the closet and opened them on the bed, then stacked the bundles of money in one of them.

She went to her dresser and grabbed slacks, sweaters, socks, and underwear, and put them in the other suitcase. She folded her pajamas and robe on top and threw in two pairs of shoes.

Where was her cosmetic bag? She got the step stool and pulled her cosmetic bag down off the closet shelf, then went into the bathroom and packed her toiletries.

Sally zipped the suitcases, then sat on the side of the bed and questioned the sanity of what she was about to do. What choice did she have? If she stayed here, she would likely end up dead like Karen Morgan.

She rolled the suitcases out to the car, loaded them in the truck, then went back for her cosmetic case and purse, realizing she'd forgotten about Kiwi.

Sally picked up an unopened bag of cat litter, the litter box, Kiwi's bowls, and a box of Friskies, and ran them out to the car.

She came back inside, took out a pad of paper, and scribbled a note.

> Sam,
>
>   I've gone to visit Nan Bingham in Jeff City. I need some time to clear my head. Don't say anything to Leslie. I'll talk to you when I get back.—Sally

She folded the note and put it in her coat pocket, then coaxed Kiwi into the cat carrier and hurried out the front door and down the steps to the car.

When she backed her Subaru out of the driveway, Sally wondered if she'd ever see the house again, or if she would be running the rest of her life.

Sam popped a couple of Tums into his mouth, lamenting that the picante sauce hadn't agreed with him.

It had been great being home with Sally—if he could call what happened really *being* with her. She seemed pleasant enough, but completely distracted. Maybe she'd eventually tell him what was bothering her. At least for now, she had reached out. And that was one step closer to rebuilding a friendship.

Sally looked good. For some reason, the creases across her forehead and laugh lines around her eyes didn't make him feel old anymore. So the packaging had changed a little. Her heart hadn't. Besides, all he had to do was look in the mirror to realize Sally wasn't the only one who had aged. Why had he ever thought a younger woman would make him happier? Sally had been his best friend, and they'd had a lot of good years together.

Sam was eager to get back in church. It was humbling having to admit how bad he'd messed up, but comforting to know it wasn't too late to turn his life around—though he'd probably blown any chance that Sally would take him back.

He looked at his watch. Maybe he'd run the Camaro over to the car wash and take a drive around Lake Jacomo. This day was dragging by, and there was a lot of weekend still left to kill.

Sally saw the I-70 exit sign up ahead and tried to decide which way to go. East? West? It really didn't matter, as long as nobody knew where she was. The note she'd left on Sam's windshield should hold him for a couple of days. And when he finally called to check on her, he wouldn't find her at Nan Bingham's.

29

Sally Cox woke up to the sound of Kiwi's meowing. The room was dark, except for daylight seeping in through a crack in the drapes. For a moment she forgot where she was.

She reached over and flipped on the light and glanced at the clock. Ten-thirty? The pill had more than done its job.

"Hey, you. Quiet down. You're not even supposed to be in here."

Sally went over to the carrier and opened it, then took Kiwi into the bathroom and let her use the litter box.

"I'm sorry, baby, but if I get caught with you, I'm going to get fined big-time. You have to go back in the carrier."

Sally reached down, picked up Kiwi, and put her on her shoulder. "Okay, if you promise to stay put, I'll let you out. But no meowing."

Sally turned on the coffeepot, the growling in her stomach letting her know that she should've thought ahead and had something handy for breakfast. She remembered seeing a McDonald's down the street, and her mouth watered for an Egg McMuffin and a big glass of orange juice. But it was too late to get breakfast there.

She sat on the side of the bed and picked up the Kansas map she had gotten when she stopped to fill the car. She'd driven halfway across the state. Did she really want to go much further?

All she needed was a nice, cozy place to hang out, where she could feel safe until she decided what to do. She had broken her first hundred-dollar bill for the motel room, and lightning hadn't struck. But she didn't want to get too used to it. When she was able, she'd put the hundred back. She couldn't handle any more guilt.

She heard church bells ringing and felt an unexpected longing—almost a groaning within. How many others had committed unspeakable acts and were afraid to go back to church? She wondered if Sam was really going to try New Hope or if he had been trying to impress her. Sally sighed. She certainly had no room to throw stones at Sam.

Kiwi's tail snaked across Sally's face and broke her concentration.

"Okay, here's the plan. We get on this highway here and drive until we find a place we like. How's that sound?"

The church bells were still ringing. For a moment, Sally was standing with Sam in front of St. Mark's, her wedding veil fluttering in the June breeze, her heart overflowing with happiness. She had been so sure it would always be that way.

She got up and put Kiwi back in the carrier. She slipped out of her pj's and into her clothes, then packed the suitcase and headed for the car. She waited until she was sure no one was watching, then slipped the carrier out of the room and put it on the passenger seat and fastened the seat belt.

It was almost laughable. She had stolen a quarter of a million dollars, and she was worried about getting in trouble for sneaking in a cat in a carrier?

Harry drove by Sally's house for the third time today and didn't see her Subaru parked in the driveway. It hadn't been there yesterday afternoon or last night either. What was the deal? Had she gone to stay at the guy's house?

He drove to the stop sign at Wells, and then turned right and pulled into the Kroger parking lot, enough money in his pocket to buy a half gallon of milk. He started to get out when he saw a red Camaro pulling in one row over. He read the license plate. It was the same car! The guy got out and walked inside. Sally wasn't with him.

Harry decided to wait until he came back and then follow him.

Sally slowed the car to thirty miles per hour and entered the city limits of Pheasant River, population 3,200. Main Street was lined with bare trees, and their branches met in the middle and formed a canopy. The quaint old buildings reminded her of Eureka Springs, where she and Sam had honeymooned.

"Kiwi, wake up. I think we've found it."

Sally wondered if there was any place to stay in a community this size. She envisioned some depressing motel with orange shag carpet and lumpy mattresses. At least they might not object to her having a cat.

Sally spotted a white church with a steeple up ahead, and a city park across the street. She came to the church and turned right down Bateman Street, quickly becoming enthralled with the neighborhood.

She came to the end of the block and saw a "Furnished Apartment for Rent" sign in the front window of a white two-story with green shutters. The place was charming.

"Wanna bet they don't allow cats?"

Sally drove around the block, talking herself out of even inquiring, and then changed her mind. She parked out front, went up on the porch, and rang the bell.

A man with unruly gray hair and thick glasses answered the door.

"My name is Sally Cox. I noticed you have an apartment for rent. I'm a writer, looking for a quiet getaway. Would you be willing to rent it for a week or two?"

"Yep. Sure would."

"How much?"

"A hunerd."

"A hundred dollars a week?"

He nodded. "Or three hunerd a month. Utilities included. You by yerself?"

"Yes—well, except for my cat. But she's no problem. She's spayed and declawed. Box trained. You wouldn't even know she was here."

"You got a cat, eh? I like those rascals. Got six or seven of my own, dependin' on which day you ask."

"May I see the apartment?"

"Sure thing. Come on in. Me and the Missus will give you the grand tour."

Sally stepped into a cozy parlor, painted Wedgwood blue and framed in white moldings. All the fabrics in the room were coordinating blue and white prints, and she guessed every accessory to be an antique. An oak fireplace adorned the center of the far wall; above it hung an oval framed sepia picture of a man and woman. In the corner was an oak staircase.

"By the way, the name's Fred Muntz. And this here's my wife Amelia."

Sally shook hands with the couple, noting the woman's soft blue eyes and the silver cross around her neck.

"Come on, dear," Amelia said. "I think you'll like the apartment. We prayed and asked the Lord to send us just the right tenant."

Sally followed them to the top of the stairs. Fred opened the door and held it. "Ladies first."

Sally stepped into an entry hall behind Amelia, then turned to the left and breathed in without exhaling. A white marble fireplace took center stage on one wall of the living room, windows on either side. The couch and chairs had been upholstered in a pleasant yellow, green, and white floral print, and matched the draperies. Hardwood floor. Crisp white walls. Lots of light.

"I love it," Sally heard herself say.

She followed Amelia into the bedroom, then stood and feasted her eyes on a cherry poster bed and three sheer-covered windows forming an alcove on the opposite wall—and a window seat ideal for Kiwi. The slanted walls gave it the cozy feel of her grandparents' attic room, where she had sleepovers with her cousin Valerie.

Sally's eyes flitted across the soft yellow and ivory color scheme, a stunning contrast to the rich wood. The room was quaint and tasteful and more inviting than she had imagined.

She had already made up her mind to take it when Amelia showed her the small but functional and cheery kitchen and the bathroom with a claw-foot tub and plenty of room in the corner for a litter box.

Amelia opened another door. "Almost forgot. This is an outside entrance. The stairs will take you down to the driveway where you can park your car. Well, dear, what do you think?"

"I'll take it for the week," Sally said. "But I might need to stay longer. How would you like me to pay you?"

Fred pursed his lips. "Oh, how about a hunerd now? We'll go from there."

"You don't want some kind of deposit?" Sally said.

"Nah, yer kitty's not gonna hurt anything, is she?"

"No. Kiwi's well-behaved and very affectionate. If you like cats, you'll get along with her just fine."

Fred winked. "A real baby, eh?"

Sally smiled. "I'll bring her in. I can see you've got her number."

Harry followed the red Camaro to an old brick apartment building not far from the Plaza. He watched the driver get out, and then waited a few seconds before following him into the building. Harry pretended to be reading the mailboxes and, out of the corner of his eye, saw the guy unlock the door to apartment 106 and go inside. Harry looked on the mailbox: *Sam Cox.* Must be Sally's brother. Or maybe her ex-husband.

He walked to the door and rang the bell. A nice-looking guy maybe ten or fifteen years younger than Harry opened it.

"Yeah?"

"Sorry to bother you. My name's Harry Rigsby, and I'm trying to run down Sally Cox. Is she here by any chance?"

Sam's eyes narrowed. "No. What makes you think she'd be here?"

"I can't seem to reach her at home and was hopin' you could tell me where I might find her. Or maybe you could contact her and have her call me."

"Why do you want to talk to Sally?"

"She took care of my mother at the nursin' home. I just wanted to thank her and give her somethin' Ma wanted her to have."

"Oh, yeah. I recognize the name now. Your mother was Elsie, right?"

"Yeah."

"Sorry. Sally's gone for a couple of days. Went to Jefferson City to visit a friend."

Rats! "Is there a number where she can be reached?" Harry said.

"I'm sure whatever business you have can wait till she gets back."

"Any idea when that'll be?"

"No. Try reaching her at the nursing home."

"Yeah, okay. Thanks."

Sam closed the door abruptly, leaving Harry at eye level with the brass numbers on the door.

He left the building, wondering how much Sam knew. And if Sally was really visiting a friend in Jefferson City.

Harry started to get in his car and noticed a white Ford Explorer parked in the back row of the parking lot, a male driver wearing a Kansas City Royals cap and sunglasses slouched behind the wheel. He remembered seeing him at Kroger's.

He pulled out of the parking lot and turned down the first side street. He drove for blocks, stopping at several stop signs, and never saw the Explorer behind him.

Satisfied that he wasn't being followed, Harry drove back to his house, determined to figure out if Sally was really with a friend in Jefferson City—or trying to pull a fast one.

Sam tried to relax and read the Sunday paper, but all he could think about was how Harry Rigsby had known where he lived. Sam had been there only a week. And his new address certainly wasn't listed in the phone book.

He couldn't imagine that Sally would've had cause to mention Sam to Harry. But even if she had, how did he get the address?

Sam thought about calling Sally at Nan's, and then decided not to. She wanted space or she wouldn't have left. He hated to admit his feelings were hurt. But after his effort to win her over, Sam felt slighted that she had left town with no more explanation than a note on his windshield. Couldn't she have at least called him?

He had missed her being with him at church. New Hope Bible Church was very different from Redeemer and would take some getting used to. But it had felt good finally owning all the garbage, and then confessing it to God. He had almost given up hope that Sally would forgive him. But at least God had.

Sam put the newspaper down. Maybe he'd take a drive, and then go see a movie. Sundays were the hardest.

Sally put the last of her things in the armoire and then lay on the poster bed, while Kiwi explored every nook and cranny of the apartment. Tucked away in this wonderful place, she finally felt safe. But the guilt weighed just as heavily. She had given Fred a hundred-dollar bill from the stash. That was two she'd have to put back.

There was a soft knock on the door. Sally got up and opened it. Amelia stood on the top step with fresh towels and a bar of soap. "Here you go, dear. If you'll put your dirty towels outside the door, I'll leave fresh ones for you every day. I'll give you fresh sheets if you stay a second week."

Sally smiled. "Thanks. I think I'm going to like it here."

"Fred and I were just saying that we had way too much roast beef for just the two of us. Would you like to join us for dinner?"

"That hundred dollars isn't going to go very far if you start feeding me."

"Nonsense. It's our pleasure."

"All right. What time?"

"We eat at six, dear. In the dining room, just off the parlor."

Harry parked his car around the corner from Sally's house. It wasn't even 6:00 PM, but it was dark enough for what he intended to do.

He cut through a couple of yards, blending into the night before slipping into the side yard of Sally's house. He waited for several minutes and, when he didn't see anyone, went through the gate to the backyard.

He stood leaning against the back of the house, annoyed that the neighbor's dog was yapping. He looked for the easiest way in and noticed a broken window with most of the glass already knocked out. His heart sank.

He hoisted himself up to the windowsill and climbed in, the sound of crunching glass under his shoes. He pulled the flashlight from his waistband and turned it on to find the place ransacked. He didn't move, the beating of his heart banging his temples. He waited several minutes and didn't hear any movement in the house.

Harry stepped over debris scattered across the floor and noticed clothes had been pulled out of drawers and off hangers in the closet. He knew Sally was too smart to have left the money there. What he wanted was her address book.

Harry took a quick look through the house, finding every room a trashy mess. He went to the kitchen and spotted the phone, then got down on the floor and dug through everything he could find. There it was!

He stuffed the address book into his coat pocket, then checked the answering machine. No messages. He stopped for a moment and listened. That stupid mutt was still barking.

Harry went out the same way he'd come in, then followed the same short cuts to the other block.

He quickly got in his car and drove out of the neighborhood, his heart racing faster than a greyhound, his eyes peeled for anyone who might be following.

30

O n Sunday evening, Sam Cox pushed open the door to his apartment building and walked down the hall to apartment 106. He started to put the key in the knob and noticed the door was ajar. He slowly pushed it open and flipped the light switch, then exhaled a sigh of disgust. The place was in shambles.

He stepped over the mess, getting madder by the second. He grabbed a baseball bat from the closet and checked behind the bathroom door.

He went to the refrigerator, looked at the list of emergency numbers, and dialed the phone.

"Kansas City Police Department. How may I direct your call?"

"I'd like to report a break-in."

"At what location, sir?"

"Shady Grove Apartments, 4500 Milton Way, apartment 106. My name's Sam Cox. I just arrived home and found my place torn apart."

"Has the intruder left?"

"Yeah. Good thing, too. I'm not a happy camper."

"Okay, sir. Try to stay calm. An officer will be there shortly."

Sam hung up the phone and looked around the room. The TV, computer, and Bose CD player were all there. The lock was still on the gun case. Why would somebody ransack the place if he wasn't going to rob it? His mind raced in all directions, and he wondered if this had anything to do with Sally.

Sam thought of Harry Rigsby and how strange it had been that he showed up at the door looking for Sally on a Sunday afternoon. Had he come back looking for her? Even if he did, why would he ransack the place?

Sam sighed and flopped on the couch. He had spent all last weekend getting things put away. He'd like to hang whoever did this.

The doorbell rang a third time. Harry closed Sally's address book and slid it under the couch, then begrudgingly got up and walked toward the door. If Gracie was here to hassle him, she could forget it.

He yanked open the front door, shocked to see the same two police officers who had come to tell him about Jonathan's death.

"Mr. Rigsby, we'd like to ask you a few questions."

"About what?" Harry said, his racing pulse almost taking away his breath

"A break-in."

"What kind of break-in?"

"May we come in?"

"Uh, yeah, sure." Harry held open the door. "You can sit there on the couch. I know nothin' about a break-in. Where was it?"

"A studio apartment at Shady Grove—on Milton Way."

Sam Cox's place? Harry tried not to show a reaction.

"Sir, where were you between two o'clock and six thirty?"

"Home mostly."

"Define *mostly*," the second officer said.

"I went to the grocery store. Took a walk. That's about it."

"Did you drop by Shady Grove Apartments looking for Sally Cox?"

"Uh, yeah. A little earlier, though. Around one o'clock."

"Why didn't you just say that?"

Harry shrugged. "That's not what you asked me."

"And what was your reason for wanting to contact Mrs. Cox?"

"She works at the nursin' home and took care of my mother. Ma died recently, and I wanted to thank Sally and give her some of Ma's jewelry. I knew she'd want Sally to have it."

"Can anyone verify that?"

Harry shook his head. "No, but I'll show you the jewelry, if you like. It's not worth much. More sentimental than anything."

"That won't be necessary. What time did you say you got home?"

"I don't know. Four o'clock. Maybe five o'clock."

"And you didn't leave after that?"

Harry leaned forward in the chair, his hands clasped between his knees. "That's right."

"Is that your Ford Falcon in the driveway?"

"Yeah, why?"

"Can you explain, sir, why your car is still hot?"

Harry felt the color rush to his face. "Maybe it was later than five o'clock. I didn't pay attention. Is it important?"

"Yes, sir. The break-in at Mr. Cox's apartment took place sometime between two o'clock and six thirty."

"Hey...wait a minute. You got it all wrong. Go ahead and search my house. Whatever the thief took, you won't find it here. I'm not you're man. Check my fingerprints. DNA. I'm tellin' you, I didn't break in that apartment."

One of the officers wrote something on the report.

Harry's mind flashed back to the guy in the white Explorer. Who was he following: Sally, Sam—or Harry?

"Okay, Mr. Rigsby. That's all for now. We may get back to you with more questions later."

Sam pushed the mess to one side of the room, then pulled down the Murphy bed and lay on his back, his hands behind his head. The break-in made no sense. Why didn't the intruder steal something? The investigating officers had dusted for prints. If Harry was responsible, he had to be a real idiot to have been so obvious.

Sam had a nagging feeling that Sally was in some kind of trouble. Her edginess after Karen's murder. The nightmares. The phantom prowler Sam was sure he saw, but who never materialized. Harry's urgent need to get in touch with Sally. And now a break-in that didn't involve a theft. Something was going on. And Sam seemed to be right in the thick of it.

He fought the urge to call Sally at Nan's. If she hadn't confided in him when they were face-to-face, what made him think she'd open up long-distance?

Maybe he should go by the house and look for something that would give him a clue as to what was going on. If Sally couldn't reach out to him, then he'd have to reach in.

Sally glanced at the clock on the buffet, surprised at how fast the evening had gone with Fred and Amelia.

"I can't remember when I've enjoyed a meal more," Sally said. "Thank you so much for inviting me."

Amelia wiped her hands on her apron and rose to her feet. "Now, dear, are you sure I can't talk you into another piece of cherry pie before you go back upstairs?"

Sally held up her hands and laughed. "I'm afraid I'd explode."

"Yep." Fred patted his belly. "I know the feelin'."

"I've never been able to make crust like that," Sally said. "Maybe sometime you could show me how you do it."

"Heavens, yes. It's not hard at all."

Sally got up and began to stack the dishes. "Let me help you get these washed."

"Nonsense," Amelia said. "You're our guest. Fred and I can clean up."

"You're too kind. But I really wouldn't mind helping."

Amelia lifted her eyebrows. "I imagine you have some writing to catch up on."

Sally hoped she wasn't blushing. "I suppose I should get to work. Thank you again for dinner. It was delicious. Good night."

"Good night, dear."

Sally went up the stairs to the apartment and shut the door. Fred and Amelia were so friendly. It had been difficult dancing around what her "book" was about. How she wished she had never lied in the first place.

Sally picked up Kiwi and carried her out to the kitchen. She double-checked Kiwi's food and water and then went into the living room and sat on the couch, admiring the details of this beautiful hideaway and wishing she had enough peace in her heart to truly enjoy it.

Sally loved being in Amelia's presence. Something about her left the air feeling fresh and clean. What would Amelia think if she knew the real Sally—the thief, not the writer.

Sam drove past New Hope Bible Church and wondered why the parking lot was full this late on a Sunday night. He pulled his Camaro in Sally's driveway and turned off the motor. He hoped she'd forgive him for invading her privacy. What choice did he have? After all that had happened, he felt compelled to investigate. Investigate *what?* If only he knew.

He walked up the steps and put the key in the lock, then gave the door a hearty push and stepped inside. He flipped the light switch and froze where he stood, his eyes slowly taking in the destruction. Even the air ducts had been pulled out of the ceiling!

"Okay, *now* I'm scared!"

Sam ran out to the car to call the police on his cell phone. He was sure of one thing: Whatever the guy was looking for, he was serious about finding it.

Harry had read every page of Sally's address book, and the only entry with a Jefferson City address was Ted and Nan Bingham. He picked up the phone and dialed.

"Hello."

"May I speak with Sally Cox please?"

There was a long pause.

"Who is this?"

"A coworker from the nursin' home where she works," Harry said. "I really need to speak with her."

"Sally's not here."

"Do you know what time she'll be back?"

"No, you don't understand. She's not staying here. Have you tried her number in Kansas City?"

"Yeah, I did. I was told she was visitin' Nan Bingham in Jefferson City."

"Really? By whom?"

"Her boss, Wanda."

"Does Wanda have a last name?"

Harry kept his voice calm and steady. "Sorry, Wanda just started workin' there. I don't remember her last name."

There was a long pause.

"Well, I'm Nan, and I haven't talked to Sally in months. I can't understand why her boss would tell you she was here. Hello...? Are you still there...?"

Harry hung up the phone and threw the address book on the table. Sally was there, all right! Her friend was covering for her.

He looked at the clock. If he left now, he could be in Jefferson City by ten.

Sam sat in the back of the squad car, drained from answering an hour's worth of questions and reeling with questions of his own.

The investigating officer got back in the car and attached something to his clipboard. "So you have no idea what the intruder might have been looking for?"

"No, I don't. I've told you everything I know. There must be a connection in the two break-ins, but darned if I know what it is. You'll have to ask Sally."

The officer looked over at him. "Mr. Cox, the Jefferson City Police are at the Binghams' house. Sally isn't there. And no one's heard from her."

"There must be some mistake. She left me a note saying that's where she was going."

"Mrs. Bingham told the officers she hadn't heard from Sally in months, but had received a call about an hour ago from a man asking to speak with Sally. He claimed to be a coworker. Mrs. Bingham told him the same thing she told the officers."

Sam's heart sank. "Then something must've happened to her. Sally wouldn't lie to me!"

"Do you know who might have placed that call?"

"No. I don't know her coworkers."

"You told Mr. Rigsby your ex-wife was visiting a friend in Jefferson City. Did you give him the name?"

"No, I told him whatever business he had with Sally could wait, to try and reach her at the nursing home. I already told you that."

There was an uncomfortable stretch of silence. Sam could feel the officer's wheels turning.

"Did you and your ex-wife get along?"

"Yeah, more or less. She's still upset with me about an affair I had. That's why we're divorced."

"So, there's tension between you?"

"Sure. But we're on speaking terms. I told you I spent Friday night at the house. Sally was upset about Karen Morgan's murder and didn't want to be by herself."

"And that's when you thought you saw a prowler outside?"

"Exactly. And that's probably who ransacked the house—and maybe even my apartment."

The officer tapped his fingers on the clipboard. "Sounds like your life would be a whole lot easier if your ex-wife just suddenly *disappeared.*"

Sam clenched his jaw. "Wait a minute. I'm the good guy, remember?"

"We have to cover every angle."

"Look, this whole thing's scaring me. Aren't you guys even going to question Harry Rigsby?"

Harry drove past the capitol building in Jefferson City, then pulled into an empty parking lot and held a flashlight on the city map, trying to get his bearings. The Binghams' home was considerably south of there.

Faced with finally confronting Sally, Harry wondered if he had guts enough to do this. What if she *didn't* know anything about the money? And got insulted that he accused her, and went whining to the police?

Then again, what were the odds he was wrong about Sally? What other reason would she have for lying about the dirt—other than she was hiding something? And if she had the money, and thought splitting it with Harry was the only way to keep him from going to the police and her from being charged with Karen's murder, how could she refuse?

Harry was aware another car had entered the lot. He took a last look at the map and memorized the route he wanted to take, then turned off the flashlight and laid it on the console.

Suddenly the back door opened. The car bounced as someone slid across the seat. In the next instant, Harry was in a choke hold, struggling to get air and trying to pull someone's arm from around his throat! He thrashed with every ounce of strength he had, until the attacker's other hand brought a knife to his throat.

"Where's Sally Cox?"

"Who?"

"Don't play games with me, Harry. Where is she?"

The sound of the man's breathing filled the stillness as he held the knife blade flush with Harry's throat.

"Visiting Nan Bingham. It's marked there on the map."

"Stop following her," the man said, "or you're going to end up like

Karen Morgan. When I let go, here's what you're going to do: one, not make a sound. Two, turn the car around and go back to Kansas City. Three, forget this ever happened. Tell anyone—or go near Sally Cox— and you're a dead man."

31

Sam Cox sat at the counter at Nick's All-Night Diner, bloated from too much chili and working on his third cup of lousy decaf. What had Sally gotten herself into? If she wasn't at Nan's, where was she? And why had she lied? What was she hiding?

It was aggravating that the police had made him feel like a suspect, but it was hard to fault them. A desperate man could have staged both break-ins and a disappearance to cover up murdering his ex-wife.

A pretty blonde came in and sat on the stool next to him, the sleeve of her coat touching his. "Hi. I hope you don't mind if I sit here."

"No, that's fine." Sam glanced down the row at mostly empty stools.

"Don't you hate Sunday nights," she said. "Unless you like to watch TV, there's absolutely nothing to do."

"Yeah, I suppose not," Sam said.

"On the other hand, things are looking up. You're here." She took off her coat and laid it on the stool next to her, then pushed up the sleeves on a tight-fitting purple sweater. "By the way, my name's Jenny."

Okay, I'm outta here. Sam reached in his pocket for his wallet. "Sorry, I was just leaving." He took out a dollar and laid it on the counter, then walked to the register. He popped a couple of Tums in his mouth, thinking Nick's chili would be with her a lot longer than any guy she'd pick up tonight.

Sam left the diner and still wasn't sleepy, so he decided to drive around. His cell phone rang, and he pulled over to the curb and pushed the talk button.

"Sally?"

"No, Daddy, it's me."

"Oh, hi, Leslie. I didn't expect to hear from you this late."

"Were you expecting Mom to call?"

"Just wishful thinking. She's been pretty upset."

"What's going on? I've left messages for two days, and she hasn't returned my calls."

Sam took his index finger and traced the emblem on the steering wheel. "Some gal who works at the nursing home was found strangled in her apartment. Your mom's taking it pretty hard."

"How awful. Was it someone she knew?"

"Yeah. They shared coffee breaks and ate lunch together."

"Do the police know who killed her?"

"Not according to the paper."

Leslie sighed. "I'm sorry about the lady, but Mom could at least have told me so I wouldn't worry."

"She's not herself, honey. Try to cut her some slack. How are you feeling?"

"A little queasy, but not too bad. Alan's been spoiling me."

Sam smiled. "Good. Wish you were closer so I could do a little of that, too."

"We've already talked about it, and we want to come visit soon, maybe in the next week or two…Daddy…? Is that a problem?"

"Uh, I don't think so. Let's talk some more about it. I'll check my work schedule."

"Okay. I know it's late there. I'll let you go. If you talk to Mom, tell her to call me, okay?"

Sam watched a blue Subaru turn into a driveway. "Sure, honey. Talk to you soon. I love you."

Sam hung up, his eyes on the young couple getting out of the Subaru. He sighed. *Lord, where is she? Please keep her safe.*

Sally turned back the yellow and ivory quilt on the poster bed and fluffed the big feather pillows. She turned off the lamp, then climbed into bed and nestled in the quiet safety the hundred-dollar bill had bought her.

Kiwi jumped up on the bed and lay next to Sally, and seconds later the cat's purring soothed her like a lullaby.

Sally had instantly hit it off with Amelia, who reminded her of Aunt Georgia who used to come visit when Sally was a little girl. The woman wasn't really her aunt, but she used to bring baked goodies and hand-sewn dolls—and laughter. Always laughter.

And Aunt Georgia never failed to take Sally to church. Her parents never went, but they didn't mind if Sally did. So she'd put on her prettiest dress, patent leather shoes, and white gloves, and accompany Aunt Georgia to the red brick church with a steeple.

They would sit as close as they could get to the pulpit, listening intently to the preacher's sermons, Aunt Georgia fanning herself with the church bulletin and saying "amen" at regular intervals. And when the congregation rose to sing hymns, Aunt Georgia sang louder than anyone else—and noticeably off key. Sally doubted she even realized how she sounded, since the lyrics seemed to pour out of her heart, not just her lips.

Aunt Georgia had a peace about her and never seemed to lose patience for more than a moment. Even the time Sally's Hershey bar had melted all over the front seat of Aunt Georgia's brand new Thunderbird, the only expression of frustration Sally heard her utter was "mercy me."

Sally smiled. That's what Amelia had said tonight when Fred knocked over the gravy boat and a river of greasy brown spilled across her white lace tablecloth. Amelia seemed far more concerned about relieving Fred of embarrassment than tending to the stain that would likely put the tablecloth out of commission.

Sally had a strong sense that Amelia and Aunt Georgia had been filled from the same fountain of goodness. If only Sally could bottle it and take a healthy dose every day.

Her eyelids grew heavy. She wondered if Sam was mad at her for leaving town and if he had figured out she hadn't gone to Nan's.

Harry fumbled to get the front door key in the lock, looking over his shoulder to see if anyone had followed him home. The door finally opened, and he hurried inside, then turned the bolt lock and slid the chain. He turned around and leaned against the door, wishing he had never heard of Sally Cox.

He peeled off his coat and tossed it on the couch, then walked in the bathroom and examined his throat. He went out to the kitchen and sat at the table, unable to stop shaking. Who was the guy who threatened him? Harry never paid attention to the man's car but had a feeling it was a white Ford Explorer.

Harry's body shook until he started to ache, his stomach feeling as though he could heave. Jon was dead. Karen was dead. And Sally was probably next—and then Harry, if he didn't keep his mouth shut. How could any amount of money be worth all that?

32

S am Cox woke up shivering and realized the covers were on the floor. What a night! He reached down and pulled the blankets up over him, his imagination already tormenting him with what might have happened to Sally. He decided he would file a missing person's report, even though it would probably add to the police's suspicion that he might have been responsible for her disappearance.

Sam got up and put on his robe, then turned on the coffeepot. He opened the front door and picked up Monday's issue of the *Kansas City Star*.

He waited till the coffee had finished brewing, then filled a mug, sat on the couch, and began reading the newspaper.

The lead story recorded the details of a domestic squabble in Mission Hills. A prominent lawyer had killed his wife and buried her on his uncle's lake property, where sheriff's deputies had just found her, five years after the murder.

Sam took a sip of coffee. Another article gave an eyewitness account of seeing an Overland Park woman being forced into a van at a grocery store parking lot by a man wearing a ski mask. The woman was later found raped and murdered at a nearby construction site.

A third article told of a carjacking behind a medical facility near the Plaza. The female owner of the vehicle had been shot and left in the parking lot, and was being treated at St. Luke's Hospital.

Sam folded the newspaper and set it on the end table. His level of concern was rising to the top, and he wondered how much longer he should withhold what he knew from Leslie.

He leaned his head back on the couch and closed his eyes. *Lord, after the way I treated Sally, I have no right to ask You for anything. But please don't let something awful happen to her. Please put someone in her path that will keep her thinking clearly. It scares me that she's out there alone.*

Sally opened her eyes to the wonderful smell of bacon frying and could imagine Amelia, an apron tied around her plump waist, standing at the stove humming. The hollow feeling in her stomach nudged her to get up and go get some groceries, but she didn't want to move. Last night's sleep was the soundest she'd had since Elsie confided in her about the money.

She glanced at the clock and saw it was only 6:58. She rolled over to go back to sleep, then remembered she needed to call the nursing home and give some excuse for not being there.

Sally climbed out of bed and took a quick shower, then went out the private entrance and down the steps to her car. She drove to the Quick Fix and bought a breakfast biscuit, a cup of coffee, and a newspaper.

"Excuse me," Sally said to the clerk. "Is there a place in town where I can buy a prepaid cell phone?"

"I'm not too up on all the new stuff, but there's a phone place over in Merritt."

"How far is that?"

"Just three miles down 14 South. Might try the Wal-Mart super store first. You'll see it on the left when you get into town. It's open 24/7."

"Thanks."

Sally got back in the car and turned south on Highway 14 toward Merritt.

Harry had taken just two sips of his morning coffee when the doorbell rang. He looked through the peephole at the faces of the two police officers who had talked to him yesterday.

Harry breathed in slowly, and then let it out. He pulled the turtleneck up around his neck and opened the door. "Good morning, officers. What can I do for you?"

"We need to talk to you about another break-in."

"*Another* one?"

"Yes, sir. Could we come in, please?"

Harry held open the door and tried to look natural. "Have a seat anywhere."

The officers sat on the couch. Harry flopped in the chair facing them.

The older officer's eyes searched his. "416 Wells Street. Sound familiar?"

Harry nodded. "Sure. Sally Cox's house."

"Mr. Rigsby, have you ever been to that residence?"

"Of course. I stopped by there several times on Saturday and Sunday tryin' to find Sally. You know that from my previous statement."

"And she wasn't home?"

"Right. That's why I went to Sam's—to see if he could tell me where she was."

"I keep asking myself why you were in such a hurry to give Ms. Cox your mother's jewelry," the older officer said. "Doesn't strike me as a pressing matter."

Harry folded his hands in his lap. "I wanted to get past the emotional stuff, you know?"

The officer nodded. "And how did you get Sam Cox's address?"

Harry's heart rate soared. The seconds ticked by. "Uh, I went by Sally's Friday night and saw a red Camaro parked out front. The lights were out in the house. I didn't want to *intrude*, if you know what I mean."

"Sir, I just asked if you had ever been to that residence, and you indicated you had—on Saturday and Sunday. Why didn't you mention Friday night?"

"Because I never got out of the car. I didn't think that counted."

"Okay." The officer rubbed his ear with the pencil eraser. "So, how did you get from seeing the car parked at Sally's to knocking on Sam Cox's door?"

"Around noon Sunday, I pulled into Kroger's to get milk and saw the guy's red Camaro. I was pretty sure it was the same one, so I followed him home. You know the rest."

"Why didn't you just ask him about Sally right there in the parking lot?"

Harry smiled and shook his head from side to side. "You know, I never even thought of it."

"Mr. Rigsby, are you aware that Sally's coworker, Karen Morgan, was found murdered in her apartment early Friday morning?"

"Yeah. I was really sorry to hear it, too. You know those two gals went to my mother's burial?"

"No, I wasn't aware of that."

"Oh, yeah. They drove all the way to Dexter Springs. Pretty special ladies. Now you know why I wanted to give Ma's jewelry to Sally." Harry sighed. "I was gonna give Karen half, but…well, it's too late now."

"Have you ever been to Karen Morgan's apartment?"

"No."

"Never?"

Harry shook his head.

The officer handed him a large black-and-white photograph. "Mr. Rigsby, is this your white Ford Falcon? Look at the license plate number."

"Yeah, why?"

"Our investigating officers took this shot in front of Karen Morgan's apartment building on Friday night. Why did you say you hadn't been there?"

"Hey, I haven't been to her *apartment*. I just drove by the scene, like a thousand other curious people. I was grateful to this woman. Kind of tore me up, you know?"

The older officer glanced at his partner, and then at Harry. "Does the name Nan Bingham mean anything to you?"

"No."

"Did you make a call to Mrs. Bingham in Jefferson City last night?"

"No. What's this about?"

"Did you make any phone calls to Jefferson City last night?"

"No."

"You realize we can subpoena your phone records?"

Harry felt flushed, his temples throbbing. "Be my guest. I don't know any lady named Bingham."

Sally sat in her car in the Wal-Mart parking lot and dialed the number at the nursing home.

"Walnut Hills Nursing Center. How may I direct your call?"

"This is Sally Cox. May I speak with Wanda Bradford please?"

"One moment. I'll ring her office."

Sally tapped the steering wheel with her fingers, wondering if Rufus Tatum would be cooperative without his jelly bean fix, and if Fay Emerson was still creating a fuss, and how Dottie Fredericks was adjusting to her new environment—and if Jeffrey Horton had come in for his shift.

"Hello, Sally," Wanda said. "You're late."

"Uh, yes. I'm so sorry I didn't call earlier. I made a last-minute decision to get away for a while. I know this leaves you in a bind, but—"

"Actually, it doesn't. A CNA who used to work for us has come back part-time and has been asking for more hours. I can use her in your absence. How are you doing?"

Sally sighed. "Not well. You were right. I can't meet the needs of my patients if my mind and emotions are elsewhere."

"Maybe things will get easier after Karen's funeral tomorrow."

"Uh, I'm afraid I won't be at the funeral."

"Oh?"

"Wanda, the truth is I can't handle it. I just can't. You must think I'm horrible."

"Of course, not," Wanda said. "The nursing home is sending flowers from all of us. I'm sure you'll be there in spirit."

"Yes…" Sally put her hand to her mouth and stifled the surge of emotion she hadn't expected.

"When do you think you'll be back to work?"

"I'm not sure. But I can't afford to lose my job. I don't have any vacation days yet."

"Sally…? You're breaking up…I can't hear you…"

Several seconds passed and all Sally heard was a loud swishing sound, and then it finally quit and she heard Wanda's voice.

"Sally?"

"Yes, the signal keeps fading. Sorry."

"Listen, don't worry about losing your job," Wanda said. "I'll talk to the director of nurses. Just take some time to deal with your emotions. You've been through quite a lot the past few weeks."

Sally wondered how she had ever thought this woman was cold and uncaring. "Thank you."

"Call me at the end of the week and let me know how you're doing."

"I will. Oh, I almost forgot. Is Jeffrey Horton scheduled in this week?"

"He was. But he called in sick."

Harry lay on the couch, his eyes drawing imaginary bars on the ceiling. He should've known better than to use his home telephone to make the call to Nan Bingham. But how was he supposed to know the cops were connecting the dots?

But even though he'd lied about the call, how could the cops prove he was attempting to do anything other than what he'd told them before—find Sally and give her his mother's jewelry? But if Sally was found murdered? Harry didn't want to think about it. He exhaled loudly, his arm dangling off the side of the couch.

He couldn't decide which would be worse: being charged for crimes he hadn't committed in the pursuit of money he'd never seen, or admitting what he thought he knew and living in fear of the attacker following through on his threat.

Sam opened the back door of Cunningham's Sporting Goods Store, pleased to see stacks of merchandise priced and ready to be put out. The stockroom clerk he had hired was even faster than Sam anticipated.

The phone rang on line five. He wondered whose spouse or significant other was calling before the store had even opened.

He heard the intercom click on. "Boss, if you're here, you have a call on line five. Sam, line five."

He walked over to the wall phone and picked up the receiver. "This is Sam."

"Hi, it's me."

"Sally! Where are you? I've been worried sick."

"So, you did call Nan's?"

"No, the police did. They were trying to reach you after the break-in."

"What break-in?"

"The house. Somebody ransacked it. Tore the place up."

"*When?*"

Sam leaned with his back to the wall. "Sometime yesterday. I found it that way and called the police."

"*You* found it? What were you doing there?"

Sam sighed. "Settle down. I hated invading your privacy, but you'd been acting strange. And had those nightmares. And then when you left town so suddenly, and Harry Rigsby came looking for you, I—"

"Harry was looking for me?"

"Yeah. He has something of his mother's he wants you to have. But he seemed a little pushy, and I told him to wait and talk to you at the nursing home. So he leaves. Then I leave for a while and come back and find my apartment ransacked."

"*What?*"

"Babe, wait. Let me back up so this makes sense." Sam put into sequence for her everything that had happened, including that the police had questioned Harry Rigsby. "Okay, how about you telling me what's going on?"

All he heard was Sally's breathing.

"Then at least tell me where you are."

"I—I really can't, Sam."

"What do you mean, you really can't?" He paced along the wall as far as the phone cord would allow. "I've done nothing but deal with the police since you left! I was about to file a missing persons report."

"Sam, stop yelling. I'm not missing. I just need time to clear my head. I told you that."

"Why don't you call and tell the *police* that? This isn't just about you anymore! After I told them you were at Nan's and you weren't, I think they started to suspect me of doing away with you, then faking the break-ins and your mysterious disappearance."

"Oh, Sam..."

There was a long pause. He heard sniffling.

"Babe, don't cry. I know you're in some kind of trouble, and I can't help you if you won't tell me what's wrong."

"I can't."

"Why not?"

"It's complicated—" Sally's voice cracked. "I don't know where to begin."

Sam softened his tone. "Try me. Nobody cares more about you than I do. I'm here for you, no matter what it is...Sally...? Are you there...? Sally, talk to me..." All he could hear was a loud swishing sound, and then the phone went dead.

Sam slammed down the receiver, then put his palms flat against the wall and hung his head.

33

Sally Cox let out a sigh of aggravation, then laid her head on the back of the driver's seat and dropped the cell phone on the passenger seat. Should she call Sam back, knowing he would only keep pressing her? Even if she somehow got the courage to tell him what she'd done, and that whoever killed Karen could be after her, how could he not involve the police? She wasn't ready for that.

Sally opened her purse and took out the piece of paper with Sam's home phone number, then entered the digits, and hit the talk button. The phone rang three times and then the answering machine clicked on.

Hello, this is Sam. Leave a message and I'll call you back...beep...

"Sam, it's me. Sorry the phone went dead. I bought a prepaid cell phone, but I can't seem to get a good signal. The only reason for my call was to let you know I'm all right. I'm sorry for what's happened there. Kiwi and I are hanging out in a little town in Kansas, and I think it's best for now. Please don't tell Leslie. I'll call her myself when I'm ready. And please don't file a missing persons report! I'll deal with the mess at the house when I get back."

If I get back! Sally hung up, wishing he were there with her. In spite of his off-the-wall, desperate fling with Allison, Sam still cared. As hard as Sally tried to hate him, she couldn't. And at the moment, she would have preferred his company to anyone else's.

Sally started the car, pulled onto 14 North, and headed back to Pheasant River. There would come a day when she would have to go back and take responsibility for what she had done. But not today.

Sally drove down the alley and pulled into the driveway of the charming white two-story. She looked up and spotted Kiwi in the window seat.

Amelia waved from the kitchen window and then disappeared. Sally carried four plastic bags of groceries up the back stairs and let herself in. She had no sooner set the groceries on the counter than she heard a gentle knock at the living room door.

She smiled. "I'll be right there." She put a pint of Ben & Jerry's Cherry Garcia ice cream in the freezer, then walked to the door and opened it, not surprised to see Amelia's smiling face.

"Hi, dear. I was wondering if you'd made plans for lunch?" Amelia said. "This is Fred's day to work at the church, and I made a yummy salmon pasta salad that's just no fun at all to eat alone."

"Oh, I love salmon."

"Splendid. How about noon? That'll give you some time to work before lunch."

"Uh, okay. That sounds great. Thanks." Sally closed the door and went to the kitchen and finished putting away her groceries.

Kiwi meowed and rubbed on one leg, and then the other.

"Poor baby, are you lonesome?" Sally picked up Kiwi and scratched her chin. "Or are you jealous I get salmon and you're having mackerel?"

Gracie and Bill Garver went through the security door at the Craddock County Sheriff's Office and up to the receptionist's window. Gracie felt Bill gently squeeze her hand.

"We're the Garvers," Bill said. "The sheriff's expecting us."

"You can go on back. He and Investigator Knolls are waiting."

Bill held open the door, and they walked down the long hallway that smelled of old wood. They stepped inside the sheriff's office and were met with warm smiles from Sheriff Baughman and Investigator Knolls.

"Please, sit down," Baughman said. "Would either of you like coffee? Hot chocolate? A soft drink?"

Gracie nodded. "Hot chocolate sounds good."

"Coffee for me," Bill said. "Black."

A half a minute later the sheriff set a cup of hot chocolate and a black coffee on the small table between Gracie and Bill.

"I was in Kansas City this past Wednesday," the sheriff said, "and took it upon myself to go speak to Harry about the notepad. He didn't budge on his story."

Gracie lifted her eyebrows. "I didn't expect he would. At least, not without a lot of prodding."

"Oh, I tried. I even told him your story made more sense than his. Didn't faze him. He still says he doesn't know anything about his mother having money—or Jon going to Layton's to dig it up."

"I talked to him after Layton mentioned the fresh dirt at the cemetery." Gracie said "He denies knowing anything, but he's plenty defensive."

Bill took Gracie's hand. "Did you talk to Layton again?"

The sheriff nodded. "Yes, I did. I can't find a snag in *his* story at all. I think he's shooting straight."

"Do you believe Harry?" Gracie said.

The sheriff leaned back in his chair, his hands behind his head. "Truthfully, I didn't know what to think. Last week, I couldn't see any reason to keep Jonathan's case open. Then I got a call from the Kansas City Police Department, asking me what I knew about Harry Rigsby. Seems there were two break-ins over the weekend, and Harry's the only suspect."

"You're kidding!" Gracie said.

"One occurred at the residence of Sally Cox, who took care of Harry's mother in the nursing home. And the other at the apartment of Sally's ex-husband, Sam Cox."

Gracie looked at Bill and then at Sheriff Baughman. "Why would Harry break in either of those places? He's a jerk, not a burglar."

The sheriff scratched his chin. "Well, that's the funny thing about this. Nothing was missing from Sam Cox's apartment."

"What about Sally's?" Bill said.

The sheriff shrugged. "Hard to say. The place was ransacked after Sally suddenly left town. Her ex told the KC police she had gone to visit a friend in Jefferson City, but when the Jeff City police went to the friend's house to inform Sally of the break-in, she wasn't there—and the friend said she hadn't heard from her in months."

Gracie's eyes widened. "First Karen Morgan is murdered, and now no one knows where Sally is? This gets more puzzling by the minute."

"There's another detail bothering me," Investigator Knolls said. "A *mature-sounding* man called Sally's friend. Said he was a coworker from the nursing home and needed to reach her. Said Sally's boss told him to call her there. The weird thing is, Sam Cox is the only one who knew where she was, and he was with the police. So who made the call?"

Sheriff Baughman raised an eyebrow. "There's more. The reason the KC police questioned Harry about the break-ins is because he had showed up at Sam Cox's apartment earlier in the day, looking for Sally."

"How strange," Gracie said.

"That's about all I'm at liberty to say," Sheriff Baughman said. "But I'm leaving Jonathan's case open for now."

Sam closed the door to his apartment and tossed his keys on the counter. He went to the freezer compartment, took out a Lean Cuisine "Fiesta Grilled Chicken" meal, and put it in the microwave.

He noticed the light blinking on his answering machine. He pushed the play button, then scrambled to get a pencil and paper when he realized it was Sally. He played her message twice, then stood for a moment, trying to absorb the impact.

How could she decide to just hang out in some little town in Kansas? What about her job? And Leslie? She couldn't just pick up and go with no explanation.

"For cryin' out loud, Sally! What the heck's going on?"

Sam yanked open the microwave and grabbed the container on both sides, hot steam scalding his fingers. He quickly set it on the stove, then held his hands under a stream of cold tap water.

He set a TV tray in front of the couch and sat down to eat his lunch.

Sally didn't trust him enough to say where she was? Or at least leave a number where he could reach her? So much for rebuilding a friendship. He wondered how much further Sally could push her old Subaru before it gave out—maybe in the middle of nowhere, leaving her vulnerable to heaven-knows-what.

He got up and slid his half-eaten lunch into the refrigerator, then reached in the cabinet for the bottle of Advil. He popped two in his mouth and washed them down with water.

Sam leaned on the counter, his arms folded, and stared out at the gray January day, feeling that his hands were tied. He remembered another gray day when he'd had these same feelings, when Sally and Leslie were on their way home from visiting Sam's parents in Sedalia and a snowstorm took a turn that forecasters hadn't predicted…

"My wife and daughter must be stuck somewhere," Sam had told the police. "They left Sedalia over six hours ago."

"I-70's a mess," the officer had said. "Blowing snow has reduced visibility to almost zero. Cars are backed up for miles. Many off the road. If they're out there, at least they're not alone. Emergency crews and sheriff's department personnel are assisting as they can. No one's going to leave them stranded."

That wasn't much consolation to Sam, though he knew Sally wouldn't have started out without a full tank of gas. Was she stuck somewhere with the heater running, praying for help? How long before she ran out of gas? Or was overcome by carbon monoxide?

He had visions of Sally and three-year-old Leslie huddled together to stay warm, desperate for help—and no one finding them until it was too late.

Sam had never felt so helpless in his life. He wasn't much of a praying man, but he got down on his knees and prayed as he never had before that God would get them home safely.

Forty minutes later, Sally and Leslie came in the front door, their coats and hair sprinkled with snowflakes, their cheeks rosy, and their spirits high.

"Daddy, Jesus gots angels!" Leslie said, her blue eyes wide with wonder. "They help us home."

Sam scooped Leslie into his arms and hugged her, the snowflakes on one of her pigtails turning to water droplets and rolling down his shirt collar.

"Sorry I didn't call," Sally said, "but I was afraid if I exited the freeway, I'd never get back on. Cars were stuck everywhere."

He caught Sally's gaze and held it and, for one blessed moment, was sure they were the two most grateful people on the planet. He pulled Sally close and planted a warm kiss on her cold cheek, then whispered, "Thank you, God."

He didn't tell Sally he had gotten on his knees and prayed the prayer of his life. But the following Sunday, he accepted Christ…

Sam blinked the stinging from his eyes. He and Sally had weathered emotional storms just as frightening and had made it through—until he walked out on her and moved in with Allison.

He went over to the couch and knelt beside it, then bowed his head. *Father, nobody knows better than You what a poor excuse for a Christian I've been. But I'm desperate for Your help. Who else can I turn to? I know Sally's in some kind of trouble, but she's never going to trust me after what I've done. Please protect her. And help her resolve whatever's hanging her up. Bring her home safely. I ask these things in the Name of Your Son, Jesus Christ.*

Sam stayed on his knees, relishing for a moment the sense that he was on holy ground, and that the God of the universe had cared enough to listen to him, Sam Cox. Adulterer. Betrayer. Spineless excuse for a believer.

Sam still could hardly fathom that God had been there for him after his fling with Allison and all the pain he had caused Sally. But like the pastor told him, how could grace be called unmerited favor if it couldn't be abused?

Sam's spirit groaned with regret. He had invited Jesus into his heart twenty-five years ago, but had dabbled at Christianity and never surrendered himself.

And now, after falling flat on his face, a total disgrace to the family of believers, the Father in heaven had forgiven him, dusted him off, and set his feet on solid ground. What kind of love was that?

Sam got up and walked over to the countertop to get his car keys. As he turned to leave, he glanced out the sliding glass doors and saw it was snowing.

Huge clumps of snowflakes were floating down out of the gray and sticking to the sidewalk. Leslie's words echoed in his head: *Daddy, Jesus gots angels! They help us home.* If his heart hadn't been so heavy, he might have smiled.

34

At precisely noon, Sally Cox opened the door to her apartment and followed the wonderful scent of bread baking down the stairs and through the blue and white parlor to the kitchen, where she found Amelia Muntz putting two white daisies into a crystal vase in the center of a drop-leaf table.

"Doesn't this look nice?" Sally said, admiring the yellow linen tablecloth and green and white floral pattern dishes.

"Oh, I'm so glad you could make it." Amelia took rolls out of the oven, put them in a basket, and set them on the table. "Why don't you have a seat, and I'll serve you."

"Amelia, I'm a tenant, not a guest of honor. You really need to let me help you."

"Nonsense. I love doing this. Sit right there so you can see out. Looks like that front's moving in."

Sally did as she was told and noticed a thick coat of gray had been painted halfway across the blue sky. "Is it supposed to snow?"

"Freezing rain. Perfect pie-making weather."

Sally smiled. "Is there *anything* you can't turn into a positive?"

Amelia poured hot tea in Sally's cup. "No, I don't believe so."

"Oh, come on. There must be something."

Amelia reached in the refrigerator and brought out two salad plates covered with fresh lettuce leaves and placed them on top of the plates on the table. "Well, I'm not particularly fond of cockroaches. No matter how hard I try, I've never found anything positive about them."

Sally laughed. "Come on, I'm serious."

"And you think I'm not?" The soft blue of Amelia's eyes reminded Sally of the aquamarine earrings Sam had given her on her fiftieth birthday.

Amelia opened the refrigerator and took out a butter dish and a serving bowl filled with pasta. She set them on the table, then sat in the chair facing Sally.

"This looks wonderful," Sally said.

"Let me say the blessing, dear. I'm anxious for you to try it." Amelia took Sally's hand and bowed her head. "Father, I am so grateful for this moment which is of Your divine choosing. I ask You to bless this food and our conversation. In Jesus' Name. Amen."

"Amen," Sally said, her mouth watering for a taste of the salmon pasta.

Amelia picked up Sally's salad plate and put a generous scoop of pasta on the bed of lettuce, then handed it back to her. "I do hope you enjoy my special recipe. I get hungry for it, and Fred just doesn't care for it the way I do."

"Mmm...this is delicious." Sally took a wheat roll from the basket, broke it in two, and buttered it. "At this rate, I'll be on a diet by the end of the month."

Amelia smiled. "So, you think you'll be staying all month?"

"Maybe. I don't know yet."

"How's the writing coming?"

"It's not, actually."

"Writer's block, dear?"

"Something like that." Sally took a bite of salmon pasta, glad to have her mouth full. She smiled at Amelia as she chewed and sensed the woman already knew she had lied at dinner last night.

"I do hope the apartment is satisfactory," Amelia said.

"Are you kidding? It's great—a steal for three hundred a month. I don't know how you can afford to rent it for that. The way you're feeding me, you'll be lucky to break even."

Amelia smiled and dropped her eyes to her plate. "I think the ripe olives give it a special something, don't you? And the red peppers."

"Mmm..." Sally nodded and kept chewing.

"I meant to ask how you found Pheasant River? We're not really on the beaten path."

Sally wiped her mouth with the napkin. "I was looking for a place to get quiet for a while. I just started driving west and ended up here. I fell in love with the town the minute I saw it."

"I'm not surprised. Fred and I did the very same thing."

The phone rang and Sally jumped, her hand over her heart.

Amelia got up and picked up the receiver. "Hello? No, I'm sorry.

I believe you have the wrong number. That's quite all right." She hung up the phone and took her spot at the table. "Aren't you feeling well, dear? You look pale."

"No, I'm fine. The phone startled me." Sally broke a second roll in two and buttered it, wondering if she would ever be able to relax. "How long have you lived here?"

"Oh, we moved here from Emporia back in the late fifties. Fred got a job at the feed store over on Second Avenue. Worked there until he retired."

"How long have you been married?" Sally asked.

"Almost seventy years," Amelia said, sounding almost giddy. "We married the month after we graduated from high school. But I fell in love with Fred when we were in kindergarten."

"How sweet. So you've known each other all your lives?"

Amelia nodded. "I can't remember a time when Fred wasn't in my life."

"That's so romantic. Probably a little scary, too." Sally wished she hadn't said it.

The white lines above Amelia's eyes formed an arch. "Because the Lord might take Fred first?"

"Do you ever think about that?"

Amelia paused and took a sip of tea. "Why, of course I do. And I have to confess I'd be jealous if Fred got to heaven before me."

"But wouldn't you be lonely?"

"Oh, I would miss Fred sorely, dear. I surely would. But knowing he was in the very presence of Jesus...well, isn't that what we all hope for?"

"I suppose so. I guess I've never thought of it that way."

"Well, when you get to be my age and have all sorts of aches and pains, you tend to think more about heaven." Amelia smiled, her eyes like jewels. "*And* that new body we're promised. But seeing Jesus face-to-face is more than I can imagine, it surely is."

Sally took a bite of her roll, her eyes studying the precious lady who reminded her so much of Aunt Georgia. "Have you been a Christian all your life?"

"I asked Jesus into my heart when I was fourteen."

"What about Fred?"

Amelia's expression turned somber. She took another sip of tea. "Fred got baptized and went to church with me. But he didn't become a believer until something happened—something terrible."

Harry Rigsby drove away from the police station in his Ford Falcon. It was getting harder and harder to make the cops believe that the only reason he wanted to contact Sally was to give her his mother's jewelry. Too much had happened with Karen and Sally for them to just blow it off.

Harry had told so many lies he could hardly keep them straight. And it had been a big mistake going to Sam Cox's apartment. If it hadn't been for that, no one would suspect him of anything.

He was pretty sure the cops didn't believe him when he said he had lied about calling Nan Bingham because he was embarrassed—that he knew he was obsessive in his desire to find Sally and give her his mother's jewelry. He stuck with his story about needing closure and to put the sadness behind him. He tried looking pitiful, but the sweat had soaked his armpits and left rings on his shirt. He didn't think they bought it.

Harry figured they wouldn't charge him with breaking and entering if they didn't have evidence. And there's no way they did. But he wondered if the attacker had his eye on him, and if the guy would think he was telling the cops everything he knew about Karen and Sally and the money.

He looked in his rearview mirror at the white SUV behind him and tried to get a good look at the driver. The vehicle made a right turn. Harry breathed in and exhaled slowly. All he wanted to do was go home and lock the door.

Sally took a bite of warm apple pie and another sip of tea. She looked over at Amelia and wondered how she could be so comfortable being transparent about such personal matters.

"After Fred embezzled the money from the bank, he was convicted and went to prison for five years." Amelia blinked to clear her eyes. "I missed him so."

"Weren't you furious with him?"

"Well, yes, I certainly was. But Fred's a good man. It was a powerful weakness with him—wanting to please me. We had so little. And he worried we wouldn't have enough. If only he had known the Lord and trusted Him to provide instead of feeling pushed to do it all himself."

"You were awfully understanding," Sally said. "Most people wouldn't be."

Amelia paused, then looked up at Sally. "We all have weaknesses, dear. Fred's just happened to be wanting to please me."

"When Fred got out of prison, is that when you moved here?"

Amelia nodded. "But no one would hire Fred. He fell into such a deep depression I was afraid he'd never come out of it. Then we started going to church. An elder named Hugo Spinner took a liking to Fred and offered him a job at the feed store." Amelia dabbed her eyes. "The beautiful thing was Hugo never made Fred feel as if he was being watched. Hugo trusted him to run the cash register and eventually gave him the keys to the store."

"Sounds like a wonderful man."

"Indeed." Amelia pushed her empty plate aside. "Hugo told Fred that God had impressed upon him that Fred and I would be used by God to heal broken hearts. Imagine that."

"And has that happened?" Sally asked.

Amelia smiled and started clearing the dishes. "We can talk about that another day."

Sam finished the last of a small pepperoni pizza and flipped on the ten o'clock news. The snow had accumulated six inches by the time he had come home from work, and the roads were extremely hazardous. He hoped he wouldn't be snowed-in tomorrow with nothing to do. He was already climbing the walls.

The phone rang. What was he supposed to tell Leslie about her and Alan coming to visit? How could Sally leave him hanging like this?

"Hello."

"Sam, it's me."

"Sally! I'm glad you called back. Is something wrong?"

"No, I'm fine. I started worrying about the police suspecting you of ransacking the house and doing away with me. Did you get that resolved?"

"Yeah, I suppose. They aren't going to do anything unless someone files a missing persons report."

"Which you're *not*, right?"

"I guess not. I wish you'd come home."

"I will. When I'm ready," she said. "What happened with Harry Rigsby?"

"Since I haven't heard anything, I doubt the police have charged him with anything. He's one strange dude."

"Yeah, I know."

Silence.

"Sal…if I promise not to send out the troops, will you tell me where you are?"

"I told you I'm in Kansas. Why do you need to know more than that?"

Sam sighed. "No reason. Will you at least give me a number where I can reach you? In case something happens to Leslie. You never know what could happen in these early months of pregnancy."

"I'll call you from time to time."

"Sally, please? It'll make me feel better to have a number. I won't tell anyone."

She sighed. "Oh, all right."

Sam grabbed a pencil and wrote down the number, then repeated it back. "I don't suppose you're going to tell me where you're staying?"

"I've rented a small apartment in the upstairs of an old house owned by a real sweet couple, Fred and Amelia Muntz. I feel peaceful here."

"Okay. Thanks for giving me that much. I'll rest better knowing I can reach you if I need to. Have you got enough money?"

"I'm fine, Sam."

"Will you call Leslie and tell her *something*. She's left messages on your machine since Saturday. She and Alan want to come visit in the next week or two. I don't know what to tell her."

"I don't think I'll be back that soon."

"Then you need to tell her that. Please don't put me in the middle."

"All right, Sam. I'll talk to her."

"Babe, you'd tell me if you were in trouble, wouldn't you? Sally…?"

There was a loud swishing sound, and the phone went dead.

Sam slammed down the receiver. "Rats!"

35

Sally Cox woke up to a wonderland of white. She crawled up in the window seat, Kiwi in her lap, and peeked through the sheers at the quaint Pheasant River neighborhood below. The snow was still coming down, and children in bright stocking caps were sledding on the downy white that covered last night's layer of ice.

Sally spotted Fred Muntz's pickup buried under a mound of white and thought back on her lunch conversation with Amelia. What must it have been like for Fred when he got caught embezzling money all those years ago? It was hard to understand how Amelia had stood by him the way she did. Sally couldn't think of another human being besides Aunt Georgia who would have reacted with such compassion and understanding.

She wondered if Sam was mad at her for not calling back when the phone went dead. At least he had Fred and Amelia's number if he needed it.

Sally was hesitant about calling Leslie, fearful that she couldn't mask her lack of enthusiasm. She ached at the thought of Leslie's child growing up with memories of some stark, ominous prison facility hemmed in barbed wire, and Grandma Sally wearing a bright orange jumpsuit with a number on the back. Not a pretty picture for the family album.

Then again, she might not live that long. She wondered if the police had charged Harry Rigsby with ransacking her house and Sam's apartment. But the feeling that someone besides Harry had killed Karen and was after her was ever present. Maybe she would call the nursing home again and see if Jeffrey Horton was back at work.

Sally hugged herself. She didn't mind being snowed in. At least she was safe inside this beautiful old house. She hoped Amelia would have time to teach her how to make good piecrust.

Sam left his snow-caked hiking boots on the mat, then went back in
his apartment, thinking it would take a few minutes for his car to heat
up enough for him to scrape off the ice.

He doubted Cunningham's would have many customers today
and had already called all but two of the employees and told them to
stay home. Sam had plenty of paperwork to keep him busy and welcomed the chance to hide in his office and get his mind off Sally.

He popped the last of a bagel and cream cheese into his mouth
and took a gulp of coffee. He spotted the piece of paper with Sally's
phone number next to the phone and jotted the number on the back
of his business card and put it in his wallet.

He wondered if he should touch base with the police officers who
took his statement about the break-ins and see if any progress had been
made. And let them know Sally was all right.

Sam looked beyond the condensation running down the sliding
glass door and saw that the ice had started to melt on his windshield.
He grabbed a Lean Cuisine meal from the freezer compartment, put
on his boots, and headed for the car.

Harry carried his bowl of Post Toasties over to the kitchen table and
sat. What a boring day this was going to be. How he hated being closed
in! At least the cops had backed off for now. And Gracie wasn't on his
case.

Harry resented feeling guilty for trying to get his mother's money.
If there was a heaven, she was probably watching him with a reproving
eye. He remembered how upset she'd gotten the one time she found
him with something that didn't belong to him...

"Where did you get this baseball glove?" his mother had said.

Harry shrugged.

His mother took him by the arm and sat him in a chair. "That was
a question, young man. Please answer me."

"Gordon's."

"Where did you get the money to pay for it?"

"Dad wouldn't give me anything!"

"That's not what I asked you."

Harry chewed his thumbnail. Why say what she already knew?

"I'll tell you what you're going to do," she said, wagging her finger. "You're going to march down there and tell Mr. Gordon you stole that baseball glove. Then you're going to work to pay him back."

"But, Ma—"

"Don't you 'But, Ma' me! There's no excuse for this."

"I just wanted a new glove like Tommy's. Mine's old and ugly."

She squatted in front of the chair, her eyes locked onto his. "That's not the way to get it. Next time you want something that bad, come talk to me about it."

"It won't do any good. Dad'll just say no."

His mother tilted his chin upward. The look in her eye told him she understood exactly how he felt. "Then we'll just have to find a way for you to earn the things you want."

"Who's gonna hire me? I'm ten."

"Well, you won't know if you don't ask."

Harry spent the next two weekends working for Mr. Gordon to pay for the baseball glove. After that, neighbors began asking him to do odd jobs. It wasn't until after Harry was grown that an elderly neighbor let it slip that Elsie had paid him to hire Harry. Looking back, he had to wonder how many of his other jobs had been secretly funded by his mother...

Harry mused. So where did *she* get the money? His old man sure didn't give it to her.

The phone rang. Who the heck was calling this early? He picked up the receiver.

"Hello?"

"Why did you talk to the police, Harry?"

He recognized the attacker's voice and fought to find his own.

"You deaf?" the man said. "I asked you a question."

"Hey, th-they came lookin' for *me*. I lied about callin' the Bingham lady's house, so they got my phone records. I told 'em I was just tryin' to reach Sally to give her my mother's jewelry—as a thank-you for her help at the nursin' home."

"We both know that's a lie, don't we, Harry? So, where is she?"

"Who?"

"Sally Cox, you moron!"

"Wasn't she at Nan Bingham's?"

"I wouldn't be calling you if she was."

"I don't know where she is, I swear!"

The sound of the man's breathing took Harry back to those terrifying moments when the guy had held a knife to his throat.

"I'm watching you, Harry. You'd better not be lying." *Click.*

Harry hung up the phone, his hands shaking, and wiped the perspiration off his upper lip. He sat for a few minutes and tried to calm down, then went out to the garage and got his shotgun. He loaded it, then brought it into the kitchen and set it in the corner.

He had never shot at a person before and wasn't even sure he was capable of it. But he shuddered at the memory of the man breathing down his neck and the knife blade at his throat.

Harry raked his hands through his hair, his feet jiggling under the table, then got up and started pacing, hating the feeling that he was being tracked.

Sally dialed Leslie's number and let it ring four times…

Hi, you've reached Alan and Leslie's. Leave a message after the beep, and we'll call you back…

"Leslie, it's Mom. I'm sorry I haven't returned your calls. I guess your dad told you a coworker of mine was murdered. I decided to take a few days off and let my emotions catch up. I'll be scarce for a while. But I'll check in with you when I can. Hope you're feeling okay. I love you."

Sally hung up, then entered the phone number for the nursing home.

"Good morning, Walnut Hills Nursing Center. How may I direct your call?"

"May I speak with Jeffrey Horton please?"

"Jeffrey's not due in till 11:00 PM. May I take a message, or would you like me to connect you with his voice mail?"

"Rachel? It's Sally Cox. Do you know if Jeffrey worked last night?"

"No. He had the flu."

"Okay, I'll try him at home. You don't happen to have his number handy do you?"

"Yeah, sure. Hang on while I look for it. Are you enjoying your time off?"

"Uh, yes, thank you."

"Okay, have you got a pencil?"

"Uh-huh." Sally wrote down the number as Rachel rattled it off. "Great. Thanks."

Sally hung up, and then dialed Jeffrey's number and got the answering machine. She turned off her cell phone and laid it on the nightstand. She picked up Kiwi, then stood at the window. Even if it *was* Jeffrey who strangled Karen, there's no way he could know where Sally was. She was sure no one had followed her.

Sally stayed in the apartment, hoping Amelia would think she was writing. She had opened the Bible in the nightstand drawer and tried to concentrate, but couldn't. All morning the smell of freshly baked pies wafted upstairs and made her hungry, not only for a taste of pie, but also for good conversation.

At two o'clock, Sally finally gave in and went down to the kitchen, where Amelia Muntz was rolling out pie dough, a dusting of flour on her hands and her nose.

"Well, there you are," Amelia said. "Isn't this the most gorgeous day?"

"The snow's pretty," Sally said. "You're working up a storm down here. How many pies have you done?"

Amelia nodded toward the pie racks. "Two apple, two cherry, and two peach. I still want to make a couple blueberry before I put them in the freezer. This is a perfect time for me to show you how I make the crusts."

"Thanks," Sally said. "I was hoping you'd say that."

"So, how is the writing going, dear?"

Sally glanced up at the icicles hanging outside the kitchen window. "Slow. I'm not feeling very creative right now."

"Such a pity—what with you coming here to get away and all."

Sally smiled. "Oh, I'm enjoying myself. Don't worry about the writing."

"Why don't we take a break and sample the pie. What kind would you like?"

Sally walked over and stood looking at the pies, her hands behind her back. "Mmm...how about peach? Oh, I don't know, cherry sounds good, too. So does apple. They all sound good."

Amelia's eyes widened. "How about a small slice of each?"

"You read my mind."

Amelia served up the pie, and Sally carried it to the table.

"I'm going to have a glass of milk," Amelia said. "May I bring you one?"

"Thank you. That sounds great."

Amelia set the milk on the table and then sat, eyeing the warm slices of pie like a kid in a bakeshop. "You know, I've been making these for Fred for almost seventy years, and I still can't stay out of them. I always have to snitch a piece. Or two. Or three." She giggled and put a bite of cherry pie into her mouth.

"Mmm...I hear you." Sally savored the first bite of peach pie, thinking she and Amelia were just little girls wrapped in wrinkled packages.

"Sally, you mentioned you were divorced. Do you have children?"

"Yes, a grown daughter—who's pregnant with my first grand-child."

"Oh," Amelia put her hands together. "I'm so happy for you. Fred and I never had children. At least none of our own."

"Was that difficult?"

"At first. But the Lord, in His mercy, has sent us many children."

Sally's eyebrows furrowed. "Were you foster parents?"

"In a sense. Remember I told you that Hugo Spinner felt impressed by God that Fred and I would be used to help heal broken hearts?"

Sally nodded.

"Well, three years later, we bought this house and converted the upstairs into an apartment and offered it for rent. The Lord has pro-vided us with a steady stream of people ever since. Hurting souls that need a quiet place to rest."

"You've been doing this for forty years?"

"Amazing, isn't it, dear? We've become quite a family. We even have a picture album. Fred and I still get Christmas cards from many of them."

Sally took her fork and moved the crumbs around on her plate. "So, you're saying the *Lord* brought each and every one of these people to you?"

"We believe so, dear. That's always been our prayer."

Sally sat quietly, her heart racing. Was it possible that God still cared enough to direct her path, even while she was running? In spite of her lies and deceit? When she hadn't even repented?

Sam sat in his office at Cunningham's Sporting Goods, working through a pile of papers and thinking about Sally. It took all the willpower he had not to call the number she had given him. He had an uncomfortable feeling that whatever was going on with Sally was somehow linked to Karen Morgan's murder.

At least she had trusted Sam with the phone number. That was progress. And he wasn't about to abuse it.

Sam was glad he had spoken earlier with the police officer who had taken his statement after the break-in. Harry Rigsby hadn't been charged with anything. Sam was frustrated that the police had no other leads and hadn't established a motive for the break-ins. He told the officer he had heard from Sally, and that she had opted to get away for a few days. At least the guy seemed to back off his suspicion that Sam had been involved in foul play.

There was a knock at the door, then the floor manager peeked his head in. "Sam, there's a man out front to see you. Says he works with Sally."

"What's his name?"

"Jeffrey Horton."

"Yeah, okay. I'll be right there."

Sam put on his name tag and went out front and spotted only one person in the store besides the two clerks. He walked over to a young man dressed in a black ski jacket and black stocking cap dotted with snow.

"I'm Sam," he said, offering his hand.

"Jeffrey Horton. I work at the nursing home with Sally. Hope you don't mind me dropping in like this, but I've tried calling Sally for a couple of days, and she's not returning my calls. I knew she was taking some time off, but when she didn't show up at Karen Morgan's funeral this afternoon, I started to worry. So, I stopped by the house. Her car wasn't there, and yellow crime scene tape had been strung across the front porch. Do you know if she's all right?"

Sam memorized everything about the young man's face. "Sally's fine. She's out of town for a few days."

"Really? I just talked to her Friday night after we found out about Karen's murder. She said she was having out-of-town company all weekend."

"Guess her plans fell through," Sam said.

"What happened to her house?"

"A break-in. The police think they know who did it."

"Good. They questioned me about a phone call to some friend of hers in Jefferson City. They wouldn't tell me much, so I thought I'd ask her about it."

"You say you work with Sally?"

"Yeah, we work in the same wing. I usually have the night shift. I leave just as she's coming on."

Sam folded his arms. "So, how do you know her—if you're gone when she's there?"

"We talk about patients before she takes over. Kind of like passing the baton." Jeffrey smiled.

"I see."

Jeffrey took a handkerchief from his pocket just in time to catch a sneeze. And then another. "Excuse me. I've been fighting a cold. Sorry to bother you. I just wanted to be sure Sally was all right."

"No problem," Sam said.

"Nice store," Jeffrey said, his hands sifting through a rack of running suits. "I need to come back when I have time to shop. Thanks for easing my mind about Sally."

Jeffrey walked to the entrance and went outside.

Sam watched through the window as he got into a yellow Volkswagen Beetle, then he wrote down the license number as Jeffrey backed out of the parking space and pulled up to the four-way stop.

He didn't know whether to trust the guy or not. What would make Jeffrey think Sam and Sally were even speaking, unless he had been spying on them?

36

ally Cox put another log on the fire, then nestled on the couch
in the apartment living room, Kiwi purring in her lap. The last
part of her afternoon with Amelia had been uncomfortable. And
yet, she wasn't sure why, other than she felt vulnerable, knowing
Amelia believed God had brought Sally here. Amelia hadn't pressured
her in the least to reveal anything. In fact, quite the opposite.

And it had never even occurred to Sally that God would care what
happened to her after she'd given Him the cold shoulder. Refused to
pray. Refused to forgive. Refused to seek His help. And especially not
after she had gotten talked into stealing Elsie's money.

Sally went to the bedroom and took the Bible out of the nightstand. She sat on the side of the bed, opened it randomly, her eyes
falling on Proverbs 10:2: *"Ill-gotten treasures are of no value, but righteousness delivers from death."*

She turned a few more pages, her eyes stopping on Proverbs 20:17:
*"Food gained by fraud tastes sweet to a man, but he ends up with a mouth
full of gravel."*

She didn't remember ever seeing those verses before. Then again,
when's the last time she read her Bible? She put the Bible back in the
nightstand and went into the living room.

She turned out the lights and curled up on the couch, mesmerized
by the flames dancing in the fireplace, and felt herself drifting off to
sleep…

Suddenly, it felt as though an inky blackness were seeping out of
her soul, causing the darkness to multiply. And breathe. And move.

Sally jumped up off the couch, turned on the lights and then
flipped on the TV. And the radio. She ran into the bedroom and got
the Bible, clutching it to her chest, her heart pounding so loudly that
she could hear nothing else.

Lord Jesus, help me! I don't want to live this way anymore!

Sam stomped the snow off his hiking boots, then opened the door to his apartment and went inside. He took off his boots and walked across the carpet, feeling water soaking his socks. He squatted and ran his hand along the carpet. It was wet in places and dry in others. How weird. He looked up at the ceiling to see if anything had leaked. He didn't see any spots.

He walked over to the kitchenette and saw puddles of water on the linoleum and a muddy print. Not again!

Sam heaved a heavy sigh, then picked up the phone and dialed the landlord.

"Hello, Shady Grove."

"This is Sam Cox in 106. Was someone in my apartment today, doing maintenance or something?"

"No."

"You absolutely sure?"

"Yeah, I'm sure. You got a problem?"

"Uh, never mind. Sorry to bother you."

Sam went to the linen closet and got a bath towel, then went to the front door. He got down on his hands and knees and started wiping up the water, just as the phone rang.

He groaned, then got to his feet and walked over and grabbed the receiver.

"Hello."

"Is this Mr. Cox?"

"Yeah."

"How are you doing this evening, Mr. Cox?"

"I'm not interested in whatever you're selling."

"Oh, I'm not selling anything. I want to save you money by giving you—"

"How about giving me a break?"

Sam hung up. He noticed there were no messages on the answering machine, but he didn't see the note with Sally's phone number, and he distinctly remembered leaving it next to the phone. He felt around the base of the phone table and noticed the carpet was wet.

Suddenly, he was filled with dread. He took out his wallet and pulled out the business card. He dialed the number he had written on the back. The worst Sally could get was mad.

"Hello?"

"Mrs. Muntz, this is Sam Cox. May I speak with Sally, please?"

"Why certainly. Maybe she's awake this time. I'll have to go up to her apartment and check. Do you mind holding, dear?"

"No, not at all."

Sam sat on the arm of the couch. He waited for what seemed like forever, then heard footsteps approaching on the other end.

"Sam?" Sally whispered. "Why are you calling me again?"

"What do you mean *again?*"

"Amelia said you called while I was napping."

"That wasn't me. I just got home from work and found my carpet wet with somebody's snowy footprints." He sighed. "I don't know who was in here, but the only thing missing is the note where I jotted down your name, the Muntz's names, and the phone number."

"I knew I shouldn't have given you the number!"

"Babe, someone broke in. It's not like I plastered it on the wall in the men's room or something. Look, it's obvious that someone's looking for you. I think it's time you leveled with me about what's going on...Sal...?"

"I can't."

"Why not?"

"I need you to stop calling me, Sam. I'm going to tell Amelia and Fred not to take any calls for me."

"Would it bother you to know that Jeffrey Horton came to see me at the store today?"

"What did he want?"

"He was worried about you. Says he's been calling, and you haven't returned his calls. Went by the house and saw the crime scene tape. Then when you weren't at Karen's funeral, he got worried. Frankly, he seemed just a little too inquisitive."

"What did you tell him?"

"That you left town for a few days. That's it. Does any of this have to do with Karen Morgan's murder?"

"Sam, I can't talk any more. Please don't call me here again." *Click.*

Sam slammed down the receiver. He fell back on the couch, his mind racing. Should he talk to the police? And tell them what: that some unknown person is looking for his ex-wife in an unknown location for an unknown reason?

He jumped to his feet and started pacing, then sat on the arm of the couch and raked his hands through his hair. He picked up the phone and hit the redial button.

"Hello?" said an elderly man.

"Yes, sir. I noticed you had an apartment for rent."

"Aw, we already rented it fer a month or so. Might try the Excelsior House down the street."

"Do you have the phone number?"

"Yes, sir. Got a pencil handy?"

"Yes, go ahead." Sam copied down the phone number and repeated it.

"Thank you very much."

He hung up and then dialed the number the guy gave him.

"Good evening, Excelsior House."

"Yes, I just called Mr. Muntz, inquiring about an apartment for rent. He's rented his and said you might have one."

"Well, now, we sure do: a big two-bedroom on the third floor. We're asking four fifty a month, utilities paid."

"Sounds great. I'd like to come take a look. Can you give me the address?"

"Yes sir, we're at 100 Bateman Street."

"Where are you in proximity to Mr. Muntz's place?"

"Muntz is down in the 300 block. We're at 100. Get on Main Street. You can only turn one direction onto Bateman—right there at the big white church."

"Yeah, I know where that is." Sam chuckled. "I'm having a senior moment. Remind me the name of the town."

"Pheasant River." The man laughed. "Don't feel bad. Sometimes I can't remember it either, and I live here."

"Thanks. As soon as the weather clears, I'll come take a look."

Sam hung up the phone. He got out his duffle bag and packed what he needed. Maybe I-70 would be cleared off enough for him to get through. Surely the sand trucks had been working all day.

He looked outside under the streetlight. The snow was still coming down. He picked up the phone and dialed his assistant manager.

"Hello?"

"Phil? It's Sam. Listen, something's come up. I need to take a few vacation days and clear up some personal business. Think you can handle it?"

"Sure. No problem. After the Christmas rush, it feels like we're all standing around looking for stuff to do anyway."

"Thanks. That big shipment from Spalding should be here before the end of the week. I don't know how long it'll take me to clear this up, but you've got my cell number. Call if you need me."

"Okay. But I'm sure we'll do fine."

Sam hung up and turned out the lights. He picked up his duffle bag, went out in the hall, and locked the front door. *Like that does any good!*

Sally sat at the kitchen table, all the lights on in the apartment. Kiwi jumped up on the table and put her paw on Sally's cheek.

"You always know, don't you?" She rubbed the cat's fur, thinking Sam would gladly take Kiwi if Sally went to prison.

No matter how many times Sally looked at her situation, she saw the same two choices: keep running for the rest of her life, hoping Karen's murderer wouldn't find her. Or take the money to the police and tell the truth, taking whatever punishment she had coming.

Sally wiped the tears off her cheeks. Her stubborn anger at Sam and at God had driven her to cash in her values for Elsie's money. How had she ever thought that would be the answer to her problems?

Sally got up and sat on the floor in front of the fire. What was done was done. This despicable failing was part of her history—her legacy. How well could she live with that?

Sam pushed his glasses up higher on his nose and focused on a pair of red taillights fifty yards beyond the whirling, dizzying mass of white coming at his windshield. It was no use. There were moments when he couldn't tell if he was on the roadway or headed for a nearby field—or a big ditch.

He spotted an exit up ahead and saw a sign advertising a Comfort Inn. How discouraging that he had been on the road for three hours and had just passed Topeka!

Sam slowly pumped the brakes, glad he'd decided to put on chains before he left, and made it down the exit without sliding. He turned left and then right, and pulled under the awning of the Comfort Inn. He leaned his head on the back of the seat and sighed with relief, then got out and went inside.

"Hello," said the man behind the counter. "I have one room left." Sam handed the guy his Visa card. "Sold. Man, it's treacherous out there."

"That's what I hear. Highway Patrol's askin' people to stay off I-70."

"They won't get any argument from me."

The man handed Sam the registration form. "Where you headed?"

"A town called Pheasant River. It's south of Salina and north of Merritt. Ever heard of it?"

"Can't say as I have."

"Well, that's where I'm going. I need to help a friend out of a jam."

"Must be some friend for you to fight this storm."

"You could say that." Sam handed him the form and took the key.

"You're upstairs in 214. Take the stairs on the left. Park wherever you can squeeze in. Continental breakfast is served in the morning from six to ten."

"Thanks."

Sam drove around to the side door and found a spot his Camaro would just barely fit into. He went inside the building and up the stairs to room 214. The place was nicer than he had anticipated. He took off his hiking boots at the door and threw his duffle bag on a chair, then got the Kansas map out of his bag and sat at the desk, tracing with his index finger the route he planned to take. Pretty simple. On a clear day, anyway. If this storm didn't let up, he wasn't sure what he would do. He glanced at his watch. It was five minutes after ten.

Sam flipped on the TV and surfed until he found a Topeka news station, then turned up the volume.

"The Kansas Highway Patrol has reported over a hundred vehicles off the road on I-70 between Topeka and Hays. Motorists are cautioned to stay off the interstate and not to venture out unless it is absolutely necessary.

"This same storm dumped a foot of snow on our Canadian neighbors and has already dropped more than eight inches of snow here in Topeka and throughout most of Kansas, as well as portions of Colorado, Nebraska, Missouri, and Iowa. Central and western portions of Kansas and eastern Colorado are expected to get another six to eight inches before daybreak…"

Sam decided to take a hot shower and let his feet thaw out. Of all times for the weather not to cooperate.

37

Sally Cox woke up shivering. For a moment, she couldn't remember where she was, then felt the Bible still clutched to her chest and realized she had fallen asleep on top of the covers. She rolled over on her back, then got up slowly and arched her back.

She turned up the thermostat, then stood at the window seat, drinking in the beauty of the snowy landscape below. As far as she could see, everything was blanketed in a fresh layer of downy white, not a footprint marring the virgin snow. *Though your sins are like scarlet, they shall be white as snow.*

Sally's vision was suddenly blurred with tears. How was she going to approach Jesus—the One who had died to set her free? How could she have put herself back in bondage and gotten caught in a trap of lies and deceit? She was a thief. And not even His forgiveness would change that fact.

How could she even begin to resolve the mess she'd gotten into? Turning herself and Elsie's money over to the police was one thing. Facing Leslie and Sam with what she had done seemed almost unbearable. But throwing herself on God's mercy seemed next to impossible.

Sally looked out beyond the white treetops at the pink glaze spread across the horizon and wondered how many more sunrises she would see before she was locked away in some dank, dreary prison.

Sally's breathing grew shallow, and she felt as though she were an animal caught in a trap, waiting for the hunter to find her and decide her fate.

Sam pulled back the drapes in his motel room and looked out at the mess in the parking lot. The snow was deep, and cars were parked haphazardly. He doubted anyone could get out without digging out. He let the drapes fall back.

The morning weather report hadn't offered much encouragement for venturing out on I-70 before afternoon, if then.

He sat on the side of the bed and put his face in his hands. *Lord, please help me get out of here and find Sally. Please don't let her do anything stupid. And Father…I'd do just about anything to win her back. If it's Your will, maybe You could help me with that, too.*

Sam got up, thinking he might as well take advantage of the continental breakfast. He heard a knock on the door and looked out the peephole and saw a man standing with a snow shovel. He opened the door.

"Hi. I'm across the hall in 213. Someone gave me this shovel to dig my car out and said to pass it on. Maybe you'll do the same."

"Wow, thanks," Sam said. "That's the best news I've heard all morning."

"Hope you get wherever you're going. I think I'm moving to Florida the first chance I get." The man smiled wryly.

Sam took the shovel and shook the man's hand. "Thanks. I really appreciate this."

Sally sat on the couch, staring at a row of shimmering icicles hanging from the eaves outside the window. Sunlight flooded the living room, taking the chill out of the air. She didn't know how long she had been sitting there, and then heard the anniversary clock on the mantel chime two.

She heard a gentle knock on the front door. Did she really want to talk to Amelia right now? Sally sighed. She got up and opened the door.

"Hello, dear. I'm wondering if you would like to have dinner tonight with Fred and me? I'm going to make my special meat loaf and new potatoes. There'll be way too much for just the two of us."

Sally smiled. "You do that on purpose."

"What's that?"

"Make too much for just you and Fred."

Amelia's soft blue eyes twinkled. "We're quite used to sharing our table with someone." She glanced over Sally's shoulder. "Would you mind terribly if I came inside and enjoyed the sunshine with you for a few minutes? This part of the house is so bright and cheery."

Sally did mind. But what could she say? "No, that's fine. Come in."

Amelia walked in the living room and stood in front of the windows, her arms outstretched as if she were absorbing the sunlight. "Isn't this splendid, dear?"

"Yes, it really is," Sally said.

Amelia sat in the chair to the right of the couch and tucked her skirt neatly around her plump legs. Kiwi jumped up and nestled in her lap.

Sally sat at the end of the couch, closest to Amelia's chair, a throw pillow under her arm. She waited in silence for several minutes, wondering why Amelia just sat there with her eyes closed and her lips moving. Sally studied her round, gentle face that seemed completely guileless and wondered what was going on in her mind.

Amelia finally opened her eyes, her face beaming. "It's impossible not to feel God's presence sitting here in all this light. Nearly takes my breath away."

Sally nodded in agreement, but didn't feel anything.

Amelia looked down at Kiwi and rubbed the cat's fur. Finally she looked up at Sally, her eyes matching perfectly the winter sky outside the window. "The Lord has impressed upon me to say something to you, Sally. I'm not sure why. But there's no doubt in my mind that He's nudging me to say it."

Sam felt as though he were crawling along I-70. The interstate was mostly snow packed, and at times, heavy drifting had caused the westbound traffic to merge into one lane. How he wished he had an SUV. Or a snowmobile. Or even a dogsled.

He took off his sunglasses and looked at the map. Salina was about fifty miles away, and Pheasant River was probably another thirty miles southwest of Salina. Had the secondary highways been cleared? Or sanded? Or even traveled enough to be snow packed?

He saw an exit up ahead and a huge truck stop. He decided to take a break and get something to eat. It was already after two o'clock. And at this rate, he doubted he could reach Pheasant River before dark.

"Read the story of the good thief," Amelia said to Sally. "That's what I feel impressed to tell you."

Sally felt the heat color her cheeks.

"Are you familiar with the story, dear?"

Sally nodded. Was this really a word from God or just Amelia's intuition?

"Let me get the Bible, dear, and we'll read it together." Amelia went to the nightstand and brought out the Bible, then sat next to Sally on the couch. "I believe we'll find it in Luke, chapter 23."

Amelia took a pair of reading glasses out of her sweater pocket and put them on, then opened the Bible and with skilled ease found the verses she was looking for. "Ah, here we are. I'll begin reading at verse 32.

"'Two other men, both criminals, were also led out with him to be executed. When they came to the place called the Skull, there they crucified him, along with the criminals—one on his right, the other on his left. Jesus said, "Father, forgive them, for they do not know what they are doing." And they divided up his clothes by casting lots.

"'The people stood watching, and the rulers even sneered at him. They said, "He saved others; let him save himself if he is the Christ of God, the Chosen One."

"'The soldiers also came up and mocked him. They offered him wine vinegar and said, "If you are the king of the Jews, save yourself."

"'There was a written notice above him, which read: THIS IS THE KING OF THE JEWS.

"'One of the criminals who hung there hurled insults at him: "Aren't you the Christ? Save yourself and us!"

"'But the other criminal rebuked him. "Don't you fear God," he said, "since you are under the same sentence? We are punished justly, for we are getting what our deeds deserve. But this man has done nothing wrong."

"'Then he said, "Jesus, remember me when you come into your kingdom."

"'Jesus answered him, "I tell you the truth, today you will be with me in paradise."'"

Amelia closed the Bible, a red ribbon marking the place, and took Sally's hand in hers, saying nothing more.

Sally clamped her eyes shut, emotion caught in her throat, realizing she had played the part of both thieves.

She replayed in her mind that scene at the cross, imagining herself in the good thief's place, receiving a full measure of Jesus' mercy and grace.

Suddenly, it was as though a healing rain began to fall from heaven on her soul, sweeping away all the shameful garbage she had been hiding.

When it seemed as though the rain had stopped, only salty streams of remorse trickled down her face.

Amelia put a Kleenex in Sally's hand. "The Lord loves you so," she whispered.

Sally wiped the tears from her cheeks. "I can't imagine why."

"Would you like me to leave you alone with your thoughts, dear?"

Sally shook her head. "No, please stay. I think it's time I finally told someone what's been going on. I can't live with it anymore."

Sally spent the rest of the afternoon telling Amelia about Sam's affair, the divorce, the financial struggles, Elsie's money, and all the events leading up to Karen's murder and Sally's leaving Kansas City.

Amelia squeezed her hand. "Mercy me, child. That's a terrible burden to be carrying around alone. I'm so glad you shared it with me."

"You must think I'm a terrible person."

Amelia turned to Sally and brushed the hair off her wet cheek. "No, we're all imperfect, dear. But now that you're at peace with the Lord, what do you plan to do to make things right?"

There was a knock on the door. "Amelia?" Fred's voice was muffled. He knocked again.

Amelia patted Sally's knee. "Let me get it, dear." She got up and opened the front door.

"Sorry to interrupt, but there's a man at the front door, wantin' to see Sally. What should I tell him?"

38

Sally Cox jumped up from the couch and looked out the window at the driveway below. In the light of dusk, she saw a red Camaro parked behind the mound of snow covering Fred's truck.

"Oh, no. It's my ex-husband! How did he find me?"

"Went to a powerful lotta trouble to git here in this weather," Fred said. "Maybe y'oughta see what he wants. Seems mighty concerned about ya."

Sally looked over at Amelia. "What should I do?"

Amelia came over and put her arm on Sally's shoulder. "The Lord has brought you to this point. I have to believe Sam's coming here is part of His plan. Perhaps you should see what he wants. He might be able to help you."

Sally sighed, not convinced.

"How 'bout I let him thaw out in the parlor while yer decidin'? He don't know it yet, but that car of his ain't goin' nowhere 'less he digs it out."

"All right," Sally said. "But I need a few minutes to gather my thoughts."

Fred nodded. "Take all the time ya need, darlin'. I just don't have the heart to keep the poor fella standin' out in the cold." He went out of the apartment and down the creaky staircase.

"If you're all right, dear, I think I'll go put my meat loaf in the oven," Amelia said.

"I'm all right—just scared to death."

Amelia's soft blue eyes held her gaze. "You've been forgiven, Sally. What happens now is secondary to that. Let's ask the Lord to help you." Amelia took her hand and bowed her head. "Our Father in heaven, holy is Your name. Thank You that You hear our requests and concerns as well as our thanksgiving and praise. Though Sally left You for a time, we know You never left her and are here with us, even now.

We're grateful she chose to confess her wrongdoing and receive Your forgiveness and mercy.

"We ask, Lord, that You give her the right words to tell Sam what has happened in her life. We ask that You protect them from the evil one, and that fear will not get in the way of honesty and resolution. Let Your perfect will be accomplished in their lives. It is in the Name of Your Son, Jesus Christ, we pray. Amen."

"Amen." Sally wiped the tears from her cheeks, and then felt Amelia's arms around her.

"The Lord will help you, dear. Trust Him."

Harry Rigsby lay on the couch, one leg up over the back, the newspaper laid across his belly. How much longer could he stay inside with all the drapes pulled, living in fear of the man who had threatened him?

He reached on the floor for the remote and turned on the TV. He surfed for a couple minutes, then turned it off. Darned reruns.

Maybe this was a good time to sort through the other box of his mother's things and throw out what he didn't want to keep. He had already looked through the box of clothes and her photographs, but he hadn't paid much attention to whatever else he had packed up at the nursing home—except for some phony diamond jewelry he told the cops he wanted to give to Sally.

Harry pulled a cardboard box out of the hall closet and carried it to the kitchen table. He took out a manila folder and dumped the contents, which appeared to be nothing but old greeting cards. He opened a few of them and read the signatures. Mostly from his mother's family. A few friends. How long had she kept these? Some of these people had been dead a long time. He stuffed them back in the manila folder and put it on the chair, the first in a pile of things to throw away.

He pulled out three small, framed photographs that had sat on the nightstand at the nursing home. The one of himself he put in the throwaway pile. In his left hand, he held up the picture of Jon that he'd always thought made him look too clean-cut; and in his right hand, the picture of his mother and father taken on their fiftieth wedding anniversary. His old man had that same obnoxious, phony half smile. Harry put both pictures on the throwaway pile.

He dug down in the box and found a pair of eyeglasses. A silk scarf. A pair of jeweled scuffs. A beaded purse. A well-worn Bible. All kinds of junk. He emptied the box, and then put it all back, except for his mother's Bible. Some inheritance.

Harry took the box out to the trash can, disappointed that the only item worth keeping was one he had no use for.

Sally looked at her reflection in the bathroom mirror. Her skin looked red and blotchy, her eyes puffy. She put a dab of moisturizer on her face and rubbed it in, and then applied foundation, blush, mascara, and lipstick. Not the best job, but a big improvement.

Lord, please help me say the right thing.

Sally went out the door of the apartment and down the steps, her chest tight, and finally remembered to exhale when she reached the bottom of the staircase.

Sam was sitting on the sofa. His face lit up when he saw her, and Sally forgot whatever it was she had planned to say.

Sam stood, a green stocking cap in his hands, a sheepish look on his face. "I hope you're not mad at me for showing up like this. But three break-ins in two days tells me we need to talk."

Sally was torn between wanting to shake him and wanting to fall in his arms and bawl. "All right. Let's talk upstairs."

Amelia peeked her head around the corner of the dining room. "There's plenty of meat loaf for both of you. It'll keep until you're ready. No need to rush."

Sally went up the stairs, Sam on her heels. She opened the door to the apartment and went inside.

"Wow, is this nice," Sam said. "I'm impressed."

Sally walked into the living room and sat on the couch. Sam sat in the same chair Amelia had sat in earlier. Kiwi jumped up and rubbed against his chest, seemingly beside herself, then made herself at home in his lap.

"Okay, I'm listening," Sam said.

Sally glanced up at him and then at her shaking hands. "I've learned some things in the past eight months—the best and the worst about myself. What I'm about to tell you is the worst. And it will disappoint you...and Leslie...But the only way I'm going to get to the other side is to walk through it. So, here goes..."

Sally started at the beginning and told Sam everything: how she had hardened her heart after the divorce and refused to ask God for help; and then in her bitterness and desperation, had resorted to justifying her and Karen stealing Elsie's money. She explained how terrified she was, and why she had run—and why she had stopped running.

"I wish I could change what I did," Sally said. "I'm so sorry."

Sam leaned against the back of the chair and shook his head from side to side. "For cryin' out loud, Sally. Why didn't you just sell the house and use the equity?"

"Everything happened so fast. I knew I was getting behind, but when the bill collectors started calling, and then I almost had an accident and hadn't paid my car insurance, I panicked. I didn't have the money or the energy to fix up the house to sell. I suppose if Elsie's money hadn't been an option, I would've been forced to. But houses aren't selling that well right now. All I could think about was getting the pressure off." Sally wiped her eyes.

"You could've gotten a second job."

"I had decided to do that. But it was exhausting to think about. Then when Karen came up with the plan to get the money, I deceived myself into believing that's what Elsie would want. What can I say? I was an idiot."

Sam looked at her, his eyes not disputing the point. "How much of the money have you spent?"

"I've broken three hundred-dollar bills. That's all."

Sam got up, his hands in his pockets, and paced in front of the fireplace. "I'll give you the three hundred. Then you can turn the entire hundred and twenty-five thousand over to the police. Maybe they'll go easy on you for having the decency to turn yourself in."

"What about the other half?" Sally said. "Someone killed Karen for it. I have to tell them."

"Let's hope you live long enough to tell the story." Sam went back to the chair and sat, his fingers tapping the sides of the chair, his foot jiggling. "How could you let yourself get mixed up in this?"

Sally's gaze met his. "I guess we never know what we're capable of until we're hurting, and someone dangles a carrot."

Sam winced, red flooding his face. "Yeah, I hear you. I'm in no position to throw stones, that's for sure."

"Well, neither am I. In a weird sort of way, I guess that's worth something."

39

Sally Cox sat with Sam at the table in the Muntz's kitchen, finishing a late dinner and looking out at a whirling mass of snowflakes visible under the streetlight.

"I thought it was supposed to stop snowing," Sally said.

Sam raised his eyebrows. "I wish. If you want to go back tomorrow, we'll have to put chains on your Subaru. Frankly, I don't think it's a good idea."

"You took a big risk coming all this way to find me."

Sam smiled. "Thanks for noticing."

"Well, I *am* grateful. Humiliated, but grateful."

Amelia walked up to the table with a tin of apple pie. "Would either of you like another piece?"

"I don't know where I'd put it," Sally said. "But it was wonderful, as usual."

Sam winked. "I could handle another piece."

"Ah, a man after my own heart." Amelia took the pie server and slid a piece of apple pie onto his plate.

"It's getting late," Sally said. "We need to decide what we're going to do."

Amelia put her hand on Sam's shoulder and winked at Sally. "Why, Sam's going to stay in our guest bedroom, of course. He can't go out in this weather. We're supposed to get another four inches."

"Please don't feel like you have to put me up," Sam said. "I had planned to stay in a motel."

"Nonsense. Why risk getting stuck in this when we have a perfectly good room down the hall?"

"Thank you. I'm really beat."

Amelia smiled. "Good, then it's settled. You two keep right on talking. I'm going to get Sam's room ready."

Sam took a bite of pie and seemed to be thinking. "When are you going to tell Leslie?"

"Let's wait till after we get back and talk to the police." Sally felt a resurgence of dread. "No point in worrying her."

"Yeah, okay."

Sally glanced at Sam and then at her empty plate. Why was he staring at her?

"I wish you'd stop worrying about the guy who called," Sam said. "The only thing I scribbled on the note was your first name, the Muntzes' names, and the phone number. Fred and Amelia didn't tell him anything."

"If you could find me this easily, so could he."

Harry put on another sweater, then walked into the kitchen, wishing he were sleepy—and warmer. He put a glass of milk in the microwave and sat at the table. He stared for a moment at his mother's Bible and couldn't remember if he'd ever opened one.

He set it in front of him and thumbed through the pages. His mother had highlighted all kinds of verses in yellow. None of it made much sense. The microwave dinged.

He got up and carried the warm glass of milk to the table. What had his mother gotten out of all this religious stuff? Her life had been difficult—and his old man a real pain. At least she'd stuck it out with him. That's more than Gracie had done with Harry.

It made more sense to him that heaven and hell didn't exist and that his best shot was right here on earth. All the more reason to feel disgusted that there wasn't any joy in his life at the moment. Then again, had there ever been?

The phone rang and startled him. He let it ring five times, relieved when it finally quit. A few seconds later, it started ringing again. After the sixteenth ring, he picked up the receiver. "Yeah, *what?*"

"Your phone etiquette needs a little work, Harry. Who are Fred and Amelia Muntz?"

"Never heard of 'em."

"I think you have."

"Look, I got no reason to lie to you."

"Really? I can think of a hundred and twenty-five thousand reasons why you might."

Harry heard voices in the background. It sounded as if the guy were at a service station. Then the connection faded in and out, and Harry figured he must've been using a cell phone.

"You'd better not be holding out on me," the man said. "I know where you live."

"I've told you the truth," Harry said. "What more do you want?"

The man laughed. "Are you kidding? The other hundred and twenty-five thousand!" *Click.*

Sally turned out the light and nestled under the covers. The darkness didn't seem threatening anymore. The picture in her mind of Amelia standing in the sunlight, her arms outstretched, feeling God's presence was one she'd pressed onto the pages of her memory.

Sally was relieved Sam had come looking for her. And as uncomfortable as she was about the future, it had felt good to stop running and finally admit the truth.

Sam had responded with as much compassion as he had disappointment, and it seemed genuine. Most of his recent attempts at connecting with her could have been construed as the actions of a man whose ego had been flattened and who was on the rebound, but this was different. Sam had plowed his way through a Kansas snowstorm to find her because he knew she needed to be found. That was more like the Sam who barged into her life the summer Larry Thompson had jilted her...

Sally had heard a tap on her bedroom window. She looked up and saw her neighbor, Sam Cox, sitting on a tree branch, motioning for her to open the window.

Sally raised the window and stuck her head outside. "What are you doing?"

"Going out on a limb."

"Very funny, Sam. I'm serious."

"So am I. How much longer are you going to pout over Larry Thompson? The slob doesn't deserve you. He's sure not worth crying over."

"It's none of your business," Sally said.

"Then whose business is it? Someone has to break up your pity party. If you hide out in your room, how will you ever meet a guy who'll treat you the way you deserve?"

Sally rolled her eyes. "The good ones are taken."

"What do you mean? *I'm* available." Sam flashed a charming smile. "I've just been waiting for that loser Thompson to show his true colors. What you need is a *real* man."

"Go home, Sam."

"And leave you to pine away by yourself? I don't think so."

"Oh, brother. Do you honestly believe anything *you* say is going to change how I feel?"

"Absolutely."

Sally sighed and shook her head. "You're something else. You've really got a lot of nerve coming here."

"Yeah. I do, don't I?" There was that charming smile again.

Without even wanting to, Sally began to look at Sam with different eyes. They dated off and on throughout the summer, and his friendship helped her to get over Larry and move on.

When school started in the fall, they went their separate ways— Sally to her senior year of high school and Sam to start junior college—but they remained close friends…

Sally turned on her side, thinking how odd it was that thirty-something years later, she and Sam had gone separate ways again, but this time discovering the worst about themselves. And yet, here they were, admitting their failings and counting on that same friendship that had held them together for more than half their lives.

Harry moved from the couch to the recliner to the bed and back to the recliner. He got up and paced in the kitchen, agonizing that somewhere out there Sally Cox and the creep who'd been threatening him had a quarter of a million dollars that should've been his. Until now, he'd had no idea how much money was involved—and almost wished he hadn't found out, since he'd never see a penny of it.

Harry tried to imagine what his mother might've been thinking when she buried it. A quarter of a million? That was some kind of secret! What had she intended it for if she wasn't going to spend it? Couldn't she have given at least *some* of it to him?

Harry sat at the table, his eyes on his mother's old Bible. A lot of good it had done her. She lived poor; she died poor—and stingy. He ran his fingers over the cracked and worn places on the cover. Why had she tried so hard to get him to believe this stuff?

He opened the Bible again and thumbed through the pages edged in faded gold. He noticed a blue envelope stuck in the Psalms. His name was on it. He opened it, pulled out a letter, and began to read:

My dear Harry,

As I write this, I'm eighty-six years old. My mind isn't what it used to be, and there are some things I want to write down. Things you need to know.

The entire time you were growing up, I taught you to be responsible, to value hard work, and to live on what you earn. I didn't want you to have financial problems and turn out to be dishonest like your father and me.

I'm sure you figured out long ago that Arnie was transporting illegal merchandise in those trucks of his. I'm not going to poison your mind with all his dirty little secrets, but he made money hand over fist, blowing it as fast as he raked it in. I was mad, so I started skimming money from the company and giving it to my brother Lou in case Arnie went to jail and I had to raise you alone.

Wanting to have enough became an obsession. And for more than thirty years, I deceived your father and cheated the government. I justified my actions by spending only what I needed and telling myself whatever money was left would secure your future.

I was kidding myself. Giving you a quarter of a million dollars that wasn't rightfully mine actually would be crueler than giving you nothing. The money never made me happy. In fact, from the moment I took the very first hundred-dollar bill, I made my own prison. I didn't want that for you.

I honestly don't know what to do with the money now that Lou's dead. He was the only other person who knew where it is, and I can't dig it up by myself. Besides, I don't have the courage to turn myself in and admit what I did—not while your father is so sick and feeble. The humiliation would kill him.

I've confessed my sin to God and take comfort in the fact that I'm forgiven. But how I wish I had trusted God to provide what I needed instead of stealing and hoarding money to secure a future my conscience never allowed me to enjoy. Though it's taken me far too long to realize it, I know that a relationship with Jesus has always been the only way to find security and happiness.

I'm sorry I can't give you an inheritance. But there is another life after this one, son. And unless you come to that realization, you're going to miss the only inheritance that matters: an eternal one. Read Mathew 6:19–21.

Ask God to reveal His Son to you. He will.

I love you,
Mother

Harry sat staring at his mother's signature. *This* was supposed to make him feel better? She sat on a quarter of a million dollars and never gave him one red cent—because she felt *guilty?*

He slammed his fist on the table, then got up and stood at the window. Some creep was going to get his hands on the entire quarter million, while Harry dined on ketchup sandwiches the rest of his life. Why hadn't she felt guilty about *that?*

40

Sam Cox opened his eyes and stared at a brass footboard and a patchwork quilt and remembered he was staying at Fred and Amelia's. He went to the window and pulled back the curtain. Everything outside was covered under a new layer of snow, and it was still coming down. So much for driving back to Kansas City.

He really wanted to get out of Pheasant River and away from the Muntzes' place. Though he had deliberately avoided alarming Sally, he was as uncomfortable about the mystery caller as she was.

He sat on the side of the bed and got dressed, trying to formulate a Plan B. Sam had slid all over the road driving to Pheasant River from the interstate, and nearly ended up in a ditch. Now after the additional snowfall, he was reluctant to go back on those same highways, especially following behind Sally. It seemed wiser to stay put until the weather cleared and the roads opened up.

Sam ached for what he knew Sally would have to face. The humiliation would be hard enough, but dealing with Leslie's disappointment would be the toughest. He couldn't imagine that Sally wouldn't have to serve some jail time.

He blinked to clear his eyes, then walked out into the hallway and toward the kitchen, hoping to find coffee. At least Sally had decided to turn herself in without being coerced. Sam's only hope was that the law would go easy on her.

Sally sat across from Amelia in the parlor, listening to her read the Psalms. For some reason, the words were soothing again, and she couldn't seem to get enough. She enjoyed watching the glow on Amelia's face as she continued reading Psalm 103.

"Verses eight through twelve are so lovely," Amelia said. "'The LORD is compassionate and gracious, slow to anger, abounding in love.

He will not always accuse, nor will he harbor his anger forever; he does not treat us as our sins deserve or repay us according to our iniquities. For as high as the heavens are above the earth, so great is his love for those who fear him; as far as the east is from the west, so far has he removed our transgressions from us.'"

Amelia looked up and smiled over the top of her glasses, then kept reading. But Sally's mind replayed the words of those verses, savoring the depth of what they would mean to her now.

The burden of guilt Sally had carried seemed lighter today. She believed she was forgiven for stealing the money. She only hoped that Leslie would be as compassionate as God had been.

Amelia finished reading Psalm 103 and closed the Bible. "Thank you for sharing my morning ritual. I start reading the Psalms and almost forget the time. I need to make breakfast."

"Let me help you," Sally said.

"All right, dear. I planned to have blueberry pancakes. The batter is already made. If you can handle the griddle, I'll fry the bacon. How's that sound?"

"Great."

Sally followed Amelia out to the kitchen and saw Sam sitting at the table, his fingers wrapped around a mug.

"Oh, good," Amelia said. "I see you found the coffee."

Sam nodded. "Yes, thank you. Tastes great."

"Did you sleep well, dear?"

"Actually, I did. The room was very comfortable. I appreciate your hospitality."

"Oh, Fred and I love opening up our home." She walked over to the stove and put her iron skillet on the largest burner. "I do hope you'll have some breakfast with us."

"I really didn't come here to impose."

"Nonsense," Amelia said. "Fred and I never feel imposed upon. Our home is the Lord's, and whomever He brings to us, we are glad to receive."

Sam looked at Sally and then at Amelia. "I think He may have brought you a handful this time."

Amelia took the bacon out of the refrigerator and placed it on the counter. "The Lord never gives us more than *He* can handle. I hope you like blueberry pancakes and bacon."

"My favorite. How'd you know?"

Amelia smiled, her eyes twinkling. "Help yourself to more coffee, if you like. Sally and I will have breakfast on the table in just a few minutes. Fred should shuffle in here any second."

Sam looked up at Sally as she heated up the griddle. "I hope you're not set on leaving this morning. The roads can't be good. They were already horrible last night before we got all this new snow."

"I'm anxious to get back to Kansas City and get this over with," Sally said. "But I don't want to end up stranded in a ditch."

Sam got up and looked outside. "I'm afraid that's exactly what might happen if we take off too soon. Amelia, have you heard the weather forecast?"

"Indeed. This storm has stalled unexpectedly, and more snow is expected to fall throughout the day."

"There's a travel advisory," Fred said, walking into the kitchen, a wet newspaper under his arm. "They're predictin' another half a foot before nightfall."

Sam sat back in his chair and sighed. "We can kiss Plan A goodbye."

"You're welcome to stay here as long as you like," Amelia said.

Fred nodded. "Got plenty of room and more vittles than we can eat by ourselves." He winked and patted his middle. "Not gonna find this kind of cookin' any place else."

"Well, I thank you for your offer," Sam said. "If we have to be snowed in, what a great place to be. But the truth is, I *am* concerned about the guy who phoned here. I didn't say anything last night because I didn't want to keep you up worrying. But I'm nervous he could find this place as easily as I did."

"Surely he wouldn't try to come here now," Amelia said, "what with the weather so dreadful and all."

Sam looked at Sally, his eyes peering over his cup. "Probably not. But I think we need to be prepared for the possibility."

Harry woke up shivering and realized he'd fallen asleep on the couch. He grabbed his shotgun off the floor, then got up and put on his coat and walked out to the kitchen. He made a pot of coffee, noting that the coffee can was almost empty.

Harry sat at the table and stared at his mother's Bible, torn between resentment and desperation. He was curious what was so important that she wanted him to read it. He looked again at her letter, then opened the Bible to Matthew 6:19 and saw his name written in the margin with a star next to it. He began to read: *Lay not up for yourselves treasures upon earth, where moth and rust doth corrupt, and where thieves break through and steal: But lay up for yourselves treasures in heaven, where neither moth nor rust doth corrupt, and where thieves do not break through nor steal: For where your treasure is, there will your heart be also.*

Harry read it again. How was he supposed to get jazzed about this when he didn't even believe in heaven?

He noticed his mother had written something else in the margin: John 3:16–18. He thumbed through the Bible until he found John, and then chapter 3. He began reading at verse 16.

For God so loved the world, that he gave his only begotten Son, that whosoever believeth in him should not perish, but have everlasting life.

Harry sighed. Not again. How many times had he heard that one? He continued reading.

For God sent not his Son into the world to condemn the world; but that the world through him might be saved. He that believeth on him is not condemned; but he that believeth not is condemned already, because he hath not believed in the name of the only begotten Son of God.

Harry rubbed the stubble on his chin, then got up and poured himself a cup of coffee. He sat again at the table and reread the verses. What did John mean when he said God's Son didn't come to condemn the world, but to save it? Save it from *what?*

The words touched something deep inside Harry. He hoped there was a heaven, but the whole thing sounded like a fairy tale. He wondered what it would be like to die and find himself somewhere else—somewhere wonderful and free from stress.

He thought again about the song "Amazing Grace" they had sung at his mother's burial. He still couldn't fathom spending ten thousand years anywhere, especially praising God and playing a harp—or whatever a person supposedly did in heaven.

Sally sat on the couch in the parlor with Fred and Amelia and agreed to Fred's suggestion with guarded optimism, feeling uneasy about putting this sweet couple at risk.

"If we're going to stay till the weather clears, it *would* make me feel safer if Sam slept on the couch in the apartment," Sally said.

Amelia looked at Fred, her head bobbing. "I think it's a fine idea."

"Then it's settled," Fred said, his eyes wide and round behind his thick lenses.

"You sure you're not uncomfortable with us staying here?" Sam said. "We can certainly find a motel. Or move down to the Excelsior House."

Fred took Amelia's hand. "The Lord sends us the folks He chooses. There's no cause for you to go movin' out. I haven't got a hankerin' to involve the police the way things are. The Lord knows what He's doin'."

Sally could hardly believe how mellow the Muntzes were. "I appreciate this so much. Sam thinks it'll work in my favor if I turn myself in voluntarily when I get to Kansas City."

"Of course, it will, dear," Amelia said. "We support you completely."

There was a loud crash upstairs.

Sally jumped, her hand over her heart, and felt Amelia take her hand.

Sam sprang to his feet and walked lightly across the wood floor and started up the stairs.

"Sam, don't!" Sally said. "You can't go up there without a weapon."

41

Sam Cox turned the handle on the door to the upstairs apartment and slowly pushed it open. He slipped inside and listened intently for any sound that would alert him as to where the intruder was. All he heard was the hammering of his own heart.

He picked up a heavy vase from the entry hall table and was distracted by Kiwi's meowing and rubbing against his leg. He quickly prodded her out the door and closed it, then paused and listened, but heard nothing. He tiptoed to the living room, wishing he had on his Nikes, and stood in the doorway, his eyes scanning the room. Everything seemed to be intact.

He took a slow, deep breath, then walked softly down the short hallway, cringing each time the floor creaked, poking his head into the kitchen and then the bathroom. He approached the door to the bedroom, and then stood outside, his pulse racing.

Sam went back to the kitchen and set the vase on the countertop. He took a knife out of the drawer, wondering if he was even capable of using it. *Lord, please protect me. I don't want to hurt anybody.*

He moved slowly toward the bedroom door, then poked his head inside and quickly withdrew it. He eased into the bedroom, then stopped, his eyes fixed on a lamp shattered on the floor next to the nightstand. He surveyed the room. Everything else seemed to be in place. He opened the closet door, noting the suitcase with the money was exactly where Sally had put it.

Sam took a moment to gather himself. On his way back to the front door, he checked the lock on the outside entrance and saw it was still in place. He breathed a sigh of relief and headed downstairs.

He walked into the parlor, greeted by three pairs of anxious eyes. Kiwi was in Fred's arms.

"Just a *cat* burglar," Sam said, giving Kiwi a scolding look. "The little scamp broke what looks like a very expensive antique lamp. I'm really sorry. I'll be glad to pay you for it."

"Nonsense," Amelia said. "I've got more accessories than I know what to do with. You should see the attic."

Sally leaned her head on the back of the couch and closed her eyes. "What were you thinking, going up there without something to protect yourself with?"

Sam shrugged. "I didn't have time to worry about it. I didn't want him to get away."

"This is making me a nervous wreck," Sally said. "I can hardly wait to turn the money over to the police."

Harry pulled back the drapes and saw the sand truck go by. He wanted to drive over to the Plaza and walk around but was afraid he might encounter the attacker again. He let the drapes fall back in place and went out to the kitchen.

From the moment I took the very first hundred-dollar bill, I made my own prison. I didn't want that for you.

His mother's words grated on him. He'd never even seen the money, and yet he was very much a prisoner of it.

He sat at the table, pulled the Bible in front of him, and reread Matthew 6:19–21. His eyes stopped on verse 21: *"For where your treasure is, there will your heart be also."*

There was no doubt where his treasure was: in the hands of Sally Cox and some goon who wanted the other half. Harry knew that his getting it had become an obsession, and that's exactly where his heart had been. He'd never thought of it that way before.

He went back to verse 19. *"Lay not up for yourselves treasures upon earth, where moth and rust doth corrupt, and where thieves break through and steal...."*

Harry sighed. He marked the place with a ribbon and closed the Bible. All his striving had gotten him zilch. Thieves had taken every cent.

Sally finished the last bite of a grilled cheese sandwich, uncomfortable with the silence around the table. "Amelia, you even make these better than anyone I know. And the chicken vegetable soup was wonderful."

"It was," Sam said. "What a perfect lunch on a cold, snowy day."

More silence followed, and Sally saw three pairs of eyes sneaking glances at her.

"You don't have to walk on eggshells," she said. "I'm just nervous about going back. I keep wondering what people are going to think. Especially Leslie."

Fred's thick lenses only magnified the kindness in his eyes. "I remember when I got caught embezzlin' all those years ago. I was plenty scared. I knew I'd done wrong, and it was too late to undo it. Goin' to prison was scary enough, but I worried about what people would think. Truth is, it didn't matter what *they* thought. My greatest fear was that Amelia would stop lovin' me."

"How could you think such a thing?" Amelia said.

Fred put his hand on hers. "She was a saint, the way she stood by me, even after I went to prison. The people who matter will stick by you, Sally. Doesn't matter what anyone else thinks."

"How long have you two been married?" Sam asked.

"Nearly seventy years."

Sam shook his head. "You're a real inspiration. Not many marriages would've survived all that."

"Amelia and me didn't go into marriage with any option other than stayin' together, for better or worse," Fred said. "Maybe that's why it worked out."

Sally rose to her feet. "Let me help you get the kitchen cleaned up. Then I think I'll take a nap."

"Oh, dear, you go right ahead," Amelia said. "Fred and I can load the dishwasher."

Sally started to stack the plates. "You can't keep waiting on us hand and foot. We'll wear out our welcome."

"Nonsense. We love doing it. Now you go rest."

"We gonna stick with the plan?" Fred said, his eyebrows raised.

"Absolutely," Sam said. "I'll go upstairs and read while she sacks out. Promise you'll call me if someone you don't know comes to the door?"

Fred nodded. "I'll do it."

Sam followed Sally through the parlor and up the stairs. Kiwi met them at the door, and Sam scooped the cat into his arms. "You've been a naughty girl, breaking Amelia's lamp like that. I thought you were past the climbing-on-everything stage."

"I think it's the newness of a different place," Sally said. "If we were here long enough, she'd quit. Listen, all this tension has been exhausting. I'm going to go crash—"

Sam put his finger to his lips. He pointed to the outside door. The lock was in place, but the knob was moving.

"Look through the peephole," Sally whispered.

Sam looked outside and saw a man in black ski jacket and a black ski mask. Sam turned around, took Sally's arm, and led her to the front door. "Babe, go downstairs and call the cops."

"Who is it?"

"Just go! Hurry!"

Sam went back to the outside door and looked through the peephole. *Lord, be with me.* He turned the bolt lock and yanked the door open.

"Oh, uh...is the lady of the house in?" the man said.

"You can stop the game playing, Jeffrey!" Sam grabbed his arm, pulled him inside, and jerked the ski mask off his face. "What're you doing here?"

"Take it easy, man," Jeffrey Horton said.

"Why were you trying to break into Sally's apartment?"

"Break in? Are you nuts? I just came to talk to her about—"

"Ever hear of knocking? Or going to the front door instead of sneaking up the outside stairs?"

Jeffrey rolled his eyes. "I knew she was upstairs because I heard the landlady go upstairs to get her when I called. Sally wouldn't take my calls, so I decided to talk to her in person."

"Wearing a ski mask?"

"Hey, man, it's freezing out there."

"Listen, you little weasel, the only way you could've known Sally was here was if you broke into my apartment and stole the number." Sam tightened his grip on Jeffrey, hoping he was strong enough to keep a man thirty years his junior pinned to the wall.

"Look," Jeffrey said, "just let me talk to her and I'll leave. What's the big deal?"

"I think we both know the answer to that," Sam said. "You and Sally can tell your stories to the police."

Jeffrey's eyes grew wide. "W—why involve the cops? All I wanted to do was talk to her."

"Yeah, right. The way you *talked* to Karen Morgan?"

Sally sat next to Sam on the couch in the parlor, her hands shaking but her resolve intact. She told the police officer about Elsie Rigsby, about digging up the money and splitting it with Karen Morgan, about Sally's decision to turn the money over to the police, and how she ended up at Fred and Amelia's. She also told them her suspicions about Jeffrey Horton.

"This is quite a story," the officer said.

"I'll be telling the Kansas City Police the exact same thing," Sally said. "Every word is the truth."

"Including the part about returning to Kansas City to turn this money over to the police?"

"Yes, sir," Sally said. "I've never had any peace about what I did. I'm anxious to turn over the money. I still have all of it…oh, except—"

"No, it's all there," Sam said. "The entire one hundred and twenty-five thousand is in that suitcase."

Sally looked up at Sam and felt her heart soften a little more.

"Wendell," Amelia said to the officer, "she's told you exactly what she told Fred and me. Why, we even prayed about it."

The officer looked at Sally. "Mrs. Cox, we would need an arrest warrant to hold you. But we don't have enough to hold Mr. Horton either. If you choose to stay voluntarily, we can keep you in protective custody until Kansas City comes to get you."

"What do you mean you can't hold him?" Sam said. "That was the whole point in our calling."

The officer nodded. "I understand. But having his hand on the doorknob wasn't a crime. All you've given us are your assumptions as to the murder, no actual facts. We can hold him for a couple hours and check to see if Kansas City is looking for him in connection with Karen Morgan's murder. If not, we have to let him go."

Sam sighed and leaned back on the couch. "At least Sally would be safe in protective custody. What do you think, babe?"

"It's probably best," Sally heard herself say.

"Now, Wendell, this here's a fine lady," Fred said. "I'd consider it a personal favor if you'd go easy on her."

The officer smiled. "Relax, Mr. Muntz. It's not like we've never had a prisoner before."

"Oh, I forgot, there was that fella back in '82." Fred winked. "I know you'll treat her right."

The officer stood up and looked at Sally. "Guess we need to get you down to the station. I don't have enough manpower to keep an eye on you here—not with all the calls we're getting with this bad weather. But we'll get somebody to look after you till Kansas City comes to get you."

"Officer, could you give us a minute?" Sam said.

"Sure. No problem."

Sally felt Sam take her hand and lead her over to the corner of the room. She stood facing him, and finally got the courage to look up at him, wondering if she could get through the next few moments.

He took his thumbs and wiped her tears, and then pulled her close and held her. "The Lord will get us through this, babe."

"It hurts so much," Sally said. "I'm so ashamed."

"Do you want me to tell Leslie? It'll take the pressure off when you finally talk to her."

Sally nodded.

"I'll be there when you get to Kansas City," Sam said. "I'll find a way to post bail, no matter how much it is."

She nestled for a moment in Sam's arms, wishing she could turn back the clock thirty years. *Lord, help me get through this.*

Sam tightened his embrace and put his lips to her ear. "I'll never stop loving you, no matter what happens."

42

Sam Cox waited outside the Pheasant River police station, antici-
pating Jeffrey Horton's release, his mind thinking back on the
tearful good-bye he'd had with Sally. He hadn't even realized the
depth of his affection until that very moment. He wondered if Sally
was turned off because he'd said he loved her. He had no right to expect
her to be receptive, but he wasn't sorry he'd said it.

Sam realized the snow had stopped falling, and the opaque gray
covering overhead was starting to show glimpses of blue sky. He took
mental inventory of everything he had packed up, feeling sure he
hadn't left anything of his or Sally's at the Muntzes.

He glanced in the rearview mirror at Kiwi in the cage in the backseat and hoped his landlord wouldn't give him a hard time about
keeping her at the apartment.

The door to the police station opened. Jeffrey Horton came out
and walked over to a white Ford Explorer and got in. Even if the police
didn't have enough to hold Jeffrey, Sam wasn't letting him out of his
sight.

Sam watched to see which way the Explorer went after stopping at
the four-way stop, then followed. It appeared that he was heading back
on 14 North to Salina. Jeffrey had the advantage in a four-wheel drive,
but Sam was confident his chains would allow his Camaro to keep up.

Sam soon was directly behind the white Explorer. Did Jeffrey recognize him? He wasn't sure until the young man made an obscene
gesture. Okay, he *did* know Sam was following him. No law prohib-
ited Sam from doing that. He wasn't about to let the guy get away with
keeping half the money—or with Karen's murder.

Sally sat staring at nothing in the chief jailer's office, vaguely aware of
the bank of monitors showing empty cells, except for one housing an

intoxicated man who kept yelling vulgarities and banging on the bars. Protective custody was probably a lot easier than what awaited her in Kansas City.

She still didn't know what she was going to say to Leslie—or Wanda. She could only imagine the gossip that would follow when her coworkers found out she was in jail for stealing Elsie Rigsby's money. It would be impossible to keep it out of the newspapers.

"Mrs. Cox, would you like a cup of coffee?" the officer asked.

"Yes, thank you. Cream, if you have it."

It had been particularly difficult watching Jeffrey Horton be released. It was hard for Sally to imagine that he was capable of murdering Karen, yet his conversation with her after the fact had seemed so weird.

But you do realize the cops don't release everything they know to the media? They always hold back something that will identify the real killer and weed out the attention seekers.

What had Jeffrey been implying? He had said something about suspecting the neighbor, Michael Rich. She wondered if the police had pursued that angle or had gotten anywhere toward solving the case.

She shuddered to think what might have happened if Sam hadn't been at the Muntzes' when Jeffrey arrived.

"Here you go, Mrs. Cox."

Sally took the Styrofoam cup and wrapped her fingers around the warmth. "Thank you."

The rich coffee aroma reminded her of Sam. Part of her was disgusted for trusting him at all. But how could she not? The man had risked his own safety, driving across miles and miles of icy roads to find her. Sam had nothing to gain by sticking by her. What did she have to offer him besides the stigma of being a convicted felon?

I'll never stop loving you, no matter what happens.

Sally blinked the stinging from her eyes and wondered which was more disconcerting: that Sam loved her—or that she still loved him.

Sam followed the Explorer's red taillights all the way to Salina. The roads weren't as bad as he had expected.

He was tired, but he hoped Jeffrey planned to drive straight through to Kansas City so Sam wouldn't have to sit in some motel parking lot, struggling to stay awake to make sure Jeffrey didn't slip away in the night. Not that Sam knew what he would do once they got to Kansas City. He couldn't follow Jeffrey around forever. But he wanted the guy to know he was being watched.

The Explorer pulled into a Chevron station, and Sam pulled up to the pump next to it and turned off the motor.

Jeffrey got out, his face red and contorted, and charged toward Sam. "Just where do you get off following me?"

"I'm going to Kansas City, Jeffrey. We're headed the same direction."

"This is intimidation."

"Call it what you want," Sam said. "It's a free country. I'm just driving home."

"You have no right to stalk me."

Sam laughed. "Look who's talking! How does it feel to have someone pursuing *you?*"

"Back off, bozo."

"What's the matter? Afraid I might find out where you're hiding the hundred and twenty-five thousand bucks that doesn't belong to you?"

Jeffrey lunged at Sam, and Sam grabbed him and shoved him against the car. "You're not going to get away with the break-ins, taking the money, or killing Karen Morgan. I'm going to be your worst nightmare until you get caught. Now, I suggest you gas your car and head on down the highway before someone inside calls the cops. Something tells me you don't need any more bad press."

Jeffrey yanked his arm free and walked back to the Explorer.

Sam swiped his credit card and topped the tank on his car, wondering how long he could keep intimidating Jeffrey before it got dangerous. He didn't even know whether or not the kid had a gun.

Lord, please help me use good sense. I don't want to get hurt. And I don't want to hurt him. I just want justice.

Harry Rigsby looked outside as darkness was about to claim the day. He let the curtain fall back and decided he couldn't stand the isolation—attacker or no attacker.

He decided to venture out and walk around the Plaza. It should be busy on a Friday night. Just being around people might help lift his mood.

He put on his scarf and coat and pulled a stocking cap over his ears. He went out to the garage and got a shovel, then opened the garage door and began to clear the driveway. The exercise felt good, and within minutes, he didn't feel cold.

Harry finished shoveling the driveway, then backed his car out of the garage and headed toward the Plaza. The roads weren't as slick as he had anticipated. There wasn't much traffic. He figured anybody with good sense had probably stayed home.

He spotted Nick's All-Night Diner and decided to splurge and enjoy a cup of coffee. Harry pulled in the parking lot, glad to see a dozen other cars. He walked in the front door and found a place at the counter.

"What can I get for you?" the waitress said.

"Coffee. Black."

"How about some homemade cherry cobbler?"

Harry agonized for a moment. "Nah, coffee's fine."

He sat and enjoyed the hum of the diner. Six other people sat at the counter, and the jukebox was playing some country western tune. He liked the cozy atmosphere and wondered why he'd never stopped in before.

The waitress put a mug of coffee on the counter—and a bowl of cherry cobbler à la mode. "Compliments of the man in the green flannel shirt," she said, nodding toward a booth along the windows.

Harry turned around, and a man about his age waved. "This is cobbler weather," the man said. "Everybody should try some."

Harry shrugged. "Okay, thanks."

"You're welcome to join me."

"Don't mind if I do." Harry picked up his coffee and the cherry cobbler and sat in the booth facing the man. "My name's Harry. And just for the record, I'm *straight*."

The man smiled and held out his hand. "I'm Albert. I'm just looking for some conversation."

"In that case, thanks." Harry shook his hand, then took a bite of cobbler.

"Amazing, isn't it?" Albert said. "They make it fresh every day."

Harry nodded. "Yeah, it's great. You a Chiefs fan?"

"Sure. Who isn't?"

"Too bad they missed their crack at the Super Bowl," Harry said. "I nearly croaked when Bentley missed that field goal. Talk about a heartbreaker."

Albert lifted his eyebrows. "I can still see that ball veering to the left of the upright."

"Kinda took the fun outta watchin' the Super Bowl, knowin' we shoulda been there. Hope the boys come back strong next season."

"I'll bet they will." Albert took a sip of coffee. "So, what do you do, Harry?"

"I just retired this past year. I gotta tell you, it's not all it's cracked up to be."

"Too much time on your hands?"

"And not enough cash flow. Truthfully, just havin' a cup of coffee out like this is a real splurge for me. I've had to tighten my belt. Sometimes the groceries don't last till my Social Security check gets deposited. Kinda depressing."

Albert seemed to be studying him.

"Did I say somethin' wrong?"

"No, not at all," Albert said. "I was just wondering if you might be interested in helping us at the soup kitchen. It's just a few hours out of your day, but you eat free."

"What soup kitchen?"

"At the Christian Center on Booth Street. Ever heard of it?"

"Nah, I don't pay much attention to religious stuff."

Albert smiled. "This isn't religious. It's just a group of people cooking nightly dinners for the homeless or anyone who's going through hard times. Everyone who works eats free, too. And it's for a good cause."

"Who pays for the food?" Harry asked.

"Different donors each week. It's a real community project."

"I don't know much about cookin'," Harry said.

Albert laughed. "Then you'll feel right at home. The recipes are easy enough that you can't mess up. Plus, it's a group effort. There's about two dozen volunteers every night. At least half are guys. It's fun."

"They're not gonna thump me over the head with the Bible and try to get me saved, are they?"

Albert's eyes twinkled. "I promise there won't be any Bible thumping."

"Pretty good food?" Harry said.

"Actually, it's quite tasty. But the best part is feeling like you're contributing something to help others. It's a real rush." Albert handed Harry his card. "Think about it. If you're interested, come to the

Christian Center tomorrow afternoon at two. I'll show you around. There's no pressure."

Harry stared at the card and wondered what it would be like to eat home-cooked meals again. And have real conversation.

"Why are you singling me out?" Harry said. "There's a lot of folks in this diner."

Albert nodded. "Yeah, there are."

"So?"

"I don't know if I can explain it. Just had a feeling you'd enjoy being a part of the group."

"I suppose you're gonna tell me *God* gave you the feelin'?"

Albert looked down, and then into Harry's eyes. "Would it really be so horrible that God was thinking of you and prodded me to ask you if you wanted to help at the soup kitchen?"

Harry rubbed his nose. "I wouldn't say horrible. More like a miracle."

Sam followed behind the white Explorer, surprised at the number of cars on the interstate. The cold temperatures had made the roadways slick again, and he was glad Jeffrey wasn't driving too fast.

He wondered where Sally was being held and how long she'd have to wait for the Kansas City police to pick her up. He knew he couldn't put off telling Leslie much longer. But since she hadn't called, he thought he'd wait as long as he could, hoping to have Sally's bail posted by the time he broke the news.

Sam couldn't shake the fact that if he hadn't divorced Sally, she would never have gotten in this mess. If only he could turn back the clock and undo the affair.

Up ahead, he saw the white Explorer start to fishtail, then spin out of control into the right lane. A blue pickup swerved to avoid a collision, then slid off the road and rolled over several times before landing in a snowy field.

Jeffrey regained control of the Explorer and kept on going.

Sam put on his flashers, then pumped his brakes until he could safely pull onto the shoulder.

He grabbed his cell phone to call 911, wondering if Jeffrey realized what had happened, or if it even fazed him that he might have just killed someone.

43

S am Cox took a sip of hot coffee, his eyes on the Medical Center chopper as it whirred upward, its eerie reverberations echoing across the frozen Kansas prairie. The man in the blue pickup had a spinal cord injury and was being airlifted to Topeka. The paramedics seemed concerned that he might have neurological damage.

Sam let his fingers thaw around the warm Styrofoam cup. He wasn't in a big hurry to get back on the interstate after what he had witnessed. As long as he'd lost sight of Jeffrey, he might as well get a motel and get some rest, finish the trip in the morning when the visibility was better.

He'd given a witness statement to the Highway Patrol. As much as he would have liked to finger Jeffrey Horton for leaving the scene of an accident, he wasn't sure the kid had even realized the blue truck was in the other lane. He reported what he saw to police, but his conscience wouldn't let him make the accusation.

Sam didn't know what he would have done had he actually followed Jeffrey home. Another confrontation might have pushed Jeffrey to violence, which wasn't something Sam was prepared to deal with. He just didn't want the guy to skip town before the Kansas City police had time to consider Sally's allegations.

Sam watched the chopper turn east toward Topeka and wondered if the victim realized how serious his injuries were. Sam had been the first one on the scene, and the guy kept saying he couldn't feel his legs. *Lord, be with him and the doctors. Help them restore his ability to walk.*

"Okay, we're done here," a highway patrolman said. "Mr. Cox, we appreciate you staying with the victim and getting the emergency calls in. You probably saved the guy's life."

"I hope he makes it," Sam said. "You have my address and phone number if you have any more questions. You might want to question

Jeffrey Horton, too. I believe that license number I gave you may be registered to someone else."

"Yeah, thanks. We'll check it out. Drive carefully."

"I will. Thanks for the coffee." Sam got back in the Camaro, his eyelids heavy, and started the car. He pulled onto the interstate, then exited at the next off-ramp. He spotted the Sunflower Motor Inn and pulled across the street and up to the front door.

He got out and walked toward the office and was shocked to see Jeffrey Horton in the lobby with a cup of coffee.

Sam flung open the door and glared at Jeffrey. "Trying to hide? You nearly killed that guy in the blue truck. They just airlifted him to Topeka."

"What're you talking about?" Jeffrey blushed and looked over at the motel manager.

"When you lost control of the Explorer, you ran a guy off the road."

"Yeah, right," Jeffrey said, rolling his eyes.

"You think I'm kidding?" Sam said. "Wait till the cops come knocking on your door."

"Listen, man, I didn't see any truck. You think I would've kept going?"

Sam searched Jeffrey's eyes. "I don't know. Would you?"

"I don't have to put up with your harassment. Stay out of my way, Sam. I'm warning you."

The manager coughed nervously. "Uh, are you gentlemen working out your problem, or do I need to call the sheriff?"

"Just a little disagreement," Jeffrey said. "I'd appreciate it if you'd put this man as far away from my room as possible."

Harry went to the pantry, looking for a midnight snack. The only thing he had was a few stale saltines. He wished he had the sardines to go with it.

He sat at the kitchen table and nibbled on the crackers. He took the business card Albert had given him out of his pocket and read it again.

Albert M. Smith, Director
Christian Center Hunger Outreach

1602 Booth Street, Kansas City, Missouri
Dinner served seven days a week at 5:00 PM
All are welcome. Come hungry. Leave filled.

Being around people had a lot of appeal right now. Not to mention a home-cooked meal. Maybe he'd take Albert up on his offer and show up tomorrow afternoon. Harry figured he could wing the cooking part, but he wondered if he'd feel awkward trying to reach out to someone less fortunate. He'd never done it before. But how hard could it be to fill a plate with food and hand it to someone?

For the first time in weeks, he was actually looking forward to something. He hoped Albert and the people at the Christian Center didn't turn out to be fanatics. All he wanted was someone to talk to and a good meal. None of that Jesus stuff thrown at him.

Sally sat in a chair in the jailer's office, her coat draped over her, and listened to a drippy faucet in the restroom across the hall.

She missed Amelia and Fred and wondered if she would ever see them again. What might have happened to her had she been holed up in some motel instead of the Muntzes' wonderful old house?

She still felt betrayed and skeptical of Sam's intentions. Yet why else would he risk the slick roads to find her unless he cared? But did she even want him to care?

She wondered if Sam had followed Jeffrey back to Kansas City as he said he would. She knew how protective he could be and hoped he wasn't doing anything foolhardy.

Sally wondered what would happen to her when the Kansas City police came to get her. Would she get a court-appointed lawyer? Would she be charged with stealing the money? Would she be able to afford bail?

Lord, please be with me through this. And help me know what to say to Leslie.

Sally wondered if Leslie would remember the incident with Jessica Kappler when the girls were fourteen...

"What's going to happen to Jessica?" Leslie had said.

Sally sat on the side of the bed and stroked Leslie's hair. "I imagine she'll be placed in juvenile detention. She's been warned about stealing numerous times before."

"She gave all the stuff back," Leslie said. "And she's sorry. Doesn't that mean anything?"

"Of course, it does. But she's done this over and over again, to the tune of thousands of dollars. Stealing is against the law. There are consequences."

Leslie sighed. "I guess when she gets out, you won't let me hang out with her anymore."

"Probably not. No one trusts a thief..."

Sally pulled her coat up around her neck, her eyes brimming with tears. She could handle losing just about anyone's respect—except Leslie's.

44

Sam Cox awoke to sunlight peeking through a crack in the thick drapes in his motel room. And Kiwi's meowing. He glanced at the clock. It was almost nine. He hadn't intended to sleep that late!

He got up and opened the bathroom door and picked up Kiwi and poured on the affection for a minute, then put her in the cage.

Sam quickly showered, shaved, and packed up the few things he had brought in and carried them out to the car. He stopped in the breakfast room off the lobby and gathered some food items and brought them back to the room. He sat at the table, enjoying his coffee, and dunking the doughnuts.

Kiwi stared at him as if she were deprived.

"Why are you giving me that look, Ms. Finicky? You don't like doughnuts."

Sam flipped on the news, hoping to find out more about last night's accident, but never saw anything. He finished the coffee and doughnuts, grabbed Kiwi's cage, and headed for the car, hoping no one was watching. He drove around to the office and dropped off the key, noting that Jeffrey's Explorer was gone.

He pulled out of the motel parking lot, got on the on-ramp to the interstate, and drove east toward Kansas City, wondering when Sally would get there and if he should be thinking about getting her an attorney.

His cell phone rang.

"Hello."

"Daddy, it's me," Leslie Saunders said. "Have you heard from Mom? I know she's taking a few days off, but I haven't heard from her, and I'm worried."

Sam took a slow, deep breath. "Well, honey, some things have happened since we talked last. I think it's time I filled you in."

Harry arrived at the Christian Center on Booth Street a few minutes before two. He drove slowly around the building and saw a few cars parked in the back lot and a huge yellow and black banner on the back of the building:

FREE DINNERS NIGHTLY.

He pulled into a parking space and saw Albert standing outside the back door, waving.

Harry got out and walked toward the building, Albert meeting him halfway, a big smile on his face.

"Glad you decided to come," Albert said, shaking Harry's hand.

"Yeah, I thought I'd give it a try."

"Friday's chicken and dumplings night. You ready to go to work?"

"Yeah, sure. Why not?" He followed Albert inside, where at least a dozen other people were already working.

"Everybody, this is Harry. He's volunteered to help. Show him the ropes."

"Nice to meet you, Harry," said a scruffy red-haired man with tattoos on his arms. "I'm Shorty. Come with me, and I'll introduce you to everyone."

Harry went from person to person, shaking hands, but felt so awkward he forgot to remember their names. The only one he remembered was Shorty's.

Shorty led him over to the counter where some volunteers were rolling out dough the way his mother had when she used to make piecrusts.

"Ever make dumplin's before?" Shorty asked.

"Nah. I'm not much of a cook. Albert said it didn't matter."

"It don't. You'll learn as you go. Come on over here, we'll put you to work."

Sally sat at a square oak table in the Kansas City Police Station. She glanced up at the black-and-white clock and saw that it was already four o'clock. She had answered the same questions over and over again, and wondered why they kept asking them.

"Are you sure you don't want an attorney, Mrs. Cox?" Investigator Sloan said.

"I don't think so," Sally said. "What I'm telling you is the entire truth. I don't have anything to hide."

Sloan leaned forward, his arms on the table. "Tell me again why you decided to keep the money."

Sally sighed. "Elsie had asked us to give the money to the poor. Karen said that with my financial situation, I could be considered poor and should keep the money—that Elsie would be glad to know she had helped me."

"And you agreed with her?"

"I talked myself into agreeing with her," Sally said. "But deep down, I never felt right about it."

"And you didn't spend it?"

"I borrowed three hundred dollars until my next paycheck, but my ex-husband already put it back for me. The entire amount is there."

Sloan glanced at his watch. "When did your ex-husband find out about the money?"

"Not until he arrived in Pheasant River on Wednesday night. I told him I wanted to turn myself in. He was going to help me do that. We were waiting for the weather to clear."

"What makes you think Jeffrey Horton killed Karen Morgan?"

Sally stared at her hands. "He had easy access to Elsie and to Karen. And the conversation I had with him the day Karen was found strangled gave me the creeps."

"Remind me," Sloan said.

Sally again went over the conversation she'd had with Jeffrey the previous Friday night. "I think the red flag went up when Jeffrey said the police don't release everything they know to the media, that they always hold back something that will identify the real killer and weed out the attention seekers."

"Why did that hit a wrong note?"

Sally shrugged. "I don't know. Something in his tone. It was almost as though he was admitting something. Plus, why would he drive all the way to Pheasant River to find me? The only way he could've known I was there is if he broke into Sam's apartment and got the phone number. The only reason I can think of why he'd want to get to me that badly is he wanted the other half of the money."

"Which you think he killed Karen for?"

Sally nodded. "Exactly."

Sloan excused himself and left the room. Sally wondered why he didn't just charge her with stealing the money and get it over with. She would gladly have signed anything at this point.

Sloan came back in the room and laid some papers in front of her. "I would like you to submit a written statement, put what happened into your own words."

"You want me to write it longhand?" Sally asked.

"Yes. Can you do that?"

"Yes, sir. Are you going to charge me with stealing the money?"

"Write out your statement, and we'll talk some more."

Harry carried to one of the stoves a tray of dough that had been cut into small circles with the top of a juice glass. He watched as one of the ladies picked up pieces of the dough and dropped them into the thick, hot chicken broth, while the other lady stirred the pot with a huge slotted spoon. The aroma made his mouth water. He tried to remember the last time he'd had chicken and dumplings.

"Mmm, this is going to be better than Cracker Barrel's," an elderly woman said. "Have the green beans come to a boil yet?"

"Yeah, they're simmerin'," Harry said. "When do we put in the rolls?"

"Now," Shorty said. "We've got room for twelve trays in the oven."

"What about the banana pudding?" Albert said.

Harry nodded. "We already did that. It's in the refrigerator."

Albert looked at his watch and smiled. "It's four-thirty. We're right on schedule. I hope you're enjoying this, Harry."

"Yeah, I am. More than I thought."

Albert put his hand on Harry's shoulder. "The best part is yet to come."

"The eatin'?"

"No, the serving."

Harry watched the volunteers bustle around the kitchen like a finely tuned machine. "How long *you* been doin' this?" Harry asked Albert.

"Ten years. It never gets old."

"How do you find time to do this and hold a job?" Harry said.

Albert smiled. "We always make time for what's important to us."

"Yeah, I suppose. What do you do for a livin'?"

"Oh, a little of this, a little of that."

"Yeah, listen to Mr. Modest over there," Shorty said. "Albert's got money comin' out his ears. He keeps lookin' for ways to give it away."

"I've been blessed with a lot," Albert said. "And I believe the more God gives you, the more He expects you to do with it."

"You really believe God gave it to you?" Harry said.

Albert nodded. "But not just for my own pleasure. There are so many worthy causes that need funding."

"You believe in that 10 percent stuff the Bible talks about?"

"Sure, I believe in tithing. But I don't think we have to stop there. Why keep more than we need?"

Harry mused. "Don't you have a big house and new car and stuff like that?"

"Not any more. I tried that route, but it never made me happy. I had it all—big mansion on Ward Parkway, a new Mercedes, a Lexus, and a Jaguar. A private yacht. Winter homes in Mexico and the Caribbean. Just don't care about it any more."

"Why not?" Harry said. "Nothin' wrong with enjoyin' what you earn."

"I know. But being involved in the street dinners is the biggest rush I've ever experienced. And it keeps happening night after night—ten years now."

Harry scratched his chin. "You got a family?"

"Yes, I do. A wife, Lillian, and two grown sons."

"What do they think about you cuttin' back?"

Albert smiled. "At first, they resented it. But after they started to get involved in ministry and realized what a blessing it is to give, they got right on board. My boys are married now, but they still get involved in all sorts of community projects."

"Ever miss what you had?" Harry said. "I can't imagine givin' up all that stuff."

"You know, I don't." Albert looked into Harry's eyes. "The minute I stopped clinging to my fortune and let the Lord guide me on how to use it, I've had peace. It's been a relief."

"Hey, I need iced tea poured into pitchers," someone said.

"I'll do it," Harry said. "Show me where it is."

Sam paced in the waiting area at the Kansas City Police Station. He couldn't shake the disappointment he'd heard in Leslie's voice when he told her what had happened. He hoped she would get over the shock before she talked to her mother.

A female officer approached Sam. "Mr. Cox? Investigator Sloan is finished questioning your wife. She's asking for you. Come this way."

Sam followed the woman to the interrogation room, where he saw Sally sitting at a big square table, across from Investigator Sloan.

"Come in and have a seat, Mr. Cox," Sloan said. "Let me tell you what we're willing to do."

Sam sat at the table, his eyes locking onto Sally's. She looked exhausted.

"Mrs. Cox has provided us with a written statement of what happened. I'm going to create a case file, give it a department case number, and then present it to the district attorney's office. It will start out as a felony theft case. But since Mrs. Cox has been completely forthcoming, we think the district attorney will let her plead to a misdemeanor charge. Unfortunately, since it's already five thirty on a Friday night, we can't get anything done until Monday or Tuesday."

"Will I have to stay in jail over the weekend?" Sally said.

"No, we don't plan to arrest you now. We need you to come to a hearing Tuesday at three o'clock."

"I'm free to go?"

"Yes, ma'am. For now."

"You don't want me to plead guilty?"

Sloan looked into Sally's eyes. "You gave us a written statement. We believe your story. Because you chose to turn yourself and the money in, we'd like to bypass a felony charge. But we need some time to work things out on the misdemeanor plea."

"Does she need an attorney?" Sam said.

"She can have one if she'd like, but there's no sense in paying an attorney when we have everything worked out already. Hopefully, we can get this case heard quickly and let her off with a misdemeanor. If we can avoid charging her with a felony, she won't lose her CNA license." Sloan looked at Sally. "We're offering you a gift, Mrs. Cox."

"Why?" she said.

The investigator folded his hands. "We deal with scum every day—people who need to be behind bars. You made a bad call. But you came forward on your own. Given your reputation and the fact that we don't believe you pose a threat to society, we're willing to ask the judge for the minimum."

"At the hearing on Tuesday?" Sally said.

Sloan nodded. "It's up to the judge. But I think he'll work with us."

"I can take her home?" Sam said.

"Yes, sir. She's free to go."

Sam pushed back his chair and rose to his feet. "What about Jeffrey Horton and Karen Morgan's murder investigation?"

"Oh, that's not over by a long shot," Sloan said. "I'm not free to comment, but we're working on some new leads."

45

Sally Cox felt Sam take her by the hand and lead her out of the Kansas City Police Station. The frigid air felt good on her face. She stood for a moment, her hair tossed about in the nippy breeze, trying to realize that she was free.

"You okay?" Sam said. "You look pale."

"I think I'm shocked. I wasn't expecting to go home. I don't even have a car. Mine is in Pheasant River."

"You can't go home anyway," Sam said. "The place is trashed. You can stay with me until we figure out what to do. I'm not going to rest easy until Jeffrey Horton is locked up."

"Me either."

"You want to go to Starbucks?" Sam said. "We could have a sandwich, talk things over."

"Sounds good. Did you ever talk to Leslie?"

Sam opened the door, and Sally slid into the passenger seat. "She called this morning," he said.

Sam shut the door and walked around to the driver's side. He got in and backed out of the parking space.

"And?" Sally said.

"She's pretty upset, babe."

"I knew she would be. Who could blame her? Who wants to find out her mother's a thief?"

"She just needs time to assimilate it, that's all."

"Sam, did you take off work again today?"

"Yeah. I've got plenty of vacation time, don't worry."

Sally blinked to clear her eyes. "You don't have to do this."

"Yes, I do."

"Why?"

"Because I care about you. I'm not going to just leave you hanging. We'll see this through together."

Sally squeezed his hand. "Thanks. I don't deserve it."

They passed by a cemetery, and Sally thought of Karen Morgan. Her death still didn't seem real. Sally regretted that she hadn't gone to Karen's funeral and wondered how many people had. Even as weird as Jeffrey was acting, it was hard for Sally to imagine that he was capable of strangling Karen.

She thought back on the night she and Karen had dug up the money and wondered where she had gotten the nerve to go along with it. Even at the cemetery, it had seemed as though the McClendons were watching them, hissing with disapproval.

It had felt good giving the money to the police. And no matter what consequences she might still have to face, at least her conscience was clear.

Harry Rigsby put a ladleful of chicken and dumplings in a bowl and put the bowl on the tray of an elderly man. "There you go, sir."

"Thank ya, kindly," the man said. "Mighty good eatin'."

Harry hadn't eaten anything yet and was surprised he didn't feel hungrier. He had been so busy helping with the street dinner that he had forgotten about himself.

"See what I mean?" Albert said.

"About what?"

"Serving being the best part."

"Uh, yeah," Harry said. "Kinda makes you forget your own troubles, eh?"

Albert smiled. "When everyone in line has been served, help yourself to whatever you want and find someone to sit with."

"Yeah, okay." Harry dished chicken and dumplings into another bowl and set it on the tray of a young boy with a red stocking cap. "Here you go."

"Thank you, mister."

Harry served the kid's mother and noticed the line was continuing to build. He wondered where all these folks were living. Most of them weren't dressed warm enough for this weather.

Harry kept serving until the line ended, then filled a tray for himself and sat next to the young boy with the red stocking cap. "Hi, I'm Harry."

"I'm Josh."

"How old are you, Josh?"

"Eleven. How old are you?"

Harry smiled without meaning to. "Sixty-five. Guess I got a few years on you."

"Mmm, this is good," Josh said, shoveling a dumpling into his mouth. "Did you cook it?"

"I helped."

The boy looked up at him, his blue eyes grateful. "Since my dad died, we always have dinner here. I don't remember seeing you before."

"This is my first time. How long since your dad died?"

"Last June. Hit-and-run driver. Mom works when she can, but it's hard to make enough. I do odd jobs to help out. But it's not easy getting a job when you're eleven."

"What do you do?"

"Oh, anything you want," Josh said. "I shovel snow. Mow and trim. Rake leaves. Clean out gutters. I can help clean up attics and garages and closets. Wash cars. I'm a hard worker."

"How much do you charge?"

"Anything anyone wants to pay me."

"Well, I'll keep that in mind. What's your last name?"

"Harper. Joshua Harper. But you can call me Josh."

Harry savored the chicken and dumplings, aware that Josh's plate was already empty.

"You want some more?" Harry said.

Josh shook his head. "No, I'm fine."

"A growin' boy like you could use a second helpin'."

"Really, it's okay. I don't want to eat more than my share."

Harry patted the boy's arm. He got up and put another scoop of chicken and dumplings in a bowl and brought it back to Josh. "There's plenty. Growin' boys need more than everybody else."

Josh looked around as if he were waiting for someone to object. "Thanks. I'm still a little hungry."

Sally sat next to the window at Starbucks, watching the icy streets glisten under the streetlights.

"Here you go," Sam said. "A large coffee with extra cream. And a ham and cheese on rye."

"Thanks," Sally said. "I'm starved." She unwrapped the sandwich and put a napkin on her lap.

"Would you mind if I said a blessing?" Sam said. "We have so much to be grateful for."

"Okay."

"Lord, we are so thankful that Sally is out of jail and that You got us both back to Kansas City safely. Please protect us from anyone who could harm us. I ask that You be with the police as they work to plead Sally down to a misdemeanor. Lord, it's almost too good to be true that she could avoid jail time after all that's happened. Please give us wisdom on how to proceed. We ask You to bless this food and let it nourish our bodies. In Jesus' name. Amen."

"Amen," Sally said. "We haven't prayed together in a long time."

"We haven't been right with God in a long time."

Sally raised her eyebrows. "Good point." She took a bite of the ham and cheese sandwich and chased it with a swallow of coffee. "Are you going to tell me about your conversation with Leslie? Or was it too awful?"

"She's having a hard time understanding how you could've been that desperate. Especially when she and Alan asked repeatedly how you were doing."

"What could I tell her, Sam? We're the parents. We shouldn't expect Leslie to solve our problems for us. I didn't want her worrying about something that wasn't her responsibility."

"I know that," he said. "But she's going to have to work through it. I think you should call her. And I wouldn't wait too long."

Sally sighed. "I will. With all the time I've had to decide what to say to her, I still don't know."

"Just tell her the truth. She loves you."

Sally blinked the stinging from her eyes. "I'm so sorry, Sam. I don't know how I talked myself into thinking what I did was all right."

"Well, I'm not without fault in this. I convinced myself that giving you the house would solve all your problems. But truth be told, it was more of a guilt offering. I knew you'd still have all the expenses. And would probably have trouble finding a job that paid anything."

"The saddest part of all is I didn't even pray about it. I was furious with you. And God. I didn't want His help. I tried to do it all myself, and when I couldn't, I got desperate."

"I haven't got any room to throw stones," Sam said. "I got the ball rolling by my affair with Allison."

Sally took another sip of coffee, wondering if she had the courage to say it, and decided she did. "Sam...what happened to us? I thought what we had was good."

Sam looked down, color flooding his face. "It was. I just panicked when I turned fifty-five and thought I was losing my youth, and then Allison came along. I'd give anything to go back and change it. The whole affair was one big fiasco."

"What if your relationship with Allison had been good?"

"It wasn't."

"But what if it had been? What would she have offered you that I didn't, besides the fact that she was fifteen years younger?"

"Absolutely nothing."

Sally traced the rim around her cup. "I thought our sex life was good. Did I miss something?"

"No, babe. You didn't miss anything. The problem was in my head. I was scared I was getting old."

Sally looked at him and smiled. "You are, Sam. We both are."

Sam rolled his eyes. "Why couldn't I see that I already had every-thing I wanted?"

"For the same reason I let Karen talk me into digging up Elsie's money and keeping it. Desperate people do desperate things."

"So, what do we do about it?" Sam said.

Sally sighed. "I don't know. We've got an awful lot of baggage to unpack."

Harry had just begun wiping the tables with Clorox water when he realized Josh Harper was standing in the doorway.

"Hey, Josh. What can I do for you, buddy?"

"Nothing. I just wanted to say thanks for the extra helping."

"No need to thank me. That's what we're here for."

"You gonna be here tomorrow night?" Josh asked.

"Hadn't given it much thought. Maybe."

"If you are, maybe we could sit together."

Harry nodded. "Sure, why not?" Harry reached in his pockets and took out two hard rolls. "You wanna take these with you?"

"Yeah, sure. If nobody's gonna eat them."

"Nah, they're extras. Those oughta taste good later when you're doin' your homework. You do homework, don't you?"

"Yeah, I do. Well, thanks again. See you tomorrow."

Josh left, and Harry continued wiping tables.

"Cute kid," Albert said. "Seems to have taken a liking to you."

"You think so?"

"Definitely."

"Know much about him?"

"Just that his dad was killed by a hit-and-run driver," Albert said. "And his mother struggles with finances. She's got some health problems that make it difficult for her to work steadily. She cleans houses when she can."

Harry stopped wiping and looked up at Albert. "Tough break. Josh seems like a neat kid."

"I saw you give him two hard rolls."

"Uh, yeah. They were extras. I was gonna take 'em, but really didn't need 'em that much."

"Felt good giving them away, didn't it?"

Harry nodded. "Yeah, it did."

"Would you like to come back tomorrow and help us out again? Shorty said you caught on fast. We could use the help."

"Sure. Why not?"

Albert slapped him on the back. "Tomorrow night we're serving meat loaf. Claudia is the queen of meat loaf. Her recipe is better than my mother's."

Harry finished wiping down the tables and then mopped the kitchen floor. He glanced up at the clock and saw that it was after seven. Where had the time gone?

46

Sally Cox helped Sam pull down the Murphy bed in his studio apartment. He opened the linen closet and handed her a set of mismatched sheets.

Sally made the bed, then threw the electric blanket over the top and tucked in the corners. "It doesn't feel right, running you out of a warm bed."

"Are you kidding? My sleeping bag is good to twenty below."

Sally sat on the side of the bed, watching as Sam pulled a nylon bag out of the closet and opened the drawstring.

"I need to call Leslie," she said.

"Use my cell phone, babe. I've got more free minutes than I'll ever use. Take as long as you need."

Sally turned on Sam's cell phone and dialed Leslie's number. *Lord, please help me know what to say.* The phone rang three times. Sally was prepared to leave a message when she heard her daughter's voice.

"Hello."

"Leslie, it's me."

"Mother! Where are you?"

"I'm at your dad's."

"Did he post bail?"

Sally cringed at the words. "It wasn't necessary. The police are working on getting the charges reduced to a misdemeanor. I go back Tuesday for a hearing."

"Will you have to go to jail?"

"Probably not. Thank God—" Sally's voice broke.

There was a long pause.

Sally fiddled with the control on the electric blanket. "Honey, I can only imagine how angry you must be, and how disappointed."

"You deceived me," Leslie said, her voice shaking. "You kept telling me you were fine. Why did you do that when you were worried about going bankrupt? Alan and I could've helped. We've got money saved."

"I didn't want to put a strain on you."

"And you think this *doesn't?*"

"I couldn't bear the thought of being a financial drain on you, Leslie. I thought if I got a second job, things would get better. Then Elsie died, and I let Karen talk me into believing that Elsie would've wanted me to keep the money. I'm so sorry... It goes against everything I believe."

"I don't get it. How come you don't have to go to jail after stealing a quarter of a million dollars?"

Sally wiped a tear off her cheek. "Probably because I voluntarily turned in my half of the money. The police thought there was a good chance the judge would let me plead to a misdemeanor instead of a felony. That way, I wouldn't lose my CNA license."

"You mean after all this, you might get to keep your job?"

"It's possible, honey. I hope so."

"Daddy said some guy you work with has been following you. Have they locked him up?"

Sally rubbed Kiwi's fur. "No. The police can't prove Jeffrey's done anything illegal. But I told them I think he may have killed Karen."

"So, why haven't they arrested him? You're still in danger!"

"Jeffrey knows I turned in the money. There's no reason for him to bother me now."

Leslie sighed. "But what if he just wants to silence you?"

"Honey, I've already told the police everything I know. If anything were to happen to me, they'd be all over Jeffrey. If anything, I think he'll avoid me."

"This is right off the ten o'clock news. Things like this happen to other people, not to us."

There were a few moments of dead air. Sally heard Leslie's sniffling.

"Honey, you can't know how sorry I am. The situation got out of control. I never felt right keeping the money, but I was terrified of going to jail. It broke my heart that I might not get to see my grandchild grow up—" Sally put her hand over the phone, trying to regain her composure, "and that I would lose your respect. You mean everything to me."

Leslie blew her nose. "I love you, Mom. I'm just trying to understand how you were capable of something like this."

"Me too, honey. If I had stayed close to the Lord, I never would've gone along with it."

"Daddy said it's partly his fault for leaving you."

Sally shook her head. "I can't blame him for this. Your father was wrong to have the affair, but I was wrong to steal the money. We both had choices."

"I guess all you can do now is pick yourself up and start over." Leslie blew her nose again. "You always said that falling down is no reason to quit."

Sally dabbed her eyes. "I love you, Leslie."

"I love you, too, Mom."

Harry Rigsby sat wide awake at the kitchen table, wishing he hadn't drunk so much coffee at the soup kitchen. He pushed the newspaper and fishing magazine aside and reached in the top drawer of a nearby cabinet and pulled out an old photograph he had taken from his mother's shoe box.

He held up the faded color shot of Jon straddling a silver and blue bicycle. What was he, nine, maybe ten? Jon looked a little like Josh Harper—and a lot like Harry, only happier than he had been at that age. Harry remembered feeling jealous when Gracie announced that she'd saved enough by cutting the grocery budget to buy the bicycle for Jon. The kid never knew how good he had it. At least Harry hadn't made him feel like an expensive inconvenience the way *his* old man had.

Harry brought the picture closer to his eyes. How did he know how he'd made Jon feel? They'd never talked about it.

Harry stuffed the picture back in the drawer and went in the living room and flopped on the couch. He picked up the remote, turned on the TV, and started surfing channels.

Gracie Garver slowly turned the pages of an old picture album. She rested her eyes on a picture she had taken on Jonathan's first birthday. The child was covered in birthday cake, all smiles, and had grabbed hold of Harry's black sweater, smearing yellow frosting across the sleeve. The disgusted look on Harry's face still irritated her.

"Honey, it's after midnight. What're you doing?" Bill stood in the doorway of the living room.

"Looking at pictures—" Her voice cracked. "I can't remember what Jon's voice sounds like."

Bill sat next to her on the couch and brushed the hair off her face. "It'll come back to you. It's stored in your heart. You don't forget a thing like that."

"I'm so afraid I will." She closed the album and fought to keep her composure. "If the snow melts over the weekend, maybe we could take a ride out to the cemetery and see if Jon's headstone has been set."

"Of course we can."

Gracie wiped a tear off her cheek. "I think Sheriff Baughman has given up on Jon's case. He couldn't get anything out of Harry, and the Kansas City police haven't charged him with anything. It really makes me mad to think that Harry finally got his hands on Elsie's money, and Jon was nothing more than a casualty in the process."

"We don't know that," Bill said. "But even if Harry's got the money, he knows you're not going let him enjoy spending it."

"Yes, but I don't really care whether or not Harry gets Elsie's money. I just want him to take responsibility for sending Jonathan to Layton's to dig it up."

Bill sighed. "Even if that's the case, would his admitting it bring Jon back? Honey, at some point you have to realize Harry wasn't responsible for Jon attacking Layton."

"Whose side are you on?"

"I just want us to get to the place where we can let it go."

"How can I let this go until I know the truth?"

"Grace, you may never know the truth. What then? Are you going to let it eat you up the rest of your life?"

47

Sally woke up on Saturday morning to the aroma of coffee brewing and let her eyes adjust to a river of sunlight streaming into Sam's studio apartment. Kiwi looked like a fuzzy orange ball curled up in front of the sliding glass door.

Sally turned on her back, her hands behind her head, and let her eyes wander around the room. Sam's apartment had a lot more character in the daylight, though she felt a twinge of sadness that he had so little.

She heard a key in the front door and pulled the covers up to her chin. The door opened and Sam walked in, a smile on his face and a sack in his hands.

"You're awake," he said. "Isn't the sun great? How long has it been since we've seen it—a week?"

"Where'd you go?"

"Down to the Breadmaker. I bought some bagels and cream cheese to go with our coffee. You hungry?"

Sally rubbed her eyes. "Probably. I'm not quite awake yet."

"You won't believe how warm it is outside. The snow's already melting. The forecast calls for the high in the midfifties." Sam smiled. "Not bad for February, eh?"

"What time is it?"

"Ten thirty. You've been out for twelve hours."

Sally sat up and fluffed the pillows, then put them behind her back. "I must've needed the rest. How about you—did you sleep?"

"Like a log. I just pretended I was under the stars."

"It was awfully generous of you to let me have the bed."

There was that charming smile. "You want coffee now?"

She nodded.

Sam poured two cups, then added a big splash of cream to Sally's. "Why don't you sit on the couch, and I'll get this bed out of the way."

Sam pushed the Murphy bed back into the wall, then picked up his coffee and sat next to Sally. "Pretty slick, eh? So what do you want to do today?"

"I haven't thought about it. I suppose I should do some laundry."

"Okay. I've got some, too." Sam blew on his coffee. "Maybe you'd like to go to a movie, get your mind off things?"

"Maybe. It's probably not a good idea just to sit around and worry about the hearing—and whether or not Jeffrey went back to work. Sam, what's going to happen if the judge lets me plead to a misdemeanor? I still have to face Jeffrey at work—or look for another job."

"I don't know, babe. At least he knows you don't have the money anymore."

"Yes, but I'm the one who accused him of killing Karen. What if he wants to shut me up? I'll never feel safe until he's locked away."

"Unfortunately, Jeffrey's not the only suspect. The police have to follow up on every lead."

"Then I wish they'd hurry up. If it's not Jeffrey, who could it possibly be?"

Harry heard the doorbell ring and grabbed his shotgun. He looked out the peephole and saw the two police officers who had questioned him about the break-ins. What now? He hid the shotgun in the closet and opened the front door.

"Mr. Rigsby, since we talked to you last, we've obtained some new information. May we come in?"

"Yeah, sure." He held open the door and let the officers in, wondering when this nightmare would end. Harry sat in the chair facing the officers. "What's this about?"

"Sir," the older officer said, "were you aware your mother had put away a huge sum of money over a thirty-year period—money she allegedly skimmed off the family business?"

"I suspected it. But Ma never admitted it to me."

"Well, apparently she told two women at Walnut Hills Nursing Center—Sally Cox and Karen Morgan."

Harry scrunched his eyebrows. "How do you know that?"

"Mrs. Cox came to us with a very interesting story. She claims your mother told her and Ms. Morgan where to find the money. And said if anything happened to her, they were to dig it up and give it to the poor." The officer retold what Sally had written in her statement. "Mrs. Cox turned in a hundred and twenty-five thousand dollars. We have reason to believe whoever killed Karen Morgan has the other half."

"Are you so sure Sally didn't kill her?" Harry asked. "She had a motive."

"I'm not free to comment on an open case. But suffice it to say, we have enough evidence to realistically rule out Mrs. Cox."

Harry's temples throbbed. Did they suspect *him*?

"Sir, is there something you want to tell us?"

Harry looked at one officer, and then the other. "Uh…yeah. Some guy's been threatenin' me. Sally told you her story. I think you oughta hear mine."

Harry started at the beginning and told them his suspicion that Jonathan had gone to Layton's to dig up the money, and that Sally and Karen had finished the job, somehow knowing it was buried behind Sophie's grave. He told them he had suspected Sally of murdering Karen and keeping all the money; and how he had driven to Jefferson City, hoping to confront Sally at Nan Bingham's, until the attacker held a knife to his throat.

The officer scribbled something on his report. "Would you tell us, sir, how you knew where to look for Sally, since Sam Cox didn't give you Mrs. Bingham's address or phone number?"

"Yeah, he did. How else could I have known?"

"He says he didn't."

Harry shrugged. "Must've forgotten what he told me."

"But you lied to us about making the call to Mrs. Bingham. Why?"

"I was wonderin' if Sally killed Karen and had the money. I wanted to talk to her before makin' any accusations. She'd been awful good to Ma."

"Okay. Why didn't you tell the police about the man who threatened you?"

"I was scared. The guy sounded like he meant business. Plus, he called my house a couple times, makin' sure I wasn't talkin' to the police. I asked what he wanted, and he said, 'the other half.' I've been holed up here, stayin' out of his way."

"What can you tell us about his voice? Was he young? Old? Did he have an accent?"

"He sounded young," Harry said. "No accent. Sounded nasally, like he had a cold or somethin'."

"Did you see what he was driving the night he accosted you?"

"No. But when I left Sam Cox's apartment, I saw some guy I'd seen at Kroger's sittin' in a white Explorer outside the buildin'. At the time, I had the feelin' he was followin' me. Could be the same guy."

"Did you get a license number?"

Harry shook his head. "No. When I left Sam's, I watched in my rearview mirror to see if the guy followed me. He didn't."

"Did you get a good look at him?"

"Nah. Just that he was wearing a Royals cap."

The officer wrote something on his report, then looked intently at Harry. "Anything else you want to tell us?"

Harry debated for a moment, then went out to the kitchen and got the letter his mother had left in her Bible and handed it to the officers. "I just found this a couple days ago."

The older officer read it out loud, and then took off his glasses. "This could explain why she told Cox and Morgan to give the money to the poor."

Harry rolled his eyes. "She sure didn't want me to have it."

"It wouldn't have mattered. Your mother owes a ton of back taxes, and her nursing care expenses will probably eat up whatever's left."

Harry folded his arms across his chest. "I tried for years to get her to admit she had it. She never would. It was a real sore spot."

The officer nodded. "Mrs. Cox told us she overhead a conversation you had with your mother at the nursing home. She pretty much confirmed what you just said."

Harry let the relief melt over him.

"We'd like you to come down to the station and file a sworn statement, outlining what you just told us," the older officer said. "This could be vital information in our investigation of Karen Morgan's murder."

"Well, I can tell you one thing. I know *nothin'* about that."

Sally strolled along the Plaza, Sam beside her, looking at store window displays and trying not to think about Tuesday's hearing. She passed by the Plaza III and was transported back to the night she'd had dinner with Karen Morgan, and then the next day when Wanda told her Karen had been found strangled.

"What're you thinking about over there?" Sam said.

"Oh, nothing—and everything. I'm walking around in a daze. Thanks for putting up with me."

"Beats doing laundry." Sam nudged her with his elbow. "You want to get dessert or something?"

"Do you mind if we just walk? It's so nice to be outside."

"You usually don't like the slush."

Sally suddenly noticed the mounds of dirty snow and the sloppy, wet street. "That's the least of my worries."

"Well, good thing you wore your boots."

Sally started to cross the street and instinctively grabbed hold of Sam's arm. She started to let go, and then didn't. How strange it felt walking arm in arm after all that had happened.

She continued walking down the sidewalk, her face tilted upward, the afternoon sun warming her. She felt someone tap her on the shoulder.

"Sally?"

She turned around and looked into the face of Wanda Bradford.

"I didn't realize you were back in town," Wanda said.

"Uh, I just got back."

"How are you doing?"

"I'm working through things. Wanda, this is my ex-husband Sam. Sam, this is Wanda Bradford, the charge nurse at Walnut Hills."

"Nice to meet you," Sam said.

Wanda shook his hand, and then looked at Sally. "Any idea when you're coming back to work?"

"Soon." Sally tried to put a smile in her voice. "I'll call the director of nurses in the middle of the week and see about getting back on the schedule."

"I'm looking forward to your coming back. No one can get Rufus Tatum to cooperate the way you do. In fact, he seems a little depressed since you've been gone."

"Well, I'm ready to get to work." Sally put her hands in her coat pocket. "Has Jeffrey Horton been out all week?"

Wanda nodded. "Poor thing has a nasty case of the flu. I warned him to get his shot, but you know how young people are. They think they're invincible. Well, don't let me keep you. I'll be anxious to see you back at work."

Sally turned around and started walking, her mind racing.

"Sounds like Jeffrey Horton's our man, all right," Sam said. "I'd love to see his face when the cops finally arrest him."

"I keep wondering why they haven't." Sally suddenly felt chilled. "What do they know that we don't?"

48

Harry Rigsby left the police station, got in his car, and headed toward the Christian Center. It was one forty-five.

He was glad to have the truth out on the table—most of it anyway. He didn't tell the police he'd gotten into Sally's house and taken the address book. It seemed irrelevant at this point, so why set himself up to be charged with something?

Harry hadn't been able to offer the police much to go on: just some guy with a cold who was probably over it. He thought it odd that the police acted as if what he'd told them had filled in the blanks. He wondered how close they were to arresting someone.

As he turned onto Booth Street, his thoughts turned to Albert and tonight's dinner at the soup kitchen. It was still a mystery to him how Albert was able to be so excited about life when he had given up everything.

Harry looked forward to seeing Josh Harper and really didn't know why. Usually he found kids annoying.

Harry pulled into a parking space in the back of the building and remembered he'd forgotten to eat lunch. He reached in his pocket and found a dollar and change. So much for eating out.

He got out of the car and walked in the back door, where he spotted four large pizza boxes on the counter—and Albert with a big smile on his face.

"Hi," Albert said. "Glad you decided to come back."

Two of the ladies opened a pizza box, each putting a couple slices on a paper plate.

"Help yourself," Albert said to Harry. "Pizza Hut was running a two-for-one, and it was just too good to pass up."

Harry took two slices of pepperoni and put them on a paper plate. "I appreciate this. I got busy with some business and forgot to eat lunch."

"Well, eat up while it's hot."

Harry stood by himself near the sink, wondering what these folks would think if they knew the police had just questioned him. He was glad when Shorty came and stood beside him.

"I was hopin' you'd be back," Shorty said.

Each time Shorty put his hand to his mouth to take a bite of pizza, Harry took a close look at the cross tattoo on his arm and the words "Jesus saves."

"You like my artwork?" Shorty said, tightening his bicep.

"It's okay. I never took you for a *cross* man—maybe a heart with some broad's name on it."

Shortly smiled. "Not any more. You a Christian, Harry?"

"My mother was. I never got into it."

"How come?"

"I dunno. Seemed like some fairy tale thinkin' people were bad and needed this God in shining armor to come save them. From what?"

Shorty's eyes narrowed. "From ourselves, man. Our carnal nature. We were made for more than *this*."

"You gonna tell me Adam and Eve blew it, so now we're all bad? 'Cause I don't buy it."

Shorty arched his eyebrows. "Looked around lately? The world's self-destructing. There's no sense of right and wrong out there. People havin' multiple sex partners. AIDS. Marriages fallin' apart. Women havin' abortions. Kids killin' kids. Terrorists thrivin' on murderin' innocent people. Executives rippin' off companies. Rapes. Murders. Pornography—"

"Hold on. That stuff's been around forever," Harry said.

"Yep. As long as there've been people. And there's still only one solution for all of it—Jesus. That's why I got the cross tattoo."

"A tattoo won't save anybody," Harry said.

"Nope. But it sure opens up some interestin' discussions." Shorty poked Harry in the ribs. "If you haven't taken a serious look at what Jesus taught—and I don't mean what other people tell you, but what you read and understand for yourself—then you're missin' what you were created for, man."

"Hey, I need a couple pairs of hands chopping onions for this meat loaf," an older woman hollered.

"I'm coming, Claudia," Albert said, winking at Harry and Shorty.

"When you finish your pizza, I think she's got about a ton of potatoes that need peeling."

Sally finished a second helping of Sam's chili and put her bowl on the end table. "I'd forgotten how good that is."

"Thanks." Sam picked up her empty bowl, rinsed it, and put it in the dishwasher. "Sorry I don't have a table and chairs in here. That's the downside of a studio apartment."

"You're sweet to let me intrude. This can't be easy for you."

Sam sat on the couch next to her. "It's easier than when I didn't know where you were. I'd ask if you wanted to go run off the chili, but I doubt the slushy street is conducive to jogging."

"Hard to believe it was just last weekend we went running," Sally said. "Feels like a lifetime ago. So much has happened."

"Yeah, it blows my mind."

Sally sighed. "I just want to get Tuesday's hearing behind me."

"I have a feeling the judge is going to go easy on you because you did the right thing."

"No, I didn't, Sam. I was going to keep the money."

"But you *didn't*. You turned it in."

Sally let Sam's words sink in, then looked up him. "I still can't believe you came to find me."

"You needed to be found."

"How come you always know that?"

There was a long pause, then he took her hand in his. "Because I'm your other half."

Sally wanted to pull her hand away and wondered why she didn't. "We're divorced, Sam. We're not *one* anymore."

Sam got up, his hands in his pockets, and stood leaning against the bookshelf. "A piece of paper can't change a spiritual reality. I feel like half of me is missing, babe. All the time. Even when I was with Allison."

"Sam, I don't want to have this conversation."

He sat beside her on the couch. "Is it because you don't miss me? And don't love me anymore? I could understand that."

"You know it isn't. I just don't know that I could ever trust you."

"But you're trusting me now."

"It's different, Sam."

"How? You've told me the darkest secret of your life, and I'm still here."

Sally blinked to clear her eyes.

"Look, I got crazy for a few months," Sam said. "And you'll never know how sorry I am. But you're the only woman I've ever loved. And all I'm asking for is that we can stay friends."

"I know, Sam. I'm just scared all the tender feelings will come back. I don't know how to draw a line and tell my emotions not to cross it. I just can't handle getting hurt again—" Sally's voice cracked.

Sam slipped his arm around her shoulder and gently pulled her close. Sally rested her head on his shoulder and allowed the scent of him to stir up tender memories.

Harry put a scoop of mashed potatoes on Josh Harper's plate. "Good to see you again, Josh."

"The line's almost gone," Josh said. "I saved a place at my table for you."

"Yeah, okay. Soon as I'm done here, I'll join you."

Harry kept greeting people and scooping mashed potatoes, but he couldn't stop thinking about a tough guy like Shorty talking plainly about Jesus. Harry had never been around someone like that before.

He saw Josh and his mother bow their heads and say grace and wondered if he was the only heathen in the crowd.

"Why don't you go eat with Josh?" Albert said. "I've had my dinner. I'll take over here."

"Okay, thanks."

Harry filled a plate for himself and went over to Josh's table and sat facing the boy.

"This is great," Josh said. "You like meat loaf, Harry?"

"Love the stuff."

"Did you make this?"

"I peeled the potatoes and helped make the Jell-O. Claudia over there," Harry nodded toward an elderly lady coming through the doorway with a tray of rolls, "*she* made the meat loaf. A family recipe."

"Harry, I'm Helen Harper, Josh's mom." The young blonde extended her hand and shook his. "Josh was hoping you'd be here tonight."

"Yeah, this is only my second time. I'm enjoyin' it. Did you go to school today, Josh?" Harry asked.

Josh smiled. "No, it's Saturday."

"All days feel alike to me. I'm retired."

"Have you got grandkids?" Josh asked.

"Nah. I don't really have any family."

Josh's blue eyes were round and wide. "I don't have a grandfather either. Maybe we could—"

"Josh," his mother said softly. "Let the poor man eat in peace."

"Oh, it's no problem, ma'am. You like sports, Josh?"

"I love sports. All kinds. Especially baseball."

"You play on a team?"

"I used to. My dad was the coach. I'm not sure whether I want to play this year."

Harry saw Helen Harper's eyes tear up and hoped she wasn't going to cry. He never knew what to do when women cried.

"What position do you play?" Harry said.

"Shortstop."

"Really? That's what I always played. Are you any good?"

Josh smiled. "Not bad."

Helen put her arm around Josh. "He was voted most valuable player on his team and played on the all-star team."

"I'm impressed," Harry said.

Josh's grin nearly took over his face. "I got a trophy and a baseball autographed by the Kansas City Royals."

"Isn't that somethin'? You'll have to show it to me sometime."

"Yeah, that'd be cool!" Josh looked thoughtful for a moment, then said, "How come you don't have any family?"

"Let Harry enjoy his dinner." Helen whispered something more to Josh, and his face fell.

"Sorry I'm talking so much," Josh said.

"Nah, I like talkin'." Harry punched Josh on the arm. "How about I get you seconds?"

"Okay."

"Can I bring you somethin' else, Helen?"

"No, thank you."

Harry was glad to get Josh another helping, but wondered if he'd feel as willing when the boy wanted to show him the trophy and auto-graphed baseball. How involved did he want to get with this kid when he'd struck out with his own?

49

Sally Cox woke up early on Sunday morning and couldn't go back to sleep. She tossed and turned, then finally decided to get up. She looked around Sam's apartment for something to read and spotted his Bible on the bookshelf.

She got up and tucked the Bible under her arm, then tiptoed back to bed and turned on the lamp. She put her pillows behind her back and opened the Bible Sam's mother had given him before she died. Sally thumbed back and forth through the gospels, then her eyes fell on the sixth chapter of Matthew, verse 24. She began reading.

"No one can serve two masters. Either he will hate one and love the other, or he will be devoted to the one and despise the other. You cannot serve both God and Money."

Sally felt an aching remorse in the deepest part of her soul. How could she have gotten so far away from what she believed? How could she have wanted money so badly that she abandoned God, whom she had sought to follow since the time she accepted Jesus at Aunt Georgia's church when she was twelve?

She knew all too well that the moment she had put her desire for money on the throne of her heart, she relinquished the very power that would have brought her through the financial struggles. If only she would have trusted God to help, she would never have made such a foolish and desperate decision—and maybe Karen Morgan would still be alive.

She wiped the tears off her cheeks and tried to read more, but her eyes wouldn't focus on the text. She marked the place with a red ribbon, then closed the Bible and hugged it, letting the reality of God's forgiveness comfort her.

"Babe, you all right?" Sam sat up in his sleeping bag, then got up and sat next to her on the side of the bed. "What's got you so upset?"

Sally opened the Bible and pointed to what she had read.

Sam read the verse, then wiped the hair off her face. "But your slate's clean, remember? No point in going back and kicking yourself all over again."

"I know God's forgiven me. But it's going to take a while for *me* to get over what I've done. I'm so disgusted with myself."

"Yeah, I hear you. I still kick myself sometimes."

There was a long pause.

Sally looked up at him, her eyes dripping with tears, her lip quivering. "I forgive you, Sam. I don't think I've ever told you that."

Sam looked away, then coughed to cover his emotion. "I never thought I'd hear you say that—" His voice failed, and he took her hand in his and sat quietly for a moment, his eyes clamped shut, his nose red.

"I don't know if the pain will ever go away," Sally said, dabbing her eyes, "but I want it to. I want what we had. Maybe God *can* fix things between us. I don't know."

Sam quickly wiped a tear off his cheek. "You caught me off guard. This is so great."

"It might take a long time, Sam. But we were better together."

Kiwi jumped on the bed and meowed until Sam put her on his lap.

Sally sat holding Sam's hand, her eyes fixed on a tiny ray of sunlight peeking in through a crack in the drapes. For the first time since he left, she felt hope. Deep, healing hope.

Sam kissed her hand and held it to his cheek. "The sun's up. Let's let some light in here."

He set Kiwi on the floor, then got up and pulled open the drapes. Light flooded the room.

Sally closed her eyes and let the warmth wash over her, feeling as though the same thing had just happened in her heart.

50

On Sunday night, Harry Rigsby carried two trays of hot rolls from the kitchen to the serving table, feeling a sense of satisfaction at having helped put a meal together for a third time. He realized he was starting to plan his days around helping at the soup kitchen.

He saw Josh and Helen Harper walk in. Josh's eyes were wide with excitement.

"Look what I brought." Josh opened a bag and pulled out a trophy and a baseball covered in autographs. "This is what I was telling you about."

Harry put the rolls in the basket and set the trays down. He took the trophy from Josh and read the inscription. "Hey, this is quite an honor bein' chosen most valuable player."

"And look at the baseball," Josh said. "There's eighteen names on it!"

Harry held the baseball and slowly turned it, letting his eyes read the signatures. "I've watched every one of these guys play."

"Me, too. Dad took me to a couple of games every season."

Harry smiled. "My kinda guy."

"Have you ever gone to see the Royals play?"

"Yeah, I used to go all the time. Haven't been for a while."

"Why'd you stop?"

"Oh, a couple of reasons. Money's been tight since I retired. Plus, I lost touch with the guys I used to go with."

Helen put her hand on her son's shoulder. "Why don't you let Harry get his work done? You can talk to him at the table."

Josh looked up at Harry. "You're gonna eat with us again, aren't you?"

"Yeah, sure. Save me a place."

Shorty walked by carrying a huge bowl of salad. "Okay, it's almost five. I think we're ready to roll." He set the salad bowl in the empty spot on the table. "You thought any more about what we talked about, Harry?"

"Some. I never heard a guy like you talk about Jesus before."

"What kinda guy am I?"

"You're a man's man, if you know what I mean. I always figured guys like us didn't need all that religious stuff."

Shorty raised his eyebrows. "Why would you think that?"

"We like to be in control, decide things for ourselves. What's the point in submitting to some authority you can't even see—that might not even be there?"

"Oh, He's there, all right. Takes more faith not to believe in Him when you look at the evidence."

"What evidence?"

Shorty glanced over at Albert, then at the line that had formed at one end of the serving table. "After we clean up tonight, let's talk some more."

Albert stood where everyone in the room could see him. "Attention everyone. Let's give the Lord thanks so we can get started. Heavenly Father, we are so grateful to share this bounty You've given us. Please pour out a blessing on each person gathered here, that they may know your Son—and be known by Him. For it is in the Name of Jesus we pray. Amen." Albert looked up and smiled. "We're glad you're here. Enjoy the food."

Harry took his place behind the table and picked up a pair of tongs. He placed a hot roll on the tray of each person that passed, recognizing a number of folks he had served the two previous nights.

Josh and Helen came through the line. Harry put two rolls on Josh's tray and winked.

Josh smiled. "Thanks. I saved you a place."

Harry greeted each person, wondering what had caused each one to become needy. He glanced over at Josh and wondered what kind of life he'd had before his father died. He felt an unexpected twinge of grief and thought again how much the boy reminded him of Jonathan.

The line finally ended, and Harry put down the tongs and started to walk toward Josh's table when Albert caught his attention.

"Harry, do you like ice hockey?" Albert held up three tickets. "There's a play-off game over at the college arena at seven. If you want to go, they're yours."

"I love hockey. How much you want for 'em?"

"Nothing. I just don't want them to go to waste. Something's come up, and I can't go."

"Don't you need me to help clean up?"

"Actually, we have more volunteers than we need tonight."

Harry took the tickets. "Thanks. I haven't been to a hockey game in years."

"If you want someone to go with, Shorty's available. But I warn you, he gets emotionally involved in the game."

Harry smiled. "Yeah?"

Albert rolled his eyes. "Oh, yeah."

Harry put the tickets in his pocket, then filled a tray for himself and sat across the table from Josh.

"How's the roast beef?"

"Great."

Helen Harper wiped her mouth with a napkin and pushed her plate aside, then looked at her watch. "Josh, we need to go. I still have to strip and wax the floors before the Heines get home from Jamaica tonight."

Josh grimaced. "Can't we stay just a few minutes? Harry just sat down."

"I'm sorry, I really need to finish this job. Their flight is scheduled to land in a few hours."

"Josh, you like hockey?" Harry reached in his pocket and pulled out the tickets.

"I *love* hockey!"

"Albert gave me three tickets, and I need two guys to go with me."

"Count me in," Shorty said, snatching a ticket from Harry's hand. "Albert said you were lookin' for company."

Harry looked at Helen. "Okay if Josh goes with us?"

Shorty leaned on the table. "You know me, Helen. Harry and I'll take good care of him."

Josh turned to his mother. "Please?"

Helen's eyes moved to Shorty, then Harry, and then back to Shorty. "Well, all right. I'm sure going to a hockey game will be a lot more fun than staying home by himself while I go wax some floors."

Sally took the dinner dishes off the end table and put them in the dishwasher. "Between what you're spending to feed me, the three hundred dollars you replaced, and your gas and motel bills, you may not make it to payday. I'll pay you back when I pick up my paycheck."

"Don't worry about it," Sam said. "My living expenses are a lot less these days."

"As soon as I put Tuesday's hearing behind me, I need to get someone to help me clean up the house."

Sam raised his eyebrows. "I think we'll need a professional. Jeffrey really trashed the place. You're not going to believe it."

"I wonder why they didn't find any evidence to prove it?"

"Maybe they have," Sam said. "I doubt the police are going to tell us anything as long as the investigation is going on."

"I'm going to have to get some repairs done, too, so I can put the house on the market."

"Let's just take it one step at a time. You've got enough on your plate right now."

Harry walked Josh Harper to his front door, while Shorty waited in the car.

"Watch your step now," Harry said, holding Josh's arm. "All I need is you to fall on this slick sidewalk. Your mother'll have my hide."

"I had such a great time," Josh said. "Thanks for asking me to go. Hockey's my next favorite sport."

Harry smiled. "No? I never would've known, the way you were carryin' on."

"*Me?* Did you hear Shorty!"

"Everybody heard Shorty."

Josh's eyes seemed to look into Harry's heart. "Thanks again for taking me. And for the banana split. I haven't had that much fun since my dad died."

"Yeah, you're welcome."

"You gonna keep coming to the dinners every night?"

Harry stood with his hands in his pockets, his feet rocking from heel to toe. "I've really enjoyed helpin'. I'll probably be around."

"Well, I guess I'd better go in." Josh put the key in the front door.

"You lock yourself in there," Harry said. "Don't open the door to anyone you don't know. Your mom should be home soon."

Josh smiled. "I'm eleven. I know what to do."

"See you tomorrow night, kid." Harry punched Josh on the arm.

"Maybe when the season opens, I'll take you to a Royals game."

Josh spun around, his eyes wide. "Wow, that'd be cool!"

"You should reconsider playin' baseball this spring. I know you miss your dad, but you love the sport."

Josh shrugged. "Doesn't matter. No one's volunteered to coach us yet."

"Somebody will. They always do."

"Have *you* ever coached a team, Harry?"

"Me? Nah, never thought about it."

"Could be fun."

"Hey, I'm sixty-five years old."

"So? You can hit the ball, can't you? And you can throw?"

"A darned sight better than you." Harry gave the boy a playful jab in the ribs.

Josh's smile spanned his face. "Then why don't we play catch and hit some balls sometime and see if you're as good as you say you are? I dare you. I think you're all talk. I'll bet you never even played baseball."

Harry's eyes narrowed. "Wait a minute. Am I being railroaded?"

The phone rang in Sam Cox's apartment. Sally looked at her watch: nine forty-five. Only Leslie would call this late.

Sam put down a magazine and picked up the phone. "Hello. Really...? Uh, yeah, sure..." He looked over at Sally, his eyebrows raised. "Thanks for the call. We'll be watching."

Sam hung up the phone and paused for a moment. "Babe, that was Investigator Sloan at the police department. They've arrested Jeffrey Horton. He said to watch the ten o'clock news."

51

Harry Rigsby was aware that Shorty had been talking since they left Josh Harper's, but Harry had been too distracted to absorb anything he was saying.

"Turn right here," Shorty said. "I've got a basement apartment in this first building."

Harry pulled into a parking space and left the motor running. "Thanks for goin' to the hockey game with me. I enjoyed it. And I know Josh had a good time."

"Isn't he a great kid? He and Helen go to my church."

"Yeah?"

"I invited them to come to the dinners after David died. That was Josh's dad."

"Horrible what happened. Too bad they never found the hit-and-run driver."

"Yeah, it's been tough on them. At least they'll see David again."

Harry turned to Shorty, his eyebrows raised. "You mean in heaven?"

"Yep. David was a believer. Which reminds me, you asked about what evidence there is that there's a God."

"Yeah, I don't see it. Like you said, the world's a real pit. So, where's the evidence?"

Shorty smiled. "His people."

"Huh?"

"The best evidence is how He changes His people."

"Like who?"

"Claudia, for one. She used to be a prostitute."

"Gimme a break, Shorty. The woman's older than I am. I'm sure she stopped *prostitutin'* a long time ago."

"Yeah, she did. Forty-five years ago. Some street preacher invited her to church, and the congregation took her under their wing and helped her get a respectable job. They introduced her to Jesus, and she trusted Him as her savior. She's been tellin' folks about Him ever since."

"So, lots of hookers get out of the business. Big deal. That's not evidence."

"Take me, then. I was doin' fifteen years for attempted murder. I was one mean dude with a violent temper—nearly beat a man to death over a stupid card game. Then some guys started comin' to the prison and told me that God is a Father who loves me and sent His Son Jesus to pay the price for my sins so I won't have to. They said He forgives us when we repent, wipes the slate clean, and let's us start over. Man, that had some appeal. At first I was cynical, but after a few weeks I started to want what they were talkin' about."

"So, what happened?" Harry said.

"I trusted Jesus to do what He said: remove my sins as far as the east is from the west—then forget about 'em. It changed my life. I could focus on Someone bigger than I am. I didn't have to be the tough guy anymore."

"So you changed, just like that?"

"Yes and no. Somethin' in my heart changed the minute I asked Jesus to take control of my life. But my temper took a while to fizzle out. Never hit nobody after that, though. I *wanted* to be different. Then after I got out of prison, I met Albert down at Nick's Diner. He hired me to repair shoes in one of his local businesses, got me trained so I could make a livin'. That's how I ended up helpin' at the soup kitchen."

Harry mused. "What do you mean your heart changed?"

"Jesus became real to me—as real as you are. And once I felt forgiven for all the hurt I caused, I started carin' about the other inmates and wantin' them to experience it, too. I did two more years in the slammer after that. But I was free. My life had a purpose nobody could mess with."

"What purpose?" Harry said.

"To point people to the whole reason we were created: to live with God forever. But it ain't gonna happen unless they accept Jesus' sacrifice on the cross. The Bible says He's the solution for sin here and now and the only way to get from here to there. Can't buy it. Can't earn it. There's just one way to heaven and a better life here: givin' your heart to Jesus. Not everyone's willin' to accept it."

"Yeah, me for one. Where's the better life you're talkin' about? Life seems pretty unfair to me, even for Christians. Look at Josh and Helen."

"Sure, life can be tough. There's a lot we don't understand or have control over. But this ain't what we were made for, man. This is a speck of time compared to eternity and the good stuff that's still to come."

"Are you sayin' this life doesn't matter?"

Shorty shook his head. "No, it matters a lot 'cause this is where we make the choice to believe or not. And where we tell other people the Good News. But there's no point in gettin' too hung up on what happens here 'cause it ain't the end of the story."

Harry thought of the verses in his mother's letter.

"I could go on and on about how knowin' Jesus causes people to change deep down," Shorty said. "Delbert, the bald guy who buys the groceries for the soup kitchen? He did time for armed robbery. Meagan, the young gal who cleans the johns? She accidentally ran over her two-year-old, then had a nervous breakdown, got hooked on prescription drugs, and spent months in rehab. Look at 'em now."

"They got saved?"

"Yep. Completely changed people. 'Course, most folks who accept Christ don't carry such *obvious* baggage. But over time He changes their attitudes and motives. You already know Albert's story: He made his fortune, then gave it up and realized he was happier without it."

Harry fiddled with the gearshift. "Albert's situation bugs me. I don't get how a guy could have anything he wants and be happier givin' it up."

"Tell you what." Shorty put his hand on the door handle. "Why don't you come to the mornin' prayer circle and listen to the testimonies? Decide for yourself whether or not Jesus changes people from the inside out. No one'll pressure you."

Harry rubbed the stubble on his chin. "Let me think about it."

Sally sat on the couch next to Sam, anxiously awaiting the ten o'clock news. She could hardly believe Jeffrey Horton had finally been arrested.

"Good evening, this is Chad Higgins."

"And Marian Monahan. Welcome to the Nightly News at Ten."

"Kansas City Police have uncovered a strange twist in connection with the Karen Morgan murder case. Our reporter Michael Rawlins is live at the police station and has the story. Michael…"

"Chad, it's been quite an evening. Less than an hour ago, Investigator Radford Sloan announced a new development in the case. But it wasn't the break we had hoped for. Let's go now to a videotape of the investigator's statement to the media.

"Good evening, I'm Investigator Radford Sloan. Earlier this evening, a twenty-three-year old Shawnee Mission resident, Jeffrey Ryan Horton, was taken into custody and filed a sworn statement that, on the night of Karen Morgan's murder, he had gone to her apartment and found the door ajar and the victim already dead on the kitchen floor.

"Horton worked with Morgan at the Walnut Hills Nursing Center and claims he went to the victim's apartment to discuss his suspicion that she knew the whereabouts of a large sum of money that belonged to a deceased patient. The department is now investigating Mr. Horton's claims."

"Chad, Investigator Sloan was questioned by reporters but opted not to make any further comment about the case. However, sources inside the police department confirm that an employee at Walnut Hills Nursing Center, Sally Cox, turned over one hundred and twenty-five thousand dollars to the Pheasant River, Kansas, police last Thursday. The money reportedly belonged to a deceased patient, Elsie Rigsby, whom Morgan, Horton, and Cox had cared for.

"Sources tell us that Morgan and Cox had conspired to obtain and split the money between them after Mrs. Rigsby died last month, and that Horton admitted to taking Morgan's half from the apartment after he found her dead.

"Sources also confirm that Ms. Cox voluntarily turned the money over to Pheasant River police and reported her suspicion that Horton was tracking her in pursuit of her portion.

"Sounds like there's a lot more to come on this story. This is Michael Rawlins, reporting live from the Kansas City Police Station. Back to you, Chad."

"Thanks, Michael. Rest assured, we're going to stay on top of this very interesting story as it unfolds. In other news tonight…"

Sally put the TV on mute, burning with embarrassment that her involvement had finally been made public.

"Honey, all things considered, you didn't look that bad," Sam said.

Her mind flashed back to the moment she had left the message on

Karen's answering machine. Jeffrey must have heard the message. How else could he have known Sally had the other half of the money? It sickened her to think about Jeffrey listening to her voice while he stood next to Karen's murdered body. She could hardly believe he hadn't even bothered to call 911 after he left.

"Sam, if Jeffrey didn't kill her, who did? And why?"

"Sounds like the police are on top of it."

"It's all so horrible. I just want it over with."

Sam squeezed her hand. "I think I should call Leslie and let her know this new development."

"Can't you just imagine the gossip at the nursing home tonight?"

"Honey, you can't worry about that. You did the right thing. Try to remember *that*."

"I wonder if I should talk to Wanda?"

"Probably couldn't hurt. But I wouldn't do it on the phone."

"She's going to think I'm awful. I doubt if I can ever work there again."

Harry pulled into the driveway and turned off the radio. If Jeffrey Horton stole the money from Karen, then he must be the creep who'd been threatening Harry. So who killed Karen?

Harry went in the house and out to the kitchen, surprised to see the light blinking on his answering machine. He pushed the play button.

"Mr. Rigsby, this is Investigator Sloan. We've made an arrest and recovered the other half of your mother's money. The story will be on the ten o'clock news. But feel free to call me if you have questions."

He went in the living room and flopped on the couch, his hands behind his head and his heart full of feelings he couldn't identify.

It was over. His mother's money was history. So, why wasn't he depressed about it anymore? He was actually looking forward to going back to the soup kitchen tomorrow night.

Harry had to admit this Jesus stuff seemed to change people—at least, the ones he'd met at the Christian Center.

He couldn't get Josh off his mind. Something about the kid had him hooked. He closed his eyes and pictured Josh's bright, eager eyes and his pleading expression, and seriously considered coaching the baseball team.

Suddenly, Harry was hit with a surge of regret that he had never gotten to know his own son at that age. He started to get up from the couch, and then lay down again, his hand over his eyes, and wept as he never had before.

God, if You're up there, You gotta help me figure all this out.

52

Early Monday afternoon, Harry Rigsby pulled into Round Hill Cemetery, parked the car, and began walking up the soggy hill, amazed that the snow had completely melted. He spotted muddy ground and walked over to the fresh grave, surprised to see Jon's headstone had been set.

He stood staring at his son's name and felt a groaning deep within. He studied the reddish marble cross and decided Gracie and Bill had done a good job picking out the headstone.

His hair tossed about by a brisk south breeze, Harry looked out beyond the cross at a sea of headstones. How many people had been buried here? What had happened to them? Were they in heaven? Hell? Nowhere? Had they been loved?

Harry wondered if anyone would even remember him when he was gone and realized to the depth of his being how alone he would be without Josh and Shorty and Albert and the others at the soup kitchen.

He lifted his eyes and looked at the clouds, wondering if Jon could see him—or if God could.

"They just set the stone," said a female voice behind him.

Harry turned and saw Gracie approaching. "I'll be out of your way in a minute."

"Actually, Bill and I were about to drive off when I saw you walk up here. There's something I need to say."

Harry spotted Bill sitting in the car, then turned his back to Gracie and stared at Jonathan's headstone. "If you came to rake me over the coals, you might as well—"

"I didn't. I wanted to apologize."

Harry turned on his heel. "Since when?"

Gracie looked at the ground, her thumbs hung on her coat pockets. "I heard on the news the police have Elsie's money, and that Sally and Karen took it. I'm sorry I accused you."

"Ma didn't want me to have it anyway. I gave the police a letter she left me in her Bible, telling me how guilty she'd felt all those years she took money and deceived my dad. Ma said she didn't want me stuck with the same burden. It's probably just as well I didn't know where it was. I would've kept it in a heartbeat. Then where would I be?"

There was a long pause. Harry sensed what she was thinking.

"Gracie, what's it gonna take to convince you I didn't know Jon went to Layton's till the cops told me? If you want me to swear right here, on our son's grave, I will."

"No, let's just put it behind us."

Harry lifted his eyebrows. "You serious?"

"Very."

"Yeah, okay." Harry nodded toward the headstone. "Looks real nice. Weird seein' Jon's name on it, though."

"I know. I miss him so much."

"Yeah, me, too. There's this eleven-year-old boy down at the Christian Center who reminds me a lot of Jon at that age. Bein' with him has made me realize what I missed."

"What are *you* doing at the Christian Center?"

"There's this soup kitchen where we serve dinners every night for anyone who wants to come. I've enjoyed helpin' out there."

Gracie stared at him.

"I know what you're thinkin', but people change."

"I'm happy for you, Harry. Just surprised, that's all."

"I'm even thinkin' about coachin' Josh's baseball team. That's the kid I was tellin' you about—Josh Harper. His dad got killed by a hit-and-run driver. The kid has no male figure in his life."

"Too bad you didn't think of that when Jon was a boy. He could've used a father, too."

"Yeah, I know." He stared at Jon's headstone until he regained his composure. "Wish I could go back. Why'd you and Bill choose a cross?"

"I don't know. It seemed appropriate."

"You guys religious now?"

"No, why?"

"I dunno." Harry put his hands in his pockets. "Some things Ma said in her letter got me thinkin' about God, heaven, Jesus—all the stuff I've heard about forever but blew off."

"Bill and I aren't into any of that."

"I wasn't either. But a couple people at the Christian Center have got me thinkin' about stuff I used to laugh at. There's this guy, Albert. He's filthy rich and could have anything he wanted. Instead, he lives simply and gives his money away. Seems genuinely happy. I envy him."

Gracie gave him a puzzled look but didn't say anything.

"I haven't decided whether or not I believe in God. But Shorty, this other guy who volunteers, he's been tryin' to convince me the best evidence that there's a God is the change in His people. Then he proceeds to tell me about some of the volunteers and their backgrounds. You wouldn't believe it: One was a prostitute; one did time for assault, one for armed robbery; another accidentally killed her kid and was hooked on prescription drugs. You'd never know it. This is the most selfless bunch of folks I've ever known. I'm startin' to look at things differently, just bein' around 'em. And for the first time in years, I wake up feelin' good and lookin' forward to somethin'."

Gracie smiled. "Well, if I believed in miracles, I'd say I'm looking at one."

Harry felt his face get hot. "I'm talkin' too much."

"No, it's nice you're finally opening up. I don't ever remember us talking like this."

"You know, in a weird kinda way, Josh is helpin' me get over Jon. Like maybe he's pullin' somethin' out of me I didn't know was in there."

"It's a shame Jon never knew that side of you. But I'm happy for your sake. I know how alone you are."

Harry pulled his coat collar up around his ears. "I've never told you what a good mother I thought you were."

Gracie's eyes welled with tears. "No, you haven't."

"I shoulda said somethin' before. Jon was a lot like me, but all the good came from you. You were the best thing that ever happened to him."

Gracie wiped the tears from her cheeks. "Thank you, Harry. I tried. I really did."

He looked up at the crisp winter sky dotted with cloud puffs and tried not to get emotional. "You suppose there's somethin' up there?"

"If you mean heaven, I honestly doubt it."

The sun felt warm on Harry's face, and for a moment he entertained the hope that maybe something better did exist. He looked at his watch. "I need to be goin', Gracie. I'm supposed to be at the soup kitchen at two."

"I'm glad I ran into you." She took his hand and gently squeezed it. "Take care of yourself."

"Yeah, I will. You do the same."

Harry trudged down the soggy hillside and got in his car, thinking he could hardly wait to see Josh Harper and tell him he'd decided to coach the team. It also occurred to him how seldom in the past four days he'd thought about how little he had.

53

On Tuesday afternoon, Sally Cox stood hand in hand with Sam outside the district attorney's office, her hands shaking, her stomach feeling as though a team of tiny gymnasts were using it as a trampoline.

"What if the judge doesn't let me plead to a misdemeanor and I end up in jail?" she said.

Sam tilted her chin upward and looked into her eyes. "You promised yourself you weren't going to do this."

"You're right." She took a slow deep breath and let it out. "Okay, I'm ready."

Sam opened the door and held it for Sally, then followed her inside.

"May I help you?" the receptionist said.

"Yes, I'm Sally Cox. I'm supposed to meet with the district attorney at three o'clock."

"Yes, ma'am, we've been expecting you. Please have a seat."

Sally sat at the end of one of the rows of mauve vinyl chairs lining the gray walls that reminded her of the hospital emergency room.

"How're you doing?" Sam gave her hand a squeeze.

"Okay," she said, trying to ignore the fact her throat was dry and chalky and her fingers were cold. "I just want it over with."

"Mrs. Cox," the receptionist said, "you'll be meeting with Assistant County Attorney Paul Rosen. Please follow me."

Sally got up, her knees shaky, and followed the woman through a door and down a hallway to a large office with a dozen people seated at desks. A short, middle-aged man with dark glasses came out of a room off to the side and extended his hand to Sally. "Mrs. Cox, I'm Paul Rosen, assistant county attorney. Let's go in my office."

"Is it all right if my ex-husband comes with me?"

"That would be fine."

Sam held out his hand. "I'm Sam Cox."

"Nice to meet you."

Sally and Sam followed him into his office and took a seat at a small, round table.

Rosen handed Sally a document, then folded his hands on the table and looked intently at her. "Let me tell you what's going to happen. First of all, I need you to read this document. It's called a 'Statements and Waivers of the Defendant and Order of the Court.' By signing this, you're waiving your right to an attorney, to a jury trial, as well as any constitutional rights that would impede your entering a plea of guilty. The document also contains a judicial confession, which is basically your written confession, which you will swear to in front of the county clerk. After that, we'll proceed to the hearing, which will be presided over by Judge William Payton. I'll give you a few minutes to read it over."

"Thank you." Sally said, wondering if she would be able to make sense of what she was about to sign. She was relieved when Sam moved his chair closer and began to review the document with her.

Sally scanned the papers and got the gist, but she was reluctant to admit she didn't understand the legalese and was nervous about waiving her rights. Had she made a big mistake agreeing to this without consulting an attorney?

"Why is it necessary for her to waive her rights?" Sam said. "I'm a little unclear about that."

"Essentially," Rosen said, "she's agreeing to forgo a jury trial and go directly to the judge for sentencing. Judge Payton has already reviewed the case and has agreed to allow her to plead to 'Failure to Report a Felony.' In other words, Mrs. Cox knew Elsie Rigby had committed the felony of Medicaid fraud but failed to report it, which is a Class A misdemeanor."

"Does that mean I won't have to go to jail?"

Rosen pushed his glasses higher on his nose. "A Class A misdemeanor carries a penalty of up to one year in jail and a fine of up to four thousand dollars. But we've explained your circumstances to Judge Payton and how forthcoming you've been. He wouldn't have agreed to work with us unless he agreed that your situation warrants leniency. Lucky for you he tends to be a reasonable man. You're not looking at jail time."

Sally couldn't concentrate after that. She scanned the document again and pretended to be reading while she waited for Sam to finish.

"Seems pretty clear." Sam took off his glasses and put them back in his pocket. "What happens now?"

Rosen looked at Sally, his hands folded on the table. "If you agree to the waivers and the confession, I'll need you to take an oath and sign the document in front of the county clerk."

"All right," she said. "I'm ready to do that."

Rosen looked at his watch, then picked up all the papers on the table and stood. "Follow me. We need to get this out of the way before you see Judge Payton."

Sam took a drink from the water fountain, then walked into the court-room and took a seat and started praying as Sally and the assistant county attorney stood before Judge Payton.

"Mrs. Cox," Judge Payton said, "do you understand the document you signed before the county clerk, which contains your judicial con-fession?"

"Yes, Your Honor," Sally said.

"And do you understand that you waived your right to an attor-ney and a jury trial?"

"I do."

"And how do you plead?"

"Guilty, Your Honor."

"I accept this plea and enter the same, and the State may proceed."

"Your Honor," Rosen said, "the State offers State's exhibit number one, which is titled, 'Statements and Waivers of the Defendant,' and which contains the judicial confession of the defendant."

Judge Payton gave a slight nod. "Received."

"We rest, Your Honor."

The judge folded his hands. "Mrs. Cox, do you have anything to say before I pronounce sentence?"

"No, Your Honor."

"Very well, then, I find the evidence substantiates your guilt, but in keeping with the plea agreement, I defer finding you guilty and sen-tence you to community service for a term of eighteen months under certain terms and conditions which the probation officer will go over with you, and which are contained in this order."

The judge took off his glasses and folded his arms, his eyes intently fixed on Sally. "Mrs. Cox, I hope you realize what happened here was a gift. The type of sentence I pronounced is called deferred adjudication. After you complete your probation, your record will show the charges dismissed, so you can say you've never been convicted of a crime.

"But don't think the court's mercy in any way lessens the seriousness of this crime. And though I find your taking the money deplorable, I also find your returning it commendable. Not everyone would have had the courage to voluntarily admit this wrongdoing to police, in spite of the consequences. I gave you a light sentence because my years of experience tell me you learned your lesson through the torment your conscience put you through before you ever turned yourself in.

"I understand you're a Christian woman. I hope not a day goes by that you don't remember how close you came to ruining your life—and thank God that you have a tender conscience and a sense of decency. That's the only reason you aren't in jail.

"Case adjourned."

Sam closed his eyes. *Thank You, Lord! Thank You!* He waited until the judge left the courtroom, then got up and went over to Sally, put his arms around her, and wept.

Sally stood on the courthouse steps, arm in arm with Sam, and looked out at the flaming pink swirls across the western sky. How immensely relieved and grateful she was for the judge's ruling. And even after meeting with the probation officer, she could hardly fathom that she had gotten off with such a light sentence.

She saw Investigator Sloan walking up the steps with a big smile on his face.

"Just the lady I wanted to see," the investigator said. "We've got Karen's killer."

Sally felt her jaw drop. "Who is it?"

"Her ex-boyfriend, Danny Edgewood. We got a DNA match from skin cells under Karen's fingernails. The guy confessed without a fight. Said he'd been out drinking with his buddies, then went to Karen's apartment to try to talk her into letting him move back in. It got ugly. He hit her a few times, then strangled her. Said he panicked and left. Never knew anything about the money."

"Then Jeffrey Horton's story makes sense," Sam said.

Investigator Sloan smiled. "I love it when that happens."

"If you had DNA, why did it take so long to figure it out?" Sally said. "Wasn't he a suspect from the beginning?"

"Edgewood had a perfect alibi. Seems he had a friend at work adjust the company travel records to show him in New York at the time of the murder. Until Horton filled in the blanks, we didn't have enough for a warrant. Well, I just came over here hoping to catch you after the hearing. It'll be on the five o'clock news."

"Thanks for the heads-up," Sam said. "This is turning out to be a pretty good day."

"How'd the hearing go?"

"The judge gave her eighteen months probation and community service." Sam squeezed Sally's hand. "Needless to say, we're thrilled."

"That's great. Judge Payton's pretty fair. He calls them the way he sees them."

"I appreciate the way you worked with me," Sally said. "I know you had a lot of input."

"You're welcome. Listen, I've got to run. Just wanted you to be the first to know we got Karen's killer. I hope you sleep better tonight."

Sally watched the investigator jog down the steps and out to his car.

"What an amazing day," Sam said. "Let's go call Leslie and tell her the good news."

54

On Wednesday morning, Sally pulled into the parking lot of Walnut Hills Nursing Center and parked Sam's Camaro at the end of a row. A blue truck was parked where Karen had always parked her Sportage.

Sally went in the employees' entrance and walked down the hall to Wanda Bradford's office, aware of the stares from other employees. She glanced at her watch. It was nine o'clock straight up. She knocked on the open door.

"Come in, Sally," Wanda said. "Close the door behind you."

Sally went in and sat in a chair in front of Wanda's desk. "Thank you for seeing me."

Wanda got up and came around to the front of the desk and sat next to Sally. "You've got some explaining to do."

"Yes, I do."

For the next forty minutes, Sally told Wanda everything that had happened from the time Elsie started talking about the money until Sally turned herself in, and also what the judge had said at his ruling yesterday.

Wanda seemed to listen intently and never said a word.

"I'm not here to ask for my job back," Sally said. "Even if the administrator agreed to let me come back, I could never work here again with everyone knowing what Karen and I and Jeffrey did. It'd be too awkward. I know you've seen it on the news, but I wanted you to hear it from me. I'm really sorry, Wanda…" Sally put her face in her hands until she gathered her composure. "All I really wanted to do in the beginning was to carry out Elsie's wish to give her money to the poor. One thing led to another, and then I was in over my head."

There was a long pause, then Wanda got up and leaned against the file cabinet. "Why didn't you tell me how much financial trouble you were in?"

Sally looked at her hands. "There wasn't anything you could've done about it. Plus, I was too embarrassed to talk to anyone."

"Except Karen?"

Sally nodded. "She had a way of drawing me out. I still can't believe I let her talk me into keeping Elsie's money. I'm so ashamed."

Wanda stood with her hands in her pockets and seemed to be thinking. "I agree with you, Sally. I don't think you could ever come back here and not be haunted by what happened. And I don't think the other employees would ever treat you the same."

"I know. I couldn't blame them."

"Did you like your work here?" Wanda asked.

"Once I got the chip off my shoulder, I really did. At least I still have my CNA license. I should be able to find a job somewhere else."

Wanda pursed her lips. "There's something you don't know. I've given notice here. I've been hired as the director of nurses at Highland Park."

"The new nursing home out on State Line?"

"Yes. My last day here will be a week from Friday."

"Congratulations," Sally said. "I'm happy for you. You'll be good at it."

Wanda came and sat next to Sally, her arms folded and her legs crossed. "Then come to work for me."

Sally repeated the words in her mind and was sure she'd heard them correctly. "Are you serious?"

"I am. Here's what I think you should do: Take a month off, catch your breath, let the dust settle. Then apply for a CNA position at Highland Park. I'll find a place for you."

"Why would you do that?" Sally said.

"Because you have a heart for this type of work. CNA licenses are easy to come by, but people who genuinely care about the elderly and know how to relate to them are not. I could use you on my team."

Sally blinked the tears from her eyes. "Goodness. I didn't come here expecting this."

"Your patients felt your absence, Sally. And so did I. What happened was unfortunate, but not unforgivable. You did give the money back, after all."

"And figuring out how to do it caused the worst eight days of my life."

"Well, it's over now. You need to move on. I'd hate to see all that compassion go to waste." Wanda smiled and rose to her feet. "Think about the offer.

Sally pulled up in front of Harry Rigsby's house and spotted his old Ford Falcon in the driveway. She got out of the car and walked up the steps and rang the doorbell. She waited a full minute and rang the bell again, aware of footsteps inside the house.

The front door opened and Harry looked at her as if he'd seen a ghost. "Why are *you* here?"

"I…I came to apologize for my role in taking your mother's money."

"A little late for that."

Sally nodded. "Words aren't enough, Harry, but they're all I've got. I'm not going to make excuses for what I did. A hundred and twenty-five thousand dollars seemed like the answer to all my financial problems, but I never had peace from the moment I decided to keep it. I could hardly wait to turn it in."

"Yeah, that surprised me. I'll give you that much. I'm not sure I would've given it back. Doesn't matter, Ma didn't want me to have it anyway."

"You knew that?"

"Not for sure, till the other day when I found a letter she left me in her Bible. She said it never made her happy. And givin' me dishonest money would be crueler than givin' me nothin'. So, that's what I got."

"She wanted the money to go to the poor," Sally said.

Harry smiled wryly. "Hey, *I* was poor. To tell you the truth, I'm not unhappy that things came down the way they did. For me, anyway."

"Really?"

"Yeah, it's forced me to focus on other things that make me grateful for what I do have. Never thought I'd say that."

"I'm sure Elsie would be proud of you," Sally said. "Listen, I'm not going to keep you any longer. But I hope you'll accept my apology, however inadequate it may seem."

Harry raised his eyebrows. "Yeah, okay."

Sally went back down the steps and started walking toward the car.

"Hey, Sally, wait!"

She stopped and looked back at Harry.

"I'm glad the judge went easy on you," he said. "You're a real nice lady."

55

Five months later…

I t's been eight hours. How long can it take?"
"A lot longer."
Sam cracked his knuckles. "You weren't in labor this long when Leslie was born."

"Hello? It took fourteen hours, thank you very much."

"I don't remember it being that long."

Sally poked him in the ribs. "That's because you weren't the one in labor."

"I wonder if the Saunders are going to make it before the baby does? Shouldn't have been more than an eight-hour drive."

Sally put her hand on his wiggling leg. "Sam, will you relax? You're going to wear yourself out before the baby gets here."

He smiled. "Am I that bad?"

Sally rolled her eyes.

Sam got up and stood at the window of the maternity waiting room of Community Hospital in Rainy Bay, Washington, his hands in his pockets, and looked out at the foggy afternoon. "Maybe the weather slowed them down. The fog seems denser than it was this morning." He came back and sat next to Sally and heaved a heavy sigh. "You think we should go back and see Leslie and give her another pep talk?"

Sally reached over and took his hand, thinking how calmly Sam handled pressure—unless it involved Leslie. "I'm sure Alan's handling things just fine."

"I wish the kids would've told us the baby's gender. The wondering is driving me nuts."

"We'll know soon enough."

The double doors opened, and Alan Saunders rushed across the hall and into the waiting room, a flush of excitement on his face. "She's dilated to ten! It won't be long." He came over and gave Sally a hug and shook Sam's hand. "Pray everything goes well."

"How is she?" Sam said.

"The epidural kicked in, so she's not in pain—just ready to get it over with. See you soon." Alan turned and hurried back through the double doors.

Sam put his hand on Sally's knee. "I don't know which I'm more excited about—seeing the grandbaby or telling Leslie and Alan that Pastor Martin married us before we left."

"Leslie's going to flip," Sally said, admiring the gold band on her left hand. "I'm surprised she didn't notice the rings."

Sally sat thinking about how willing her parole officer had been to allow her to leave the state so she could be here for the birth of her grandchild. It seemed as though everyone involved wanted to see her life restored.

Sally silently prayed for Leslie, aware of Sam turning the pages of a magazine and the TV on and the hands moving around the clock.

"It's been over an hour," Sam said. "I wonder what's—"

The double doors opened and Alan came rushing into the room, his eyes brimming with tears. "It's a girl! Emily Elizabeth!" He shook Sam's hand, then fell into Sally's arms. "Mom, she's so beautiful!"

Sally kissed her son-in-law on the cheek and tasted salt.

"How's Leslie?" Sam said.

"On cloud nine. She's anxious to see you. Come on. You guys can hold Emily before the nurses get busy with her."

Sam took Sally's hand and followed Alan through the double doors and down the hall to a nice room with flowered wallpaper.

Leslie was sitting up in the bed, joy and fatigue in her round blue eyes and a rosy glow on her cheeks. She held a tiny bundle with a pink cap.

Sally drew in a breath, her hands to her mouth, and affixed the image to the scrapbook of her heart.

"Come meet your granddaughter," Leslie said.

Sam nudged Sally. "Go on, babe. You go first."

Sally walked over to the bedside, her husband behind her. She brushed the hair from her daughter's face and kissed her, then gently took her granddaughter into her arms and looked into the child's beautiful dark eyes.

"Hello, Emily," Sally said softly. "I'm your grandmother. I've always wondered what this day would be like…" Suddenly, the past, present, and future collided, sending a river of emotion down Sally's cheeks.

She was aware of voices, and that Leslie and Alan had noticed the wedding rings, and Sam had his arm around her, and Alan's parents had entered the room.

But for one glorious and very private moment, Sally let her heartstrings be tied to her granddaughter's—and her thanksgiving rose to the throne of grace, amazed that the God of second chances had given her the desire of her heart.

AFTERWORD

"For the love of money is a root of all kinds of evil.
Some people, eager for money, have wandered from the
faith and pierced themselves with many griefs."

1 TIMOTHY 6:10

Dear Reader,

Few of us will ever find ourselves in such desperate financial straits that we're willing to turn a cold shoulder to God and take matters into our own hands the way Elsie Rigsby and Sally Cox did.

But most of us have gone through times when there were more bills than money to pay them, and after doing all we knew to do, we had to rely on God to open a door of provision.

He *is* faithful. How different these two women's lives would have been had they remained faithful to Him and allowed Him to provide a solution to their very legitimate need. But by abandoning their only Source of help, Elsie and Sally were wide open to deception and its painful consequences.

On the other hand, Harry's financial struggle was the result of a lifetime of careless spending in the pursuit of pleasure, with no thought given to the future. It's not uncommon today even for believers to become saddled with the bondage of credit card debt or even bankruptcy, either because they don't have enough, or because they want more than they can afford.

When we acknowledge that our money is a blessing from God, and that He is Lord over it, it *cannot* become our nemesis. And though we may encounter times of financial testing, believers need never worry that God will not meet our needs, if we have sought Him first according to Matthew 6:31–33:

"So do not worry, saying, 'What shall we eat?' Or 'What shall we drink?' or 'What shall we wear?' For the pagans run after all these things, and your heavenly Father knows that you need them. But seek first his kingdom and his righteousness, and all these things will be given to you as well."

Friends, money isn't evil; it's morally neutral. It's our attitude about money that can get us into trouble. But regardless of the reason we find ourselves struggling with finances, the solution is the same: We must seek God first and with all our hearts, and adhere to the sound principles about money He has given us in His Word, so that we will have everything we need—and won't compromise our beliefs and our witness, bringing even worse circumstances upon ourselves.

I invite you to join me for the next adventure, book one in the Seaport series, *A Shred of Evidence,* where we will catch up with Ellen and Guy Jones from Baxter. Will Ellen be able to abandon her nose for news and simply write novels? Or will she find herself in the throes of community skirmishes? And will Guy become a Christian and support Ellen in her walk with God? Or will he continue to be as irritating as a rock in her shoe? Watch for *A Shred of Evidence,* in March 2005.

I love hearing from my readers. You can write to me through my publisher at letstalkfiction.com or through my website at www.kathyherman.com. I read and respond to every e-mail and greatly value your input.

In Him,

Kathy Herman

DISCUSSION GUIDE

1. Have you ever experienced financial hardship as a result of circumstances beyond your control? Or someone else's poor spending habits? Or your own? How did you feel?

2. Why do you think Elsie Rigsby made such a desperate decision? Why do you think she regretted it even though she never got caught?

3. Did Elsie's sin have an impact on her relationship with the Lord? With Arnie? Harry? Jonathan? Sally? Karen? Jeffrey?

4. Do you think God overlooks desperate behavior the times we deceive ourselves into thinking the ends justify the means? Why or why not?

5. Could you relate to Sally's financial despair? Her anger at Sam? At God?

6. At what point did Sally's thinking get her into trouble? What should she have done?

7. If you had been in Sally's shoes, how tempted might you have been to keep Elsie's money? If it had been a hundred dollars instead of one hundred and twenty-five thousand, would it have made any difference in your choice? Should it have?

8. Did you feel compassion for Harry Rigsby? To what extent were his choices influenced by his upbringing? His own greed?

9. Do you think (be honest) there are times when money makes people happy? If so, explain.

10. Do you think Malachi 3:8–12 is a call for believers to tithe? If so, why? And what do you believe are the benefits?

11. Which aspect of your finances do you find the most difficult to trust the Lord with? The easiest? Do you think believers should handle finances differently than unbelievers? If so, in what way?

12. What do you understand from Matthew 6:21: "For where your treasure is, there your heart will be also"? Can you look at your life and tell where your heart is? Can others? Should they be able to?

13. Which character's struggle could you best relate to? Why?

14. Which character's struggle could you least relate to? Why?

15. What did you take away from this story?

THE
BAXTER SERIES

by Kathy Herman

Page-turning inspirational suspense novels that will keep
your attention to the very end.

TESTED BY FIRE
Book One

Book one in the Baxter Series is a
CBA bestseller!

ISBN: 1-57673-956-2

DAY OF RECKONING
Book Two

"Kathy Herman's *Day of Reckoning* is a
suspenseful story with intriguing twists
and turns. Prepare to get hooked!"
—*Randy Alcorn, author*

ISBN: 1-57673-896-5

VITAL SIGNS
Book Three

Life and death hang in the balance in this the third novel in the bestselling Baxter series. A deadly virus strikes and violence threatens the uneasy community of hometown Baxter.

ISBN: 1-59052-040-8

HIGH STAKES
Book Four

"Mystery and murder, an offbeat heroine on a secret mission, and changed lives… Herman brings it all vibrantly to life in this winning addition to the Baxter series."
— *Lorena McCortney, author*

ISBN: 1-59052-081-5

A FINE LINE
Book Five

The final book of bestselling author Kathy Herman's suspenseful Baxter series explores the effects of a small-town mayors alleged infidelity—nothing goes unseen in a small town.

ISBN: 1-59052-209-5

LEARN MORE ABOUT THESE NOVEL FROM BESTSELLING
AUTHOR KATHY HERMAN.
LOG ON TO WWW.KATHYHERMAN.COM TODAY!

What readers are saying about Kathy Herman and the Baxter series:

"I had to write to you to express the excitement I've found from your writing. Reading Christian fiction has provided such an incredible spiritual and mental awakening in me. I have been a fan of Dee Henderson, Teri Blackstock, and the Left Behind series. After going through most of their books, I was desperate to find another author. My best friend suggested *Tested by Fire*. It is the *best* book I've ever read."—*Lori in Ontario, Canada*

"I read *Tested by Fire* earlier in the week and immediately had to go find the other books in the series. The books are so good and hold my attention from start to finish. I am a huge fan."—*Shelby in Virginia*

"*Day of Reckoning* kept me on edge until the end. The twist was definitely unexpected. The book prompted me to look into my heart and deal with bitterness. The book also makes me want to be more like the Kennsington family—faithful and prayerful through it all. What an excellent piece of literature!"—*Creshanda in Texas*

"I don't know that I have ever felt the Spirit of the Lord in such a way as I did reading the first three of the Baxter series. I read all three within four days. I am waiting anxiously for the last two of the series to be delivered."—*Mike in North Carolina*

"I love the suspense as well as the encouragement in my own walk with our Lord. *Vital Signs* has been my favorite, perhaps because it was the first one I read, yet all are great. I can't wait to read the new one this summer."—*Janet in Minnesota*

"I just finished reading *A Fine Line*. Wow! This book was intense! *High Stakes* was my favorite of the series, but I believe this one has taken its place. The point you brought out in praying for men because of the temptations they face was a good reminder for me to evaluate what I wear and say and to pray for the men in my life. Thank you!"—*Christina in the U.S.A.*

"I loved *all* the books, and I'm sorry to know the series is over, but excited to begin reading your new books. I keep looking for authors who can weave suspense and mystery while bringing Christ into the characters' lives. Keep up the great work as He leads you to a deeper depth and knowledge of His Word."—*Donna in California*

"I *love* your books. I hadn't ventured into suspense/mystery, but after discovering your books, boy am I glad I did! I finished the first one in one night and was back at the bookstore the next day to buy the rest. I am looking forward to *Poor Mrs. Rigsby!*"—*Rebecka in Michigan*

3/1 4

CPSIA information can be obtained at www.ICGtesting.com
Printed in the USA
LVOW11s1717100314

376777LV00002B/442/P

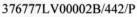